East of E[den]

Steinbeck

DATE DUE

Nov 5 '73			
Nov 19 '73 pd			
		WITHDRAWN	
GAYLORD			PRINTED IN U.S.A.

SONS

PEARL S. BUCK

SONS

NEW YORK

THE JOHN DAY COMPANY

ABOUT THE AUTHOR

Pearl S. Buck was born in Hillsboro, West Virginia, and in childhood was taken by her parents to China where she has lived since, except for the time she spent in the United States while studying at Randolph-Macon College. She has taught at the University of Nanking and at the Government University in Nanking under two national régimes. She now lives in Nanking.

Sons is Mrs. Buck's third published novel; the first being *East Wind: West Wind*, and the second *The Good Earth*, chosen as the Pulitzer Prize novel of 1931. Mrs. Buck is now translating the classic Chinese novel *Shui Hu*, written in the 13th century by Shih Nai-an. She has contributed articles and stories to various magazines, among them *The Atlantic Monthly*, *The Nation, Asia* and *Cosmopolitan*.

SONS

I

WANG LUNG lay dying. He lay dying in his small, dark, old earthen house in the midst of his fields, in the room where he had slept as a young man, upon the very bed where he had lain on his marriage night. The room was less even than one of the kitchens in that great town house, which was his also, where his sons and their sons now lived. But he was content to die here in the midst of his lands, in this old house of his fathers, in this room with its rude, unpainted table and benches, under his blue cotton bed curtains, since die he must.

For Wang Lung knew that his time had come to die, and he looked at his two sons who were beside him and he knew they waited for him to die, and his hour was come. They had hired good physicians to come from the town, and these came with their needles and their herbs and they felt his pulse long and looked at his tongue, but in the end they gathered their medicines together to depart and they said,

"His age is on him and none can avert his destined death."

Then Wang Lung heard those two sons of his whisper together, who had come to stay with him in this earthen house until he died, and they thought him sunken in sleep, but he heard them, and they said staring at each other solemnly,

"We must send south for his other son, our brother."

And the second son answered, "Yes, and we must send at once, for who knows where he is wandering under that general he serves?"

3

And hearing this, Wang Lung knew they prepared for his funeral.

Beside his bed stood his coffin which his sons had bought for him and placed there for his comfort. It was a huge thing, hewn of a great tree of ironwood, and it crowded the small room, so that who came and went must circle and press about it. The price of this coffin was nearly six hundred pieces of silver, but even Wang the Second had not begrudged the spending, although usually money passed through his fingers so slowly it seldom came out so much as it went in. No, his sons did not begrudge the silver, for Wang Lung took a vast comfort in this fine coffin of his, and every now and then, when he felt able, he stretched out his feeble yellow hand to feel the black, polished wood. Inside there was an inner coffin also, planed to smoothness like yellow satin, and the two fitted into each other like a man's soul into his body. It was a coffin to comfort any man.

But for all this Wang Lung did not slip off into death so easily as his old father had done. It was true his soul was ready to start on its way half a score of times, but every time his strong old body rebelled that it must be left behind, its day ended, and when the struggle began between these two, Wang Lung was frightened at the warring he felt in himself. He had ever been more body than soul and he had been a stout and lusty man in his time, and he could not lightly let his body go, and when he felt his soul stealing away he was afraid, and he cried out in a hoarse gasping voice, wordlessly as a child cries.

Whenever he cried out thus, his young concubine, Pear Blossom, who sat by him day and night, reached out and soothed his old hand with her young hand, and his two sons hastened forward to comfort him with the tales of the funeral

4

they would give him, and they told him over and over all they planned to do. The eldest son stooped his great, satin-clad body to the small, shriveled, old, dying man, and he shouted into his ear, "We will have a procession more than a mile long, and we shall all be there to mourn you, your wives weeping and mourning as they should, and your sons and your sons' sons, in white hempen garments of woe, and all the villagers and the tenants from your land! And your soul's sedan shall go first and in it the picture we have had an artist draw of you, and after it is to come your great, splendid coffin, wherein you will lie like an emperor in the new robes we have waiting for you, and we have rented embroidered cloths of scarlet and of gold to be spread over your coffin as it is carried through the streets of the town for all to see!"

Thus he shouted until his face was red and he was breathless, for he was a very fat man, and when he stood erect again to pant more easily, Wang Lung's second son took up the tale. He was a small, yellow, crafty man, and his voice came out of him through his nose and piping and small, and he said,

"There will come the priests also, who shall chant your soul into paradise, and there will come all the hired mourners and the bearers in red and yellow robes who shall carry the things we have prepared for you to use when you are a shade. We have two paper and reed houses standing ready in the great hall, and one house is like this and one like the town house, and they are filled with furniture and with servants and slaves and a sedan chair and a horse, and all you need. They are so well made and so made of paper of every hue that when we have burnt them at your grave and sent them after you, I swear I believe there will be no other shade so fine as yours, and all these things are to be carried in the procession for everyone to see, and we pray for a fair day for the funeral!"

5

Then the old man was vastly cheered and he gasped out, "I suppose—the whole town—will be there!"

"The whole town, indeed!" cried his eldest son loudly, and he flung out his big, soft, pale hand in a large gesture. "The streets will be lined on either side with all the people who come to see, for there has not been such a funeral, no, not since the great House of Hwang was at its height!"

"Ah—" said Wang Lung, and he was so comforted that once more he forgot to die, and he dropped into one of his sudden, light slumbers.

But even this comfort could not go on forever, and there came an hour in the early dawn of the sixth day of the old man's dying when it ended. The two sons were wearied with their waiting for the hour, for they were not accustomed to the hardships of a cramped house like this where they had not lived since they were young, and, exhausted with their father's long dying, they had gone to bed in the small inner court he had built long ago in the days when he took his first concubine, Lotus, in the days when he was in his prime. They told Pear Blossom when they went at the beginning of the night that she was to call them if their father began his dying again suddenly, and they went to their rest. There upon the bed which Wang Lung had once thought so fine and where he had loved so passionately, his eldest son now lay down and he complained because the bed was hard and rickety with age, and he complained because the room was dark and close now that the season was spring. But once down he slept heavily and loudly, and his short breath caught in his thick throat. As for Wang the Second, he lay upon a small bamboo couch that stood against the wall and he slept lightly and softly as a cat sleeps.

But Pear Blossom did not sleep at all. She sat the night through in the still way she had, motionless upon a little

6

bamboo stool so low that as she sat beside the bed her face was near the old man's, and she held his dried old palm between her own soft palms. She was young enough in years to be Wang Lung's daughter; yet she did not look young, either, for she had the strangest look of patience on her face, and all she did was done with the most perfect, tutored patience, which is not like youth. Thus she sat beside the old man who had been very kind to her and more like her father than any she had ever known, and she did not weep. She looked at his dying face steadfastly hour after hour, as he slept a sleep as still and nearly as deep as death.

Suddenly at that small hour when it is blackest night and just before dawn breaks, Wang Lung opened his eyes, and he felt so weak that it seemed to him his soul was out of his body already. He rolled his eyes a little and he saw his Pear Blossom sitting there. He was so weak he began to be afraid, and he said whispering, his breath caught in his throat and fluttering through his teeth, "Child—is this—*death?*"

She saw him in his terror and she said quietly and aloud and in her natural voice,

"No, no, my lord—you are better, you are not dying!"

"You—are sure?" he whispered again, comforted with her natural voice, and he fixed his glazing eyes upon her face.

Then Pear Blossom, seeing what must come, felt her heart begin to beat hard and quick, and she rose and bent over him and she said in her same, soft, usual voice,

"Have I ever deceived you, my lord? See, your hand I hold feels so warm and strong—I think you are growing better every moment. You are so well, my lord! You need not be afraid—no, fear nothing—you are better—you are better—"

So she soothed him steadily on, saying over and over how well he was and holding his hand close and warm, and he lay smiling up at her, his eyes dimming and fixing, his lips

7

stiffening, his ears straining to catch her steady voice. Then when she saw he was dying indeed, she leaned down close to him and she lifted her voice clear and high and she called,

"You are better—you are better! No death, my lord—it is not death!"

Thus she comforted him and even as he gathered his last heart beats together at the sound of her voice, he died. But he could not die peacefully. No, although he died comforted, yet when his soul tore itself out of him, his choked body gave a great leap as though of anger and his arms and legs flung themselves out and so strongly that his bony old hand jerked upward and struck Pear Blossom as she leaned over him. It struck her full in the face and with a blow so sharp she put her hand to her cheek and she murmured,

"The only blow you ever gave me, my lord!"

But he gave her no answer. Then she looked down and saw him lying all askew and as she looked his last breath went out of him in a gust and he was still. She straightened his old limbs then, touching him lightly and delicately, and she smoothed his quilts decently over him. With her tender fingers she closed his staring eyes that saw her no more, and she gazed for an instant at the smile, still on his face, which had come when she told him he was not dying.

When she finished all this, she knew she must go and call his sons. But she sat down upon the low stool again. Well she knew she must call his sons. But she took the hand that had struck her and she held it and bowed her head upon it and she wept a few silent tears while she was yet alone. But hers was a strange heart, sad in its very nature, and she could never weep and ease it as other women do, for her tears never brought her comfort. . . . She did not sit long, therefore, but rose and went and called the two brothers, and she said,

"You need not hasten yourself, for he is dead already."

8

But they answered her call and they did hasten themselves and they came out, the elder with his satin under robes all rumpled with sleep and his hair awry, and they went at once to their father. There he lay as Pear Blossom had straightened him, and these two sons of his stared at him as though they had never seen him before and as though they were half afraid of him now. Then the eldest son said, whispering as though there were some stranger in the room,

"Did he die easily or hardly?"

And Pear Blossom answered in her quiet way,

"He died without knowing he did."

Then the second son said,

"He lies as if he slept and were not dead at all."

When these two sons had stared for a while at their dead father they seemed filled with some vague and confused fear, because he lay there so helpless for them to gaze upon, and Pear Blossom divined their fear and she said gently,

"There is much to be done for him yet."

Then the two men started and they were glad to be reminded of living things again, and the elder smoothed his robes over himself hastily and passed his hand over his face and he said huskily,

"True—true—we must be about his funeral—" and they hastened away, glad to be out of that house where their father lay dead.

II

Now before Wang Lung had died one day he commanded his sons that his body was to be left in its coffin in the earthen house until he was buried in his land. But when his sons came to this time of preparation for his funeral they found it very irksome to come and to go so far from their house in the town, and when they thought of the forty and nine days which must pass before the burial, it seemed to them they could not obey their father, now that he was dead. And indeed it was a trouble to them in many ways, for the priests from the town temple complained because they must come so far to chant, and even the men who came to wash and to dress Wang Lung's body and to put his silken burial robes on him and to lift him into his coffin and seal it, demanded a double fee and they asked so much that Wang the Second was in horror.

The two brothers looked at each other, then, over the old man's coffin, and they each thought the same thing, that the dead man could say no more. So they called the tenants and told them to carry Wang Lung into the courts where he had lived in the town house, and Pear Blossom, although she spoke against it, could not prevail with them. When she saw her words useless, she said quietly,

"I thought the poor fool and I would never go to that town house again, but if he goes we must go with him," and she took this fool, who was Wang Lung's eldest daughter and a woman grown in years, but still the same foolish child she had been all her life, and they followed behind Wang Lung's coffin as it went along the country road, and the fool went laughing because the day was fair and warm with spring and the sun shone so brightly.

Thus did Pear Blossom go yet again to the court where she had lived once with Wang Lung alive, and it was to this court that Wang Lung had taken her on a certain day when his blood ran full and free even in his age, and he was lonely in his great house. But the court was silent now, and on every door in the great house the red paper signs had been torn off to show that death was here, and upon the great gates open to the street white paper was pasted for a sign of death. And Pear Blossom lived and slept beside the dead.

One day as she thus waited with Wang Lung in his coffin, a serving maid came to the door of the court and by her Lotus, Wang Lung's first concubine, sent word that she must come and pay her respects to her dead lord. Pear Blossom must return a courteous word, and so she did, although she hated Lotus who had been her old mistress, and she rose and waited, moving a candle here or there as it burned about the coffin.

It was the first time Pear Blossom had seen Lotus since that day when Lotus knew what Wang Lung had done and she sent word to him that she wished never to see Pear Blossom again because she was so angry that he had taken into his own court a girl who had been her slave since childhood. She was so jealous and angry that she pretended not to know if Pear Blossom lived or died. But the truth was she was curious, and now that Wang Lung was dead she had told Cuckoo, her servant,

"Well, if that old man is dead, she and I have no more to quarrel over and I will go and see what she is like now." Thus filled with her curiosity she had waddled out of her court, leaning upon her slaves, and she chose an hour when it was still too early for the priests to be there chanting by the coffin.

Thus she came into the room where Pear Blossom stood waiting, and she had brought candles and incense for decency's sake, and she commanded one of her slaves to light these before the coffin. But while the slave did this, Lotus could not keep her eyes from Pear Blossom and she stared avidly to see how Pear Blossom had changed and to see how old she looked. Yes, although Lotus wore white shoes of mourning upon her feet and robes of mourning, her face did not mourn and she cried to Pear Blossom,

11

"Well, and you are the same small pale thing you ever were, and you are not changed. I do not know what he ever saw in you!" And she took comfort in this, that Pear Blossom was so small and colorless and without any bold beauty.

Then Pear Blossom stood by the coffin, her head hanging, and she stayed silent, but such a loathing filled her heart that she frightened herself and she was humbled by the knowledge that she could be so evil and hate even her old mistress like this. But Lotus was not one who could keep her old wandering mind even on hatred, and after she had stared her fill at Pear Blossom, she looked at the coffin and muttered,

"A pretty heap of silver his sons paid for that, I'll swear!" And she rose heavily and went and felt of the wood to appraise it.

But Pear Blossom could not bear this coarse touch upon the thing she watched so tenderly and she cried out suddenly and sharply,

"Do not touch him!" And she clenched her little hands on her bosom and drew her lower lip between her teeth.

At this Lotus laughed and she cried out, "What—do you still feel so toward him?" And she laughed in easy scorn, and she sat awhile and watched the candles burn and sputter, and wearying of this soon, she rose and went out into the court to go away. But looking everywhere in her curiosity, she saw the poor fool sitting there in a patch of sunlight, and she called out,

"What—is that thing still alive?"

Pear Blossom went and stood beside the fool at this, and her loathing filled her heart still, so that she could scarcely bear it, and when Lotus was gone, she went and found a cloth and she wiped again and again the place on Wang Lung's coffin where Lotus had put her hand, and she gave the fool a little sweet cake, and the fool took it merrily, since she had not expected it, and she ate it with cries of joy. And Pear Blossom watched her sadly for a while and at last she said, sighing,

"You are all I have left of the only one who was ever kind to me or saw me for more than slave." But the fool only ate her cake, for she neither spoke nor understood any who spoke to her.

So Pear Blossom waited the days out until the funeral, and those days were very silent in the courts except for the hours when the priests chanted, for not even Wang Lung's sons came near him unless they must for some duty. They were all somewhat uneasy and afraid in that whole house because of the earthy spirits a dead man has, and since Wang Lung had been so strong and lusty a man, it could not be expected that these seven spirits of his would leave him easily. Nor did they, for the house seemed full of new and strange sounds, and servant maids cried out that they felt chill winds seize them at night in their beds and toss their hair askew, or they heard mischievous rattling at their lattices, or a pot would be knocked out of a cook's hand, or a bowl drop from a slave's hand as she stood to serve.

When the sons and their wives heard such servants' talk they pretended to smile at it for foolishness of ignorance, but they were uneasy, too, and when Lotus heard these tales she called out,

"He was ever a wilful old man!"

But Cuckoo said, "Let a dead man have his way, mistress, and speak well of him until he is under ground!"

Only Pear Blossom was not afraid, and she lived alone with Wang Lung now as she had when he was living. Only when she saw the yellow-robed priests did she rise and go to her room and there she sat and listened to their mournful chanting and to the slow beating of their drums.

13

Little by little were the seven earthy spirits of the dead man released, and every seven days the head priest went to the sons of Wang Lung and said,

"There is another spirit gone out of him." And the sons rewarded him with silver every time he came and said this.

Thus the days passed, seven times seven, and the day drew near for the funeral.

Now the whole town knew what day the geomancer had appointed for the funeral of so great a man as Wang Lung and on that day in the full spring of the year and close upon summer, mothers hastened their children at the morning meal so they would not dally and be too late to see all that was to be seen, and men in their fields left off farming for the day, and in the shops the clerks and the apprentices in trades plotted to see how they could stand and see the procession pass for this funeral. For everyone in that whole countryside knew Wang Lung and how he had been poor once and a man on the land like any other and how he grew rich and founded a house and left his sons rich. Every poor man longed to see the funeral because it was a thing to ponder on that a man as poor as himself had died rich, and it was a cause for secret hope in every poor man. Every rich man would see the sight because they knew the sons of Wang Lung were left rich, and so must every rich man pay his respects to this great old dead man.

But in Wang Lung's own house that day there were confusion and noise, for it was no easy thing to have so vast a funeral set forth in order, and Wang the Eldest was distracted with all he had to do, and since he was the head of the house, he must have oversight of all, of hundreds of people and mourning fitted to each as was his station, and the hiring of the sedan chairs for the ladies and children. He was distracted and yet he was proud of his importance and that all came running to him and bawling to ask what to do in this and that, and being agitated so that the sweat ran down his face like in mid-summer, his rolling eye fell upon his second brother who stood calmly there, and this coolness angered Wang the Eldest in the midst of his heat, and he cried out,

"You leave all to me and you cannot even see that your own wife and children are dressed and sober-faced."

At this Wang the Second answered with a secret sneer, and very smoothly,

"Why should anyone do anything when you can be pleased only with what you do yourself? Well we know, my wife and I, that nothing else will please you and your lady, and we do desire to please you first!"

So even at his funeral Wang Lung's sons bickered together, but this was partly because they were both secretly distraught because their other brother had not come home yet and each blamed the other for the delay, the elder son that his second brother had not given the messenger money enough if he had to travel far to find the one he sought, and the second because his elder brother had delayed in sending the messenger for a day or two.

There was only one peaceful in all that great house on this day and it was Pear Blossom. She sat in her mourning robes of a white hempen cloth that were lesser in degree of mourning only to those that Lotus wore and she sat quietly and waited beside Wang Lung. She had robed herself early and she had dressed the fool in mourning, too, although that poor creature had no notion of what this was all about and laughed continuously and was disturbed by the strange garments she wore so that she tried to pull them off. But Pear Blossom gave her a cake to eat and saw to it that she had her strip of red cloth to play with and so she soothed her.

15

As for Lotus, she was never in such a pother as she was this day, for she could not sit in the usual sedan, being so mountainous as she was now, and she tried this chair and that as it was brought to her and she was shrieking that none would do and she did not know why they made chairs so small and narrow now-a-days, and she wept and was beside herself for fear she would not be able to join in the procession of so great a dead man as her husband. When she saw the fool all dressed in mourning she fixed her anger there and she cried out in complaint to Wang the Eldest,

"What—is that thing to go, too?" And she complained that the fool ought to be left behind on such a public day.

But Pear Blossom said softly and positively,

"No, my lord said I was never to leave this poor child of his and this was the command he laid on me. I can quiet her for she listens to me and is used to me and we will trouble no one."

Then Wang the Eldest let the matter pass because he was so torn with many things to be done, and with the knowledge that hundreds of people waited for the day to begin; and seeing his anxiety, the chair bearers seized the chance of necessity and they demanded more money than they ought to have and the men who carried the coffin complained that it was so heavy and so far to the family burial place, and tenants and idlers from the town flooded into the courts and stood about everywhere useless and gaping to see what could be seen. To all this was added another thing and it was that Wang the Eldest's lady was continually upbraiding him and complaining that things were not managed well, so that in the midst of all this Wang the Eldest ran about and sweated as he had not in many a day, and although he shouted until he was hoarse no one heeded him greatly.

Whether they would ever have finished the funeral that

day or not none knows, except the most opportune thing happened, and this was that suddenly Wang the Third came in from the south. At this very last moment he came in and they all stared to see what he had become, for he had been away from home ten years and they had not seen him since that day when Wang Lung took Pear Blossom to himself. No, he had left in the strangest passion on that day and he had never come home again. He left a wild, tall, angry lad, his black brows drawn down over his eyes, and he left hating his father. Now he came back a man, the tallest of the three brothers and so changed that if it had not been for his two black brows frowning as ever and his mouth still surly, they would not have known him.

He came striding into the gate in his soldier's garb, but it was not the garb of a common soldier either. The coat and the trousers were of a fine dark cloth and there were gilded buttons on his coat and he had a sword girdled to his leather belt. Behind him marched four soldiers with guns over their shoulders, all good enough men except for one who had a harelip; yet he, too, was stout and strong as any in body.

When these came marching through the great gate a silence fell over the confusion and the noise and every face turned to see this Wang the Third, and everyone was silent because he looked so fierce and so used to command. He went with firm long steps through the crowd of tenants and priests and idlers who pressed everywhere to see all that could be seen, and he said in a loud voice,

"Where are my brothers?"

Now one had already run to tell the two brothers that their other brother was here and so they came out not knowing how to receive him, whether respectfully, or as a younger brother who was a runaway. But when they saw this third brother clad as he was and the four fierce soldiers behind him motionless at his command, they were quickly courteous, and as courteous as they would have been to a stranger. They bowed and sighed heavily at the sadness of the day. Then Wang the Third bowed also deeply and properly to his elder brothers, and he looked to the right and to the left and he said,

"Where is my father?"

Then the two brothers led him into the inner court where Wang Lung lay in his coffin under the scarlet coverings embroidered in gold, and Wang the Third commanded his soldiers to stay in the court and he went alone into the room. When Pear Blossom heard the clatter of leathern shoes upon the stones she took one hasty look to see who came and she saw and turned herself away quickly with her face to the wall and she stood thus turned away.

But if Wang the Third saw her at all or marked who she was he made no sign of it. He bowed before the coffin and he called for the hempen robes that had been prepared for him, although when he drew them on they were too short for him, for his brothers had not thought him so tall a fellow as he was. Nevertheless, he drew the robes on and he lit two fresh candles he had bought and he called for fresh meats to be brought as a sacrifice before his father's coffin.

When all these things were ready he bowed himself to the ground before his father three times, and he cried out very properly, "Ah, my father!" But Pear Blossom kept her face steadfastly to the wall and she did not turn herself once to see what went on.

When Wang the Third had finished his duty he rose and said in his swift short way, "Let us proceed if affairs are ready!"

Then it was the strangest thing that where there had been so much confusion and noise and men bawling here and there at each other, now there were silence and willingness to obey, and it seemed that the very presence of Wang the Third and of his four soldiers was power, for when the chair bearers began again their complaint that they were making to Wang the Eldest in such surly tones, their voices grew pleading and mild and their words reasonable. Even so Wang the Third drew his brows together and stared at the men so that their voices grew faint and died away and when he said, "Do your work and be sure you shall be justly treated in this house!" they fell silent and went to the chairs as though there were some magic in soldiers and guns.

Each man went to his place and at last the great coffin was carried out into the courts and hempen ropes were put about it and under it and poles like young trees slipped through the ropes and the bearers put their shoulders under the poles. There also was the sedan for Wang Lung's spirit and in it they had placed certain possessions of his, the pipe he smoked for many years and a garment he had worn and the picture they had hired an artist to paint of him after he was ill, since he had never such a likeness made before. True, the picture did not look like Wang Lung and it was only a picture of some old sage or other, but still the artist did his best and he brushed in great whiskers and eyebrows and many wrinkles such as old men do have sometimes.

So the procession started, and now the women began their weeping and wailing and loudest of all was Lotus. She pulled her hair awry and she had a new white kerchief and put it to her eyes, to one and to the other, and she cried out in great sobs,

"Ah, he who was my support is gone—is gone—"

And all along the streets people stood thick and pressed together to see Wang Lung pass this last time, and when they saw Lotus they murmured and approved the sight and they said,

"She is a very proper woman and she mourns a good man gone." And some marvelled to see so large and fat a lady weeping so stoutly and with such a clamor and they said, "How rich he was to have her able to eat herself to such a size as this!" And they envied Wang Lung his possessions.

As for the wives of the sons of Wang Lung, they wept each according to her nature. The lady of Wang the Eldest wept decently and as much as she should, touching her eyes from time to time with her kerchief and it was not right that she weep as much as Lotus. The concubine her husband had, who was a pretty plump girl newly wed a year or so before, looked at this lady and wept when she wept. But the country wife of Wang the Second forgot to weep for it was the first time she had ever been carried through the streets of the town like this on men's shoulders and she could not weep for staring about her at all the hundreds of faces of men and women and children standing pressed against the walls and crowded into doorways, and if she remembered and put her hand to her eyes she peeped through and saw and forgot again.

Now it has been said from ancient times that all women who weep may be divided into three sorts. There are those who lift up their voices and their tears flow and this may be called crying; there are those who utter loud lamentations but whose tears do not flow and this may be called howling; there are those whose tears flow but who utter no sound and this may be called weeping. Of all those women who followed Wang Lung in his coffin, his wives and his sons' wives and his maid servants and his slaves and his hired mourners, there was only one who wept and it was Pear Blossom. She sat in her sedan and she pulled the curtain down so no one could see her, and there she wept silently and without a sound. Even when the mighty funeral was over and Wang Lung was in his land and covered with it, when the houses and servants

20

and beasts of paper and reed had been burned to ashes, when the incense was lit and smouldering and his sons had made their obeisances and the mourners had howled their due time out and been paid, when all was finished and the earth heaped high over the new grave, then when no one wept because it was over and there was no use in any more weeping, even then Pear Blossom wept on in her silent way.

Nor would she go back to the town house. She went to the earthen house and when Wang the Eldest urged her to return with them to the town house and live with the family, at least until the inheritance was divided, she shook her head and she said,

"No, I lived here with him longest and I have been most happy here and he left me this poor child to care for. She will be irksome to the First Lady if we go back there, and that one does not love me either, and so we two will stay on here in my lord's old house. You are not to trouble about us. When I need anything I will ask you for it, but I can need only a very little and we shall be safe here with the old tenant and his wife and I can take care of your sister thus, and so fulfil my lord's command he laid on me."

"Well, if you so wish it, then," said Wang the Eldest as though he were unwilling.

Yet he was pleased, too, for his lady had spoken against the fool that she was such a thing as ought not to be about the courts, especially where there were women bearing children, and now that Wang Lung was gone it was true that Lotus might be more cruel than she dared to be when he was alive, and so trouble come forth. So he let Pear Blossom have her way, and she took the fool by the hand and led her to that earthen house where she had nourished Wang Lung in his age. She lived there and cared for the fool and she went only so far away as Wang Lung's grave.

Yes, thereafter she was the only one who went often to Wang Lung, for if Lotus came it was only at such few seasons as a widow must in decency go to her husband's place of burial and she took care to go at such hours as people were about to see how dutiful she was. But Pear Blossom went secretly and often and whenever her heart grew too full and lonely, and she took care to go when no one was near, at times when people were secure in their houses and asleep in the night, or if they were busy and away in their fields. At such lonely times she took the fool and went to Wang Lung's grave.

But she did not weep aloud there. No, she leaned her head down on his grave and if she did weep a little sometimes she made no sound except to whisper a time or two,

"Ah, my lord and my father, and the only father I ever had!"

III

Now although this mighty old man of the land was dead and in his grave he could not be forgotten yet, for he was due the three years of mourning which sons must give their father. The eldest son of Wang Lung, who was now head of the family, took the greatest care that everything should be done decently and as it should be, and when he was not sure of how this was, he went to ask his wife. For Wang the Eldest had been a country lad in his childhood and he had grown up in the midst of fields and villages before his father grew rich enough by a lucky chance and his own cleverness to buy this great town house for them all. Now when he went to his wife secretly for her counsel she answered coldly, as though she despised him somewhat for what he did not know, and yet she answered him carefully, too, for she cared enough not to be ashamed in this house,

"If the tablet where his soul lives for the time is set up in the great hall, then prepare the sacrificial food in bowls before it and let our mourning all be made thus—"

And she told him how everything should be and Wang the Eldest listened and then went out from her and gave the commands as his own. Thus the garments of second mourning were arranged for them all and cloth bought and tailors hired. For a hundred days the three sons were to wear white shoes and afterwards they might wear pale grey ones or of some such lifeless hue. But they were not to wear any silk garments, neither the sons of Wang Lung nor his wives, until the full three years were over and the final tablet for the resting place of Wang Lung's soul was made and inscribed and set in its true place among the tablets of his father and his grandfather.

Thus Wang the Eldest commanded and the mourning garments for each man and woman and grandson were prepared as he said. He made his voice very loud and lordly now whenever he spoke, since he was head of this house, and he took as his right the highest seat in any room where he sat with his brothers. His two brothers listened, the second one with his small narrow mouth awry as though he smiled inwardly, for he felt himself secretly always wiser than this elder brother of his, because it was to the second son that Wang Lung in his lifetime had entrusted the stewardship of the lands, and he alone knew how many tenants there were and how much money could be expected each season from the fields, and such knowledge gave him power over his brothers, at least in his own mind. But Wang the Third listened to the commands of his elder brother as one does who has learned to hear commands when it is needful to hear them, but still as one whose heart is not in what he does and as though he were eager to be away.

The truth was that each of these three brothers longed for the hour when the inheritance was to be divided, for they were agreed it must be divided, since each had in his inner heart a purpose for which he wished to have his own given him, and neither Wang the Second nor Wang the Third would have been willing for the lands to be wholly in the power of their elder brother, so that they must be dependent on him. Each brother longed in his own way, the eldest because he wanted to know how much he would have and if it would be enough or not for his household and his two wives and for his many children and for his secret pleasures he could not deny himself. The second brother longed because he had great grain markets and he had money loaned out and he wanted his inheritance free so that he could enlarge himself in his making of money. As for the third brother, he was so strange and silent that no one knew what he wished and that dark face of his never told anything at all. But he was restless and it could be seen at least that he was eager to be away, although what he would do with his inheritance no one knew and no one dared to ask. He was the youngest of the three but they were all afraid of him and every servant, man and maid, leaped twice as quickly when he called out to them as they did for anyone else, and they went slowest of all for Wang the Eldest, for all his loud and lordly voice.

Now Wang Lung had been the last to die in his generation, so long and lustily had he held to life, and there was no one left of his time except a cousin of his, a wandering rascally soldier, and the brothers did not know where he was, for he was only a small captain in some wandering horde that was but half soldier and more than half robber and turning to whatever general paid them best, or to none if it suited them

24

better to rob alone. The three brothers were glad enough not to know where this cousin of their father's was unless they could know he was dead.

But, since they had no other older relative, by common law they must ask some worthy man among their neighbors to come in to divide the inheritance before an assembly of honest and good citizens. And as they talked together one evening as to who this should be, Wang the Second said,

"There is none nearer us and more to be trusted, my elder brother, than Liu, the grain merchant, under whom I had my apprenticeship as a clerk, and whose daughter is your lady. Let us ask him to divide our inheritance, for he is a man whom all hold just, and rich enough so that he will not be envious for himself."

When Wang the Eldest heard this he was displeased secretly because he had not thought of it first and he answered weightily,

"I wish you would not be so quick to speak, brother, because I was just about to say let us invite the father of the mother of my sons to do it for us. But since you have said it, let it be and we will ask him. Nevertheless, I was just on the point of saying so myself, and you are always too quick and speaking out of your place in the family."

At this rebuke the elder brother stared hard at Wang the Second and breathed heavily with his thick lips pursed, and Wang the Second drew his mouth down as though he could have laughed but did not. Then Wang the Eldest looked away hastily and he said to his younger brother,

"And how does it seem to you, my little younger brother?"

But Wang the Third looked up in his haughty half-dreaming way, and he said,

"It is nothing to me! But whatever you do, do it quickly."

Wang the Eldest rose then as though he would make all

haste, although as he came into these middle years of his life he could not make haste without confusion, and if he even walked quickly his feet and hands seemed too many for him.

But the matter was arranged at last and Liu the merchant was willing, for he had respected Wang Lung for a shrewd man. The brothers invited also such of the neighbors as were high enough for them and they invited certain high men of the town who were both rich and stable in their position, and these men gathered on the appointed day in the great hall of Wang Lung's house, and each took his seat according to his rank.

Then Wang the Second, when Liu the merchant called upon him to give an account of all the lands and moneys to be divided, rose and gave the paper on which all was written into the hands of Wang the Eldest and Wang the Eldest gave it to Liu the merchant and Liu received it. First he opened it and put his great brass spectacles across his nose and he muttered the account over to himself, and they all waited in silence until he had done. Then he read it over again aloud, so that all the men sitting there in that great hall knew that Wang Lung when he died had been lord over a mighty number of acres of land, in all more than eight hundred acres, and seldom had anyone in those parts ever heard of so much going under the name of one man and scarcely under one family, even, and surely not under any since the time of the great Hwang family's height. Wang the Second knew it all, and he would not look surprised, but the others could not but let their wonder leak out, however much they held their faces straight and calm for propriety. Only Wang the Third seemed not to care and he sat as he always did, as though his mind were elsewhere and he were waiting impatiently for this to be done and over so that he might go away where his heart was.

Besides all this land there were the two houses which were

Wang Lung's, the farm house in the fields and this great old town house that he bought from the dying lord of the House of Hwang, when that house had fallen into decay and its sons scattered. And besides houses and lands, there were sums of money lent here and there and sums of money in the grain business and there were bags of money lying idle and hidden, so that the money itself was half as much as the value of the lands.

But there were certain claims to be decided before all this inheritance could be divided between the brothers and, besides certain small claims to a few tenants and some tradesmen, the chiefest were those of the two concubines that Wang Lung had taken in his lifetime: Lotus, whom he took out of a tea house for her beauty and for his passion and for the satisfaction of his maturity when his country wife palled upon his flesh, and Pear Blossom, who had been a slave in his own house when he took her to comfort his old age. There were these two, and neither of them was true wife and both but concubines, and a concubine cannot be reproached overmuch if she choose to seek another when her master is dead if she is not too old. Still, the three brothers knew that if these did not wish to go out then they must be fed and clothed and they had the right to remain in the house of the family so long as they lived. Lotus indeed could not go out to another man, seeing how old and fat she was, and she would be glad to stay snugly in her court. So it was that now when the merchant Liu called for her, she rose out of a seat near the door, and she leaned on two slaves and wiping her eyes with her sleeves, she said in a very mournful voice,

"Ah, he that fed me is gone, and how can I think of another and where can I go? I am in my age now, and I need but a little to feed me and to clothe me and give me a little

27

wine and tobacco to lighten my sad heart, and the sons of my lord are generous!"

Then the merchant Liu, who was so good a man he thought all others good, too, looked at her kindly and he never remembered who she was nor that he had ever seen her anything except a good man's wife, and he said with respect,

"You speak well and becomingly, for the one gone was a kind master, and so I have heard from all. Well, I will decree thus, then; you are to be given twenty pieces of silver a month and you may live on in your courts and you are to have your servants and slaves and your food and some pieces of cloth yearly besides."

But when Lotus heard this, and she listened to catch every word, she rolled her eyes from one son to the other and she clasped her hands piteously and she set up a piercing wail and she said,

"But twenty? What—but twenty? It will scarcely buy me my sweetmeats I need because I have so small a little appetite and I have never eaten coarse and common foods!"

At this the old merchant drew off his spectacles and he stared at her astonished and he said sternly,

"Twenty pieces a month is more than many a whole family has, and half would be generous enough in most houses and not poor houses, either, when the master is dead!"

Then Lotus began to cry in good earnest and there was no pretence in her now and she cried for Wang Lung as she had never done yet and she cried,

"Would that you had not left me, indeed, my lord! I am cast aside and you have gone into the far places and you cannot save me!"

Now the wife of Wang the Eldest stood behind a curtain near and she drew it aside now and made signs to her husband that this behavior was indecent before all these goodly people here, and she was in such an agony that Wang the Eldest fidgeted on his chair and tried not to see her and yet he must see her, and at last he rose and called out loudly above the din that Lotus made,

"Sir, let her have a little more so that we can get on!"

But Wang the Second could not bear this and he rose in his place and called out,

"If it is to be more, then let my elder brother give it from his share, for it is true that twenty pieces are enough and more than enough, even with all her gaming!"

This he said, because as she grew older Lotus grew fond to passion of gaming and what time she did not eat or sleep she gamed. But the wife of Wang the Eldest grew the more indignant and she made violent signs to her husband that he must refuse to do this and she whispered loudly,

"No, the shares must be given to the widows before the inheritance is divided. What is she more to us than to them?"

Now here was a pother and the old peaceful merchant looked in dismay from one to the other, and Lotus would not cease her din for one moment, so that all the men were distracted with such confusion. So it would have gone on for longer except that Wang the Third was outraged and he rose suddenly and stamped his hard leathern shoes upon the tiles and he shouted,

"I will give it! What is a little silver? I am weary of this!"

Now this seemed a good way out of the trouble, and the lady of Wang the Eldest said,

"He can do it, for he is a lone man. He has no sons to think of as we have."

And Wang the Second smiled and shrugged himself a little and smiled his secret smile as one who says to himself, "Well, it is no affair of mine if a man is too foolish to defend his own!"

But the old merchant was very glad and he sighed and took out his kerchief and wiped his face, for he was a man who lived in a quiet house, and he was not used to such as Lotus. As for Lotus, she might have held to her din for a while longer except there was something so fierce about this third son of Wang Lung's that she thought better of it. So she ceased her noise suddenly and sat down, well pleased with herself, and although she tried to keep her mouth drawn down and grieved, she forgot very soon and she stared freely at all the men, and she took watermelon seeds from a plate a slave held for her and cracked them between her teeth that were strong and white and sound still in spite of her age. And she was at her ease.

Thus it was decided for Lotus. Then the old merchant looked about and he said,

"Where is the second concubine? I see her name is written here."

Now this was Pear Blossom and not one of them had looked to see whether she was here or not and they looked now about the great hall and they sent slaves into the women's courts, but she was not anywhere in that house. Then Wang the Eldest remembered he had forgot to summon her at all, and he sent for her in great haste and they waited an hour or so until she could come and they drank tea and waited and walked about, and at last she came with a maid servant to the door of the hall. But when she looked in and saw all the men she would not go in, and when she saw that soldier she went into the court again, and at last the old merchant went out to her there. He looked at her kindly and not full in the face so as to dismay her, and he saw how young she still was, a young woman still and very pale and pretty, and he said,

"Lady, you are so young that none can blame you if your life is not over yet, and there is plenty of silver to give you a good sum and you may go to your home again and marry a good man or do as you will."

But she, being all unprepared for such words, thought she was being sent out somewhere and she did not understand and she cried out, her voice fluttering and weak with her fright,

"Oh, sir, I have no home and I have no one at all except my dead lord's fool and he left her to me and we have nowhere to go! Oh, sir, I thought we could live on in the earthen house and we eat very little and we need only cotton clothes for I shall never wear silk again, now that my lord is dead, not so long as I live, and we will not trouble anyone in the great house!"

The old merchant went back into the hall then and he asked the eldest brother, wondering,

"Who is this fool of whom she speaks?"

And Wang the Eldest answered, hesitating, "It is but a poor thing, a sister of ours, who was never right from her childhood, and my father and mother did not let her starve or suffer as some do to these creatures to hasten their end and so she has lived on to this day. My father commanded this woman of his to care for her, and if she will not wed again let some silver be given her and let her do as she wishes, for she is very mild and it is true she will trouble no one."

At this Lotus called out suddenly, "Yes, but she need not have much, because she has ever been but a slave in this house and used to the coarsest fare and cotton clothes until my old lord made himself silly in his old age about her white face, and doubtless she wheedled him to it, too—and as for that fool the sooner she is dead the better!"

This Lotus called out and when Wang the Third heard it he stared at her so terribly that she faltered and turned her head away from his black eyes, and then he shouted out,

31

"Let this one be given the same as the old one and I will give it!"

But Lotus demurred, and although she did not dare to say it loudly, she muttered,

"It is not meet that elder and younger be treated as one and equal—and she my own slave!"

So she muttered and it seemed she might fall to her old noise again, and the old merchant seeing this said with all haste,

"True—true—so I decree twenty-five pieces to the elder lady and twenty to the younger—" And he went out and said to Pear Blossom, "Go back to your house and be at peace again, lady, because you are to do as you will and you shall have twenty silver pieces a month for your own."

Then Pear Blossom thanked him prettily and with all her heart and her little pale mouth quivered and she was trembling because she had not known what would happen to her and it was a relief to know she might live on as she had and be safe.

With these claims ended, then, and the decision made, the rest was not hard and the old merchant went on and he was about to divide lands and houses and silver equally into four parts to give two parts to Wang the Eldest as head of the house, and one part to Wang the Second and one part to Wang the Third when suddenly this third son spoke out,

"Give me no houses and lands! I had enough of the land when I was a lad and my father would have me be a farmer. I am not wed, and what do I want with a house! Give me my share in silver, my brothers, or else if I must have house and land, then do you, my brothers, buy them from me and give me silver!"

Now the two older brothers were struck dazed when they heard this, for whoever heard of a man who wanted his whole inheritance in silver, which can escape a man so easily and leave no trace behind, and will not have house and land, which can remain to him for a possession? The elder brother said gravely,

"But, my brother, no good man in this whole world goes unwed all his life and sooner or later we will find you a woman, since our father is gone, whose duty it was to do it, and you will want house and land then."

Then the second brother said very plainly, "Whatever you do with your share of the land we will not buy it from you, for there has been trouble in many a family because one has taken his inheritance in silver and spent it all and then has come howling back, crying out that he is defrauded of lands and inheritance, and the silver is gone then and no proof that it ever was beyond a bit of paper that could be written by anyone, or else men's bare words, and these are no proof. No, and if the man himself does not do this, his sons will and their sons' sons and it means strife into the generations. I say the land must be divided. If you wish it I will see to your lands for you and send you the silver they bring to you every year, but you shall not have your inheritance in silver."

Now the wisdom of this struck everyone, so that although the soldier said again, muttering it, "I will have no house nor land!" no one paid heed to him this time except that the old merchant said curiously,

"What would you do with so much silver?"

To this the soldier answered in his harsh voice, "I have a cause!"

But not one of them knew what he meant and after a time the old merchant decreed that the silver and the lands should be divided and if he truly did not wish a share in this fine town house he might have the old earthen house in the country, which was worth little indeed, seeing it was made out of

33

the earth of the fields at the slight cost of a little labor. He decreed beyond this that the two elder brothers should have a sum ready, too, for Wang the Third's marriage, as it was the duty of elder brothers to the younger, if the father was dead.

Wang the Third sat in silence and heard all this and when it was decided at last and all divided fairly and according to law the sons of Wang Lung gave a feast to those who had sat to hear the division, but they still did not make merry or wear silk, because the time of their mourning was not yet over.

Thus were the fields upon which Wang Lung had spent his whole life divided and the land belonged now to his sons and no more to him, except that small part where he lay, and this was all he owned. Yet out of this small secret place the clay of his blood and bones melted and flowed out to join with all the depths of the land; his sons did as they pleased with the surface of the earth but he lay deep within it and he had his portion still and no one could take it from him.

IV

Now Wang the Third could scarcely wait for the inheritance to be divided, and as soon as it was finished he made ready with his four men and they prepared to go out again to those parts from which he had come. When Wang the Eldest saw this haste he was astonished and he said,

"What—and will you not wait even until the three years of mourning are over for our father before you set out on your business again?"

"How can I wait three more years?" returned the soldier passionately, and he turned his fierce and hungry eyes to his brother as he spoke. "So far as I am away from you and this house, men will not know what I do nor is there one to care if he did know!"

At this Wang the Eldest looked curiously at his brother and he said with some passing wonder,

"What thing is it that presses you so?"

Then Wang the Third stayed himself in the act of girdling his sword to his leather belt. He looked at his elder brother and saw him, a great soft man, his face full and hung with fat, and his lips thick and pouting, and all his body clothed in soft pale flesh, and he held his fingers apart, and his hands were soft as a woman's with his fat, the nails long and white and the palms pink and soft and thick. When Wang the Third saw all this he turned his eyes away again and he said in contempt,

"If I told you you would not understand. It is enough if I say I must return quickly, for there are those who wait for me to lead them. It is enough if I say I have men under my command ready to do my bidding."

"And are you paid well for it?" asked Wang the Eldest, wondering and not perceiving his brother's scorn, since he held himself to be a goodly man.

"Sometimes I am and sometimes I am not," said the soldier.

But Wang the Eldest could not think of anyone's doing a thing for which he was not paid and so he said on,

"It is a strange business which does not pay its men. If a general commanded me and paid me nothing I would change to another general if I were a soldier like you and a captain with men under me."

But the soldier did not answer. He had a thing in his mind to do before he left and he went and found his second brother and he said to him privately,

"You are not to forget to pay that younger lady of my

35

father's her full share. Before you send me my silver take the extra five pieces every month out of it."

The second brother opened his narrow eyes at this and since he was one who did not easily understand the giving away of such sums he said,

"Why do you give her so much?"

The soldier replied in some strange haste, "She has that fool to care for, too."

And he seemed to have more to say but he would not say it and while his four soldiers tied his possessions together in a bundle he was very restless. He was so restless he walked out to the city gate and he looked out toward where his father's lands had lain and where the earthen house was that was his own now, for all he did not want it, and he muttered once,

"I might go and see it once, since it is mine."

But he took his breath deeply again and he shook his head and he went back to the town house. Then he led out his four men and he went quickly and he was glad to be gone, as though there were some power over him here yet from his old father, and he was one who would have no power over him of any kind.

So did the other two sons yearn also to be free of their father. The eldest son longed to have the three years of mourning past and he longed to put the old man's tablet away into the little loft over the great hall where the other tablets were kept, because so long as it stood where it did every day in the hall it seemed as though Wang Lung were watching these sons of his. Yes, there his spirit was, seated in the tablet, watching his sons, and his eldest son longed to be free to live for his pleasure and to spend his father's money as he would. But he could not, so long as that tablet was there, put his hand freely into his girdle and take his pleasure where he would, and there were these years of mourning to be passed, when it is not decent for a son to be too merry. Thus upon this idle man, whose mind was ever running upon secret pleasures, the old man still laid his restraining power.

As for the second son, he had his schemes too, and he longed to turn certain of the fields into money because he had a plan to enlarge his grain business and buy over some of the markets of Liu the merchant who grew old and whose son was a scholar and did not love his father's shops, and with so large a business Wang the Second could ship grain out of that region and even to foreign countries near by. But it is scarcely seemly to do such great things while mourning is yet going on, and so Wang the Second could but possess himself in patience and wait and say little except to ask his brother as though idly,

"When these days of mourning are over what will you do with your land—sell it or what?"

And the elder brother replied with seeming carelessness, "Well, I do not know yet. I have scarcely thought, but I suppose I must keep enough to feed us, seeing I have no business as you have and at my age I can scarcely begin a new thing."

"But land will be a trouble to you," said his brother. "If you are a landlord you must see to the tenants and you must go yourself to weigh out grain and there are many very wearisome such things for a landlord to do if he is to make his living at all. As for me, I did these things for my father, but I cannot do them for you, for I have my own affairs now. I shall sell all but the very best land and invest the silver at high interest and we will see who will get rich the more quickly, you or I."

Now Wang the Eldest heard this with the greatest envy for he knew he needed a great deal of money and more than he had, and he said weakly,

"Well, I shall see, and it may be I will sell more than I thought I would, perhaps, and put the money out at interest with yours, but we shall see."

But without knowing it when they talked of selling the land they dropped their voices low as though they were afraid the old man in the land might hear them still.

Thus these two waited with impatience for the three years to be over. And Lotus waited, too, and grumbled as she waited, because it was not fitting for her to wear silk these three years and she must wear her mourning faithfully and she groaned because she was so weary of the cotton things she wore and she could not go out to feasts and be merry with her friends except secretly. For Lotus in her age had begun to make merry with some five or six old ladies in other well-to-do houses and these old ladies went about in their sedans from this house to that to game and to feast and to gossip. None of them had any cares now that they could not bear children any more and if their lords lived they had turned to younger women.

Among these old ladies Lotus complained often of Wang Lung and she said,

"I gave that man the best of my youth and Cuckoo will tell you how great a beauty I was so that you may know it is true, and I gave it all to him. I lived in his old earthen house and never saw the town until he was rich enough to come here and to buy this house. And I did not complain; no, I held myself ready for his pleasure at any moment, and yet all this was not enough for him. As soon as I was old at all he took to himself a slave of my own, a poor pale thing I kept out of pity for she was so weak she was little use to me, and now that he is dead I have only these few paltry bits of silver for my pains!"

Then this old lady or that would commiserate her, and

38

each pretended she did not know that Lotus had been only a singing girl out of a tea house, and one would cry out,

"Ah, so it is with all men, and as soon as our beauty is gone they look about for another, even though they used our beauty heedlessly until it was gone! So it is with us all!"

And they all agreed upon these two things, that all men were wicked and selfish and they themselves were most to be pitied of all women because they had sacrificed themselves so wholly, and when they were agreed upon these things and each had shown how her lord was the worst, they fell with relish to their eating and then with zest to their gaming, and so Lotus spent her life. And since it is a servant's due to have what her mistress earns at gaming, or else a share in it, Cuckoo was zealous to urge her on to such a life.

But still Lotus longed for the days of her mourning to be over so she could take off her cotton robes and wear silks again and forget that Wang Lung had lived. Yes, except for the certain times when she must for decency's sake go to his grave and weep and when the family went to burn paper and incense to his shade, she did not think of him except when she must draw on those mourning robes in the morning and take them off at night, and she longed to be rid of this so she need not think of him at all.

There was only Pear Blossom who was in no haste, and she went as she always did and mourned by that grave in the land. When no one was by to see her she went and mourned there.

Now while the two brothers waited they must live on together in this great house, they and their wives and children, and it was not easy living because of the hostility of their wives to each other. The wives of Wang the Eldest and Wang the Second hated each other so heartily that the two men were distracted by them, for the two women could not keep their

39

anger to themselves, but each must pour it forth to her husband, when she had him alone.

The wife of Wang the Eldest said to him in her proper, pompous way, "It is a strange thing I can never have the decent respect which is my due in this house to which you brought me. I thought while the old man lived I must endure it because he was so coarse and ignorant a person that I was shamed before my sons when they saw what they had for a grandfather. Yet I bore it all because it was right for me so to do. But now he is dead and you are the head of the family, and if he did not see what your brother's wife is and how she treats me, and he did not see it because he was so ignorant and unlearned, you are the head and you see it and still you do nothing to teach that woman her place. I am set at naught by her every day, a coarse, country woman and irreligious, too."

Then Wang the Eldest groaned in himself and he said with what patience he could muster,

"What does she say to you?"

"It is not only in what she says," the lady replied in her chill way, and when she talked her lips scarcely moved and her voice did not rise or fall. "It is in all she does and is. When I come into a room where she is she pretends to be at some task from which she cannot rise and give me place, and she is so red and loud I cannot bear her if she speaks at all, no, not even if I see her pass, even."

"Well, and I can scarcely go to my brother and say, 'Your wife is too red and too loud and the mother of my sons will not have her so,'" replied Wang the Eldest, wagging his head and feeling for his tobacco pipe in the girdle under his robe. He felt he had said a very good thing and he dared to smile a little.

Now the lady was not one who was ever quick to answer and the truth was she could not answer many times as

40

quickly as she longed to do, and one reason she hated her
sister-in-law was because the country wife had a sharp witty
tongue, although it was coarse, too, and before the towns-
woman could finish a speech she set out to make slowly and
with dignity, the country wife had with some roll of her eyes
and with some quick word interspersed put to naught the
townswoman and made her seem absurd so that when the
slaves and servants who stood by heard it they had to turn
away quickly to hide their smiles. But sometimes a young
maid turned too late and her laughter burst out of her with a
great squeak before she could stop herself and then others
must needs laugh as though at the noise she made, and the
townswoman was so angry she hated the country wife with all
her heart. So when Wang the Eldest said what he did, she
looked at him sharply to see if he made sport of her too, and
there he sat in a reed chair he had for his ease, and there he
was smiling his soft smile, and she drew herself up very hard
and she sat erect and chill upon the stiff wooden chair she
always chose, and she dropped the lids over her eyes and
made her mouth very small and tight and she said,

"I know very well you despise me, too, my lord! Ever
since you brought home that common creature you have
despised me, and I wish I had never left my father's house.
Yes, and I wish now I could give myself to the gods and
enter myself a nun somewhere and so I would if it were not
for my children. I have given myself to building up this house
of yours to make it more than a mere farmer's house, but you
give me no thanks."

She wiped her eyes with her sleeves carefully as she said
this, and she rose and went into her room and soon Wang
the Eldest heard her reciting aloud some Buddhist prayer.
For this lady of late years had recourse to nuns and to priests
and she had grown very scrupulous in her duty to the gods

and she spent much time in prayers and chants and the nuns came often to teach her. She made a parade, too, of being able to eat but a very little meat, although she had not taken the strict vows, and she did all this in a rich man's house where there is no need for such worship as a poor man must give to the gods for safety's sake.

So now, as she always did when she was angered, she began to pray aloud in her room and when Wang the Eldest heard it he rubbed his hand ruefully over his head and he sighed, for it was true this lady of his had never forgiven him that he had come to the taking of a second woman into his house, a pretty, simple girl he saw on the street one day at a poor man's door. She had sat on a little stool beside a tub washing clothes, and she was so young and pretty he looked at her twice and thrice as he passed, and he passed again and again. Her father was glad enough to let her go to so goodly a rich man and Wang the Eldest paid him well. But she was so simple that now he knew all she was Wang the Eldest did sometimes wonder how it was he had longed for her as he had, for she was so simple that she feared his lady very much and had no temper at all of her own, and sometimes when Wang the Eldest called for her to come to his room at night she even hung her head and faltered,

"But will my lady let me tonight?"

And sometimes when he saw how timid she was Wang the Eldest grew angry and vowed he would take a good, robust, ill-tempered wench next who would not fear his lady as they all did. But sometimes he groaned and thought to himself that after all it was better so, because at least he had peace between his two women, seeing that the younger one obeyed her mistress abjectly and would not so much as look at him if the lady were by.

Nevertheless, although this somewhat satisfied the lady, still she never ceased to reproach Wang the Eldest, first that he had taken any other woman at all, and then if he must, that he had taken so poor a thing. As for Wang the Eldest, he bore with his lady and he loved the girl still sometimes for her pretty childish face, and he seemed to love her most whenever his lady spoke most bitterly against her, so that he managed by stealth and by schemes to get the girl who was his own. He would answer when she feared to come to him,

"You may come freely for she is too weary to be troubled by me tonight."

It was true enough that his lady was a woman of a chill heart and she was glad when her days of child-bearing were over. Then Wang the Eldest gave her the respect that was her due and he deferred to her by day in everything and so did the girl, but by night the girl came to him, and so he had peace with his two wives in his house.

Still the quarrel with the sister-in-law was not so easily settled, and the wife of Wang the Second was at her husband too, and she said,

"I am sick to death of that white-faced thing who is your brother's wife, and if you do not something to separate our courts from theirs, I shall take my revenge one day and bawl in the streets against her, and that will make her die of shame she is so puling and so fearful lest one does not bow deep enough every time she comes in. I am as good as she is and better, and I am glad I am not like her and that you are not like that great fat fool, even though he be the elder brother over you!"

Now Wang the Second and his wife agreed very well. He was small and yellow and quiet and he liked her because she was ruddy and large and had a lusty heart, and he liked her because she was shrewd and a good wife in the house and she spent money hardly and although her father had been a farmer and she was never used to fine living, now that she could have it she did not crave it as some women would have. She ate coarse food by choice and wore cotton rather than silk, and her only faults were a tongue too ready for gossip and that she liked to chatter with the servants.

It was true she could never be called a lady since she liked to wash and to rub and work with her own hands. Yet since she was so she did not need so many servants and she had only a country maid or two whom she treated as friends, and this was another thing her sister-in-law held against her, that she could not treat a servant properly but must look on them all as her equals, and so bring the family to shame. For servants talk to servants, and the elder wife had heard the maids in her sister-in-law's house boast about their mistress and how much more generous she was than the other and how she gave them bits of dainties left over and bits of stuffs for shoes, if she were in such a mood.

It was true the lady was hard with her servants, but so she was with all and she was hard with herself, too, and she never came forth as the other one did, who ran anywhere with her garments faded and worn and her hair awry and her shoes soiled and turned under at the heel, although her feet were none too small, either. Neither had the lady ever sat as the country wife did, who suckled her child where she sat or stood, with her bosom all out.

Indeed, the greatest quarrel these two ever had was because of this suckling, and the quarrel drove the two brothers at last to find a way of peace. It happened on a certain day that the lady went to the gate to enter her sedan, for it was the birthday of a god who had a temple in the town, and she went to make an offering. As she passed into the street there was the country wife at the gate with her bosom all bare like a slave's, and she was suckling her youngest child and talking to a

44

vendor from whom she bought a fish for the noon meal of the day.

It was a hideous coarse sight and the lady could not bear it, and she set herself to reproach her sister-in-law bitterly, and she began,

"Truly it is a very shameful sight to see one who should be lady in a great house do such a thing as I would scarcely allow a slave of mine—"

But her slow and sedate tongue could not match the other's, and the country wife shouted out,

"Who does not know that children must be suckled and I am not ashamed I have sons to suckle and two breasts to suckle them at!"

And instead of buttoning her coat decently she shifted her child triumphantly and suckled it at her other breast. Then hearing her loud voice a crowd began to gather to see the fray and women ran out of their kitchens and out of their courts, wiping their hands as they ran, and farmers who passed set their baskets down awhile to enjoy the quarrel.

But when the lady saw these brown and common faces she could not bear it and she sent the sedan away for the day and tottered into her own courts, all her pleasure spoiled. Now the country wife had never seen such squeamishness as this, for she had always seen children suckled wherever their mothers happened to be, for who can say when a child will cry for this and that and the breast is the only way it will be quieted? So she stood and abused her sister-in-law in such merry ways that the crowd roared with laughter and was in high good humor at the play.

Then a slave of the lady's who stood by, curious, went and told her mistress faithfully all that the country wife said and she whispered,

"Lady, she says you are so high that you make my lord go

45

in terror for his life and he does not even dare to love his little concubine unless you say he may and then only so long as you say, and all the crowd laughed!"

The lady turned pale at this and she sat down suddenly on a chair beside the table in the chief room and waited and the slave ran and came back again and said breathlessly,

"Now she is saying you care more for priests and nuns than you do for your children and it is well known what such as they are for secret evil!"

At such vileness as this the lady rose and she could not bear it and she told the slave she was to command the gateman to come to her at once. So the slave ran out again in pleasure and excitement, for it was not every day there was such an ado as this, and she brought the gateman in. He was a gnarled old laborer who had once been on Wang Lung's land and because he was so old and trusty and he had no son to feed him when he grew old he had been allowed to see to the gates. He went fearful of this lady as they all did and he stood bowing and hanging his head before her and she said in her majestic way,

"Since my lord is at his tea house now and knows not of all this unseemly commotion and since his brother is not here either to control his house, I must do my duty and I will not have the common people on the streets gaping like this at our house and you are to shut the gates. If my sister-in-law is shut out, let her be shut out, and if she asks you who told you to shut the gates say I did, and you must obey me."

The old man bowed again and went out speechless and did as he was commanded. Now the country wife was still there and she enjoyed it mightily when the crowd laughed at her and she did not see the gates closing slowly behind her until they were closed almost to a crack. Then the old gateman put his lips to the crack and he whispered hoarsely,

46

"Hist—mistress!"

She turned then and saw what was happening and she made a rush and pushed the gates and ran through, her child still at her breast, and she shrieked at the old man,

"Who told you to lock me out, you old dog?"

And the old man answered humbly, "The lady did, and she said I was to lock you out because she would not have such a din here at her gates. But I called to you so you would know."

"And they are her gates, are they, and I am to be locked out of my own house, am I?" And shrieking thus the country wife bounced into her sister-in-law's courts.

But the lady had foreseen this and so she had gone into her own rooms and barred the door and she had fallen to her prayers, and although the country wife knocked and beat mightily upon the door, she had no satisfaction and all she heard was the steady, monotonous drone of prayers.

Nevertheless, be sure the two brothers heard of it that night each from his own wife, and when they met in the street the next morning on their way to the tea house they looked at each other wanly, and the second brother said, his face in a wry smile,

"Our wives will drive us into enmity yet and we cannot afford to be enemies. We had better divide them. You take the courts you are in and the gate that is upon the main street shall be your gate. I will stay in my own courts and open a gate to the side street and that will be my gate, and so can we pursue our lives peacefully. If that third brother of ours ever comes home to live he may have the courts where our father lived and if the first concubine is dead then hers where she is adjoining it."

Now Wang the Eldest had been told many times in the night by his lady every word of what had passed and he was so pressed by his lady that this time he swore to her he would not be mild and yielding; no, this time he would do what was fitting for the head of the house to do when the mistress of the house is so outraged as this by one who is her inferior and ought to pay her deference. So now when he heard what his younger brother said he remembered how hard pressed he had been in the night, and he said feebly in reproach,

"But your wife did very wrong to speak of my lady as she did before the common crowd and it is not enough to let it pass so easily. You should beat her a time or two. I must insist you beat her a time or two."

Then Wang the Second let his little sharp eyes twinkle and he coaxed his brother and he said,

"We are men, you and I, my brother, and we know what women are and how ignorant and simple the best of them are. Men cannot concern themselves in the affairs of women and we understand each other, my elder brother, we men. It is true that my wife behaved like a fool and she is a country woman and nothing better. Tell your lady I said so and that I send my apologies for my wife. Apologies cost nothing. Then let us separate our women and children and we will have peace, my brother, and we can meet in the tea house and discuss the affairs we have together and at home we will live separately."

"But—but—" said Wang the Eldest, stammering, for he could not think so fast and so smoothly as this.

Then Wang the Second was clever and he saw immediately that his brother did not know how he was to satisfy his lady and so he said quickly,

"See, my elder brother, say it thus to your lady: 'I have cut my younger brother's house off from us and you shall never be troubled again. Thus have I punished them.'"

The elder brother was pleased, then, and he laughed and rubbed his fat pale hands together and he said,

"See to it—see to it!"

And Wang the Second said, "I will call masons this very day."

So each man satisfied his wife. The younger one told his wife,

"You shall not be troubled by that prudish, proud towns-woman any more. I have told my elder brother I will not live under the same roof with her. No, I will be master in my own house and we will divide ourselves, and I will not be under his heel any more, and you not at her beck and call."

And the elder one went to his lady and said in a loud voice, "I have managed it all and I have punished them very well. You can rest your heart. I said to my brother, I said, 'You shall be cut off from my house, you and your wife, and your children, and we will take the courts we have by the great gate, and you must cut a little side gate on to the alley toward the east, and your woman is not to trouble my lady any more. If that one of yours wishes to hang about at her door suckling her children like a sow does her pigs in the street, at least it will not disgrace us!' So have I done, mother of my sons, and rest yourself, for you need not see her any more."

Thus each man satisfied his wife, so that each woman thought herself triumphant and the other altogether van-quished. Then the two brothers were better friends than they had ever been and each felt himself a very clever fellow and one who understood women. They were in high good humor with themselves and with each other and they longed for the days of mourning to be over soon so that they might set a day to meet at the tea house and plan the selling of such land as they wished to sell.

So the three years passed in this varied waiting and the

time came when the mourning for Wang Lung could be ended. A day for this was chosen from the almanac and the name of that day had the proper letter in it for such a day, and Wang the Eldest prepared everything for the rites of the release from mourning. He talked with his lady and again she knew all that was fitting and she told him and he did it.

The sons and the sons' wives and all who were near to Wang Lung and had worn mourning these three years dressed themselves in gay silks and the women put on some hue of red. Then over these they put the hempen robes they had worn and they went outside the great gate, as the custom was in those parts, and there a heap of spirit money in gold and silver had been made and priests stood ready and they lit the paper. Then by the light of the flames they who wore mourning for Wang Lung took it off and stood manifest in the gay robes they wore underneath.

When the rites were complete, they went into the house and each congratulated all that the days of sorrow were over, and they bowed to the new tablet that had been made for Wang Lung, for the old one was burned, and they put wine and sacrifices of cooked meats before the tablet. Now this new tablet was the permanent tablet and it was made, as such are, of a very fine hard wood and it was set into a little wooden casket to hold it. When it was made and varnished with very costly varnish of black, the sons of Wang Lung searched for the most learned man in the town to inscribe it for them with the name and the spirit of Wang Lung.

There was none more learned than the son of the old Confucian scholar who had once been their teacher, a man who had gone up in his youth to the imperial examinations. True, he had failed, but still he was more learned than those who had not gone at all, and he had given all his learning to his son and this son was a scholar too. When he was invited to

50

so honorable a task as this, therefore, he came swinging his robes as he walked and setting his feet out as scholars do, and he wore his spectacles low upon the end of his nose. When he was come he seated himself at the table before the tablet, having first bowed as many times as he ought to it, and then, pushing back his long sleeves and pointing his brush of camel's hair very fine and sharp, he began to write. Brush and ink slab and ink and all were new, for so they must be at such a task, and thus he inscribed. When he came to the last letter of the inscription he paused for a time before he wrote the very end, and he waited and closed his eyes and meditated so that he might catch the whole spirit of Wang Lung in the last touch of the last word.

And after he had meditated awhile it came to him thus: "Wang Lung, whose riches of body and soul were of the earth." When he thought of this it seemed to him that he had caught the essence of Wang Lung's being, so that his very soul would be held fast, and he dipped his brush in red and set the last stroke upon the tablet.

Thus was it finished, and Wang the Eldest took his father's tablet and carried it carefully in both his hands and they all went together and set the tablet in that small upper room where the other tablets were, the tablets of the two old farmers who had been Wang Lung's father and grandfather. Here their tablets were in this rich house, and they would never have dreamed when they were alive of having tablets such as only rich people have, and if they thought at all of themselves when they would be dead, it was only to suppose their names would be written upon a bit of paper by some fellow a little learned and pasted to the earthen wall of the house in the fields and so stay until it wore away after a while. But when Wang Lung had moved into this town house he had tablets made for his two ancestors as though they had lived here, too, although whether their spirits were there or not, no one could know.

Here then was Wang Lung's tablet put also, and when his sons had done all that should be done they shut the door and came away, and they were glad in their secret hearts.

Now it was the proper time to invite guests and to feast and to be merry, and Lotus put on robes of a bright blue flowered silk, too bright for so huge and old a creature, but no one corrected her, knowing what she was, and they all feasted. And as they feasted they laughed together and drank wine and Wang the Eldest shouted again and again, for he loved a great merry gathering,

"Drink to the bottom of your cups—let the bottom be seen!"

And he drank so often that the dark red came up from the wine in him and flushed his cheeks and eyes. Then his lady, who was apart with the women in another court, heard he was about to be drunken and she sent her maid out to him to say, "It is scarcely seemly to be drunken yet and at such a feast as this." So he recalled himself.

But even Wang the Second was cheerful this day and did not begrudge anything. He took opportunity to speak secretly with some of the guests to see if any wished to buy more land than he had, and he spread it about here and there secretly that he had some good land to part with, and thus the day passed, and each brother was satisfied because he broke the bond under which he had been to the old man who lay in the earth.

There was one who did not feast among them and Pear Blossom sent her excuse saying, "The one I care for is a little less well than usual and I beg to be excused." So, since no one missed her, Wang the Eldest sent word she was to be excused if she liked from the feasting and she alone did not take off her mourning that day, nor the white shoes she wore nor the white cord that bound her hair where it was coiled. Neither did she take these signs of sadness from the fool either. While the others feasted she did what she loved to do. She took the fool by the hand and led her to Wang Lung's grave and they sat down. Then while the fool played, content to be near the one who cared for her, Pear Blossom sat and looked over the land, and there it was spread in its small green fields laid edgewise and crosswise and fitted into each other for as many miles as her eyes could reach. Here and there a spot of blue stood or moved where some farmer bent over his spring wheat. So had Wang Lung once bent also over the fruit of his earth when it had been his turn to have it for his own, and Pear Blossom remembered how in his old age he had dwelled on those years before she was born and how he loved to tell her of them and of how he had been used to plough this field and plant that one.

So did this time pass and so did this day pass for the family of Wang Lung. But his third son did not come home even for such a day. No, wherever he was he remained there and he busied himself in some life of his own and apart from them all.

V

Now as the branches of some great old tree spring out from the stout trunk and strain away from that trunk and from each other, straining and spreading each upon its own way, although their root is the same, so it was with the three sons of Wang Lung, and the strongest and most wilful of the three was Wang the Third, Wang Lung's youngest son, who was a soldier in a southern province.

On the day when Wang the Third had received the news

53

that his father lay dying he was standing in front of a temple outside the city where his general lived, for there was a piece of bare ground before that temple, and he marched his soldiers to and fro and he taught them feints and postures of war. So he was doing when his brothers' messenger came running and panting and, breathless with the importance of the message he bore, gasped forth,

"Sir, and our third young lord—your father, the old lord— lies dying!"

Now Wang the Third had had no dealing with his father at all since the day he had run away from home in a mighty fit of anger because his father took into his own court, when he was already a very old man, a certain young maid who had been reared in the house, who was Pear Blossom, and Wang the Third had not known he loved her until he heard what his father had done. That same night he ran into his father's court, for he had brooded the whole day since he heard, and he was so surcharged with his brooding that he dashed into the room where his father sat with the maid. Yes, he dashed into that room out of the hot darkness of a summer's night and there she sat, still and pale, and he knew surely he could have loved her. Then such a sea of anger rose in him against his father that he could not bound it, for he was given to anger, and he knew if he stayed to let it swell it must have burst his heart, and he flung himself out of his father's house that very night, and because he had always longed to adventure forth and to be a hero under some banner of war, he spent the silver he had by him and went south as far as he could and took service under a general famous at that time in a rebellion. And Wang the Third was so tall and strong and fierce a youth and his face so dark and angry and his lips hard and pressed over his great white teeth, that the general had marked him at once and wanted him near himself and he had raised Wang the Third up very quickly and much more quickly than usual. This was partly because he was so silent and changeless a young man that the general came to trust him and partly because Wang the Third had such a fierce and angry temper that when it was roused he did not fear to kill nor to risk being killed, and there are not many men so brave as this to be hired. Besides this, there was a war or two and war is a time when soldiers may rise rapidly and so it was with Wang the Third, for as men above him were killed or displaced the general gave him higher and higher office until from a common soldier he had risen to be a captain over many men, and so he had been when he set out for his father's house.

When Wang the Third heard what the messenger had to say he sent his men away and he walked alone over the fields and the messenger walked a distance behind him. It was a day in early spring, such a day as his father Wang Lung had been used to stir himself and go out and look over his land and on such a day he would take his hoe and turn over the earth between the rows of his wheat. There, although there were no signs of new life to any other eye than his, to his eye there was a swelling and a change, the promise of a new harvest out of the earth. Now he was dead, and Wang the Third could not imagine death on such a day.

For in his own way did Wang the Third feel the spring also. Where his father had gone out restless to his land Wang the Third grew restless, too, and every spring he turned his mind to a plan he had, and it was to leave the old general and set out upon a war of his own and entice such men as would to come under the banner he would set up for himself. Every spring it seemed to him a thing he could do and at last a thing that he must do, and as year after year he planned how he could do it, it grew into his dream and his ambition, and so great had it grown that in this very spring he had said to himself he must set out on it, and he could not any longer endure the life he led under the old general.

For the truth was that Wang the Third was very bitter against the old general. When he had first come to the banner under which he served, the general was one of those who led in a rebellion against a wicked ruler and he had been still young enough then so he could talk of revolution and how fine a thing it was and how all brave men must fight for a good right cause, and he had a great rolling voice and words slipped easily from his tongue and he had a trick of moving men beyond what he felt himself, although those who heard him did not know this.

When Wang the Third had first heard these fair words he was very moved, for his was a simple heart, and he swore to himself he would stand by such a general as this in so good a cause, and his deep heart was filled with the purpose.

It astonished him, therefore, when the rebellion was successful and the general came back from his wars and took this rich river valley for his place to live, to see this man, who had been a hero in wars, settle himself with zest to these things he now did, and Wang the Third could not forgive him that he had forgotten himself like this, and in the strangest way it seemed to Wang the Third he had been robbed or defrauded somehow of something, although he did not know what, either, and it was out of this bitterness the thought had first come that he would leave this general he had once served with all his heart in war, and that he would pursue alone his own path.

For in these years power had passed out of the old general and he grew idle and he lived off the land and went no more out to any wars. He let himself grow huge in flesh and he ate the richest meats every day and drank wines from foreign countries that do eat out a man's belly they are so fiery, and he talked no more of war but all his talk was of how this cook had made such a sauce upon a fish caught out of the sea, and of how that cook could pepper a dish to suit a king, and when he had eaten all he could eat then the only other game he knew was women and he had fifty wives and more and it was his humor to have women of every sort, so that he had even a strange woman with a very white skin and leaf-colored eyes and hair like hemp, whom he had bought for a price somewhere. But he was afraid of her, too, because she had so much discontent in her that she was festering with some bitterness and she would mutter to herself in her own strange tongue as though she cast a spell. But still it amused the old general and it was a thing to boast of that he could have such a one, even, among his women.

Under a general like this the captains grew weak and careless also and they caroused and drank and lived off the people and all the people hated the general and his men very heartily. But the young men and the brave grew restless and stifled with inaction and when Wang the Third held himself above them all and lived his plain way and would not even look at women, these young men turned to him, one after the other, this handful and that, this brotherhood and that, and they said among themselves,

"Is it he who can lead us out?"

And they turned their eyes to him expectantly.

There was but one thing that held Wang the Third back from his dream now and it was that he had no money, for after he left his father's house he had no more except the paltry bit he received at the end of each month from the old general, and often he did not have even that, for sometimes the general had not enough to pay his men, since he needed so much himself and fifty women in a man's house are rapacious and they vie with one another in their jewels and their garments and in what they can secure by tears and coquetry out of an old man who is their lord.

So it seemed to Wang the Third he could never do what he hoped unless he became a robber for a while and his men a robber band, as many like him have done, and when he had robbed for a time until he had enough, he could wait for a lucky war and make terms with some state army or other somewhere and demand to be pardoned and received into the state again.

But it was against his stomach to be a robber, too, for his father had been an honest man and not such a man as falls easily into robbery in any famine or time of war, and Wang the Third might have struggled on for more years yet and waited for a chance, for now he had dreamed so long that it had come to be a certainty in him that heaven itself had marked out his destiny for him even as he dreamed and he had but to wait until his hour came and he could seize it.

The one thing which made it well-nigh impossible for him to wait, for he was not a man of patient temper, was that his soul had come to loathe this southern country where he lived and he longed to be out of it and away to his own north. He was a man of the north and there were days when he could scarcely swallow one more time the endless white rice these southerners loved and he longed to set his great hard white teeth into a stiff sheet of unleavened wheaten bread rolled about a garlic stalk. Yes, he made his own voice harsher and louder even than its nature was because he hated so heartily the smooth oiled courtesies of these southern men, who were so smooth they must be tricky since it is against nature to be always gentle, and he thought all clever men must have hollow hearts. Yes, he scowled at them often and

58

was angry with them often because he longed to be in his own country again where men grew tall as men ought to be and not little apes as these southerners were, and where men's speech was scant and plain and their hearts stern and straight. And because Wang the Third had so evil a temper men were afraid of him and they feared his black brows' frowning and his surly mouth and because of these and his white long teeth, they made a nickname for him and they called him Wang the Tiger.

Often in the night in the small room he had for his own Wang the Tiger would roll upon his hard and narrow bed and seek for a plan and a way to do what he dreamed. Well he knew if his old father died he would have his inheritance. But his father would not die, and gnashing his teeth Wang the Tiger muttered often into the night,

"The old man will live clean through my own prime and it will be too late for me to grow great if he does not die soon! How perverse an old man is he that he will not die!"

So at last in this spring he had come to the place where, however unwilling he was to do it, yet he had made up his mind he must turn robber rather than wait on and scarcely had he made up his mind when the news came of his father's dying. . . . Now having this news he walked back across the fields, his heart swelling and pounding in his bosom because he saw the way that was set out before him clear and plain for him to follow, and it was so great a comfort he need not be a robber that he could have shouted had he not been so silent a man by nature. Yes, far above every other thought was this; he had not been mistaken in his destiny and with his inheritance he would have all he needed, and heaven guarded him. Yes, far above every other thought was this; now he could take the first step out upon that upward and endless road of his destiny, for he knew he was destined to be great.

But none saw this exultation upon his face. None ever saw anything upon that fierce changeless face of his; his mother had given to him her steadfast eye and her firm mouth and her look of something rocklike in the very substance of which his flesh was made. He said nothing therefore but he went to his room and prepared himself for the long journey north, and he told off four trusty men whom he commanded to come with him. When his scanty preparations were made, he marched to the great old house in that city which the general had taken for his own use and he sent a guard in to announce him, and the guard came back and called out that he was to enter. Then Wang the Tiger marched in, bidding his men wait at the door, and he went into the room where the old general sat finishing his noon meal.

The old man sat crouching over his food as he ate and two of his wives stood to serve him. He was unwashed and unshaven and his coat was loose upon him and not buttoned, for he loved now as he grew old to go unwashed and unshaven and careless of his looks as he had when he was young, for he had been in his day a very low and common working man except that he would not work and fell to robbery and then he rose out of robbery at a turn of some war or other. But he was a genial merry old man, too, very reckless in all he said, and he always welcomed Wang the Tiger, and respected him because he did those things he was too indolent to do himself now in his fat old age.

So now when Wang the Tiger came in and made his obeisance and said, "One came today to say my father is dying and my brothers wait for me to come to bury him," the old general leaned back easily and said, "Go, my son, and do your duty to your father and then come back to me." Then he fumbled in his girdle and wrenched at it and brought out a handful of money and he said, "Here is a largesse for you and do not deal too hardly with yourself on your travels."

And he leaned far back in his chair and called out suddenly he had something in a hollow tooth, and one of his wives plucked a long slender silver pin from her hair and gave it to him and he busied himself and forgot Wang the Tiger.

So had Wang the Tiger gone back to his father's house, and with his impatience seething in him, he waited until the inheritance was divided and he could hasten away again. But he would not set out upon his plan until the years of mourning were over. No, he was a scrupulous man, and he chose his duty to do it if he could, and he waited, therefore. But it was easy for him to wait now, for his dream was sure at last, and he spent the three years in perfecting every means and in saving his silver and in choosing and watching what men he hoped would follow him.

Of his father he thought no more since he had what he needed, except as the branch may think of the trunk from which it sprang. Wang the Tiger had no more thought of his father than that, for he was a man whose usual thoughts ran deep and narrow and there was room in him for only one thing at a time, and in his heart space but for one person. That person now was himself, and he had no dream except his one dream.

Yet that dream had enlarged itself this much. In those days when he was idle in his brothers' courts he saw something his brothers had that he had not and he envied them this one possession. He did not envy them their women nor their houses nor goods nor all the prosperous airs they had nor the bows men gave them everywhere. No, he envied them only this, and it was the sons they had. He stared at all those lads of his brothers', and he watched them as they played and quarrelled and clamored, and it came to him suddenly for the first time in his life that he wished he had a son of his own, too. Yes, it would be a very good thing for a lord of war to have a son of his own, for no blood is wholly loyal to a man except his own, and he wished he had a son.

But when he had thought of it for a while, he put the wish away again, at least for the present, for it was not the hour now for him to pause for a woman. He had a distaste for women and it seemed to him no woman could be aught but a hindrance to him at this beginning of his venture. Nor would he have any common woman he could leave and not count a wife, for if he took a woman for the hope of a son, he wanted true son from true wife. He put his hope away for a while, then, and he let it lie in his heart and deep in the future.

VI

Now while Wang the Tiger was preparing to go forth out of the south and for himself at last, there was a certain day when Wang the Second said to his elder brother,

"If you have the leisure tomorrow morning come with me to the tea house on the Street of the Purple Stones and let us talk together of two things."

When Wang the Eldest heard his brother say this he wondered to himself, for he knew the land must be talked about but he did not know what else, and so he said,

"I will surely come, but what other thing is there to talk about?"

"I have a strange letter from that third brother of ours," replied Wang the Second. "He makes us an offer for as many sons as we can spare, because he sets out on some great endeavor, and he needs men of his own blood about him, because he has no sons of his own."

"Our sons!" repeated Wang the Eldest astounded and his great mouth ajar with his astonishment and his eyes staring at his brother.

Wang the Second nodded his head. "I do not know what he will do with them," he said, "but come tomorrow and we will talk." And he made as though to pass on his way, for he had stopped his brother upon the street as he came back from his grain market.

But Wang the Eldest could not finish with anything so quickly and he had always time and to spare for anything that came up, and so he said, being in a mood to be merry these days now that he had come into his own,

"It is easy enough for a man to have sons of his own! We must find him a wife, Brother!"

And he narrowed his two eyes and made his face sly as though he were about to say a good piece of wit. But Wang the Second seeing this smiled a very little and he said in his wintry way,

"We are not all so easy with women as you are, Elder Brother!"

And he walked on as he spoke, for he was not minded to let Wang the Eldest begin upon his loose talk now when they stood there in the street and people passing to and fro and ready to stop and listen to any tale.

The next morning, therefore, the two brothers met at the tea house and they found a table in a corner where they might look out and see anything there was to be seen but where men could not easily hear what they had to say to each other and there they took their places, and Wang the Eldest sat in the inner seat, which was the higher place and his own by right. Then he shouted for the serving man of that house and when he came Wang the Eldest ordered this and that of food, some sweet hot cakes and some light sorts of salty meat such as men eat in the morning to tempt their stomachs, and a jug of hot wine and some other meats that men eat to send the wine down so that its heat will not rise and they be drunken early in the day, and he ordered on of such things as struck his fancy, for he was a man who loved good food. Wang the Second sat and listened and at last he fidgeted in his seat and was in an agony for he did not know whether or not he would have to pay his share of all this and at last he called out sharply,

"If all these meats and foods are for me, Brother, then I will not have them, because I am an abstemious man and my appetite is small and especially in the morning."

But Wang the Eldest said largely,

"You are my guest for today and you need not mind for I will pay."

So he set his brother at rest, and when the meats were come, Wang the Second did his best to eat all he could, seeing he was a guest, for it was a trick of his he could not keep from, that although he had plenty of money he could not keep from saving all he could and especially if it was something for which he had not paid anything. Where other men gave their old garments and any unwanted thing to servants he could not bear to do it, but must take them secretly to a pawnshop keeper and get a little out of it. So when he was a guest he must needs stuff himself as best he could, although he was a spare man with a lean belly. But he forced himself and ate all he could so that he was not hungry for a day or two afterward, and it was strange for he did not need to do it either.

Yet so he did this morning and while the brothers ate

64

they did not talk at all but ate on and when they waited for the servant to bring a new dish they sat in silence and looked about the room where they sat, for it is a thing very ill for a man's appetite if he begin to discuss some matter of business while he eats, and it closes his stomach against its food.

Now although they did not know it, this was the very tea house to which their father Wang Lung had once come and where he had found Lotus, the singing girl whom he took for his concubine. To Wang Lung it had seemed a place of wonder, and a magic and beautiful house with its paintings of pretty women on silken scrolls hung upon the walls. But to these two sons of his it was a very usual place and they never dreamed of what it had been to their father, or how he had come in timidly and half ashamed as a farmer among townsmen. No, the two sons sat here in their silken robes and they looked about them at their ease and men knew who they were and made haste to rise and bow to them if the brothers looked their way, and servants made haste to wait on them and the master of the house came himself with the serving man who carried the jugs of heated wine and he said,

"This wine is from jars newly opened and I broke their clay seals with my own hand for you, sirs." And he asked again and again if all were to their liking.

Yes, so it was with these sons of Wang Lung, although in a far corner there still hung that silk scroll upon which Lotus was painted, a slight girl with a lotus bud in her little hand. Once Wang Lung had looked at it with his heart beating hard in his bosom and his mind all confusion, but now he was gone and Lotus was what she was, and the scroll hung here grimed with smoke and specked with flies' filth and no one ever looked at it or thought to ask, "Who is that beauty hanging hidden in the corner?" No, and these two men who were Wang Lung's sons never dreamed it was Lotus or that she could ever have looked like that.

They sat here now respected of all and ate on, and although Wang the Second did his best yet he could not keep up eating so long as his elder brother did. For when Wang the Second had eaten all and more than he could Wang the Eldest ate on robustly and he drank his wine and smacked his full lips over its flavor and ate again until the sweat stood out on him and his face was as though it had been oiled. Then when even he had done the best he could he sat back in his seat and the serving man brought towels wrung out of boiling water and the two men wiped their heads and necks and hands and arms, and the serving man took away the broken meats that were left and the dregs of wine and he wiped the bones and bits of food from the table and he brought fresh green tea, and so the two men were ready to talk together.

By now it was mid-morning and the house was filled with men like themselves who had come out of their homes to eat in peace away from their women and children, and having eaten to talk with friends and sup tea together and to hear the latest news. For there can be no peace for any man in his house where women and children are, since women shriek and call and children are bawling and weeping, for so their nature is. But here in this house it was a peaceful place with the busy hum of men's voices rising everywhere in good talk. In the midst of all this peace, then, Wang the Second drew a letter out of his narrow bosom and he drew the paper from the envelope and laid it upon the table before his brother.

Wang the Eldest took it up and he cleared his throat and coughed loudly and he read it muttering the letters to himself as he read. When the scanty words of common greeting

66

were written, Wang the Tiger wrote on, and his letters looked like him because they were straight and black and he brushed them boldly upon the paper,

"Send me every ounce of silver you can, for I need all. If you will lend me silver, I will repay it at a high interest on the day when I achieve what I set out to do. If you have sons over seventeen send them to me also. I will raise them up and raise them higher than you dream, for I need men of my own blood about me that I can trust in my great venture. Send me the silver and send me your sons, since I have no son of my own."

Wang the Eldest read these words and he looked at his brother and his brother looked at him. Then Wang the Eldest said, wondering,

"Did he ever tell you at all what he did beyond that he was in an army with some southern general? It is strange he does not tell us what he will do with our sons. Men do not have sons to cast out like that into something they do not know."

They sat for a while in silence and drank their tea, and each thought with doubt that it was a wild thing to send sons out not knowing where and yet each thought jealously of the words, "I will raise your sons high," and each thought to himself that since he had a son or two old enough he might after all spare a son on the chance. Then Wang the Second said cautiously,

"You have sons who are more than seventeen."

And Wang the Eldest answered, "Yes, I have two over seventeen, and I could send the second son, and I have not thought what I would do with any of them, they grow up so easily in a house like mine. The eldest must not go out, since he is next to me in the family, but I could send the second one."

67

Then Wang the Second said, "My eldest is a girl, and the one after her is a son, and that one could go, I suppose, since your eldest son is at home to carry on the name."

Each man sat and mused over his children then and thought what he had and what worth their lives could be to him. Wang the Eldest had six children by his lady, but of these two were dead in childhood, and he had one by his concubine, but his concubine was ripe to give birth again in a month or two, and of these children he had every one was sound except the third son whom a slave had dropped when he was but a few months old, so that his back grew twisted in a knot on his shoulders, and his head was too large for him and it set into this knot like a turtle's head into its shell. Wang the Eldest had called a doctor or two to see it and he had even promised a robe to a certain goddess in the temple if she would cure the child, although in usual times he did not believe in such things. But it was all useless, for the child would carry his burden until he died, and the only pleasure his father had out of it was that he made the goddess go without her robe, since she would not do anything for him.

As for Wang the Second, he had five children in all, and three were sons, the eldest and youngest being girls. But his wife was in her prime yet and the line of his children was not ended either, doubtless, for she was so robust a woman she would bear on into her middle age.

So it was true that out of all these children a son or two could be spared out of so many, and thus each man thought when he had meditated awhile. At last Wang the Second looked up and he said,

"How shall I answer our brother?"

The elder brother hesitated then, for he was not a man to decide anything quickly for himself, having leaned for many years upon the decisions of his lady and said what she told him to say, and this Wang the Second knew and he said cunningly,

"Shall I say we will send a son apiece and I will send as much silver as I am able?"

And Wang the Eldest was glad to have it said thus and he answered, "Yes, do so, my brother, and let us decide it. I will send a son gladly, after all, because my house seems so full sometimes with brats squalling and the big ones bickering that I do swear I have not a moment's peace. I will send my second one and you your eldest, and then if anything untoward comes, there is my eldest son left to carry our name on."

So it was decided and the two drank tea for a while. Then when they were rested they began to talk of the lands, and of what they would sell. Now to both of these men as they sat and whispered together came a strong memory and it was of a certain day when they had first spoken of selling the land, and their father Wang Lung was in his age and they did not know he had strength enough to come creeping out after them to hear what they said as they stood in a certain field near the earthen house. But he did come and when he heard them say "sell the land" he had cried out in mighty anger,

"Now, evil, idle sons—sell the land?"

And he had been so angry he would have fallen if they had not held him up on either side, and he kept muttering over and over, "No—no—we will never sell the land—" and to soothe him, for he was too aged to be so angry, they had promised him they would never sell it. Yet even as they promised they smiled at each other over his nodding old head, foreseeing this very day when they would come together for this very purpose.

Eager as they were, therefore, upon this day, to heap up

69

money now, the memory was still strong in them of the old man in the land so that they could not speak as easily of selling the land as they had thought they could, and each was held back in his own heart by some caution that perhaps the old man was right after all, and each resolved to himself that he would not at once sell all; no, hard times must come and if business grew bad they would still have enough land to feed themselves. For in such times as these none could be sure what day a war might come near or a robber chief seize the countryside for a time or some curse or other fall upon the people, and it was better to have something that they could not lose. Yet they were both greedy after high interest from the silver that land will bring when it is sold, and so they were torn between their desires. Therefore when Wang the Second said,

"What lands of yours will you sell?" Wang the Eldest replied with a caution that sat strangely upon him,

"After all, I have not a business as you have, and there is nothing I can do except to be a landlord, and so I must not sell more than enough to bring me in ready cash to use, and I must not sell all."

Then Wang the Second said, "Let us go out to our lands and see all we have and where it is and how it lies, the distant and scattered pieces also. For our old father was so greedy for land that in his middle years he would buy it anywhere when it was cheap in a famine year, and we have lands all over the countryside, and some fields but a few paces in size. If you are to be landlord, it will be easier for you to have yours near together and so easy to control."

This seemed good and reasonable to them both, and so they rose, after Wang the Eldest had paid out his money for the food they had eaten and the wines, and something over and above for the serving man. They went out then,

Wang the Eldest first, and as they went men rose here and there in the room to bow and let it be known to all that they were acquainted with these two great men of the town. As for the two brothers, the eldest nodded freely and easily to all and smiled, for he loved this homage; but the younger one went with his eyes downcast and he nodded a little and very swiftly and he looked at no one, as though he feared if he were too friendly one might stop him and draw him aside and ask to borrow money of him.

So the two brothers went out to their land, and the younger one set his steps slow to match the pace of his elder brother, who was fat and heavy and unused to walking. At the city gate he was weary already and so they hailed two men who stood there with donkeys saddled and for hire, and the brothers bestrode these beasts and went out the gate.

That whole day did these two brothers spend upon their land, stopping at a wayside inn to eat at noon, and they went far and wide to every scattered field and they eyed the land sharply and saw what the tenants did. And the tenants were humble before them and anxious, since these were their new landlords, and Wang the Second marked every piece it was best to sell. All the lands that were their third brother's they so marked for sale, except the little that was about the earthen house. But with common accord the two brothers did not go near that house, no, nor near to that high hillock under a great date tree, where their father lay.

At the end of the day they drew near again to the city upon their weary beasts, and at the gate they dismounted and paid the men the price they had agreed upon. The men were weary too, having run behind the beasts all day, and they begged for a little more than the price, having run so far and so long that their shoes were worn somewhat the worse. Wang the

Eldest would have given it but Wang the Second would not and he said,

"No, I have given you your just due, and it is not my business what happens to your shoes."

And he walked away as he said it and would pay no heed to the muttered curses of the men. So the two brothers came to their own house and as they parted they looked at each other as men do who have a common purpose, and Wang the Second said,

"If you are willing, let us send our sons this day seven days, and I will take them there myself."

Wang the Eldest nodded then and walked wearily into his own gate for he had never done such a day's work as this in his whole life, and he thought to himself that a landlord's life was very hard.

VII

ON the appointed day, therefore, Wang the Second said to his elder brother,

"If it be that your second son is ready, then mine is too, and I will take them tomorrow at dawn and go to that southern city where our brother is, and present them to him and he may do as he likes with them."

Then Wang the Eldest that same day when he was idle called his second son to him and he looked at the boy well to see what he was and how he would be for the purpose for which he was destined. The lad came when he was called and stood before his father waiting. He was a lad small in stature and very fragile and delicate in his looks, not beautiful either, and very timid and easily afraid, and his hands were always trembling and moist in the palms. He stood before his father now, twisting his trembling hands together without knowing he did, and his head hung down but every now and again he looked up quickly and cornerwise at his father and then hung his head down again.

Wang the Eldest stared at him awhile, seeing him for the first time alone and out of his place among the other children, and he said suddenly, half musing,

"It would have been better if you had been the eldest and the eldest in your place, for he is better framed than you are to be a general, and you look so weak I do not know whether you can stick on a horse or not."

At this the lad fell suddenly to his knees and he forked his quivering fingers together and he implored his father,

"Oh, my father, I do hate the very thought of being a soldier and I thought I would be a scholar for I love my books so! Oh, my father, let me stay home with you and my mother, and I will not even ask to go away to a school—no, I will read and study as best I can alone, and I will never trouble you for anything if you will not send me away to be a soldier!"

Now although Wang the Eldest would have sworn he had said nothing at all about this matter, still the thing had leaked out somehow, and the truth of it was that Wang the Eldest could keep nothing to himself. He was such a man that without his knowing it every time some thought came to him or he laid some secret plan his very puffs and sighs and his half sentences and his portentous looks betrayed him. He would have sworn he had told no one, but he had told his eldest son and he had told his concubine in the night and he had told his wife last, coming to her, indeed, perforce, to have her approval. He put the matter so well to her, too, that the lady thought her son would step into being a general at once and she was willing, although she felt, after all, it was no more than he was fit for as her son. But the eldest son who was a clever lad and knew more than anyone dreamed he did, because he had such a finicking languid air and he seemed to see nothing, had tormented his younger brother and had sneered at him and said,

"You are to be made into a common soldier to follow that wild uncle of ours!"

Now this younger lad of Wang the Eldest's was indeed such a one that he could never even see a fowl killed without running somewhere to vomit, and he could scarcely bear to eat flesh at all he had such a puny stomach, and when he heard his brother say this he was beside himself with fear and he did not know what to do. He could not believe it and he was sleepless the whole night and he could do nothing, either, except to wait until he was called, and so he had thrown himself before his father to beg for mercy.

But when Wang the Eldest saw his son kneeling and begging like this he was angry, for he was a man who could be mulish and full of temper when he knew he had power, and he cried out, stamping his foot upon the tiled floor,

"You shall go, for this is such a chance as we cannot refuse, and your cousin is going too, and you ought to be glad to go! When I was young I would have rejoiced at such a chance and it did not come. No, I was sent south to nothing at all and even there I stayed but a little time because my mother died and my father bade me come home. And I never dreamed of disobeying him; I would not have dreamed of it! No, I had no such chance to grow great through an uncle's high position!"

And then Wang the Eldest sighed suddenly, because there came to him this thought, that if he had been given such a chance as this his son had, how great he could have grown by now and how noble he would have looked in a soldier's gilded coat and bestride a great high horse of war, for so he imagined generals did look, and he saw himself a great huge man as a general ought to be. Then he sighed again and he looked at this little wretched son of his and he said,

"I would have liked a better son than you to send, it is true, but I have not one old enough except you, and the eldest cannot leave home, for he is my chiefest heir and next to me in the family, and your younger brother is hunchback and the next but a child. You must go, then, and all your weeping is no help to you, either, for you must go." And he rose and went out of the room quickly so that he need not be troubled any more by this son of his.

But the son of Wang the Second was no such lad as this. He was a merry boisterous boy who had had smallpox when he was three years old from too strong a pox his mother had pushed into his nose with her thumb to make him safe against the disease, and he had kept his pocks all his years until now he was called by everyone, "Pocks" instead of his name, even by his own parents. When Wang the Second had called to him and said, "Get your clothes into a bundle because tomorrow you go south with me, for I shall give you to your soldier uncle," he capered and ran about in glee because he was one who was always ready to see what was new and he loved to make a boast of what he had seen.

But his mother looked up from a pot she stirred upon some coals in a little earthen stove there by the kitchen door, and since she had not heard of the thing before she cried out in her loud way,

"What do you spend good silver to go south for?"

Wang the Second told her then and she listened and stirred, but her eyes were fastened sharply meantime upon a maid who cleaned a fowl there and she watched lest the maid take the liver or the unlaid eggs secretly and so she heard only the last of what her husband said, and it was this,

"It will be a venture and I do not know what he means by raising the lad up, but there are other sons to put into the business, and we have only this one old enough. Besides, my brother sends one."

When his wife heard these last words, she brought her mind to the thing and she said at once,

"Well, and if their sons are to be raised to a high position we must send ours, or else I shall be forever hearing my sister-in-law talk of her son who is a military hero. It is true this son of ours ought to be doing something he is so big and so full of his clownish tricks. And as you say, we have the others for the shop."

So Wang the Second the very next day took these two lads each with his garments, but the son of Wang the Eldest had his in a good pigskin box and he was fastidious. Although his eyes were still red with weeping, and he delayed to see that his man servant carried it properly with the top uppermost so that his books should not be all askew within. But the son of Wang the Second owned no book, and he had his few clothes tied into a large blue cotton kerchief and he carried this himself, and he ran as he went and shouted aloud over everything he saw. It was a clear bright day in spring and the streets of the town were full of the first produce of the fields and everyone was busy buying and selling. To this lad it was a good year and a bright day and he was setting forth on a journey which he had never done before, and his mother had cooked him a dish he loved to eat that morning, and so he was very merry. But the other lad walked along decorously and slowly and in silence and he hung his head down and he scarcely looked at his cousin, and from time to time he wet his pale lips as though they were very dry.

Thus Wang the Second walked with the two lads and he mused on his own affairs, for he was never one to pay heed to children, and so they came to the north of the town where the place was to mount the fire wagon, and Wang the Second paid money and they mounted. Then the son of Wang the Eldest was put to much shame because his uncle had bought the cheapest places that could be bought, thinking it good enough for two lads, and so this youth found he must go into a carriage where very common people sat, who reeked of garlic, and their cotton clothes were unwashed and smelled of poverty, and here was he in his good blue silk gown and he must sit among them. But he did not dare to complain for he was afraid of his uncle's secret scorn, so he could only take his place and put his box between him and the common farmer fellow that sat next, and he looked piteously at his servant who must leave him now, but still he did not dare to say anything.

But Wang the Second and his son looked little better than any because Wang the Second had put on himself a cotton robe that morning when he rose, for it seemed to him he had better not look too fine before his third brother, lest he seem richer than he would seem. As for his son, he did not own a silk robe yet and his stout cotton clothes were stitched by his mother and cut full and loose and long for him to grow to fit. And Wang the Second looked at his nephew and said in his wry way,

"It is ill to travel all day in such fine clothes as you wear. You had better take off that silk robe of yours and fold it and put it into your box, and sit in your under garments and so spare your best."

The boy muttered then, "But I have better than this, and it is what I wear every day at home." Nevertheless, he did not dare to disobey and so he rose and did what his uncle said.

Thus they went all that day by land, and Wang the Second stared at the fields and the towns through which they passed, appraising all he saw, and his son cried out at every new thing, and he longed to taste the fresh cakes of every vendor when they stopped, only his father would not have it. But the other lad sat pale and timorous, and he was sick because the carriage went so fast, and he leaned his head upon his pigskin box and said nothing all day, and he shook his head even at food.

Then they went by sea also two days in a small and crowded ship, and thus at last they came to the town where they must find the one they sought, and when they came out of the ship and were upon land again, Wang the Second hired rikshas, and put the two lads into one and he took one himself. The puller of the lads complained bitterly of his double burden, but Wang the Second explained to him they were but young lads and not men yet, and one of them pale and thin and less than usual because of his seasickness, and at last by haggling and paying a little more, but not so much as another vehicle cost, the puller was somewhat willing. And the rikshas came to the name of the house and street which Wang the Second gave them, and when they stopped, he drew the letter out of his bosom and he compared the letters written over the gate with those in the letter and they were the same.

He came out of his riksha then and he bade the two lads come out of theirs, and after he had haggled awhile with the pullers, because the place was not so far as they had said, and he paid them a little less than the price agreed upon at first, he took the box at one end and the two lads took it at the other end, and they started to walk through the great gate, on either side of which stood two stone lions.

But there was a soldier standing there beside one of the lions and he cried out,

"What, do you think you can come through this gate as you please?" And he took the gun off his shoulder and pounded its butt upon the stones and he was so fierce and rude in his looks that the three stood dazed, and the son of Wang the Eldest began to tremble, and even the pocked lad looked grave for a moment, because he had never stood so near a gun before.

Then Wang the Second hastened to draw his brother's letter out of his bosom and he gave it to the soldier to see and he said,

"We are the three mentioned here and this is our proof."

But the soldier could not read and so he shouted for another soldier and he came and after he had stared awhile at them and heard their whole tale he took the letter. Yet he could not read either, and after he had looked at it he took it inside somewhere. After a long time he came back and he pointed inside with his thumb and he said,

"It is true enough—they are relatives of the captain and they are to go in."

So they picked up the box again and they went in and past the stone lions, although the man with the gun looked after them as though he were unwilling and very doubtful still. Nevertheless they followed the other soldier and he led them through ten courts or so, every court filled with soldiers who idled there, some eating and some drinking, and some sitting naked in the sun to pick the vermin out of their clothes, and some lying asleep and snoring, and thus they went on to an inner house and there in its central room sat Wang the Tiger. He sat there at the table waiting for them and he wore good dark clothes of some rough foreign stuff and they were fastened with buttons of brass upon which were stamped a sign.

When he saw these relatives of his come in he rose quickly

79

and shouted to the soldiers who served him to bring wine and meats and he bowed to his brother, and Wang the Second bowed also, and bade the two lads bow, and they all seated themselves according to rank, Wang the Second in the highest seat and then Wang the Tiger, and the two lads in side seats below them. Then a serving man brought the wine and poured it out, and when this was done Wang the Tiger looked at the lads and he said in his sudden, harsh way,

"That ruddy one looks stout enough but I am not sure what wisdom he has behind that pocked face. He looks a clown. I hope he is not a clown, Elder Brother, because I do not like too much laughter. He is yours?—I see a smack of his mother in him. As for the other one—is that the best my eldest brother can do?"

When he said this the pale lad hung his head deeper than ever and it could be seen that a light chill sweat stood out on his upper lip and he took his hand and wiped it furtively away, looking doggedly down all the time he did this. But Wang the Tiger continued to stare at them steadily with his hard black stare, until even the pocked lad who was always so ready did not know where to look, so that he turned his eyes this way and that and moved his feet and gnawed his fingernail. Then Wang the Second said in apology,

"It is true they are but two poor things, my brother, and we are grieved that we had none more meet for your kindness. But my elder brother's eldest son is chiefest heir, and the one after this one is a hunchback, and this pocked one is my eldest and my next but a child, and so these two are the best we have for the time."

Then Wang the Tiger, having seen what they were, told a soldier to lead the lads into a side room and let them eat their meat there, and they were not to come again unless he called for them. The soldier led them away then, but the son of

80

Wang the Eldest cast piteous looks back at his uncle and Wang the Tiger seeing him waver like this called,

"Why do you linger?"

Then the lad stopped and said in his feeble way, "But am I not to have my box?"

Wang the Tiger looked then and saw the fine pigskin box beside the door and he said with some measure of contempt,

"Take it, but it will be no use to you for you shall strip off those robes and get into the good stout clothes that soldiers wear. Men cannot fight in silk robes!"

The lad turned clay-colored at this and went without a word and the two brothers were left alone.

For a long time Wang the Tiger sat in silence, for he was never one to make talk for courtesy's sake, and at last Wang the Second asked him,

"What is it of which you think so deeply? Is it something about our sons?"

Then Wang the Tiger said slowly, "No, except I thought how that most men so old as I am have sons of their own growing up and it must be a very comforting sight to a man."

"Why, so might you have them if you had wed soon enough," said Wang the Second, smiling a little. "But we did not know where you were for so long and my father did not know either and he could not wed you as he would have. But my brother and I will do it willingly, and the money for it is there when you need it for such a thing."

But Wang the Tiger put the thought from him resolutely and he said,

"No, it will seem strange to you, but I do not stomach a woman. It is a strange thing but I have never seen a woman—" and he broke off there for the serving man came in with meats, and the brothers said no more.

When they had eaten and the dishes were taken away again

and tea was brought Wang the Second made ready to ask what thing it was that Wang the Tiger wished to do with all his silver and with these lads, but he did not know how to begin to ask it, and before he had decided on a skilful way, Wang the Tiger said suddenly,

"We are brothers. You and I understand each other. I depend on you!"

And Wang the Second drank some tea and then he said cautiously and mildly,

"Depend upon me you may, since we are brothers, but I should like to know what your plan is so that I can know what I am to do for you."

Then Wang the Tiger leaned forward and he said in a great whisper and his words rushed out fast and his breath was like a hot wind blowing into Wang the Second's ear,

"I have loyal men about me, a good hundred and more, and they are all weary of this old general! I am weary, too, and I long for my own country and I never want to see one of these little yellow southern men again. Yes, I have loyal men! At my sign they will march out with me in the dead of a certain night. We will make for the north where the mountains are, and we will march to the far north before we entrench ourselves to make a war of revolution if this old general comes after us. But he may not stir—he is so old and so sunken in his eating and drinking and his women, except that among my hundred are his best and strongest men, men not of the south but out of fiercer, braver tribes!"

Now Wang the Second had always been a small and peaceful man, a merchant, and while he knew there was always a war somewhere he had had nothing to do with wars except once when in a revolution soldiers had been quartered in his father's house, and he knew nothing of how war is begun or waged except that if it is waged too near the prices of grain

high and if it is distant then prices fall again. He had
er been so near a war as this, even in his own family was
s war! His narrow mouth gaped and his small eyes widened
d he whispered back, "But what can I do to help in this,
ho am so peaceful a man as I am?"

"This!" said Wang the Tiger and his whisper was the grat-
g of iron upon iron. "I must have much silver, all my own,
d I must borrow of you and at the least interest you will
give me until I can establish myself!"

"But what security?" said Wang the Second, breathless.

"This!" said Wang the Tiger again. "You are to lend me
what I need and what the land will bring until I can gather
a mighty army and I will establish myself somewhere north
of our own region and I will make myself lord of that whole
territory! Then when I am lord I will enlarge myself and my
lands, and I shall grow greater and more great with every
war I wage until—" He paused and seemed to look off into
some distant age, into some distant country, as though he saw
it plain before him, and Wang the Second waited and then
could not wait.

"Until what?" he said.

Wang the Tiger rose suddenly to his feet. "Until there is
none greater than I in this whole nation!" he said, and now his
whisper was like a shout.

"What will you be then?" asked Wang the Second astounded.

"I shall be what I will!" cried Wang the Tiger, and his
black brows flew up over his eyes suddenly and sharply and
he smote the table with the flat of his hand so that Wang the
Second leaped at the crack, and the two men stared at each
other.

Now all this was the strangest thing of which Wang the
Second had ever heard. He was not a man who could dream

83

great dreams and his greatest dream was to sit down at ni
with his books of accounts and look over what he had s
that year and plan in what safe sure ways he could enlar
himself the next year in his markets. Now, therefore, he s
and stared at this brother of his and he saw him tall an
black and strange and his eyes shining like a tiger's eyes, an
those straight black brows like banners above his eyes. Thu
staring Wang the Second was lifted out of himself so that h
was afraid of his brother and he did not dare to say anything
to thwart him for there was a look in the man's eyes that w·s
half crazed and it was so mighty a look that even Wang the
Second could feel in his pinched heart the power of this man,
his brother. Still he was cautious, though, and still he could
not forget his habit of caution, and so he coughed dryly and
said in his little dry voice,

"But what is there in all this for me and for us all and
what security if I lend my silver to you?"

And Wang the Tiger answered with majesty, and he
brought his eyes back to rest upon his brother,

"Do you think I will forget my own when I have raised
myself up and are not you my brothers and your sons my
brothers' sons? Did you ever hear of a mighty lord of war
who did not raise up all his house as he rose? Is it nothing
to you to be the brother of—*a king?*"

And he gazed down into his brother's eyes, and Wang the
Second suddenly half believed this brother of his, although
unwillingly too, for all this was the strangest tale he had ever
heard, and he said in his sensible way,

"At least I will give you what is your own and I will lend
you what I can spare, if it be that indeed you can rise like this,
for doubtless there are many who do not rise so high as they
think they can. At least you shall have your own."

Then some fire went suddenly out of Wang the Tiger's

eyes and he sat down and he pressed his lips together straight
and hard and he said,

"You are cautious, I see!"

His voice was so hard and cold that Wang the Second was
a little afraid and he said to excuse himself,

"But I have a family and many little children and the
mother of my sons is not old yet and she is exceedingly fertile, and I have all these to plan and care for. You are unwed
yet and you do not know what it is to have so many depend-
ing on you for everything, and food and clothing costing more
every year!"

Wang the Tiger shrugged himself and he turned away, and
he said as if carelessly,

"I do not, indeed, but hear me! Every month I will send my
trusty man to you and you will know him by his harelip. You
are to give him as much money as he is able to carry. Sell my
lands as quickly and as well as you are able, for I shall need
a thousand pieces of silver a month."

"A thousand!" cried Wang the Second, and his voice was
cracked and his eyes idiotic in his surprise. "But how can you
spend it?"

"There are a hundred men to be fed and clothes and arms
to be bought. I must buy guns before I can increase my army
if I cannot capture them quickly enough," said Wang the
Tiger speaking very fast. Then suddenly he was angry. "You
are not to ask me this and that!" he roared, smiting the table
again. "I know what I must do and I must have silver until
I can establish myself and be lord over a territory! Then I
can tax the people, as I will. But now I must have silver.
Stand by me and you shall have a certain reward. Fail me—
and I can forget you are my blood!"

When he said these last words he thrust his face very near
to his brother's and Wang the Second, looking into those fierce

eyes hooded beneath the heavy black brows, drew back hastily and coughed and said, "Well, and of course I will do it. I am your brother. But when will you begin?"

"When can you sell my parcel of land?" asked Wang the Tiger.

"The wheat harvest will come before many months," said Wang the Second slowly, musing as he spoke and hesitating, for he was dazed with all he had heard.

"Then men will have money," returned Wang the Tiger, "and you can sell something before rice is put in, doubtless."

Now this was true enough and Wang the Second did not dare to oppose this strange brother of his at all for he was afraid of him, and he knew he must manage the thing somehow. So he rose and said,

"If there is such haste as this I must return at once and see what I can do, for harvests are quickly spent and then men think themselves poor again and hard-worked with what land they have to plant and more land will seem too much for them."

So he would not stay at all for he wanted to be away out of this place where there were such fierce men and guns and weapons of war everywhere. He stayed only to go into the next room where the lads had been sent and they were sitting on a bench before a small unpainted table upon which food was placed. It was the broken meats of what Wang the Tiger had put before his brother, but it was good enough for these lads, and Wang the Second's son stuffed it into his mouth very willingly, his bowl to his lips. But the other lad was dainty and accustomed to better than what was left over after others had eaten, and he sat and picked a little rice up with his chopsticks and did not touch the meats. Then Wang the Second felt some strange unwillingness to leave these lads and especially his own, and he had a doubt for a moment as to whether it was not a hazard he should not have taken for his son. But the thing was begun now and he could not undo what was begun, so he merely said,

"I return, and my only command on you both is that you are to obey your uncle in every single point, for you are his now, and he is a fierce and impatient man and he will not bear anything from you. But if you are obedient and will do all he says, you may rise to what you do not know. There is some destiny written for your uncle."

Then he turned quickly and went away, for he could not help it that his heart was a little heavy to leave his son, more than he could have thought it would be, and to ease it he muttered to himself,

"Well, such a chance does not come to every lad, and if it is chance it is a fair one. He will not be a common soldier after all, but an official of some sort if the thing succeeds."

And he determined he would do well and do all he could to make it succeed; at least for his son's sake he would do all he could.

But the pale lad who was Wang the Eldest's son began to weep when he saw his uncle go and he wept aloud, and Wang the Second hurried away. Yet the sound of that weeping pursued him, and he made haste to reach the gate where the lions were, so that he could hear it no more.

VIII

Now began this strange enterprise which, if Wang Lung's soul had not been in some far country, could have made his body rise out of that land of his where he slept, because in his lifetime he had hated above anything else war and soldiers, and here was his good land being sold for such a cause. But he slept there and he slept on and there was no one to stay these sons of his in what they did; no, there was no one except Pear Blossom and she did not for a long time know what they did. These two elder sons feared her for her faithfulness to their father and so they hid their plans from her.

For when Wang the Second had come back to his house he told Wang the Eldest to come to the tea house where they could talk in peace and there over their bowls of tea they talked. But this time Wang the Second chose a secret hidden corner where two walls came together without any window or door in either wall, and they sat so they could see who came near and they bent their heads over the table and talked in whispers and hints and broken words. Thus Wang the Second told his brother what Wang the Tiger planned, and whereas now he was come back to his own house again and into the common ways of his usual life the plan of the soldier had seemed more and more a dream and an impossible dream, the eldest brother seized on it as he listened as a thing wonderful but easy to do, too. The truth was that this huge and child-like man grew excited as the plan unfolded before him, for he saw himself raised above his highest fancy—brother to a king! He was a man of little learning and less wisdom and besides one who loved to see plays and he had seen many old plays which tell of the deeds of ancient and fabled heroes, who were at first but common men and then by the skill of their arms and by their wit and guile, they rose high enough to found dynasties. Now he saw himself the brother of such an one, and more than that, the elder brother of such an one, and his eyes glistened and he whispered hoarsely,

"I always said our brother was like no other lad! It was I who besought our father to take him out of the fields and hire a tutor for him and teach him what he ought to know as a

88

landlord's son. Doubtless my brother will not forget what his eldest brother did for him, and how if it had not been for me he would have been but a hind on my father's land!"

And he looked down pleased with himself, and he smoothed over his great belly the rich purple satin robe he wore, and he thought of his second son and how the family would all rise, and he himself would be perhaps a nobleman; doubtless he would be made a nobleman when his brother was a king. There were stories of such things in the books he had read and he had seen these things in the playhouse. Then Wang the Second, who had been more and more dubious as he came back to himself, and indeed the fierce enterprise seemed very far from this quiet town, when he saw the mind of his elder brother flying into the future he grew jealous and his very caution made him greedy and he thought to himself,

"I must be careful lest haply there is a little in what my younger brother dreams, and lest perhaps he does even succeed in a tenth part of what he dreams. I must be ready to share his success with him and I must not draw back too far," and he said aloud, "Well, but I have to furnish him the silver and without me he could do nothing. He must have what he needs until he can establish himself, and how I am to get so much I do not know. After all, I am but a little rich man, and scarcely counted rich by those who are lords of wealth. The first few months I can get it by selling his land, and then we can sell some land, you and I. But what shall we do if he is not established by that time?"

"I will help him—I will help him—" said the elder brother hastily and he could not at this moment bear to think that anyone should do more for this younger brother than he did.

The two men rose then in the haste of their common greed and Wang the Second said,

"Let us go out to the lands once more and this time we will sell!"

Now this time, also, when the two brothers went out to the land they remembered Pear Blossom and they did not go near that earthen house. No, they bestrode two donkeys that stood among many at the city gate to be hired by their masters and thus they went out along the narrow paths between the fields, and the donkey keepers, who were young lads, ran after them and beat the donkeys upon the thighs and shrieked at them to urge them on, and they went to the north and away from that house and that bit of land. The beast that Wang the Second rode went willingly enough, but the other swayed upon its delicate feet beneath the mighty weight of Wang the Eldest, for this man grew fatter every month, and it was plain that in another ten years or so he would be a marvel in the town and the countryside, seeing that now, when he was but turned his forty-fifth year, he was so round and full about his middle and his cheeks hanging and thick as haunches. So they must wait a little for the burdened beast, but still they went well enough, and in that one day they visited all the tenants which were on the lands that had been marked before for sale. And Wang the Second inquired of every man if he would buy the land he worked and if he would then when, and how soon he could pay for it.

Now it so happened that it had been decided, since Wang the Tiger wished for silver, that they would give him the largest single piece of land and it was the farthest from the town and tilled now under one farmer, a prosperous good man, who had begun humbly enough as a laborer upon Wang Lung's own land and he had married a slave out of the town house, a strong, honest, noisy woman, who worked hard while she bore her children and she drove her husband to work harder too than he would have, left alone. They had

90

prospered, and each year they rented more of Wang Lung's land until they had a number of acres under them and they had to hire men to help with the labor of it. But still they themselves worked, for they were a saving, thrifty pair.

To this man the two brothers came this day and Wang the Eldest asked him saying,

"We have more land than we wish and we need silver to venture in other affairs, and if you want to buy these pieces you till, well enough and we will sell them to you."

Then the farmer's round, ox-like eyes opened and he let his mouth go agape under the shelf of his teeth and he said, his voice hissing and spitting against his teeth when he spoke, for so his way was and he could not help it,

"I did not dream your house was ready to sell its land already, seeing how fastened to the land the old man your father was!"

Then Wang the Eldest drew down his thick mouth and he looked very grave and he said,

"For all his love of it he has left us a very heavy burden to bear. We have his two concubines to care for, and neither of them is our mother, and the elder one loves her good wines and her fine foods and she must have her gaming every day, and she is not clever enough to win at it every day either. Money from the lands comes in slowly and it is dependent upon the whims of Heaven. And such a house as we have must spend money generously, for it would be unseemly of us and unworthy of us as our father's sons if we let our family look poor and mean and poorer than when he was alive. So we must take some of the land for our livelihood."

But Wang the Second had fidgeted and coughed and frowned while his brother made this ponderous speech and it seemed to him his brother was little better than a fool, for if it is seen that one is eager to sell his goods, the price goes down. He made haste to say now in his turn,

"But there are many who inquire after our land to buy it because it is well known in these parts that the lands our father bought are good and the best in this countryside. If you do not want the land you hire, then let us know quickly, for there are others who wait for it."

Now this shelf-toothed farmer loved the land he tilled, and he knew it every foot and how each bit lay, how that field sloped, and how this one must be ditched if he was to secure the harvest. Much good manure had he put into the land, too, not only the excrements of his own beasts and of his household, but he had labored and gone into the town and carried out for this long distance buckets of the town's waste. He had risen often and early in the morning to do this. Now he thought of all those stinking loads he had carried and of all his labor gone into these fields, and it seemed to him an ill thing indeed if now it were all to pass to another man. So he said hesitating,

"Well, I had not thought of owning the land myself yet. I thought in my son's time perhaps it might be ready to sell. But if it is to be sold now I will think what I can do and I will tell you tomorrow when I have thought of it. But what is your price?"

The two brothers looked at each other then and Wang the Second said quickly before the elder brother could speak, for he feared that one would say too little,

"The price is just and fair; fifty pieces of silver for a field the size of the sixth of an acre."

Now this was a high price and too much for land so far from town as this and it was more than could be paid for it, and they all knew this, but still it was a start to the bargain. Then the farmer said,

"Such a price I cannot pay, poor as I am, but I will tell you tomorrow when I have thought."

Then Wang the Eldest grew too anxious for the money and he said,

"A little more or less will not spoil the bargain!"

But Wang the Second cast him an angry look and he plucked his brother by the sleeve lest he say more foolishness yet and he led him to go away again. But the farmer called after them,

"I will come tomorrow when I have thought!"

This he said, although what he meant was that he must talk with his wife, but it would seem very small in a man if he said he held what his wife thought to be of any account, and so he put it thus to save his own pride.

When the next day came after he had talked with his wife in the night he went to the town where the two brothers lived, and there he bickered and bargained with them and he bargained as once Wang Lung had in that very house for the land that house owned, a house now scattered and dispersed of which only these bricks and stones were left. But a price was agreed upon at last, a third less than Wang the Second had said, and this was fair enough and the farmer was willing because it was a price his wife had mentioned he might take if so be he could get the land for no less. When the land was thus sold, the farmer said,

"How will you have the purchase money, in silver or in grain?"

And Wang the Second said quickly, "Half in silver and the rest in grain."

This he said thinking if he took the grain he could sell it a time or two and turn a little extra silver on it and it would not be robbing his brother either, since it was no one's affair save his own if the grain were turned a time or two and the profit was due him for all this labor. But the farmer said,

"I cannot muster so much silver. I will give you a third in silver and a third in grain now and the last third I promise from next year's harvest."

Then Wang the Elder rolled his eyes in his lordly way and he stamped his foot and shifted his chair where he sat with them in the great hall and he said,

"But how can you tell what the skies will be next year and what rains will come and how will we know what we are to have?"

But the farmer stood there very humble before these rich townsmen, who were his landlords, and he sucked his teeth before he spoke and then he said patiently,

"We on the land are at the mercy of heaven always, and if you cannot share the risk you must take the land again as security."

So it was settled at last, and on the third day the farmer brought the silver, not all at once but in three times, each time with a roll of it wrapped in a blue cloth and hidden in his bosom. Each time he took the silver out slowly and his face drew together as though he were in some pain and he put the silver down on the table hardly, as though he did it with sorrow, and so he did, for into this silver had gone so many years of his life, so many pounds of his flesh, so much of the strength of his sinew. He had collected from every place where he had hid his little stores of gain and he had borrowed all he could, and he could not even have had this except by bitter, frugal living.

But the two brothers saw only the silver and when they had set their seal upon the receipt of it and the farmer had sighed and gone away, Wang the Eldest cried with contempt,

"Well, and the farming folk always cry out and make such

an ado because they live so hard and have so little. But any of us would be willing to gain silver like this man has been able to do, and it has not been hard for him, I dare say! If they can heap it up like this from the land, I swear I shall press harder upon my tenants after this!"

And he pushed back his long silken sleeves and smoothed his soft pale hands and he took up the silver and let it slip through his fat fingers that were dimpled at the knuckles as a woman's are. But Wang the Second took up the money and Wang the Eldest watched him unwillingly as he did it, and Wang the Second counted it swiftly and skilfully into tens once more, although it had been well counted already. Into tens he counted it all and wrapped it up neatly as clerks do in some sheets of paper he had. Wang the Eldest stared at it unwilling to see it go and at last he said longingly,

"Need we send it all to him?"

"We need send it," said Wang the Second coldly, seeing his brother's greed. "We must send it now or his venture fails. And I must take the grain and sell it and be ready for the day when his trusty man comes."

But he did not tell his brother he would turn the grain over a time or two, and Wang the Eldest did not know these tricks a merchant has, and so he could only sit and sigh to see the silver go away. When his brother was gone he sat on awhile, feeling melancholy, and poor as though he had been robbed.

Now Pear Blossom might never have heard of all this that went on, for Wang the Second was cunning beyond all and he never hinted of anything he did, no, not even when at the proper time he took to her the allowance of silver that was hers. Twenty-five pieces he took to her every month as Wang the Tiger had said he must, and the first time he did it she said in her soft voice,

95

"But where does this five come from, for I know only twenty was given to me, and I do not need even so much, only for this poor child of my lord's. But this five I have not heard of."

To this Wang the Second replied,

"Take it, for my younger brother said you were to have it and it comes from his share."

But when Pear Blossom heard this she counted out five pieces with all speed, her small hands trembling, and she pushed the money to one side as though she feared it might burn her, and she said,

"I will not have it—no, I will have nothing except my due!"

At first Wang the Second had thought he would press her, but then he remembered what a risk he ran when he loaned money for this venture of his brother's, and he remembered all the trouble he had for which he received no pay, and he remembered all the possibility there was that the venture might fail. When he thought of all this he scraped up the silver she had set aside and he put it carefully into the bosom of his robe and he said in his small, quiet voice,

"Well, it may be better so, since the other and the elder has as much, and it is true you should have a little less. I will tell my brother."

But seeing what her temper was he forebore to say the very house she lived in belonged to that third son, for it suited them all to have her live there with the fool. He went away, then, and he never said more to Pear Blossom than this, and except for such casual meetings for some purpose or other, Pear Blossom did not see the family in the great town house. Sometimes, it is true, she saw Wang the Eldest pass at the turn of the season, in the spring when he came out to measure the seed for his tenants as a landlord must, although he did but stand by very high and important while some agent he had hired measured it. Or he came out sometimes before the harvest to appraise what the fields had, so that he could know whether or not his tenants lied to him when they cried out as they always did of this and that and what a bad year it had been for them and how much or how little it had rained.

So he came and went a few times a year, and each time he was sweating and hot and ill-tempered with his labor, and he grunted his greeting to Pear Blossom if he saw her, and although she bowed decorously if she saw him, she did not speak if she could help it, because he grew such a great blowsy man and he had a way of leering his eyes secretly at women.

Nevertheless, seeing him come and go, she supposed that the land was as it had always been, and that Wang the Second saw to his lands and the third brother's, and no one thought to tell her anything. She was not indeed one with whom it was easy to gossip, because she was still and distant in her manner to all except children, so that, although she was gentle, yet there was that about her that made people fear her, too. She had no friends at all except that of late she had acquainted herself with some nuns who lived in a nunnery not far away, a quiet house built of grey bricks, and set behind a green willow hedge. These nuns she received gladly when they came to teach her their patient doctrines, and she listened to them and brooded upon them after the nuns were gone, for she longed to learn enough to pray for Wang Lung's soul.

So might she never have known about the selling of the land except that in that very year when the farmer had bought the first parcel of land the little hunchbacked son of Wang the Eldest followed his father at a distance, so that the man did not know it, when he came out to the harvest fields.

Now this lad was the strangest little lad and he was not like any of the children in the courts of the great house. His mother had disliked him from the hour he was born for some reason that none knew, perhaps because he was less ruddy and good to see than her other children or perhaps because she was weary then of child-bearing and weary of him before he was born. But because of her dislike she had given him at once to a slave to suckle and this slave did not love him either because they had taken her child away from her for his sake, and she said he had an eye too wise for his age, that looked evil in his baby face. She said he was full of malice, too, and that he bit her wilfully when he suckled, and once she screeched as she held him to her breast and she dropped him upon the tiles of the court where she sat under a shade tree with him, and when they came to see what was amiss she said he had bit her until she bled, and she held her breast out for them to see, and it was true it did bleed.

From that time on this lad grew hunched, and it was as though all his strength of growing went into this great knot he carried on his shoulders, and everyone named him Hunchback and by that name did even his parents call him. Seeing what a poor thing he was and that there were other sons there was no trouble taken over him and he did not have to learn his letters or do anything at all, and he learned early to stay out of men's sight, and especially out of the sight of other children, who mocked him cruelly for the burden he bore. He prowled about the streets or he walked far out in the countryside alone, limping as he walked, and carrying that great load of his upon his back.

On this harvest day he had followed his father unseen and he kept out of his father's sight, for well he knew his father's ill temper on such days as he must go to his land, and he followed him out as far as the earthen house. But Wang the Eldest passed on to his fields, and the hunchback stayed to see who it was that sat at the door of the house.

Now it was only Wang Lung's poor fool, and she sat there

98

in the sun as she always did, but she was a woman grown in body now and more than that for she was nearly forty years old and there were white streaks in her hair. But she was still the same poor child and she sat there grimacing and folding her bit of cloth, and the hunchback wondered at her, for he had never seen her before, and in his malicious way he began to mock her and make grimaces, too, and he snapped his fingers so loudly under her nose that the poor thing shrieked in fear.

Then Pear Blossom came running out to see what went wrong and when the lad saw her he ran limping and hobbling into the pointed shadows of the bamboo grove, and from there he peered out like a little savage beast. But Pear Blossom saw who it was and she smiled her gentle sad smile and she drew out of her bosom a small sweet cake, for she carried such cakes with her to coax the fool sometimes when she grew stubborn suddenly from some strange caprice and was unwilling to obey. This cake she held out to the hunchback, and he stared at her first and at last he crept out and seized the cake and stuffed it all into his mouth at once. Then enticing the child she got him to come and sit beside her upon a bench at the door and when she saw how this poor lad sat himself down all askew and how small and weary his face looked under the great burden on his back, and his eyes so deep and sorrowful she did not know whether he was man or child except he was so small, she reached out her arm and she laid it about his crooked body, and she said in her pitying soft way,

"Tell me, little brother, if you are the son of my lord's son or not, for I have heard he had one like you."

Then the child shook her arm off sullenly and nodded and made as if he would go away again. But she coaxed him and gave him another cake and she smiled at him and said,

99

"I do believe you have a look about your mouth like my dead lord's, and he lies now under that date tree there. I miss him so sorely that I wish you would come here often because you have some look of his."

This was the very first time that anyone had ever said such a thing to the hunchback before, to wish him there, for he was used, even though he was a rich man's son, to have his brothers push him aside and to have the very servants careless of him and serve him last because they knew his mother did not care for him. Now he stared at her piteously and his lips began to quiver and suddenly he wept, although he did not know why he did, and he cried out in his weeping,

"I wish you would not make me weep so—I do not know why I weep so—"

Then Pear Blossom soothed him with her arm about that knotty back of his and although he could not have said so, the lad felt it was the sweetest touch he had ever had upon him and he was soothed without knowing why or how he was. But Pear Blossom did not pity him too long. No, she looked at him as though his back were straight and strong as other lads' are, and after this day the hunchback came often to the earthen house, for no one cared where he went or what he did. Day after day he came, until his very soul was knit to Pear Blossom. She was skilful with him, too, and she made as though she leaned on him and needed his help to care for the fool, and since no one had ever looked to the lad for help of any sort before, he grew quiet and gentle and much of his evil spirit went out of him as the months went on.

If it had not been for this lad, then, Pear Blossom might never have known how the land was being sold away. Nor did the lad know he told her, for he talked to her of everything as it came into his mind and he prattled of this and that and he said, one day,

"I have a brother who will be a great soldier. Some day my uncle is to be a great general, and my brother is with him learning how to be a soldier. My uncle is to be a very king some day, and then my brother will be his chief captain, for I heard my mother telling it so."

Pear Blossom was sitting on the bench by the door when the lad said this, and she looked away over the fields and she said in her quiet voice,

"Is your uncle so great, then?" She paused awhile and then she said again, "But I wish he were not a soldier because it is so cruel a thing to be!"

But the lad cried, boasting a little, "Yes, he is to be the greatest general and I think a soldier, if he is a brave, good hero, is the most magical thing a man can be. And we are all to be great with him. Every month my father and my second uncle send my soldier uncle silver against the time he will be great and a hideous great harelipped man comes for the silver. But some day we are to have it all back again, for I heard my father tell my mother so."

Now when Pear Blossom heard this a small strange doubt came into her mind and she pondered a little and then she said gently as though it were a matter of no account and as though she asked from idle curiosity,

"And where does so much silver come from, I wonder? Does your second uncle loan it from his shop?"

And the lad answered innocently and proud of his knowledge,

"No, they sell the land that was my grandfather's, and I see the farmers come in every day or so and they take a roll out of their bosoms and unwrap it and there the silver is, shining like stars when it falls upon the table in my father's room. I have seen it more times than a few and they do not mind if I am standing by because I am of such little worth."

101

Then Pear Blossom rose so quickly that the little lad looked at her wondering, for she moved usually very softly, and she checked herself then and said to him in the gentlest way,

"I have only just thought of something I must do. Will you look after my poor fool for me while I am gone? There is no one whom I trust as I do you."

This the lad was proud to do for her now and he forgot what he had said and he sat there proudly holding a bit of the fool's coat in his hand while Pear Blossom made ready to go. So he sat and Pear Blossom saw him thus when she had drawn a dark coat about her and had set forth in all haste across the fields. There was that in these two poor creatures, that even now stayed her a moment to look back at them, and it drew her heart out and curved her lips into a smile of sad tenderness. But she hastened on, for if she looked at these two with love, and she loved no one else now, there was such an anger in her heart as must out, and if it were a quiet anger, seeing her anger was always so and she could have no other kind, still it was a firm anger, too, and she could not rest until she went and found the brothers and found out what they truly did with the good lands they had from their father, even the land he had bid them keep for the generations to come in his family.

She hastened through the fields upon the narrow foot paths and she was alone and there was no one to be seen in these byways except here and there in the distance the figure of a man in his blue cotton work garments bending over his land. Seeing these her eyes filled with tears as they often did now and too easily in these days, for she remembered how Wang Lung used to go about on these very paths and how he loved the earth so that he would stop sometimes and pick up a handful of it and turn it over in his fingers, and how he would never lease it longer than a year because he would keep it his own—and here were these sons of his selling it away from him!

For although Wang Lung was dead, he lived on for Pear Blossom and, to her, his soul was always hovering about these fields and she felt he surely knew it if they were sold. Yes, whenever a small chill breeze smote her suddenly on the face by day or by night, or a little whirling wind wheeled along the roadway, such winds as others fear because these winds are so strange it is said they must be souls flying past, Pear Blossom lifted her face and smiled when such a wind smote her, and this because she believed it might be the soul of the old man who had been like a father to her and dearer than the father who sold her to him.

So with this feeling of his presence, she hastened through the land and it lay fair and fruitful before her, for there had been no famine these five years, and there would be none this year either, and the fields lay tended and fruitful and waving with the tall wheat which was still too green for harvest. She passed by such a field now and a little wind rose out of the grain and rippled it so that it bent silvery and smooth as though a hand had brushed over it and she smiled and wondered what wind it was and lingered an instant in her purpose until the wind sank into the grain again and left it still.

When she came to the town and to the gate where the vendors spread their stores of fruits she bent her head and kept her eyes steadfastly upon the ground and she did not once look up to meet the eyes of anyone. No one paid heed to her, either, for she was so small and slight and not young as she had once been, and clad as she was in her dark robe and her face without powder or red paint, she was not one for men to see above any other woman. Thus she went. If any had looked at her tranquil pale face he would not have dreamed that a good deep anger burned in her and that she was going bent on bitter reproof, and brave for the hour.

When she reached the great gate of the town house she passed through it without calling out she was come. The old gateman sat there on the threshold nodding, his jaw ajar and showing the only three teeth he had scattered here and there in his mouth, and he gave a start as she passed, but he knew her and he nodded again. She went as she had planned straight to the house of Wang the Eldest, for although she disliked him heartily, she had more hope of moving him than the greedy heart of Wang the Second. She knew, too, that Wang the Eldest was seldom purposely unkind and she knew that if he were foolish, yet he had a kind, loose heart sometimes, too, and he could be kind if it did not trouble him too much at the moment. But she feared the cold narrow eyes of the second son.

She entered the first courts and a slave was there idling, a pretty girl who had slipped out to catch the eye of a young serving man who waited in the court for something, and Pear Blossom said to the slave in her courteous way,

"Child, tell your mistress I am come for something if she will see me."

Now the lady of Wang the Eldest had been somewhat friendly to Pear Blossom after Wang Lung died, and far more friendly than she had ever been to Lotus, because Lotus was so coarse and so free with what she said, and Pear Blossom never spoke in such ways. Of latter times when they had met at some common family day of ceremony the lady used even to say to Pear Blossom,

"You and I, after all, are nearer to each other than to these others, for the eyes of our hearts are finer and more delicate."

And of late she had said, "Come and talk with me sometimes about the things the nuns and priests say of the gods. You and I are the only devout ones in this house."

104

This she said when she had heard that Pear Blossom listened to the nuns from that nunnery not far from the earthen house. So Pear Blossom asked for her now, and the pretty slave came out soon, her eyes creeping here and there to see if the young serving man were still there or not, and she said,

"My lady says you are to come and sit down in the great hall and she will come as soon as she finishes the round of prayers she is making on her rosary that she has vowed to make every morning."

So Pear Blossom went in and sat down in a side seat in the great hall.

Now it happened that on this day Wang the Eldest had risen very late for he had been to a feast the night before in a certain fine inn in the town. It had been a noble feast with the best of wines and behind every guest's chair a pretty singing girl was hired to pour out his wine for him and to sing and to prattle and to do anything else the guest to whom she was appointed might like her to do. Wang the Eldest had eaten mightily and had drunk more than he usually did, and his singing girl had been the prettiest little lisping maid, not more than seventeen years old, but still so wise in her coquetry that she might have been a woman used to men for ten years and more. But Wang the Eldest had drunk so well that even this morning he did not remember all that had happened the night before, and he came into the hall smiling and yawning and stretching himself, not seeing that anyone was there before him. Indeed the truth was his eyes were slow to see anything this morning, because he was smiling and thinking inwardly of the little maid and how she had slipped her small cool fingers into his coat against his neck to tease him when he played with her. And, thinking of this he said to himself that he would ask his friend who had been host where this maid lived and to what public house she belonged and he would seek her out and see what she was.

Thus yawning loudly he stretched his arms above his head and then he slapped his thighs to waken himself and he came sauntering into the great hall clad only in his silken undergarments and his feet were bare and thrust into silken slippers. Then his eye fell suddenly on Pear Blossom. Yes, she stood there straight and quiet as a shadow in her grey robe, but trembling because she loathed this man so much. He was so astonished to see her there that he let his arms drop suddenly and he broke off his yawn unfinished and stared to see her. Then seeing it was really she he coughed in embarrassment and said courteously enough,

"I was not told anyone was here. Does my lady know you are here?"

"Yes, I sent one to tell her," said Pear Blossom, and as she spoke she bowed. Then she hesitated and she thought to herself, "It is better if I do speak now and speak out what I have to say to him alone." And she began to speak quickly and more quickly than her wont was, the words hurrying and pressing upon each other, "But I have come to see the Eldest Lord. I am so distressed—I cannot believe it. My own lord said, 'The land is not to be sold.' And you are selling it— I know you are selling it!"

And Pear Blossom felt a rare slow red come up into her cheeks and she was suddenly so angry she could scarcely keep from weeping. She bit her lips and lifted her eyes and looked at Wang the Eldest, although she loathed him so she could scarcely bear to do it, and even while she did it for Wang Lung's sake, she could not but see how fat and yellow and loathly this man's neck was where he had left his coat unbuttoned, and how the flesh hung pouched under his eyes, and how his lips puffed out full and thick and pale. Then when

106

he saw her eyes steadfastly upon him he was confused for he feared very much the anger of women and he turned away and made as though he must button up his coat for decency's sake. He said hastily over his shoulder,

"But you have heard an idle tale—but you have had a dream!"

Then Pear Blossom said more violently than anyone had ever heard her say anything,

"No, I do not dream—I had it from the lips of one who spoke the truth!" She would not tell where she had heard it lest the man beat his poor hunched son, so she held back the name of the lad but she went on, "I do marvel at my lord's sons that you disobey him like this. Although I am weak and worthless I must speak and I will tell you this, my lord will avenge himself! He is not so far away as you think, and his soul hovers over his land still, and when he sees it gone he will have ways to avenge himself upon sons who do not obey their father!"

Now she said this in such a strange way and her eyes grew so large and earnest and her soft voice so chill and low that a vague fear fell upon Wang the Eldest, and indeed he was a man easily afraid in spite of his great body. No one could have persuaded him to go alone among grave lands at night and he believed secretly the many tales told about spirits; although he laughed falsely and loudly, still secretly he did believe. So when Pear Blossom spoke thus he said hastily,

"There has been only a little sold—only a little of what belonged to my younger brother, and he needs the silver and a soldier cannot want land. I promise you no more shall be sold."

At this Pear Blossom opened her mouth to speak but before her voice could come the lady of Wang the Eldest entered and she was plaintive this morning and vexed with her lord because she had heard him come in drunken and talking of some maid or other he had seen. She saw him now and cast him a scornful look so that he made haste to smile and nod negligently as though naught were amiss, yet watching secretly too, and he was secretly glad Pear Blossom was here, for his lady was too proud to speak her full mind if he were not alone. He grew voluble and made a great fuss to feel the teapot on the table to see if it were hot and he said,

"Ah, here is the mother of my sons, and is this tea hot enough for you? I have not eaten yet and was but now on my way to the tea house for a sup of tea there, and I will go my way and not disturb you—well I know ladies have that to say to each other which is not for us men to hear—" and laughing falsely and hollowly and uneasy beneath his wife's haughty silence and the stiff looks she threw at him, he bowed and made such haste away that his flesh shook on him.

The lady said nothing at all while he was there but she seated herself and held her back straight and away from the chair, for she would never lean at all, and she waited for him to be gone. Indeed she did look a very perfect lady, for she wore a smooth satin coat of a blue grey hue, and her hair was combed and coiled and smooth with oil although it was scarcely mid-day yet and at an hour when most ladies do not do more than turn upon their beds and reach out a hand for their first drink of tea.

When she had seen her lord gone, she heaved a sigh and she said solemnly,

"There is no one who knows what my life is with that man! I gave him my youth and my beauty, and I never complained however often I had to bear, even after I had three sons, even after he went and took to himself a common daughter of the people, a maid such as I might have hired for a servant. No,

I have borne with him in all he did, although I am wholly unused to such low ways as he has."

She sighed and Pear Blossom saw that for all her pretences she was truly sad, and she said to divert her,

"Well we all know how good a wife you are and I have heard the nuns say you do learn the good rites more quickly than any lay sister they have ever taught."

"Do they say so?" cried the lady greatly pleased, and she began to talk of what prayers she said and how many times a day and how some time she would take the vow against all meat eating, and how it behooved all of us who are mortal to think gravely of the future, since there are but heaven and hell for final resting places for all souls until the bitter round of life begins again, and the good have their reward and the evil theirs also.

So she prattled on and Pear Blossom did but half listen and with the other half of her heart she wondered heavily if she could believe what the man said when he promised to sell no more land, and it was hard for her to believe he could be true. And suddenly she was very weary and she took the moment when the lady was silent for an instant to sup tea, and she rose and said gently,

"Lady, I do not know what your lord tells you of his affairs, but if you can bring to his mind sometimes what his father's last command was, that the land was not to be sold, I pray you will do it. My own lord labored all his life to bring together these lands that his sons of a hundred generations might rest upon a sure foundation, and it is surely not well that already in this generation they should be sold. I beg your help, lady!"

Now this lady had indeed not heard how much of the land was sold, but she would pretend there was nothing she did not know and so she said with great certainty,

"You need not fear that I will let my lord do anything that is unseemly. If land is sold it is only the distant bit that belongs to the third brother, because he has schemes to be a general, and to raise us all up, and he needs silver more than land."

Now when Pear Blossom heard this same thing said over again she was somewhat reassured and she thought it must be true, if it were thus said again, and so she took her leave a little comforted. She bowed and said her farewells in her soft still way, giving every deference to the lady so that she left her complacent and pleased with herself. And Pear Blossom returned to the earthen house.

But Wang the Eldest saw his brother in the tea house to which he went and Wang the Second was there eating his noon meal, and he dropped himself down heavily beside the table where his brother sat alone and he said pettishly,

"It does seem as though men can never be free from the nagging of women, and as if I had not enough of it in my own house that last woman of our father's must come and tell me she hears a rumor of the land being sold and she clamors to get me to promise it is not to be sold!"

Then Wang the Second looked at his brother, and his smooth thin face curved into its slight smile and he said,

"What do you care what such an one says? Let her say! She is the least in my father's house and she has no authority of any kind. Pay no heed to her and if she mentions land to you, talk to her of anything except the land. Mention this and that to her but let her see you pay her no heed because she has no power to do anything. She should be glad she is fed every month and allowed to live on in that house."

The serving man came at this moment with the account, and Wang the Second looked at it sharply and cast it up in his mind and found it correct. He took the few coins out then that were needed, and he paid the money out slowly as though he did protest that the charge should not have been wrong somehow. Then he bowed a little to his brother and went away, and Wang the Eldest stayed on alone.

In spite of what his brother said he felt some melancholy sitting with him and he wondered with a touch of fear what Pear Blossom had meant when she said the old man was not far away even though he was dead. And as he thought he grew very uneasy so that at last he called to the serving man and he ordered a rare and dainty dish of crabs to divert himself and make him able to forget what did not please him.

IX

TWICE and thrice did Wang the Tiger send his trusty harelipped man to his brothers and twice and thrice did the man bring back silver to his captain. He carried it on his back and wrapped in blue cloth as if it were some poor possession of his own and he was clad in a coarse blue coat and trousers and he was barefoot except for rough straw sandals. No one on the road seeing this man plod along in the dust with his load in a bundle on his back would have dreamed that he carried rounds of silver there or that he was anything more than some common fellow, although if anyone had taken thought to look more closely than usual he would have seen that the man sweated strangely under so small a load as he had. But no one looked at him as closely as this, since he was so poorly clad and his face was common and coarse and like a hundred others to be seen in a day except for his split lip, and if anyone stared at him a moment it was only to wonder at this hideous lip of his and at the two teeth he had growing out of the roots of his nose.

Thus safely the trusty man brought the silver to his captain, and when Wang the Tiger had enough buried under his tent to last him three months until he could establish himself, he set the day for his going forth for himself. He gave his own secret signal and the word ran among the men who were ready to go with him and on a certain day after the cutting of the rice harvest and before the cold came down out of the north, on a certain night when there was no moon until dawn and then but a warped thing hung crookedly in the sky, these men crept out each from his bed where he slept and they left the banner of the old general under whom they served.

A hundred men in all so crept forth on that dark night, and every man rose in utter silence and rolled his quilt and tied it upon his back and took up his gun if he had one, and he took his neighbor's also if he could do it without waking the man, although this was not easy for by custom every man slept with his gun under his body in such a way that if anyone moved to take it from him he was awakened and could cry out. This was because a gun was so precious a thing and it could be sold for a heap of silver and sometimes men stole a gun to sell if they lost too heavily at gambling or if they were unpaid for many months when there was no war on, and no looting, and so no silver coming in. Yes, if a soldier lost his gun it was a grievous thing, for guns are brought from very distant and foreign parts of the world. On this night, therefore, the men who crept forth took what they could, but they did not get in all more than twenty guns or so beyond their own, because the soldiers all slept so warily. Still, twenty was good and they could enlarge their number by twenty men.

All these hundred soldiers were the stoutest men and the

best that had fought under the old general, his bravest and most daring, his most ruthless and experienced among the younger soldiers he had. They were very few from the south and nearly all were come from wild inner provinces where men are bold and lawless and not afraid of dealing death. Such men were the more easily caught by the proud looks and the tall straight body of Wang the Tiger, and they admired his silences and his sudden angers and his ferocity, and they admired him the more because there was nothing now to worship in the fat old general who grew so fat he could not even climb his horse any more unless two men hoisted and heaved his legs over the saddle. Yes, there was not anything to fire a young man in such as he and so they were ready to desert him and to follow a new hero.

Each man with his gun then and each with his horse if he had one rose in the dead of that night at the signal, and the signal was when any man felt three light strokes upon his right cheek he was to rise instantly and buckle on his belt with his ammunition and take up what he had for a gun, and mount his horse or come on foot if he had not one, to a certain spot in a shallow valley that lay in the top of a mountain five miles away. There was an old temple there, deserted except for an aged hermit, dazed in his head, who lived among the ruins, and poor shelter though this was, it would shelter them until Wang the Tiger could shape them into an army and lead them on to the place he would choose.

Now Wang the Tiger had already prepared everything there and days before he had sent out the trusty man and his pocked nephew and they had wines set in the temple in jars and some live pigs and fowls and even three fat oxen penned into an empty cell where some priest had lived once. These Wang the Tiger had bought from farmers round about, and he was an honorable man and paid for all he took, and he would not, as some soldiers do, take what the poor have and pay nothing for it. No, he had his trusty man pay close to the full value and so the beasts were driven up the mountain to that temple and the pocked lad stayed there to watch them.

The trusty man had bought three great iron cauldrons, too, and he carried them up the mountain one by one over his head, and he set them on little ovens he built out of the old bricks of the ruined temple. But more than this he did not buy, for Wang the Tiger had it in his mind to go quickly away from this place and as quickly as he could to the north to some fastness there where he would be safe from the old general. Not that he wanted to go near the northern capital, either, lest he have to contend too soon with the state soldiers who come out sometimes against such lords of war as Wang the Tiger had it in his mind to be. Still, he feared neither of these very much, for the old general's wrath was short-lived these days, and as for the state it was a time when one dynasty ended and no new dynasty had come up to take its place, and so the state was weak and robbers flourished and lords of war strove heartily together for highest place and there was nothing to restrain them.

To this temple, then, did Wang the Tiger come on that dark night and he took with him the pale son of Wang the Eldest, and it was a puzzle to him often to know what he would do with this timorous, down-cast youth. The pocked youth had rejoiced in the adventure and he had gone out merrily enough to do what he was told, but this other one hid himself out of sight and now when Wang the Tiger roared at him to follow him he crept shivering behind his uncle, and when Wang the Tiger flashed the light of his flaming torch on him he could see the lad was all of a sweat and Wang the Tiger shouted at him in scorn,

114

"How is it you sweat when you do nothing?"

But he did not stay to hear if there were any answer. He strode on through the night and the lad's faltering footsteps followed.

There at the pass at the top of the mountain which led to the ruined temple Wang the Tiger set himself down upon a rock and he sent the lad into the temple to help with the food. He stayed there alone and he waited to see who would come to his banner that night out of all who had promised. Then men came in pairs and singly and in eights and tens, and Wang the Tiger rejoiced to see each one, and he called out to each,

"Ha, you are come!" and he called out, "Ha, you noble good fellows!"

Whenever he heard footsteps of those who came to join him as they came up the ruined stone steps of the temple path he took the smouldering torch he held in his hand and he blew it into flame and let its light fall over the faces and he exulted to see this good man he knew and that among those who came. Thus the one hundred assembled themselves, and Wang the Tiger told them off, and when all had come that he knew would come he commanded that the oxen be killed and the fowls and the pigs too. Then the men set themselves heartily to such a task, for they had not eaten very good meat in many a day. Some lit the ovens and set them roaring and some fetched water from a mountain stream that ran near there, and others killed the beasts and skinned them and hewed them in pieces. But when they had plucked the fowls they stuck them upon spits of green wood that were forked branches the men hacked from the trees about the temple, and these fowls they roasted whole before the fires.

Then when all was ready they spread the feast upon the stone terrace in front of the temple, a ruined terrace where the weeds were forcing the old stones apart. In the center was a great old iron urn, higher than a man is tall, but even it was crumbling into red dust it was so old. By this time it was day and the newly risen sun streamed down upon the men and the cool sharp mountain air made them famished, and they all crowded laughing and eager about the smoking food. And everyone ate and was filled full, and there was joy everywhere because it seemed to all that a new and better day was beginning for them under this new leader, young and brave, and he would take them into new lands where there were food and women and all the plenty a lusty man needs.

When they had satisfied their first hunger and before they fell to again they broke the clay seals of the wine jars and into each man's bowl he carried they poured out wine, and they drank and laughed and shouted and they cried out to each other to drink to this and to that, and most of all to their new leader.

Out of the shadows of the bamboo thicket the poor dazed hermit watched them beside himself with wonder, and he muttered to himself, thinking they were devils. He stared to see them eat and drink so lustily and the water ran out of his mouth when he saw them tearing the smoking meats apart. But he did not dare to come out for he did not know what devils they were come suddenly like this into the quiet valley where none but himself had lived these thirty years alone, tending a bit of land to feed himself. And as he stared, one of the soldiers, being stuffed with food and drowsy with wine, threw away the thigh bone of an ox he chewed upon and it fell at the edge of the thicket. Then the hermit put forth his scrawny hand and seized it and drew it silently into the shadows and he put the bone to his own mouth and sucked and gnawed it, and he trembled strangely for he had not eaten meat all these years and he had forgotten the flavor of it and how good it was. And he could not but suck and mumble at the bone, although he groaned within himself as he did it, knowing through all his daze that for him this was a sin.

Then when they had eaten all they could and the remnants were strewed about the court, Wang the Tiger rose with a sharp swift leap and he leaped upon a monstrous old stone turtle that stood to one side and a little above the terrace at the base of a great old juniper tree. This turtle had once marked some famous grave place and it had borne on its back one past day a high stone tablet extolling the virtues of the one dead, but the tree in its indomitable growing had pushed this tablet aside so that at last it fell and now it lay split upon the ground with its letters rubbed away by wind and rain, while the tree grew on.

Upon this turtle Wang the Tiger leaped and he stood and looked down upon all his own men. He stood proudly with his hand upon the hilt of his sword and one foot thrust forward upon the turtle's head, and he looked at them in his arrogance, his black brows drawn down, and his eyes glittering and piercing. And as he looked on these men who were his, his heart swelled and swelled until it seemed his body would burst with it, and he thought to himself,

"These are my own men—sworn to follow me. My hour is come!" And aloud he cried and his proud voice rang through those silent woods and echoed in the ruined courts of the temple, and he said, "Good brothers! This is who I am! I am a man humble as yourselves. My father farmed the land and I am from the land. But there was a destiny for me beyond the tilling of the fields and I ran away when I was but a lad and I joined the soldiers of the revolution under the old general.

"Good brothers! At first I dreamed of noble wars against

117

a corrupt ruler, for so the old general said his wars were. But his victory was too easy, and he became what we know he is, and I could not longer serve under such an one. Now, seeing that the revolution he led had no such fruition. as I dreamed, and seeing as I do how the times are corrupt and every man fights for himself, it came to me as my destiny that I must call for all good fellows who were restless and unpaid under the old general, and that I must lead these forth to hew out for ourselves a place to be our own, free from corruption. I do not need to tell you that there are no honorable rulers, and the people cry out under the cruelties and oppressions of those who ought to treat them as fathers treat their sons. This has been so from the old days, even five hundred years ago, when good brave fellows banded together to punish the rich and to protect the poor. So shall we do also! I call on you, brave and good fellows, to follow where I go! Let us swear to live and to die together!"

There he stood, shouting this out in his great deep voice, his eyes shining and darting here and there over the men who squatted on the stones before him, his brows now drawn, now springing up like flags unfurled, lighting and changing from instant to instant the look upon his face. When he had finished speaking, every man leaped to his feet and a mighty shout went up from them,

"We swear! A thousand thousand years to our captain!"

Then one man who was more waggish than the others cried out in a squeaky high voice,

"I say he looks like a black-browed tiger, I say!"

And so Wang the Tiger did look, he was so slender and long and he moved so smoothly and his face was narrow at the chin and wide at the cheek bones and very high, and his eyes were wild and watchful and shining, and there above them were his long black brows, pressing down and shadowing his eyes so that when he drew them down his eyes seemed peering and shining out of some cavern. When he lifted his brows up his eyes seemed to spring out from under them and his whole face opened suddenly as though a tiger sprang forth.

Then all the men laughed fiercely and they took up the cry and they shouted,

"Ha, the Tiger, the Black-browed Tiger!"

As for the poor dazed hermit, he did not know what to make of all this shouting of tigers through the valley, and it was true there were tigers roaming in these hills, and he feared them more than anything. Now when he heard these great shouts he looked here and there in his thicket and he ran and hid himself in a small wretched room at the back of the temple where he slept, and he drew the rude bar across the door and he crept into his bed and pulled the ragged quilt over his head and there he lay shivering and weeping and wishing he had not tasted the meat.

Now Wang the Tiger had all a tiger's caution, too, and he knew that his venture was but barely begun and he must take thought of what was ahead of him. He let the men sleep for a while until the wine they had drunk was worn away and the fumes passed off from them, and while they slept he called out three of his men whom he knew to be clever tricky fellows and he told them to disguise themselves. One he bade strip himself except for his ragged inner trousers, and he bade him smear mud and filth on himself as a beggar does and go begging in the villages near the town where the old general was encamped, and he was to hear and to see what he could and to find out whether the old general was making ready to give chase or not. The other two he told to go into a market town and buy at some pawnshop a farmer's garments and his baskets and pole and they were to buy produce and carry it

119

into the city and loiter and see what men said and if any talked of what had happened and of what might happen now that the old general's best men had run away from him. At the mouth to the pass Wang the Tiger set his trusty harelipped man to watch and to search the countryside with his keen eyes, and if he saw any movements of more than a few men anywhere he was to run without delay and bring the word to his captain.

When this was done and these men gone and the others had slept away their wine, Wang the Tiger took stock of all he had. He set down with a brush upon paper the number of his men and how many guns he had and how much ammunition and what the clothing of the men was and what their shoes were, whether good for a long march or not. He commanded his men to file past him and he looked closely at every one, and he found he had a hundred and eight good lusty men, not counting his two lads, and not one among them was too old and only a few were diseased, beyond sore eyes or the itch or such small things that anyone may have and these cannot be counted illness. Now as his men went past him slowly thus, they gaped and stared at the marks he made upon the paper, for not more than a scant two or three of them could read or write, and they were more in awe at Wang the Tiger than ever, because besides the skill at arms he had this wisdom also, that he could brush marks upon a piece of paper and he could look at them again and see meaning there.

And Wang the Tiger found he had besides his men a hundred and twenty-two guns and every man had his belt full of ammunition, and besides this Wang the Tiger had eighteen boxes of bullets he had taken secretly from the general's store to which he had had access. These he had sent one by one and his trusty man had brought them here and stored them behind the crumbling old Buddha in the temple, because there the roof was best and leaked least, and the Buddha sheltered them from rains driving in the gaping doors.

As for clothing, the soldiers had what they wore and it was enough until winter winds came and each man had his quilt to sleep in.

Wang the Tiger was well pleased at all he had and there was enough left of food to feed them three days more, and it was his plan then to march out by night as quickly as he could to his new territories in the north. Even if he had not loathed these southern lands he would have marched to another place, because the old general was so indolent that for ten years and more he had not moved from this place and he lived upon the people taxing them heavily beyond what they could afford to pay, and he took shares of their grain, too, and this he had done until the people were poor and there was nothing more to be had from them, and so Wang the Tiger must seek fresher lands.

Neither was it in his purpose to fight a battle with the old general over this stretch of over-taxed land, and he planned he would move on to the regions near his own home, for there were hills there to the northwest where he might shelter his men, and if he were pursued too hotly he could retreat into the more inaccessible parts, into those places where mountains are fierce and wild and the people are savage, and even lords of war seldom go there save at such times when they are driven into robbery and retreat. Not that he thought of retreat now; no, it seemed to Wang the Tiger that his way lay open before him, and he had only to be fearless and press on and make his name great in the land, and he set no defines to his greatness.

Then the ones whom he had sent out came back and one said,

"The news is everywhere that the old hive of bees has divided and a new swarm has come out and everywhere people are frightened because they say they are sucked so dry and they say the land cannot feed two hordes."

And the one who was the beggar said, "I hung about the very old camp and I smeared mud and filth on my face, so that no one could see what I was, and I listened and watched as I whined for alms, and the whole camp is astir and the old general is shouting and screeching and ordering this and that and taking it back again and saying something else, and he is all askew with his confusion and anger and his face is all purple and swollen. I dared so much as that, even, and I went close to see him, and he shouted out and I heard him, 'I did not dream that black-browed devil could do a turn like this, and I trusted him with everything. Yes, and people do say the northerners are more honest than we! I wish I had him skewered here upon my gun, the cursed thief and son of a thief!' And he cries out every word or two that his men are to take up arms and pursue us and give battle!"

The man paused and chuckled and he was that same fellow who loved to joke in his squeaky way, and now he said, and his voice went squeaking higher and higher and he grinned through his mud,

"But I did not see a single soldier move at all!"

Then Wang the Tiger smiled a little and grimly and he knew he had nothing to fear, for those men had gone unpaid for nearly a year and they stayed on only because they could be idle and yet fed. But if they were to fight they must be paid before they would do it and Wang the Tiger knew that when it came to such a point the old general would not pay them and so in a day or two his anger would cool and he would shrug himself and go back to his women, and his soldiers would sleep in the sun and wake to eat and sleep again.

As for Wang the Tiger, he set his face to the north and he knew he need fear no one.

X

THREE days did Wang the Tiger allow his men to feast and they ate all they could and they drank the jars of wine down to the very lees. When they were fed as they had not been in many months and stuffed and full with their feeding, and when they had slept until they could sleep no more they rose up strong and quarrelsome and lusty. Now all these years Wang the Tiger had lived among soldiers and he had learned well how men are and he knew how to manage strong, common, ignorant fellows, how to watch their moods and make use of these and how to seem to give liberty and yet hold all he could within the leash of his own will. So when he heard his men fall easily into quarreling and when they threatened each other over nothing at all or over nothing more serious than that one fell over another's outstretched legs as he tried to sleep, and when he saw how some began to think of women and long after them, he knew the hour was come when some new hard thing must be begun.

Then he sprang upon the old stone turtle again and he crossed his arms on his breast and he cried out,

"Tonight when the sun is gone behind the edge of the flat fields at the foot of the mountain we must start upon the journey to our own lands! Let every man take heed to himself, and if he has it still in his mind to return to easy feeding and sleeping under the old general let him return now and I will not kill him. But if, having set out with me tonight, any man turns back from the oath we have sworn, then I will stick him through with my sword!"

When he said these last words Wang the Tiger drew out his sword as swiftly as a flash of lightning plays across a cloud, and he thrust it straight out at the listening men and they were so startled they fell back one upon the other and they looked at each other in terror. Wang the Tiger stood waiting and staring and as he waited there were five among the older men who looked doubtfully at each other and at that sharp glittering sword he held thrust at them, and without a word they rose and crept away and down the mountain and they were seen no more. Wang the Tiger watched them go, and he held his sword out still motionless and shining, and he shouted,

"Is there any other one?"

There was a great silence over the men and not one moved for a time. Then suddenly a slight stooped figure stirred on the edge of the crowd and it made haste to creep away, and it was the son of Wang the Eldest. But when Wang the Tiger saw who it was he roared out,

"Not you, you young fool! Your father has given you to me, and you are not free!"

And he sheathed his sword as he spoke and he muttered with contempt as he did it, "I would not dip this good blade into such pale blood. No, I will whip you soundly, as one whips a child!" And he waited until the lad stood still again, his head hanging down as he always held it.

Then Wang the Tiger said in his usual voice,

"Let it be so then. See to your guns and tie your shoes fast upon your feet and gird yourselves, for tonight we make a mighty march. We will sleep by day and march by night so that men will not know we are moving through the countryside. But every time we come into the territory of a lord of war I will tell you what his name is, and if any ask you who we are you must say, 'We are a wandering band who come to join the lord of these lands.' "

Thus it came about that when the sun fell and there was yet a little light of day but the stars were out too, without a moon, the men filed raggedly to the pass, each man girded and with his bundle on his back and his gun in his hand. But Wang the Tiger had the extra guns given only to the men he knew best and whom he could trust for there were many among these men of his who were untried as yet and he could spare a man better than a gun. Such as had horses led them down the mountain and at the foot of the mountain before they set out on the highway to the north Wang the Tiger paused and he said in his harsh way,

"Not one of you is to stop except where I say and we will make no long stop until dawn at a village which I shall choose. There you may eat and drink and I will pay for it."

So saying he leaped upon his own horse, a high red beast with thick bones and long curled hair that had come from the plains of Mongolia, very strong and tireless. It had need so to be this night, for under him Wang the Tiger had put many pounds of silver he carried, and what he could not take he had given to his trusty man to carry and to certain others in lesser amounts, so that if one yielded to a temptation such as may assail any man, no great quantity would be lost. But strong as his beast was Wang the Tiger would not let it go at its full best. No, he was kind at heart and he held his horse reined in and kept it walking, mindful of those men who had no horses and must walk. On either side of him, also, rode his two nephews and he had bought asses for them, and the short legs of the asses could not match his own horse's stride. Some thirty odd of his men were on horses and the rest afoot, and Wang the Tiger divided his horsemen and put half before and half behind and the walking men between.

So through the silent night did they march, mile after mile, stopping now and then when Wang the Tiger shouted that they might rest for a little time and moving again when he gave the command. And his men were sturdy and uncomplaining and they followed him well, for they hoped much from him. Wang the Tiger was pleased with them, too, and he swore to himself that if they did not fail him neither would he fail them and in the days when he was great he would raise up every one of these first followers of his. Thus watching them and thinking of them as dependent upon him and trustful of him, even as children are in those who care for them, there arose in Wang the Tiger's heart a tenderness toward these men of his, for he was a man who could be thus tender secretly, and he was kind to his men and he let them rest a little longer now and then when they threw themselves upon some grassy plot of land, or under juniper trees such as are planted about graves.

Thus they marched for more than twenty nights, and by day they rested in such villages as Wang the Tiger appointed. But before they came to any village he took care to inquire who the lord of that territory was, and if any asked who this horde was and where they went, Wang the Tiger had his answer ready and smooth upon his tongue.

At every village, though, the people set up a mighty lamentation when they saw them coming, not knowing how long such wandering soldiers would stay or what they would eat or what women they might desire. But Wang the Tiger in these first days had very high purposes and he held the leash tightly over his men, and the more tightly because he had so strange a coldness in his own heart against women that he was the more impatient if other men were full of their heat, and he said,

"We are not robbers nor bandits and I am no robber chief! No, I shall hew out for myself a better road than that to greatness and we will win by skill of arms and by honorable means and not by preying upon the people. What you need you are to buy and I will pay for it. You are to have your wage every month. But you shall not touch any woman unless it be such as are willing and accustomed to men for money and their living, and go to them only when you must. Take care for yourselves that you do not go to those who are too cheap and who carry a vile death in them and strew it about. Keep yourselves from such. But if I hear that any man of mine has taken unlawfully a virtuous wife or a virgin daughter, that man will I kill before he has time even to say what he has done!"

Now when Wang the Tiger spoke like this every man of his stopped to hear and to think for there were those eyes of his glittering under his brows and well these men knew that for all his good heart their captain did not fear to kill a man. The young men murmured with admiration, for indeed Wang the Tiger was in these days their hero, and they called out, "Ha, the Tiger—Ha, the Black-browed Tiger!" So they marched on or they stayed at his command and every man obeyed Wang the Tiger or hid it very well if he did not.

There were many reasons why Wang the Tiger had chosen to settle upon lands not too far from his home, and among them was that he would be near to his brothers and so certain of the revenue they would give him for a time until he could establish taxes for himself, and he would be spared the danger of losing his silver by robbery along the way until it was brought to him. Moreover, if he met a reverse very sudden and great, such as is possible sometimes to any man if Heaven turns against him, he could disappear among his own folk, and his family was so great and rich he would be safe. Therefore he shaped his way steadfastly toward the town where his brothers lived.

But on the day before they came into sight of the town walls, Wang the Tiger grew impatient with his men for they lagged at marching and when night came and he commanded them to set out they were slow to move and Wang the Tiger heard some of them muttering and complaining, and one said,

"Well, now, and there are better things than glory and I do not know if we did well to come after a wild fierce fellow like this!" And another said, "It is better to have time to sleep and to have no need for wearing one's legs to the knee, even though there be less to eat!"

The truth was these men were very weary for they were not used to marching so steadfastly, for in these later years the old general had lived so softly his laxness had spread throughout his men. And knowing well how fickle ignorant men are, Wang the Tiger cursed them in his heart that now when they were nearing their northern lands they could fall into complaining. He forgot that while he had been rejoicing in this north and filled with content that he could buy hard-baked bread and sniff the good stout garlic again, these were still strange things to his men. His trusty man said to him secretly one midnight as they rested under a juniper tree,

"It is time we let them rest somewhere three days or so on end and time to feast them and give them a bit of extra silver."

Wang the Tiger leaped to his feet and he shouted,

"Show me the man who talks of straggling, and I will put a shot into his back!"

But the trusty harelipped man drew Wang the Tiger aside and he whispered peaceably,

"No, now, my captain, do not talk thus. Cease your anger. These soldiers are only children at heart, and they will show such strength as you would not believe true if they have the

128

hope of some little joy ahead, even a small reward such as a dish of meat or a jug of new wine or a day's leisure to gamble. They are as simple as this, as easily pleased and quickly sad. The eyes of their minds are not open as yours are, my captain, so that they can remember to see what is more than a day ahead."

Now while this trusty man pleaded thus he stood in a patch of faint moonlight, for the moon had been new and now was full again as they marched, and he was very hideous to see in this light. But Wang the Tiger had tried him so often and knew him to be true and sensible, and he no longer saw the man's split lip, but he saw only his good common brown face and his faithful humble eyes, and he trusted him. Yes, Wang the Tiger trusted this man, although he did not know who he was, for the man never said anything of himself, and if he were very hard pressed he said only,

"I am native to a very far place and if I told you what place you would not know the name it is so far."

But it was rumored that he had committed a crime. It was said he had had a beautiful wife, a pretty girl who could not bear his looks, and she had taken a lover, and this man had found the pair together and he killed them and fled. Whether the tale was true or not none knew, but true it was that this man had attached himself to Wang the Tiger at first for no other reason except that the young man was so fierce and beautiful, and because of his very beauty a marvel to this poor, hideous fellow. And Wang the Tiger felt this love in the man, and he valued him above all others, because the man followed him for no reason of gain or position, but because of this strange love that asked for no return except to be near him. So he leaned on the man's loyalty, and he always heard what he had to say. Now he knew the man was again right, and so Wang the Tiger went to where his men lay outstretched

129

and weary and in silence under the juniper trees, and he said more kindly than his wont was,

"Good brothers, we are hard upon my own town, and near to the village where I was born, and I know every road and path in these parts. You have been brave and tireless all these weary days and nights, and now I shall prepare your reward. I will lead you into the villages round about my own hamlet, but not into that one place, because the folk there are our own, and I would not offend them. And I will have cattle bought and killed and pigs also, and ducks and geese roasted, and you shall eat your fill. Wine you shall have, too, and the best wine in this country is made here, and it is a heady bright wine and the fumes rise quickly. And every man shall have three pieces of silver for his reward."

Then the men were cheered and they rose and they laughed and shouldered their guns and they marched that same night to the town and they passed it and Wang the Tiger led them to the hamlets beyond his own. There he halted and he chose four small hamlets and quartered his men in them. But he did not quarter them there arrogantly as some lords of war will. No, he went himself from village to village first in the early dawn when smoke was beginning to steal out of the open doors, as fires were lit for the first meal, and he sought the village heads and he said courteously,

"Silver I will pay for everything and no man of mine is to look at a woman not free to him. You must take twenty-five men."

But in spite of all his courtesy the village elders were distressed because they had had lords of war promise them before this and yet pay nothing and they looked askance out of their eyes at Wang the Tiger and they stroked such beards as they had and murmured together in their doorways, and at last they asked for some earnest of Wang the Tiger's good faith.

Then Wang the Tiger took out his silver liberally, for these were countrymen of his, and he left an earnest in the hand of every village elder and he said to his own men privately before he left them,

"You are to bear in mind that these folk were friends of my father and this is my own land and the people who see you see me. Speak courteously and take nothing without pay, and if any man of mine looks at a woman who is not public, I will kill him!"

Seeing how fierce he was his men promised him loudly and with many good sound curses on themselves if they failed to do what he said. Then when they were all quartered and food was being prepared for them and he paid out enough silver to change the sour looks of the villagers to smiles, when all was done he looked at his two nephews and he said to them with rough good humor, for indeed it was pleasant to him to be in his own country,

"Well, lads, your fathers will be glad to see you, I swear, and for these seven days I will rest too, for our war lies just ahead."

And he turned his horse toward the south and he passed by the earthen house without stopping for he did not pass near on purpose, and his two nephews followed him on their asses. So they drew near to the town and they went through the old gates again and came to the house. And for the first time in all these months a pale cheer was upon the face of the son of Wang the Eldest and he made a little haste toward his home.

XI

SEVEN days and seven nights did Wang the Tiger stay in the great house in the town and his brothers feasted him and treated him as an honored guest. Four days and four nights he stayed in the courts of his elder brother and Wang the Eldest did all he could to win his younger brother's favor. But all he knew to do was to give him those things he himself counted pleasure, and so he feasted Wang the Tiger every night and he took him to the tea houses where there are singing girls and players on the lute, and he took him to playhouses. Yet it did seem as if Wang the Eldest gave himself pleasure more than he did his brother, for Wang the Tiger was a strange man. He would not eat more than he needed to stay his hunger and then he stopped and sat on in silence while others ate, and he would not drink more than he liked.

Yes, he sat on at feast tables where men made merry and ate and drank until they sweated and must needs take off this robe and that garment and some even went out and vomited what they had eaten so as to have the pleasure of eating more. But Wang the Tiger would not be tempted, no, not by the finest soups nor the most delicate flesh of sea serpents that are sold very dearly because they are so rare and hard to catch, nor would sweets tempt him nor anything made from fruits nor lotus seeds candied, nor honey nor any of those things which men will usually eat, however filled their bellies be.

And although he went with his elder brother to those tea houses where men go to play and toy with women, he sat stiff and sober and his sword hung from his belt and he would not unloose it and he watched everything with those black eyes of his. If he did not seem displeased neither was he pleased and he seemed to see no singing girl above another in beauty of voice or face, although there were more than one or two who noted him and yearned over his dark strength and his good looks so that they made every effort and they went and put their little hands on him even and they drew out their glances long and sweet and languid and fastened upon him. But he sat on as he was, rigid and unmoved and staring at all alike, and his lips were as surly as ever, and if he ever did say anything it was not the things to which pretty women are accustomed, but he would say,

"This singing is like the cackling of jays to me!" And once when a little soft creature, painted and pouting, looked straight to him and sang her little warble, he shouted out, "I am weary of all this!" and he rose and went away and Wang the Eldest had to follow him although it went against him sore to leave so good a play.

The truth was that Wang the Tiger had from his mother his scanty sparing tricks of speech so that he never said anything he need not say and his speech when it came was so bitter and true that after a time or two men feared it when his lips so much as moved.

Thus he spoke one day when the lady of Wang the Eldest was of a mind to come and urge him a little and say a good word or two for her second son. She came into the room where Wang the Tiger sat drinking tea one afternoon and Wang the Eldest sat by a small table drinking wine. She came in with mincing steps and with much modesty and very proper downcast looks, and she bowed and simpered and did not so much as look at the men, although when he saw her come in Wang the Eldest wiped his face hurriedly and poured out a bowl of tea for himself instead of the wine he had there hot in a pewter jug.

She came in plaintively and tottering on her little feet and

133

she sat down in a lower seat than her right was although Wang the Tiger rose, too, and motioned her to sit higher. But the lady said, and she made her voice weak and delicate as she did now-a-days unless she forgot herself or grew angry,

"No, I know my place, Brother-in-law, and I am but a weak and worthless woman. If ever I forget it, my lord takes pains to make me remember again, seeing that he holds so many women better and more worthy than I."

This she said and she cast an oblique look at Wang the Eldest so that he broke into a light sweat and murmured in a feeble way,

"Now, lady, when did I ever—"

And he began to cast over in his mind if there had been any special thing he had done of late of which she could have heard adversely. It was true he had found and sought the singing girl who was young and coy and who had pleased him so well at a feast one night, and he had begun to visit her and to pay her a regular sum and he had thoughts of establishing her somewhere in the town on a bounty as men do when they do not care to add the trouble of a new woman to their courts, yet desire her enough to keep her for themselves for a time at least. But this thing he had not yet accomplished, for the girl's mother lived and she was such a greedy old hag that she would not come down to Wang the Eldest's price for her daughter. So he thought his lady could not have heard of it before the thing was done and he wiped his face with his sleeve again and looked away from her and drank his tea heavily in loud sips.

But the lady was not thinking of him this time and she went on without heeding his muttering and she said,

"I have said to myself that humble as I am and a mere woman, yet I am my son's mother and I ought to come and thank my brother-in-law for what you have done for our worthless second son, and though my thanks can be nothing to one like you yet it is my pleasure to do what I ought and so I do it spite of every burden and slight I have to bear."

Here she cast another of her looks at her lord and he scratched his head and looked at her foolishly and was all in a sweat again because he did not know what she was about to say and being so fat he sweat at nothing at all. But she went on,

"So here be my thanks, Brother-in-law, and worthless though they are they come from a sincere heart. As for my son, I will say that if there is a lad worthy of your kindness he is that one and he is the kindest, best and gentlest lad and such a wise head as he has! I am his mother and although it is said mothers see the best always in their children, still I will say again that we gave you the best son we have, my lord and I."

All this time Wang the Tiger had sat and stared at her as his way was when anyone spoke, and he stared so strangely one could not know whether he heard what was said or not, except when his answer came, and it came now, brutal and blunt,

"If that is so, Sister-in-law, then I am sorry for my brother and you. He is the timidest, weakest lad I ever did see and his gall is no larger than the gall in a white hen. I wish you could have given me your eldest son. He is a good wilful lad and I could break him and make him into something of a good wilful man, obedient to me and none other. But this second son of yours is always weeping and it is like carrying a leaking dipper with me everywhere. There is no breaking him for he has nothing in him and so no making him, either. No, both my brothers' lads disappoint me, for your lad is so soft and timid his brains are washed out in tears, and the other one is good and lusty and rough enough for the life but he is thoughtless and he loves his laughter and he is a clown, and I do not know how high a clown can go. It is an evil thing for me that I have no son of my own to use now when I need him."

Now what the lady might have said to such a speech as this none knows, but Wang the Eldest was trembling for he knew no one had ever spoken to her so plainly as this before, and the high red was flooding into her face and she opened her lips to make sharp answer. But before her voice could shape the words, her eldest son came out suddenly from behind a curtain where he was listening and he cried out eagerly,

"Oh, let me go, my mother—I want to go!"

There he stood before them all, eager and beautiful in his youth, and he looked quickly from one face to the other. He wore a bright blue gown the color of a peacock's feathers, such as young lords love to wear, and shoes of foreign leather, and he had a jade ring on his finger and his hair was cut in the newest fashion and smoothed back with fragrant oil. He was pale as young men in rich houses are pale who never need to labor or be burned by the sun, and his hands were soft as a woman's hands. Yet there was something very lusty in his looks too, for all his beauty and paleness, and he had a good, impatient eye. Nor did he move languidly when he forgot himself and forgot that it was the fashion for young men about town to be languid and careless of anything. No, he could be as he was now, his languor all laid aside, when he was full of the flame of a desire.

But his mother cried out sharply,

"Now this is the greatest nonsense I ever heard, for you are the eldest son and after your father the head of the house, and how can we let you go to wars and perhaps even go to a battle and be killed? We have spared nothing at all for you and we have sent you to every school in this town and hired scholars to teach you, and we have loved you too well to send you south to a school even, and how can we let you go to war?" Then seeing that Wang the Eldest sat there silent and hanging his head she said sharply, "My lord, am I to take this whole burden on myself, too?"

Then Wang the Eldest said feebly,

"Your mother is right, my son. She is always right, and we cannot spare you to such hazard."

But the young man, although he was nearly nineteen years old, began to stamp his feet and to weep and to storm and he ran and beat his head against the door lintel and he cried out,

"I shall poison myself if I cannot do what I like!"

Then his parents rose up in great dismay and the lady cried out that the young lord's servant was to be sent for, and when the man came running in terror, she cried to him,

"Take the child to some place for play and divert him and see if this anger can go out of him!"

And Wang the Eldest made haste to take a good handful of silver out of his girdle and he pressed it upon his son and said,

"Take it, my son, and go and buy yourself something you like or use it for a game or whatever you like."

At first the lad pushed the silver away and made as if he would not have such consolation, but the man servant coaxed and besought him, so that after a while the youth took the silver as though very unwillingly, and then flinging himself about and crying out that he would go, and he would go with his uncle, he suffered himself to be led away.

When it was over the lady sank upon a chair and she sighed piteously and she gasped,

"He has always had such—a spirit—we have not known

137

how to do with him—he is much harder to teach than the one we gave you!"

Now Wang the Tiger had sat gravely and watched all that passed, and now he said,

"It is easier to teach where there is a will than where there is nothing. I could make that lad if I had him and all this storming is because he has not been taught."

But the lady had been too put about to endure more and she would not bear it to have it said her sons were not well taught. So she rose in her majestic way and she said, and she bowed,

"Doubtless you have much to say to each other," and she went out.

Then Wang the Tiger looked at his eldest brother with a grim pity and they said nothing for a time, only Wang the Eldest began to drink his wine again, but not with any zest now, and his fat face was mournful. At last he said more thoughtfully than he usually spoke, and he sighed heavily before he spoke,

"There is a thing that is a riddle to me and it is this, that a woman can be so yielding and delicate and pliant to man's will when she is young and when her years come on her she grows another person altogether and is so scolding and troublesome and devoid of all reason as to keep a man dazed. I swear sometimes I will keep off all women, for I do believe my second one will learn of the first one, and they are all so." And he looked at his brother with a strange envy and with eyes as sorrowful as a great child's and he said sadly, "You are fortunate and more fortunate than I; you are free of women and you are free of land. Twice bound I am. I am bound by this accursed land my father left me. If I do not attend to it we have nothing from it, for these accursed country folk are all robbers and leagued against the landlord,

138

however just and good he be. And as for my steward—who has ever heard of an honest man who was a steward?" He drew down his thick mouth plaintively and he sighed again and looked again at his brother and said, "Yes, you are fortunate. You have no land and you are bound to no woman at all."

And Wang the Tiger replied in greatest scorn,

"I do not know any women at all."

And he was glad when the four days were gone and he could go to the courts of Wang the Second.

Now when Wang the Tiger came into his second brother's house he could not but marvel to see how different it was from the other's, and how full of high good humor, in spite of bickering and quarreling among the children, too. And all the noise and good humor swelled and centered about Wang the Second's country wife. She was a noisy, boisterous creature and whenever she spoke her voice rang through the house she was so ruddy and loud. Yet, although she lost her temper a score of times a day and knocked this child's head against that one's or flung her arm out, with its sleeve forever rolled above her elbow, and slapped some child's cheek with a crack so that the house was full of roaring and bawling from morning until night and every servant was as loud as the mistress, yet she was fond too, in her rough way, and she would seize a child who passed and nuzzle her nose into his fat neck. And while she could be so saving of money, yet when a child came crying for a penny to buy a lump of candy or a bowl of some hot sweet stuff from a passing vendor or a stick of haws dipped in sugar or some such thing children love, she always reached into her deep bosom and fumbled out a penny. Through this noisy lusty house Wang the Second moved quiet and serene and filled with his secret plans, and he was always well pleased with them all and he and his wife lived content with each other.

For the first time Wang the Tiger in these days laid aside for the present his plans of glory and while his men rested and feasted he lived in his brother's house and there was something here in Wang the Second's house that he liked. He saw why his pocked nephew came out of this home merry and laughing and how the other one was always timid and fearful and he felt the content between Wang the Second and his wife and he felt the content the children had too, although they were not washed often nor did any servant take heed of them beyond seeing them fed by day and put into some bed or other at night. But every child was merry out of all the crew, and Wang the Tiger watched them everywhere with some strange moving in his heart. There was one boy of five years or so and Wang the Tiger watched him most, for he was the roundest, fairest boy and Wang the Tiger yearned for him somehow. But when he reached his hand out diffidently to the child, or found a penny and held it to him, the boy was suddenly grave and put his finger in his mouth and stared at Wang the Tiger's grave looks, and ran away, shaking his head. And Wang the Tiger was as pained by this refusal as though the boy were a man, although he tried to smile and make it nothing.

Thus Wang the Tiger waited for these seven days to pass, and his rare idleness made him more thoughtful than he usually was, and seeing these two houses full of children he felt afresh his lack that he had no son to be knit to him. And he thought on and a little about women, for this was the first time he had lived freely in a house where there were wives and maid servants and young slaves running here and there, and there was some strange sweet stir in him sometimes when he saw a slender maid with her back turned

140

to him at some task she had and he could remember once Pear Blossom had looked so about these very courts, where he had been a lad. But when the maid turned and he saw her face his old confusion fell on him, and the truth was there had been in that youth of his such a sealing of his fountains that at the sight of any woman's face there was some stopping in his heart and he turned himself away.

Still in his idleness and with this faint stir in him too, he was restless and one afternoon he told himself he would go and pay his respects to Lotus, for it was in Lotus's courts he used most often to see Pear Blossom in those old days, and he had a secret fancy to see the rooms again and the court. He went then to Lotus, having first sent his servant to announce his coming, and Lotus rose from the table where she sat gaming with her friends, the old ladies of other houses. But he would not sit long. No, he cast his eyes about this room, and he remembered it, and then he wished he had not come and he rose and was restless again and would not stay. But Lotus did not understand his brooding looks and she cried out,

"Stay, for I have sugared ginger in a jar and I have sweetened lotus root and such things as young men love! I have not forgotten what young men are like, no, for all I am so old and fat, I do remember how you all are!"

And she laid her hand on his arm and she laughed her thick laugh and leered at him. Then he loathed her suddenly and he stiffened himself and bowed and made his excuses again and he went away quickly. But he heard the cackling laughter of the old women as they gamed and it followed him through the courts.

Yet even as he went his remembrance made him more restless and he said to harden himself that his life was very far from here now and he must be on his way, and as soon as he had visited once his father's grave as it was his duty to do and especially before he went on with his venture, he would be away once more and out of these courts.

So on the next morning, the sixth day, he said to Wang the Second,

"I will not stay longer than to burn a little incense at my father's grave, else my men will be growing lax and lazy and there is a long fierce road ahead. What have you to say of the moneys I need?"

And Wang the Second said,

"Nothing except that I will give you every month what we have agreed."

But Wang the Tiger cried impatiently, "Be sure I will return you one day all you lend me! Now I go to my father's grave. Do you, then, see that the two lads are ready for me and that they are not drunken or overfed tonight for we set forth at dawn tomorrow!" And he went away, half wishing he need not take his elder brother's son again, but not knowing how to refuse, lest it breed jealousy. And as he went he took a little incense from a store kept in the house and he went out to his father's grave.

Now these two, father and son, had been very far apart when they lived, and even Wang the Tiger's childhood had been bitter because his father had said he must stay on the land, and Wang the Tiger had grown up hating the land. He hated it now and as he drew near to the earthen house which was his he hated it; although it had been his childhood home, he did not love it because it had been a prison to him once and he had thought he would never be free of it. He did not go near it, but he circled around and drew near through a small grove of trees to the hillock where were set the graves of the family.

As he drew near with his swift steps he heard a low soft

sound as though one wept and when he heard it he wondered who could weep at that grave, for he knew Lotus was gaming and well he knew it could not be she. He softened his striding then, and he drew near, and he peered through the trees. There was the strangest sight he had ever seen. Pear Blossom leaned her head upon his father's grave and she sat crouched in the grass in the way that women have when they weep and think no one near and they can weep on uncomforted. Not far from her sat his sister, the fool, whom he had not seen these many years and now although her hair was nearly white and her face shrunken and small she sat in a spot of autumn sunlight and played at a bit of red cloth, folding and refolding it and smiling to see the sun on it so red. And holding to her coat faithfully, as a child does who has been bid to do something for one he loves, sat a small, twisted, hunched boy. He had his face turned sorrowfully to the weeping woman and his mouth was all puckered and he was near to weeping, too, for her sake.

Wang the Tiger stood there, stricken motionless with his surprise, and he listened to Pear Blossom mourning on in that soft low way she had as though the weeping came from some innermost part of her, and suddenly he could not bear it. No, all his old anger fell once more against his father, and he could not bear it. He dropped the incense there where he stood and he turned and walked quickly away, breathing heavily in great sighs as he went, although he did not know he did.

He rushed back over the land and he only knew he must be away from this place, this land—this woman—he must be at his own business. He walked back through the hard autumn sunlight, falling brilliant and clear across the fields, but he saw none of it and noted no beauty.

At dawn he was up and on his red horse and the horse was curveting and impatient in the chill air and his hoofs thudded heavily upon the cobbled street and the pocked lad, well fed with all he had eaten for his morning meal, was on his ass and they rode around to the gate of Wang the Eldest to fetch that other lad. But before they could wait at all a man servant came running out of the gate and he cried as he ran somewhere,

"What a thing of evil is this—what a curse upon this house!" And he ran his way somewhere.

Then Wang the Tiger felt his impatience rise in him and he shouted out,

"What curse is it? Curse it is that the sun is near the horizon and I am not on my way yet!"

But the man did not look back. Then Wang the Tiger cursed very heartily and he cried to the pocked lad,

"That cursed lad your cousin is nothing but a burden to me and never will be else! Go and find him and tell him he is to come or I will not have him!"

The pocked lad slid down at once from his small old ass and ran in and more slowly Wang the Tiger came down from his horse and went to the gate and gave the reins over to the gateman to hold for him. But before he could go further the lad was out again, white as a spirit and breathing as fast as though he had run around the town walls. He gasped out between his breaths,

"He will never come again—he is hung and dead!"

"What do you say, you small monkey!" shouted Wang the Tiger and he leaped and ran into his brother's house.

There was confusion indeed and men and women and servants and all were gathered about something in the court, and above the din and shouting a woman's loud shrieks were heard, and it was the lad's mother who so cried. But Wang

144

the Tiger pushed them aside and in the center of the crowd was Wang the Eldest. His fat face was yellow as old tallow and all shaken with tears, and he held supported in his arms the body of his second son. The lad lay there outstretched in the court, under the bright morning sky, dead, and his head hung back over his father's arm. He had hanged himself with his girdle upon the beam in the room where he slept with his elder brother, and the brother had not known it until he woke in the morning, for he slept hard after wine at some merrymaking the night before. When he woke in the pale dawn and saw the slight form dangling he thought at first it was a garment and he wondered why it hung there but when he looked again he screamed and so woke the house.

Then Wang the Tiger, when one had told him this tale and a score of others helped in the telling, stood and looked down on this dead son with the strangest feeling, and he pitied this lad for a while as he never had when the lad was alive. He was so very small and slight now he was dead. And Wang the Eldest looked up and saw his brother there and he blubbered,

"I never dreamed this child of mine would choose death to going with you! You must have treated him very ill to make him hate you like this! Well for you that you are my brother, or I would—I would—"

"No, Brother," said Wang the Tiger more gently than he was used to speak, "I did not treat him ill. He even had an ass to ride when others older than he walked. But neither did I dream he was brave enough to die. I might have made something of him after all if I had known he had in him the power to die!"

He stood and stared awhile. But bustle began suddenly when the serving man who had run somewhere returned with a geomancer and with priests and their drums and with all those whose duty it is to come with such an untoward death, and in the commotion Wang the Tiger went away and waited in a room alone.

But when he had waited and done all that he should do as brother in so sad a house he mounted his horse and he rode away. And as he went he was sadder than he had been and he was compelled to harden himself and to remember again and again how he had never beaten the lad or treated him ill in any way and none could have known he had this despair in him to take his own life, and Wang the Tiger told himself it was so destined by heaven and not any man could have averted this thing, for so the life of everyone is wholly with heaven. Thus he forced himself to forget the pale lad and how he had looked when his head lay over his father's arm, and Wang the Tiger said to himself,

"Even sons are not all blessing, it may be."

When he had comforted himself like this he was better, and he called heartily to the pocked lad,

"Come, lad, there is a long road before us and we must set out upon it!"

XII

THEN Wang the Tiger struck his horse with the braided leathern whip he carried and he let the beast have its full way and the horse sped over the countryside as though it were winged. It was a day fit to start upon so high a venture as Wang the Tiger's, for the sky was cloudless and the wind blew keen and cool and full of vigor and it turned the trees this way and that and wrenched at them and whipped the late leaves from their branches and it stirred the dust in the roadways and whirled itself over the shorn grain lands. In Wang the Tiger's heart a recklessness rose like the very wind itself and he purposely took his way far from the earthen house and he made a wide circle from the place where Pear Blossom lived and he said to his own heart,

"All the past is finished and I look forward to my greatness and to my glory!"

So the day began and the sun rose full and enormous and glittering over the edge of the fields, but he looked at it unblinking, and it seemed to him that heaven itself set its seal upon him in such a day as this and he would achieve his greatness, for greatness was his destiny.

Early in the morning he came to the hamlets where his men were, and his trusty harelipped man came out to meet him and he said,

"It is very well, my captain, that you have come, for the men are rested and full of food and they are chafing to be on to more freedom."

"Round them out, then, when they have had their morning meal," shouted Wang the Tiger, "and let us be on our way and half way to our own lands by tomorrow."

Now during these days that Wang the Tiger had been in the house of Wang the Second he had been thinking much of what lands he should take for his own rule and he had talked with his brother who was cautious and wise, and it seemed to them that the lands just over into the borders of the next province were very good lands for the purpose and the best to be had. These regions were far enough from Wang the Tiger's home so that if dire need came he would not be taking from those who were his own people and yet near enough so that if he were vanquished in a war he could take refuge among his own. Moreover, it was near enough so that the silver he would need until he was established could be brought to him easily and without too great risk of robbers. As for the lands themselves, they were famous good lands where the famine did not strike too often, and some of the lands were high and some were low, and there were mountains to serve for retreat and hiding. There was besides all this a certain highway that was a passage between the north and south for travellers coming to and fro, and such travellers could very well be taxed also for revenues and the right to pass that way. There were two or three large towns too, and a small city, so that Wang the Tiger need not be wholly dependent upon the people who tilled the earth. These lands had another value also, and it was that they sent out the best grain to the markets for wine and the people were not very poor.

There was but one hindrance to all these goods, and it was that there was already a lord of war over that region and Wang the Tiger must first drive him out if he was to prosper to the utmost, for there is no region rich enough to maintain two lords of war. Now what this lord was or who he was or how strong he was were things Wang the Tiger did not know, for he could not find out anything sure from his brothers except that they had heard him called the Leopard, because he had such a strange slanting forehead sloping back into his head as leopards' foreheads do, and he ruled the people harshly, so that they hated him.

Therefore Wang the Tiger knew he must go secretly to those lands and not in any bold array. No, he must go stealthily, separating his men into small bands so that they would not look more dangerous than bands of deserting soldiers, and he would seek out some retreat in a mountain and from that vantage he would search out the country with his trusty men and see what sort of a lord of war he had to fight and from whom he must take the lands he felt were already his by destiny.

As he planned, so he did. When his men were gathered out of the hamlets and when he had seen each man fed and

148

warmed with good wine against the chill winds that contended with the heat of the mounting sun, when he had taken care that all was paid for and he had asked the villagers, "Did my men do anything in your houses they should not?" and had heard them answer volubly, "No, they did not, and we wish all soldiers were like yours," then Wang the Tiger was well pleased and he drew his men far out beyond the villages and he told them as they stood about him of the lands to which he would lead them and he said,

"There are the best lands anywhere and there is only one lord to fight against. There is such heady wine, too, in that land, as you have never tasted before!"

When the men heard this they shouted with joy and they clamored,

"Take us there, our captain—we have longed for such lands!"

Then Wang the Tiger answered them, smiling his grim smile,

"It is not so easy as this, for we must search out the strength of the lord who holds it. If his men are too many for us, we must seek ways of winning them away from him, and every man of you must be a spy to see and to hear. Nor must anyone know why we are come or we are undone. I will go myself first to see where we can make our camp, and my trusty harelipped man shall stay at the border at a hamlet there called the Valley of Peace. He will stay at an inn there that I have heard of, and it is the very last inn on the street and there is a wine flag hanging out of the door. He is to wait for you and give you the name of the place I shall set for us to gather. Now you are to break up into threes and fives and sevens and saunter as though you were runaways, and if any man asks you where you go, ask him where the Leopard is for you come to join him. To everyone I will give three pieces of silver for food until we meet. But there is one thing I say to every man. If it comes to my ears that any man has injured a humble man or looked at a woman not free to him I shall not ask what man it is but I will kill two men for every such man I hear about."

Then one man called out, "But, my captain, are we never to be free to do the things soldiers may?"

And Wang the Tiger shouted at him, "When I give the command you are free! But you have not fought for me yet, and shall you have the rewards of battle when there has been no battle?"

The man was silent then and he was afraid, for Wang the Tiger was known to be very sudden in his tempers and swift with his sword and he was not a man whom one could move with a witty word or a merry saying fitly spoken. Yet he was known to be just, too, and these men who followed him were good enough and they knew what was fair. It was true they had not fought yet and they were willing to wait so long as they were fed and sheltered and paid.

Then Wang the Tiger watched them as they scattered into groups and when they were so scattered, he paid them from the store he had, and with the pocked lad on his ass and the harelipped trusty man upon a mule Wang the Tiger had bought for him at a hamlet, the three started alone toward the northwest.

When Wang the Tiger came to the border of that region of which he had heard he forced his red horse up a large, tall grave of some rich man's that stood there, and from this vantage he looked out over the land. It was the fairest land he had ever seen and it spread itself out before him, rolling in little low hills and in wide shallow valleys that were already faintly green with the newly sprouted winter wheat. To the northwest the hills rose suddenly into jagged mountains full of cliffs cut clearly against the bright sky of the day. The houses of the people of that land were scattered in small villages and hamlets, good earthen houses not fallen into decay, and many had the roofs newly thatched with straw from that year's harvest. There were even a few houses of brick and tile. In every dooryard near enough for him to see there were ricks of straw and he could hear the distant cackling of hens that had laid their eggs, and now and again the wind blew to him where he stood fragments of some song a farmer sang as he cultivated his fields. It was a very fair land and his heart leaped to see how fair it was. But he had no mind to go through clad as he was in a soldier's garb and on his red horse and let a rumor of war loose too early upon the people. No, he looked and he planned out for himself a winding way to the mountains where he could hide himself and his men and seek out the strength of his enemy before any could even know he was come.

At the foot of the low hill upon which this tall grave and many other graves were, was a little village, the border village of which he had told his men. It stretched out its few furlongs of one street, and Wang the Tiger turned his horse there and he rode through it, with the pair behind him. It was at that time of the morning when farmers return to their own hamlets, and the village tea house was full of farmers drinking tea or supping up bowls of noodles made from wheaten flour or buckwheat. They had their baskets emptied from the markets piled on the ground beside them as they ate, and they looked up in wonder when they heard the clattering of hoofs upon the street and they stared with jaws ajar as Wang the Tiger passed. He looked back at them, too, to see what sort of men they were, and he was very pleased to see how goodly they were, how brawny and brown and hearty and how well fed and he said to himself freshly he had chosen his lands very well if it could breed such men as these. But, save that he looked at them, he went with unusual modesty and as one goes who passes through a place a guest and going on to some other far place.

At the end of the street there was the wine shop he had heard of and he told the pair to wait outside, and he halted his horse and dismounted and he pushed aside the curtain at the door and went into the shop. There was no one there for it was a very small place with but a table or so for guests, and Wang the Tiger sat down and slapped the table with his hand. A lad came running out then and seeing how fierce a man was there he ran back to his father, who was the keeper of the shop, and the man came out and wiped the table with his torn apron and he said, courteously,

"My lord guest, what will you have for wine?"

"What have you?" returned Wang the Tiger.

The shop keeper answered him, "We have the fresh sorghum wine made in these parts. It is the best wine and shipped over the whole earth, I suppose, even to the emperor in the capital."

At this Wang the Tiger laughed in some scorn and he said, "Have you not heard in this little village that we have no emperor these days?"

At this a great look of terror came over the man's face and he said in a whisper,

"No, and I had not heard it! When did he die? Or was his throne taken by violence, and if it was, who is our new emperor?"

And Wang the Tiger marvelled that there could be a man so ignorant as this and he replied with some slight scorn,

"We have no new emperor these days at all."

"Then who rules us?" said the man in consternation as at some new disaster newly fallen on him unawares.

"It is a time of striving," said Wang the Tiger. "There are many rulers and it is not known which can seize the highest seat. It is such a time as any man may use to rise to glory."

This he said, and the ambition that was the greatest part of him soared up suddenly and he cried to his own heart, "And why may not that one be I?" But he said nothing aloud; he only sat and waited for his wine beside the small unpainted table.

Then the man when he had fetched the jug of wine came back and it could be seen from his sober face that he was much troubled and he said to Wang the Tiger,

"It is a very evil thing to have no emperor, for this is to have a body without a head and this means wild movements everywhere and none to guide us all. It is an ill thing you have told me, my lord guest, and I wish you had not told me for now I shall not be able to forget it. Humble as I am, I shall not be able to forget it, and however peaceful our village is I shall be afraid every day for the next."

And with downcast looks the man poured the warm wine into a bowl. But Wang the Tiger did not answer for he had his thoughts elsewhere than on this humble soul, and as for him he was glad it was such an hour as it was. He poured out the wine and drank it down quickly. It spread through his blood, hot and strong, and he felt it mount to his cheeks and fume through his head. He did not drink above a few bowls of it then, but he paid for it and for a bowl more and this he took out to his trusty harelipped man. The man was very grateful for it, too, and he took the bowl in both his hands and supped as best he could, lapping it somewhat as a dog does to taste it and then throwing his head back and pouring it down his throat because his upper lip was so little use to him, divided as it was.

Then Wang the Tiger went back into the shop and he said to the keeper,

"And who rules you here in this region?"

The man looked east and west at this but there was no one near and so he said in a low voice,

"It is a robber chief who is called the Leopard. He is the cruellest bitter fellow. Every one of us must pay a tax to him or he comes sweeping down on us with all his ne'er-do-wells, he and his men like a flock of evil crows to pick us clean. Well do we all wish we could be rid of him!"

"But is there no one to contend with him?" asked Wang the Tiger, and he sat down as though it were a small careless thing he said and of no importance to him. And to seem more careless he said, "Bring me a pot of mild green tea. The wine stays like fire in my throat."

And as the man fetched the tea he answered Wang the Tiger, "Not one to contend, my lord guest. We would complain of him to those above if it were of use so to do. Once we did go to our county court and the highest magistrate in our region lives there. We told him our case and we asked him to send his soldiers out and to borrow soldiers from the one yet above him and see if together they could not drive out this fellow who oppresses us. But, sir, when those soldiers came they were such cruel men and they so lived in our houses and took our daughters and so ate their fill of what they would and did not pay us that they grew to be a burden we could not bear. No, and besides this they were such cowards that they ran at the very smell of a battle and the robbers grew all the more arrogant. So we went then and begged the magistrate to take his soldiers off from us again and he did at last. But it was a very bitter thing at best, for many of the soldiers went and took service under the robbers, giving as excuse that they had not been paid for long and they must eat, and w were worse off than before for a soldier has a gun to take with him where he goes. And as if it were not enough, that magistrate of ours who lives in the county seat there sent out his tax gatherers and put a heavy tax upon us all, on men on the lands and on keepers of shops, too, because he said the state had been put to such a cost to protect us that we must pay them for it. Well enough we knew he and his opium pipe were the state, and so since that time we have never asked for any help, choosing rather to pay so much and so much to the Leopard every feast day and so keep him in bounds. It is well enough while we have no famine and we have had so many good years now that heaven will surely send us a bad year soon, and there must be many bad years in store for us. Then I do not know how we shall do."

To all of this long tale Wang the Tiger listened carefully as he drank his tea. Then he asked again,

"Where does this Leopard live?"

Then the wine shop keeper took Wang the Tiger by the sleeve and he led him to a small window at the east of the shop and he pointed with his crooked forefinger, stained with wines, and he said,

"There is a mountain yonder with two crests and it is called the Double Dragon Mountain. Between the two crests is a valley and in that valley is the robbers' lair."

Now this was what Wang the Tiger waited to hear and so he affected the more negligence of it and he said carelessly, smoothing his hard mouth with his hand,

"Well, I shall stay away from that mountain then. And now I must be on the way to my home northward. Here is the silver I owe you. As for the wine, it is as you say it is, a very good bright heady wine."

Then Wang the Tiger went out and he mounted his horse again and with the two behind him he rode round about so as not to pass any more villages. He rode over the tops of circling hills and through lonely places although he was never far from men either, because that place was so well tilled and so full of hamlets and villages. But he kept his eyes fixed on that double-crested mountain and he guided his horse to the south of it to a certain other lower mountain he saw that was partly wooded with pine trees.

All through that day they rode in silence, for no one spoke to Wang the Tiger if he did not speak first, unless there were some very pressing thing to be said. Once the lad began to sing a little under his breath, because he was such an one as found silence wearisome, but Wang the Tiger hushed him sternly, for he was in no mood for any merry noise.

At the end of the afternoon but before the sun was set they came to the foot of that wooded mountain toward which they had been many hours riding, and Wang the Tiger dismounted from his weary horse and began to climb some rude stone steps that led upward. These he followed and the pair behind him also, their beasts stumbling over the stones, and as they went the mountain grew wilder and there were cliffs over which the road led and streams burst forth here and there between the rocks and the trees, and the grasses grew thick and deep. The mosses upon the stones also were soft and showed but little sign of the passage of human feet except in the very center, as though only one or two persons ever passed this way. When the sun was set they had reached the end of this mountain road and it ended at a temple built of rough stone and set with its back to the cliff so that indeed this cliff was its innermost wall. The temple was very nearly hidden by trees but it could be seen because its faded red wall gleamed out in the setting sun. It was but a small temple, old and ruinous, and its gates were closed.

Wang the Tiger went up to it and for a while he stood with

his ear pressed against the closed gate. But he heard nothing and so he beat upon it with the handle of his leathern whip. No one came for a long time and then he beat very furiously and with anger. At last the door opened a little and the face of a shorn and shaven priest looked out, a very old and shriveled face. And Wang the Tiger said,

"We seek for shelter here tonight," and as he spoke his voice rang out hard and sharp and clear in that quiet place.

But the priest opened the door a very little more and he answered in a little piping voice,

"Are there no inns and tea houses in the villages? We be but a scant handful of men who have left the world and have but the poorest of food without any meat and we drink only water." And his old knees shook in his robes when he looked at Wang the Tiger.

But Wang the Tiger pushed his way in through the gates and past that old priest and he called to his lad and the trusty man,

"Here is the very place for which we seek!"

He went in then without any heed at all to the priests. He went into the temple through the main hall where the gods were, and they were like the temple, very aged and their gilt peeling from their clay bodies. But Wang the Tiger did not even look at them. He passed them and went into the inner side houses where the priests lived, and he chose out a small room for himself better than the others and cleaned not too many days ago. Here he ungirdled his sword, and the trusty man went hither and thither and found food and drink for him, although it was only a little rice and cabbage.

But that night as Wang the Tiger laid himself down upon the bed in the room he had chosen he heard a deep, low wailing come out of the hall where the gods were and he rose and went out to see what it was. There the five old priests of the temple were and the two little acolytes they had who were farmers' sons left there for some prayer answered. They all knelt and wailed to the Buddha who sat leaning on his fat belly in the center of the hall and as they wailed they prayed the god to save them. A torch burned there and the flame flew this way and that in the night winds and in the light of the flying flame these knelt and prayed aloud.

Now Wang the Tiger stood and looked at them and listened to them and he found that they prayed to be protected against him and they cried,

"Save us—save us from the robber!"

When he heard this Wang the Tiger shouted out heartily and the priests leaped to hear his sudden voice and they stumbled to their feet entangled in their robes with their haste, all except one old priest who was the abbot of that temple and he fell flat on his face, thinking his last hour was come. But Wang the Tiger shouted,

"I shall not hurt you, you old baldheads! Look, I have silver to spare, and why should you be afraid of me?" And as he spoke he opened his girdle purse and he showed them the silver he carried there and it was true there was more silver in it than they had ever seen and he said on, "Beyond this I have more silver and I want nothing of you except shelter for a little while such as any man may claim in his need from a temple."

The sight of this silver did comfort the priests very much and they looked at one another and they said among themselves,

"He is some military captain or other who has killed a man he should not have killed, or who has lost his general's favor and so he must hide for a little time. We have heard of such."

As for Wang the Tiger he let them think what they would

and he smiled his slight and mirthless smile, and he went back to his bed.

The next day at dawn Wang the Tiger rose and he went out to the gate of the temple. It was a morning of mists and the clouds filled the valleys and covered this mountain top from every other and he was alone and hid from the world. Nevertheless, the chill in the air reminded him that winter must soon come and he had much to do before snows set in, for his men depended on him for food and shelter and for clothing against the cold. So he went into the temple again and he went into a kitchen where his trusty man and the lad slept. They had covered themselves with straw and they still slept and the breath whistled through the man's split lip. They slept fast enough, although already an acolyte was feeding straw carefully into the mouth of the brick oven and from under the wooden lid of the iron cauldron on the bricks a bubble of steam leaked out. When the acolyte saw Wang the Tiger he shrank back and hid himself.

But Wang the Tiger paid no heed to him. He shouted to his trusty man and seized him and shook him, and bade him rise and eat and get gone to the inn, lest some of the men pass that morning. Then did the trusty man stagger up out of his sleep rubbing his two hands over his face and yawning hideously. But he shuffled into his clothes and he dipped a bowl into the simmering cauldron and supped some of the scalding sorghum gruel the acolyte brewed there. Away he went down the mountain, then, a goodly enough man if one saw only his back and not his face, and Wang the Tiger watched him go and valued him for his faithfulness.

Then as Wang the Tiger waited that day for his men to gather to him in this lonely place, he planned what he would do and whom he would choose for his trusty men to be his helpers and take counsel with him. He portioned out cer-

159

tain labor to certain numbers of men also, to these to be spies, and to these to forage for food and to others to gather fuel and to others cooking and the mending and cleaning of weapons, to each man his share in their common life. And he thought that he must remember to keep a hard hand over them all, and to reward them only where reward was due and he would order all under his complete command. Life and death should be in his own hand.

Beyond this he planned how each day he would spend certain hours training his men in feints and postures of war so that when his times of struggle came they would be ready. He dared not waste his bullets for the guns at practice, seeing he had not many beyond his need yet. But he would teach them what he could.

So he waited restless in that still mountain top and before the day was ended there were fifty and more men who had found their way to him again and by the end of the next day nearly fifty more. The few left never came and it seemed they had deserted to some other cause. Wang the Tiger waited two more days but they did not come, and he grieved, not because of the men but because with each he had lost a good gun and a belt of bullets.

Now when the old priests saw this horde of men gathering into their peaceful temple they were beside themselves and they did not know what to do. But Wang the Tiger comforted them and he said over and over,

"You shall be paid for everything and you need not fear."

But the old abbot answered in his feeble way, for he was very aged and the flesh upon his bones was dried and shriveled with his age,

"It is not only that we fear no return, but there are things for which silver makes no restoration. This has been a very quiet place and its very name is The Temple of Holy Peace.

We few have lived out of the world these many years in this place. Now here are all your lusty hungry men and peace is gone with their coming. They crowd into the hall where the gods are and they spew their spittle everywhere and they stand anywhere, even before a god himself, and pass their water as they please and they are coarse and wild in all they do."

Then Wang the Tiger said, "It is easier for you to move yourselves and your gods than for me to change such things in my men, for they are soldiers. Move your gods then into the innermost hall and I will tell them that to that one place they shall not go. So may you be at peace."

Thus the old abbot did, then, seeing that there was no other way, and they moved every god on its pedestal, except the gilt Buddha who was too large and they feared if he fell he would burst into pieces and bring disaster upon them all. The soldiers lived in the hall with him then and the priests covered his face with a piece of cloth so that he might not see and be angered by what sins they could not avoid.

Then Wang the Tiger chose out from his men the three he would have as his trusty men. First he took the harelipped man and after him two others, one nicknamed the Hawk, because he had a very curious hooked nose in the middle of his thin face and a narrow, down-drooping mouth, and one nicknamed the Pig Butcher. The Pig Butcher was a great thick fat red man, and his face was large and flat and his features smashed upon it as though a hand had smeared him in the making. But he was a lusty fellow, and it was true enough he had once been a pig butcher, but he had killed a neighbor in a brawl and he would often bemoan it and say, "If I had been eating my rice and had chopsticks in my hand I could never have killed him. But he quarreled with me when I had my chopping knife in my hand and the thing seemed to fly out of its own accord." Nevertheless, the man having died of his bleeding, the Pig Butcher had need to run away to save himself from the court. He had one strange skill. Coarse and thick as he was, he had swift and delicate speed in his hand so that if he took a pair of chopsticks he could pluck the flies out of the air as they flew, one by one he plucked them, and many times his fellows would bid him to do this for them to see and they roared with laughter to see such skill. With this exactness he could prick a man as delicately and spill his blood out neatly and swiftly, too.

Now these three men were very canny men, although not one could read or write. But for such a life as theirs they needed no learning in books, nor did they dream such learning could be useful to them. Wang the Tiger called them to his room when he had chosen them and he said,

"I shall look to you as my three trusty men above the others to watch them and to see if any betrays me or fails in what I have commanded. Be sure you shall have a reward on the day when I rise to glory."

Then he sent the Hawk out and the Pig Butcher too, and he kept only the harelipped trusty man and to him he said with great sternness,

"You I set above those other two and it is your duty to see if they, too, fail me in loyalty."

Then he called the three together again and he said, "As for me, I shall kill anyone whose loyalty is even brought to question. I will kill him so swiftly that the next breath he had planned as a thing of course shall be left half taken and hanging in the air."

Then his harelipped man answered peaceably, "You need not fear me, my captain. Your own right hand shall betray you before I do so."

162

Then the other two swore eagerly also, and the Hawk said loudest of all,

"Shall I forget you took me as a common soldier and raised me up?" This he said, for he had his own hopes in him, too.

Then the three made their obeisances before Wang the Tiger to show their humility and their faithfulness, and when this was over Wang the Tiger chose out certain tricky clever men and he sent them out through the land everywhere to spy out what the news was about his enemy. He commanded,

"Make all haste and find out what you can so that we can establish ourselves before the great cold begins. Find out how many men follow the Leopard and if you come upon any of them talk to them and test their loyalty to him and see if they can be bribed away or not. I will bribe everyone I can because your lives are more precious to me than silver, and I shall not waste one life if I can buy a man instead."

Then these men took off their soldiers' garb and they wore their old ragged inner garments and Wang the Tiger gave them money to buy what they might need of common upper clothes. They went down the mountain then and into the villages and the pawnshops and bought the old worn clothes that farmers and common men pawn for a few pence and never redeem again they are so poor. Thus clad the men wandered all through that countryside. They idled at inns and at tables where men gamed to pass the time away and they stayed at wayside shops and everywhere they listened. Then they came back and told everything to Wang the Tiger.

Now what these men told was the same that Wang the Tiger had heard in the wine shop and it was that the people of these lands hated and feared this robber chief, the Leopard, because every year he demanded more of them if he was not to come and lay waste their houses and fields. His excuse was that each year he had a greater horde of men to feed and he beat off other robbers from the common people and for this he ought to be paid. It was true that his band grew very large and larger every year because every idler in that whole region who did not wish to work and all who had committed some crime fled to the lair in the Double Dragon Mountain and joined the Leopard's banner. If they were good fellows and brave they were very welcome and if they were weak and cowards they were kept to serve the others. There were even some women who went there, bold women whose husbands were dead and who did not care for fame, good or ill, and some men when they went took their wives with them, and some women were captives and held for the men's pleasure. And it was true, too, that the Leopard did hold off other robber chiefs from this whole region.

But in spite of this the people hated him and they were unwilling to give him anything. Yet whether they wished it or not they gave, for they had no weapons. In olden days they might have risen with forks and scythes and knives and such simple tools, but now that the robbers had foreign guns, these were of no avail; nor was any courage or anger of avail against so leaping a death as this.

When Wang the Tiger asked his spies how many men followed the Leopard he had strange answers, for some said they had heard five hundred and others said two or three thousand and others said more than ten thousand. He could not find out what the truth was and he only knew that it was more by many than the men he had. This gave him much to ponder upon and he saw that he must use guile and keep his guns until the last sharp battle and he must avoid even this if he could. So he pondered as he sat and listened to what his spies said, and he let them say on freely, knowing that an ignorant man tells most when he does not know it. And the

164

man who loved to be merry, the same one who had named his captain the Black-browed Tiger, said, making his little weak voice high and boasting,

"As for me, I am so fearless I pushed my way in to the largest town which is the seat of this whole county and I listened there and they are afraid there, too. Every year this Leopard makes a demand at the feast days and the merchants must give him a vast heap of silver or he says he will attack the town itself. And I said to the fellow who told me, and he was a vendor of pork balls, the very best I ever did eat—they have rare pigs here, my captain, and they put garlic into their meats, and I am glad if we stay here and I said, 'But why does your magistrate not send his soldiers out to fight and do battle with this robber for the people's sake?' And that maker of pork balls—he was a good fellow too, and he gave a bit of a broken ball more than I paid for—and he said, 'That magistrate of ours sits sunken in his opium and he is afraid of his own shadow and the general he keeps for his army has never been to war at all and he does not know how to hold a gun—a little fuming, fussy fellow he is who cares more how his soup is brewed than what happens to us! As for that magistrate you should see the guards he keeps about him and he pays them more and more lest they turn against him or be bribed by someone and he spends out money like one pours tea on the ground out of a cold pot. And with all this he is so afraid he shivers and shakes if the Leopard's name is even mentioned and he moans to be free and yet does not make a stir of his hand and every year he pays out more to the Leopard to keep him off.' So this vendor told me and when I had eaten the pork and saw he was in no mind to give me more even if I paid for one more, I went on and I talked with a beggar who sat picking the lice out of his garments in a sunny spot between two walls. He was a wise old man, too, who begged all his life in the streets of that town. He was the cleverest old man and he bit off the head of every louse he pinched and he crunched them. He was well fed, I swear, with all the lice he had! And he said when we had talked of many things that the magistrate this year seemed more of a mind to do something because those higher had heard how he let a robber rule in his regions and there were many who craved his place and they are bringing an accusation against him at the higher court that he does not do his duty and if he must come down there are a dozen who will strive for his place, because these regions are so good and full of revenue. And the people grieve over this, too, for they say, 'Well, we have fed this old wolf and he is not so greedy as he was and if a new one comes in ravenous he must be fed from the very start again.'"

Thus Wang the Tiger let his men talk as they would and they did as ignorant men will, telling all they heard and guffawing and making merry, for they were full of high hopes and they had faith in their captain, and everyone was fed and pleased with the land and with the hamlets they had passed through. For although the people had to feed these two, the Leopard and the magistrate, still they had enough left to feed themselves well enough, too, for it was such a goodly land and much was left them. And Wang the Tiger let them talk, and if much they said was no worth, still they often let fall something he wanted to know and he could sift the wheat from the chaff, for he was much wiser than they.

As this fellow ceased his piping, Wang the Tiger laid hold on the last thing he had said, that the magistrate feared lest he lose his place and he thought deeply on this, and it seemed to him that here was the secret of the whole venture, and through this weak old man he might seize the power over these lands. The more he listened to his men the more sure he

166

grew that the Leopard was not so strong as he had thought, and after a time he made up his mind that he would send a spy to the very strongholds of the robbers' lair and see what men were there and all the Leopard had for strength.

He looked about his men as they sat that night at their evening meal, sitting on their haunches and every man with a roll of hard bread to gnaw and a bowl of grain gruel to sup, and for a time he could not decide which of them to send and none seemed clever and wise enough. Then his eye fell on his nephew, the lad he kept near him, and he was at this instant gorging himself, his cheeks puffed and full with food. Wang the Tiger did but walk away to his own room and the lad followed him instantly as it was his duty to do, and Wang the Tiger bade him close the door and stand to hear what he said, and he said,

"Are you brave enough for a certain thing I shall tell you?"

And the lad said sturdily, still chewing his great mouthful, "Try me, my uncle, and see!"

And Wang the Tiger said, "I will try you. You are to take a little sling such as lads use to kill birds and you are to go to that double-crested mountain and go about evening time and pretend you have lost your way and are afraid of the wild beasts on the mountain, and you are to go crying at the gates of the lair. When they let you in then say you are a farmer's son from the valley beyond and you came up the mountain to look for birds and you did not see how swiftly the night came down and you are lost and beg a night's shelter from this temple. If they will not let you stay then beg them at least for a guide to the pass and use your eyes—see everything and see how many men there are and how many guns and what the Leopard is like and tell me everything. Can you be so brave as this?"

Wang the Tiger fixed his two black eyes on the youth and

he saw the lad's ruddy face turn pale so that the pocks stood out like scars on the skin, but he spoke up well enough and he said, although somewhat breathless,

"I can do it."

"I have never asked you anything," said Wang the Tiger sternly, "but perhaps your clownishness can be of some use now. If you are lost and do not use your wits or if you betray yourself it is your own fault. But you have that merry, silly face and I know you look more simple than you are, and so I have chosen you. But play the part of a simple witless lad and you are safe enough. If you are caught—can you be brave enough to die and be silent?"

Then the good red came surging back into the boy's face and he stood there sturdy and strong in his coarse clothes of blue cotton, and he said,

"Try me, my captain!"

Then Wang the Tiger was pleased with him and he said, "Brave lad! It is the test and if you do well you are worthy to move higher." And he smiled a little as he stared at the boy and his heart that so seldom moved at anything except his gusts of anger now moved a little toward this boy, yet not for the boy's sake either for he did not love him, but it moved with some vague yearning and he wished again he might have a son of his own; not like this lad, either, but a strong, true, grave son of his own.

So he bade the boy put on such clothes as a farmer's son wears and girdle a towel about his waist and he had him put on old worn shoes on his bare feet, for he had a long way to go and rough rocks to clamber over. The lad made a little sling then such as all boys have and made out of the small forked branch of a tree and when it was made he ran lightly down the mountainside and he disappeared into the woods.

Then during the two days he was gone Wang the Tiger

ordered his men as he planned he would and he apportioned out the work to them all so that none could be idle and mischievous. He sent his trusty men out into the countryside to buy food and he sent them separately and they bought meat and grains in small quantities so that none might suspect they bought for a hundred men.

When the evening of the second day was come Wang the Tiger went out and he looked down the rocky steps to see if the lad was come. Deep in his heart he feared for the lad and when he thought of him perhaps cruelly dead he found some strange compassion and remorse in his heart and as night came on and the new moon rose he looked toward the Double Dragon Mountain and he thought to himself,

"I should have sent a man I could spare, perhaps, and not my own brother's son. If he is cruelly dead, how shall I meet my brother? Yet I could only trust my own blood, too."

He watched on after his men slept and the moon came clear of the mountains and swung high in the heavens, but still the lad did not come. At last the night wind grew very chill and Wang the Tiger went in and his heart was heavy because he found what he had not known before, that he would miss the lad a little if he never came back, because he had such merry tricky ways and he could not be angered.

But in the small late hours of the night as he lay awake he heard a little beating on the gate and he rose himself and in haste and he went out. There the lad was when Wang the Tiger had drawn away the wooden bar, and he looked very weary and spent but still good humored. He came limping in and his trousers were torn from his thigh and blood had streamed down his leg and dried. But he was still in high humor.

"I am back, Uncle," he cried in a spent small voice, and

Wang the Tiger laughed suddenly and silently in the way he
had if he were truly pleased and he said roughly,

"What have you done to your thigh?"

But the lad answered lightly, "It is nothing."

Then Wang the Tiger made one of the few jokes he ever
made in his life, because he was so pleased, and he said,

"I hope the Leopard did not claw it!"

The lad laughed aloud at this for he knew his uncle meant
it for laughter, and he sat down on the step into the temple
and he said,

"No, he did not. I fell upon a briary tree, for the moss is
damp with dew and slippery, and the tree scratched me like
this. I am starving, Uncle!"

"Come and eat then," said Wang the Tiger, "eat and drink
and sleep before I hear your tale."

And he told the lad to come into the hall and sit down and
he roared out for a soldier to bring food and drink for the
once to serve this lad. But the noise of it woke this man and
that and one after the other waked and they came crowding
into the court lit by the light of the high moon and they all
wanted to hear what the lad had seen. Then Wang the Tiger,
seeing how after the lad had eaten and drunk, that he was
so important and excited with the success of his venture that
he was far from sleep, and seeing that dawn was now near,
he said,

"Tell it all now, then, and afterwards go to your sleep."

So the boy sat on the altar before the Buddha whose face
was covered and he said,

"Well, and I went and I went, and that mountain is twice as
high as this one, Uncle, and the lair is in a valley round as a
bowl at the top, and I wish we could have it for ours when
we take the region. They have houses and everything there
like a little village. And I did what you said, Uncle. I went

crying and limping to the gates at night with my dead birds in my bosom, and some of the birds on that mountain are the strangest, brightest hue. One I struck was bright yellow all over like gold and I have it yet, it was so pretty—" and as he spoke he drew out of his bosom a yellow bird and it hung in his hand soft and dead and like a handful of limp gold there. Wang the Tiger was in all haste to hear the lad's tale and he chafed at this childishness of a dead bird, but he restrained himself and let the lad tell his tale in his own way, and so the lad went on and he laid his bird carefully on the altar beside him and he looked from one face to another of the men who listened to him, and beside him flared the torch Wang the Tiger had caused to be lit and thrust into the ashes of the incense urn on that altar, and the lad said,

"Well, and when they heard the beating on the gate they came from within and first they opened a very narrow crack and peered to see who it was. And I cried piteously and said, 'I am far from my home—I have wandered too far and the night has come down on me and I am afraid of the beasts of the wood and let me come into this temple!' Then the one who opened shut the gate again and he ran and asked some one and I cried on and moaned as piteously as I could," and here the lad moaned to show them all what he did and all the men roared with laughter and admired him and here and there one called out,

"The little monkey—the little pocked devil!"

The lad grinned all over his pocked face with delight and he told on and he said,

"They let me in at last and I was so simple as I could be and after I had eaten wheaten bread and a bowl of gruel I pretended to be frightened and to know where I was and I began to cry, 'I want to go to my home. I am afraid here because you are the robbers and I am afraid of the Leopard!' and I ran to the gate and wanted to be let out and I said, 'I would liefer be among wild beasts after all!'

"Then they all laughed because I was so simple and they comforted me and said, 'Do you think we will hurt a lad? Wait until morning and you may go your way in peace.' So I ceased my shivering and crying after a while and I pretended to be more at ease and they asked me where I had come from and I told them the name of a village I had heard was on the other side of the mountain. Then they asked me what I had heard about them and I said I had heard they were very heroic, fearless men and their leader not a man, but a man's body with a leopard's head on it, and I said, 'I would like to see him, but I would be afraid, too, to see such a sight.' They all laughed at me, then, and one said, 'Come and I will show you him,' and he led me to a window and I looked in out of the darkness and there were torches burning inside, and there the chief sat. He is truly a curious and monstrous fellow, Uncle, and his head is wide at the top and slopes at the brow so that he does look like a leopard, and he sat drinking with a young woman. She was very fierce, too, and still she was pretty, but fierce, and they drank together from a jug of wine. First he drank and then she drank."

"How many men were there in that place and what their guns?" asked Wang the Tiger.

"Oh, many men, Uncle," said the lad earnestly. "Three times our number of fighting men and many serving men and there are women and there are little children running everywhere and some lads like me. I asked one of them who his father was and he said he did not know because they had no separate fathers there and they only knew their mothers but not their fathers. And that is a strange thing, too. All the fighting men have guns but the serving men have only sickles and knives and such homely things. But at the head of the cliffs about the lair they have great heaps of round rocks piled to roll down upon any who attack them, and there is only one pass into that lair, for there are cliffs everywhere about it and guards always at the pass. Only the guard slept when I came by and I crept past him. He slept so that I might have taken his gun for it lay there on the rock beside him and he snored so that I might have taken it. But I did not, though I was tempted, for they might have thought I was not what I seemed."

"Did the fighting men seem large and brave?" asked Wang the Tiger again.

"Brave enough," replied the lad. "Some are big and some small, but they talked among themselves after they had eaten and they paid no heed to me for I stayed with the lads after a while, and I heard them complain against the Leopard because he would not divide the spoils according to their law, and he kept so much for himself and he was greedy with all the pretty women and he would not let the other men have them until he was tired of them. He did not share as brothers should share, they said, and he held himself too high, although he was born a common fellow, and he cannot read and write, and they are weary of his highness."

Now this pleased Wang the Tiger greatly when he heard it and he mused on as the lad told his story of this and that and what he had to eat and how clever he was and Wang the Tiger mused and planned, and after a while he saw that the lad had told all and only repeated his words and searched his brain for a last thing so that he might keep the attention and the admiration of the men as long as he could. Then Wang the Tiger rose and he commended the lad and bade him go to sleep now and he told the men to be at their tasks for it was dawn, and the torch was burned down and its flickering flame pale in the light of the rising sun.

173

He went into his room, then, and he called his trusty men to him and he said,

"I have mused and planned and I believe I can do this thing without losing a life or a gun, and we must avoid battle, since they are so many more than we are in that lair. The thing to do when one kills a centipede is to crush its head and then its hundred legs are in confusion and they run hither and thither against each other and they are harmless. We will kill the poisonous head of this robber band thus."

The men stared astounded at such boldness and the Pig Butcher said in his loud coarse way,

"Captain, it sounds well, but you must first catch the centipede before you can cut off its head!"

"So shall I," returned Wang the Tiger, "and here is my plan. You are to help me. We are to garb ourselves very fine and bravely as heroes do, and we will go to the magistrate of this region and say we are braves and wandering soldiers and that we seek for service under him, secret service as a private guard, and we will give as our pledge that we will kill the Leopard for him. He is anxious now for his seat and he will be eager for our help. Here is the plan. I will tell him he is to pretend truce with the robbers and invite the Leopard and the next to him to a mighty feast. Then when the moment comes, and he can mark it by a wine cup dropped from his hand and shattered, you and I will rush from where we are hidden and fall upon the robbers and kill them. I will have our men scattered through the town secretly everywhere and they shall fall upon such of the smaller robbers as will not come to my banner. So we will kill this centipede's head and it is not a thing hard to do."

Now all of them saw this thing was feasible and they were struck with admiration and they agreed heartily to it. After they had talked a little more of how it would be managed,

Wang the Tiger dismissed them and he called his men into the temple hall. He sent his trusty men to see that the priests were not near where they could hear him and then he told his gathered men what his plan was. When they heard it they shouted loudly,

"Good! Good! Ha, the Black-browed Tiger!"

And Wang the Tiger heard them as he stood there beneath the veiled god and although he said nothing and he was very proud and silent and aloof, yet there surged up in him such a deep pleasure in his power that he lowered his eyes and stood there grave among his men. When they were still once more and waited to hear what else he might tell them, he said,

"You are to eat and drink well, and then garb yourselves as commonly as you can, but still as soldiers, and take your guns and scatter yourselves through the city only not too far from the magistrate's court. When I send out my shrill whistle you are to come. But wait the number of days until I call." And he turned to his trusty harelipped man and he said, "Pay every man five pieces of silver for wine and lodging and the food he needs."

This was done and every man was content. Then Wang the Tiger called his three trusty men to him and they dressed themselves bravely and concealed short swords in their garments and they took up their guns and they all went away together.

As for the priests, they rejoiced very much to see these wild fellows go. But when Wang the Tiger saw them rejoicing he said,

"Do not rejoice too soon, for we may come back. But if we can find a better place we will not." He paid them well, nevertheless, and above what he owed he gave them a sum and he said to the abbot, "Mend your roofs and repair your house and buy yourselves each a new robe."

The priests were overjoyed at such generosity and the old abbot was somewhat ashamed and he said,

"You are a good man after all, and I shall pray before the gods for you and how else can I reward you?"

To this Wang the Tiger answered, "No, do not trouble yourself with gods, for I have never had faith in them very much. But if in after days you hear of one called the Tiger, then speak well of him and say the Tiger treated you well."

The old abbot stared and stammered in a daze and he said he would, he would! And he held the silver clasped preciously against his bosom in his two hands.

XIII

STRAIGHT to the city did Wang the Tiger lead his trusty men and when they were come to it then straight to the gates of the magistrate's court they went. When Wang the Tiger was come to the gate he said boldly to the guards that leaned idly against the stone lions there,

"Let me in, for I have something private to say to the magistrate."

Now the guard at the gate demurred, for Wang the Tiger did not show any silver at all, and when Wang the Tiger saw the man's unwillingness he shouted once and his trusty men leaped forward and pointed their guns at the man's breast. He turned green-skinned and fell back and so they passed through, making their shoes clatter upon the stones of the court. There were those idling about the gates who had seen what happened and not one dared to move against them. Then Wang the Tiger cried roughly and fiercely and he drew his black brows down over his eyes,

"Where is the magistrate?"

But not a man moved and when Wang the Tiger saw he grew suddenly angry and he took his gun and pricked the man nearest him in the belly, and the man leaped in terror and cried out,

"I will take you to him—I will take you to him!" And he ran pattering ahead, and Wang the Tiger laughed silently to see his terror.

So they followed him and they passed through court after court. But Wang the Tiger did not look east or west. He kept his face straight and furious and his trusty men did the same thing as much as they could. At last they came to an innermost court, very beautiful and set out with a pool and a terrace of peonies and some old pine trees. But the lattices of the rooms upon it were drawn down and there was silence everywhere. The man who led them halted on the threshold and coughed and a servant came then to the lattice and he said,

"What do you wish? Our lord sleeps."

But Wang the Tiger shouted out loudly, and his voice seemed to crash about him in that quiet court,

"Wake him, then, for I have something of greatest importance to tell him. He must wake, for it concerns his very seat!"

The servant stared at them uncertainly, but he saw how full of authority was Wang the Tiger's look, and he surmised these men must be messengers from some higher court. He went in then and shook the sleeping old magistrate and the old man woke out of his dream and he rose and washed himself and put on his robes and he went and sat down in his hall and he told the servant to bring them in. Then Wang the Tiger went in boldly and loudly and he made a proper obeisance before the old magistrate, but still he did not bow too deeply nor full of reverence.

The old magistrate was full of terror at the fierceness of

177

these men before him and he rose in haste and invited them to be seated and he had cakes and wine and fruits brought. And he spoke the usual courteous words that are spoken to a guest, and Wang the Tiger returned the scantest courtesy that he could. At last when these rites were over he said plainly,

"We have heard from those above that you, most honorable, are oppressed by robber bands and we are come to offer our good arms and our skill to help you be rid of them."

Now all this time the old magistrate had been wondering and trembling and when he heard this he said in his cracked and quavering voice,

"It is true I am so plagued, and I am not a man of arms myself, but a scholar, and I do not know how to deal with such men. It is true I have a general I hire, but he is paid by the state so much whatever he does, and he does not like a battle, either, and the people of this region are so wilful and foolish that in a battle we do not know whether or not they would take the side of the robbers against the state even, they are so easily angered by a little rightful tax. But who are you, and what your honored surnames, and where the place where your ancestors resided?"

But Wang the Tiger said no more than this, "We are wandering braves, and we offer our arms where they are needed. We have heard this land is ridden by a pest of robbers and we have a plan, if you will hire us."

Now whether or not the old magistrate would in common times have listened to strangers like this none can tell, but it was true that at this time he was very fearful lest his living be taken from him and he had no son and he could not at his age hope for another living. He had an old wife and a hundred lesser relatives of one sort and another all dependent on him and his place, and in his helpless age his enemies grew strong and greedy, and so he grasped at anything that might deliver him out of his troubles. He lent his ear now, having sent away his servants, except a few for guard, and Wang the Tiger told his plan, and when he had heard it he seized eagerly upon it. There was only one thing he feared and it was that if they failed and did not kill the Leopard, the robbers would take very bitter revenge. But when Wang the Tiger saw what the old man feared he said carelessly,

"I can kill a leopard as easily as a cat, and I can cut off his head and let the blood drip, and my hand will not falter. I swear it!"

And the old magistrate mused and thought how old he was and how his own soldiers were weak and cowardly and it seemed to him there was no other chance for him but this. And he said,

"I see no other way."

Then he called his servants back and he bade them bring meats and wines and prepare a feast and he treated Wang the Tiger and his trusty men as honored guests. Wang the Tiger waited then and he planned with the old magistrate and they laid every part of their plan very well, and as they planned they did in the next few days.

The old magistrate sent emissaries to the robbers' lair and he told them to say he was growing old and he was leaving his post and another would come to take his place. But before he left he wished to make sure that no enmity stayed after him and he wished the Leopard and his chiefs would come and dine and feast with them and he would recommend them to the new magistrate. When the robbers heard this they were wary, but Wang the Tiger had thought of this, also, and he told the magistrate to spread rumors everywhere that he was going away. The robbers asked among the common people, therefore, and they heard the same story. So they believed it, then, and they felt it would be a good thing if the new magistrate could be influenced in their favor and fear them and pay the sums they demanded and it would spare them battle. They accepted the truce the old magistrate held out to them, and they sent word they would come upon a certain night when the moon was dark.

Now it happened that on that day rains fell and the night was dark and full of mists and winds, but the robbers held to their word and they came in their best robes and with their weapons sharp and clean and bright, and every man held his sword drawn and glittering in his hand. The courts were filled with the guard they brought and some stood out in the streets about the gates to guard against treachery. But the old magistrate did his part very well, and if his withered old knees shook in his robes, still he kept his face peaceful and his voice courteous, and he caused all weapons among his own men to be put aside, and when the robbers saw no weapons except their own they were more at ease.

The old magistrate had caused the best sort of feast to be prepared by his own cooks and this feast was to be spread forth for the chiefs in the innermost hall but the robber guards were to be fed in the courts. Now when all was ready the old magistrate led the chiefs to the hall of feasting, and he assigned the seat of honor to the Leopard, and after many refusals and bows of courtesy the Leopard took it, and the old magistrate sat in the host's seat. But he had taken care before to have it near a door, for he planned when the moment came for him to throw down his wine bowl as a signal that he would escape and hide until all was over.

So the feast began, and at first the Leopard drank cautiously and glowered if any of his chiefs drank too easily. But the wine was very good, the best good wine of all that region, and the meats that were brought in were cunningly seasoned to make men thirsty, and they were such meats as the robbers had never tasted who knew only their rough coarse fare. Such hot and delicate dishes they had not dreamed of, for they were from birth but coarse fellows and unused to any dainties. At last their reserve gave way and they ate and drank fully and recklessly, and so their guards did also in the courts, and the more easily they, since they were not even so wise as their chiefs.

Now Wang the Tiger and his trusty men watched from a curtain round a latticed window near the door through which they were to charge. Every man held his sword drawn and ready and they listened for the crash of the porcelain wine bowl which was to be their sign. There came a moment when the feast had lasted three hours or more, and it was a moment when the wine flowed at its freest, and the servants bustled here and there and the robbers were full of meat and wine and heavy with all they had in their bellies. Suddenly the old magistrate began to tremble and his face turned ashy and he faltered out,

"The strangest pain has struck my heart!"

He lifted his wine bowl in all haste but his hand shook so that the delicate thing seemed to shiver out of his hand and fell upon the tiles and he staggered up and out of the door.

Then before they could draw a breath in surprise, Wang the Tiger blew his whistle and he shouted once to his men and they charged through the door upon the robber chiefs and each trusty man sprang upon the one whom Wang the Tiger had already appointed to him. But the Leopard Wang the Tiger kept for himself to kill.

Now the servants had been told that when they heard the shout they were to bar every door, and when the Leopard saw this he leaped to his feet and dashed to the door through which the old magistrate had staggered. But Wang the Tiger sprang upon him and pinned his arms, and the Leopard had but a short sword he had plucked as he leaped, and not his own sword, and he was helpless. Each man thus fell upon his enemy and the room was full of cries and curses and struggling men and no trusty man looked to see what any other did, until he had killed the one appointed to him. But some robbers were easily killed because they were fumbling and drunken, and as each trusty man killed his enemy he went to Wang the Tiger to see how he did and to help him.

Now the Leopard was no mean enemy and although he was half drunken he was so swift with his flying feet and he could kick and fence so well that Wang the Tiger could not end him with a single sword thrust. But he would not have help for he wanted this glory and he struggled with the Leopard. And indeed when he saw how bravely this man fought and how desperately with only the poor weapon he had snatched, Wang the Tiger was moved to admiration, as a brave man is even against a foe if he be brave also, and he was sorry he must kill the man. But still he must, and so he drove the Leopard into a corner with his flying sword, and the man was too full fed and too drunken to do his best. Moreover, it was hopeless for the Leopard who had taught himself all he knew, and Wang the Tiger had been taught in an army and he knew the skill of weapons and every sort of feint and posture. The moment came then when the Leopard could not defend himself quickly enough and Wang the Tiger drove his sword into the man's vitals and twisted it strongly once and blood and water rushed out. But as the Leopard sank and died he gave Wang the Tiger such a look that Wang the Tiger never did forget it his whole life long it was so wild and fierce. And the man did indeed look like a leopard, for his eyes were not black as are the eyes of common mortals, but they were pale and yellow as amber. When Wang the Tiger saw him still at last and lying dead and his yellow eyes staring he said to himself that this was a true Leopard, for besides his eyes, his head was wide at the top and sloped back in the strangest, beast-like way. The trusty men gathered then to praise their captain, but Wang the Tiger held his bloody sword, forgetful of it, and he stared down at the dead man still, and he said sorrowfully,

"I wish I need not have killed him, for he was a fierce, brave man and he had the look of a hero in his eyes."

But even as he stood and looked sadly at what he had had to do, the Pig Butcher shouted out that the Leopard's heart was not yet cold, and before any knew what he was about he had stretched out his hand and taken a bowl from the table and with the swift delicate skill that was lodged so curiously in his coarse hand he cut a stroke into the Leopard's left breast and he pinched the ribs together and the Leopard's heart leaped out of the cleft and the Pig Butcher caught it in the bowl. It was true the heart was not cold and it quivered a time or two there in the bowl and the Pig Butcher stretched out the bowl in his hand to Wang the Tiger and he called out in a loud, merry way,

"Take it and eat it, my captain, for from old times it has been said the heart of a brave foe eaten warm makes one's own heart twice as brave!"

But Wang the Tiger would not. He turned away and he said, haughtily,

"I do not need it." And his eye fell on the floor near the chair where the Leopard had sat to feast and he saw the Leopard's sword glittering there. He went and picked it up. It was a fine steel sword such as cannot be made this day, so keen that it could cut through a bolt of silk and so cold it could divide a cloud in two. Wang the Tiger tried it upon the robe of a robber who lay dead there and it melted through

183

to the man's bone even before he pressed it at all. And Wang the Tiger said,

"This sword alone will I take for my share. I have never seen a sword like this."

Just then he heard a gagging noise and it was his pocked lad who had stood staring at the Pig Butcher, and he was suddenly sick and vomited at what he saw. And Wang the Tiger hearing it said kindly, for he knew it was the first time the lad had seen men killed,

"You have done well not to be sick before this. Go out into the cool court."

But the lad would not, and he stood his ground sturdily and Wang the Tiger was pleased at this and he said,

"If I am Tiger, you are fit to be a Tiger's cub, I swear!"

And the lad was so pleased he grinned, and his teeth shone out of his white sick face.

When Wang the Tiger had thus done what he promised he would he went out into the courts to see what his men had done with the lesser robbers. It was a cloudy dark night, and the shapes of his men were but a little more solid and dark than the night. They waited and he commanded that torches be lit, and when they were flaring he saw that only a few men lay dead and he was pleased, for he had commanded that men were not to be wantonly killed and that they were to have the chance to choose if they would change their banner or not, if they were brave.

But Wang the Tiger's work was not done yet. He was determined to storm the lair now that it was weakest and before the robbers who were left had any time to reinforce themselves. He did not stay even to see the old magistrate, but he sent word saying, "I will not claim a reward until I have stamped out this nest of snakes." And he called to his men

184

and they went through the dark night across the fields to the Double Dragon Mountain.

Now Wang the Tiger's men did not follow him very willingly for they had fought already this night and the march was a good three miles or so and they must perhaps fight again and many of them had hoped to be allowed to loot in the city as a reward for their battle. They complained to him then saying,

"We fought for you and we risked our lives and you have not let us take any booty either. We have never served under so hard a master for we have never heard that soldiers must fight and have no booty; no, and not so much as touch a maid, either, and we have held ourselves off until we fought for you, and still you give us no freedom."

At first Wang the Tiger would not answer this but he could not bear it when he heard several of them muttering together and he knew he must be cruel and hard or they would betray him. So he turned on them and slashed his fine sword whistling through the air and he roared at them,

"I have killed the Leopard and I will kill any and all of you and care nothing. Do you have no wisdom at all? Can we despoil the very place which we hope to be ours and turn the people against us with hatred the very first night? No more of these cursed words! When we come to the lair you may loot anything and take it all, except that you are not to force a woman against her will."

Then his men were cowed and one said timidly, "But, captain, we were only joking." And another said, half wondering, "But, captain, it was not I who complained, and if we do loot the lair where are we to live, for I thought we were to have the lair."

Then Wang the Tiger answered sullenly, for he was still angry,

185

"We are no robber band and I am no common robber chief. I have a better plan if you will but trust me and not be fools. That lair shall be burned to the ground and the curse of those robbers shall pass from this countryside, so that men need fear them no more."

Then his men were more astonished than ever, even his trusty men, and they said, one speaking for all,

"But what shall we be, then?"

"We shall be men of battle, but not robbers," answered Wang the Tiger very harshly. "We will have no lair. We shall live in the city and in the magistrate's own courts and we shall be his private army and we need fear no one for we shall be under the name of the state."

Then the men fell silent in very awe of the cleverness of this leader of theirs, and their evil humor passed from them like a wind. They laughed aloud and they trusted to him, and they mounted the steps eagerly that led to the pass to the lair, and about them the fogs wreathed and curled in those mountains, and their torches smoked in the cold mists.

They came suddenly to the mouth of the pass and a guard was there so astonished he could not run, and one of the men, being very merry, ran him through with his sword before he could speak. Wang the Tiger saw this but he did not reprove his man for once, because it was but one he killed, and it is true that a captain cannot hold ignorant and wild men too closely in check, lest they turn and rend him. So he let the man lie dead and they went on to the gates of the lair.

Now this lair was indeed like a village and it had a wall of rock hewn out of the mountain and welded together with clay and lime so that it was very strong and there were great iron-bound gates set into the wall. Wang the Tiger beat upon those gates, but they were locked fast and strong, and no answer came. When he beat again and still no answer came,

186

he knew that those within had heard of what had befallen their leader, and doubtless some of the robbers had run back and warned the others, and either they had fled from the lair or they had entrenched themselves within the houses and prepared for attack.

Then Wang the Tiger bade his men prepare fresh torches out of the dried autumn grass that was about the lair and they set fire to these torches of twisted grass and they burned a hole in the wooden part of one of the gates, and when the hole was big enough one slipped through it and unbarred the gates swiftly. They all went in then, and Wang the Tiger led the way.

But the lair was as still as death. Wang the Tiger stood to listen and there was not a sound. Then he gave the command that every man was to blow his torch to flame and the houses were to be set on fire. Every man ran to the task and they yelled and screeched as the thatched roofs of the houses caught fire and as the whole lair began to burn suddenly people began to run out of the houses as ants will run out of a hill. Men, women, and little children streamed out and they ran cowering here and there and Wang the Tiger's men began to stab them as they ran until Wang the Tiger shouted that they were to be allowed to escape, but that the men might go in and take their goods.

So Wang the Tiger's men rushed into such houses as were not too ablaze and they began to drag out booty of silken pieces and yards of cloth and garments and anything they could carry. Some found gold and silver and some found jars of wine and food and they began to eat and drink gluttonously and some in their eagerness perished in the very flames they themselves had lit. Then Wang the Tiger seeing how childish they were sent his trusty men to see that they did not come to harm and so not many perished.

As for Wang the Tiger, he stood apart and watched it all, and he kept his brother's son near him and he would not let the lad loot anything. He said,

"No, lad, we are not robbers and you are my own blood and we do not rob. These are common, ignorant fellows and I must let them have their way once in a time or they will not serve me loyally, and it is better to let them loose here. I must use them for my tools—they are my means to greatness. But you are not like them."

So he kept the lad by him, and it was very well he did, for the strangest thing happened. As Wang the Tiger stood there leaning on his gun and watching the flaming houses that were beginning already to smoke and to smoulder, the lad suddenly gave a great scream. Wang the Tiger whirled and he saw from above a sword descending down upon him. Instantly he lifted his sword up and met it and the blade slipped down the smooth sword and it fell a little on his hand, but so little it was scarcely a wound, and fell to the ground.

But Wang the Tiger leaped into the darkness, swifter than a tiger, and he laid hold on someone and he dragged it out into the light of the fires, and it was a woman. He stood there confounded, holding her by the arm he had caught, and the lad cried out,

"It is the woman I saw drinking with the Leopard!"

But before Wang the Tiger could say a word, the woman had twisted and writhed and turned herself, and when she found he held her fast and beyond her strength to free herself, she threw back her head and she spat full into Wang the Tiger's eyes. Now he had never had such a thing happen to him before and it was such a filthy, hateful thing that he lifted his hand and slapped her upon the cheek as one slaps a wilful child, and his hard hand left the marks of his fingers there purple upon her cheek, and he shouted,

"That for you, you tigress!"

This he said without thinking what he said and she shouted back at him viciously,

"I wish I had killed you, you accursed—I meant to kill you!"

And he said grimly holding her fast still,

"Well I know you did, and if it had not been for my pocked lad here I would have lain dead this instant with my skull cleft!" And he called to some of his men to bring a rope from somewhere and bind her and they bound her to a tree there by the gate until he could know what to do with her.

Now they bound her very tightly and she struggled and chafed and cut her flesh but she could not so much as loosen herself, and as she struggled she cursed them all and especially Wang the Tiger with such curses as are seldom heard anywhere they were so rich and vile. Wang the Tiger stood and watched while the men bound her and when she was safely tied and tight and the men had gone to their pleasure again, he walked back and forth then in front of her and every time he passed he looked at her. Each time he looked more steadfastly and with more wonder, and he saw she was young and that she had a hard, bright, beautiful face, her lips thin and red and her forehead high and smooth and her eyes bright and sharp and angry. It was a face narrow and bright as a fox's face. Yes, it was beautiful, even now when she had it twisted with hate for him every time he passed her and each time he passed she cursed him and spat at him.

But he paid no heed to her. He only stared at her as he went in his silent way and after a time as the night wore on to dawn she grew weary for they had tied her so tightly that she was in much pain and at last she could not bear it. At first she did not curse and only spat, and after a while she suffered so she did not spit either and at last she said, panting and licking her lips,

"Loosen me even a little, for I am in such pain!"

But Wang the Tiger did not heed this, either, and he only smiled hardly, for he thought it was a trick of hers. She begged him thus every time he came near her but he would not answer. At last one time he came past and her head hung down and she was silent. Still he would not go near her, for he would not be spit on again and he thought she feigned sleep or faintness. But when she did not move for several times he passed, he sent the lad to her, and the lad went and took her by the chin and turned her face up, and it was true she had fainted.

Then Wang the Tiger went to her and he looked at her closely, and he saw that she was fairer than he had even seen her to be in the dim and flickering light of dying fires. She was not more than five and twenty, and she did not look a common farmer's daughter or a common woman and he could not but wonder who she was and how she came to be here and where the Leopard had found such a one. He called a soldier then to come and cut her down and he had her trussed still, but more lightly and not hung against a tree. He bade them lay her on the ground and there she lay and she did not come to herself until it was dawn and the sunlight was beginning to creep through the morning mists.

Then at this hour Wang the Tiger called his men and he said,

"The time is up. We have other things to do than this."

His men ceased their quarrelling over booty slowly and they gathered at his call for he made his voice very loud and fierce and he held his gun cocked and ready for any who would not obey him, and he said, when his men were come, "Collect every gun and all the ammunition there is, for these are mine. I claim these as my share."

When his men had done this, Wang the Tiger counted the guns and there were a hundred and twenty guns and a goodly amount of ammunition, too. But some of the guns were old and rusty and of little value, and these Wang the Tiger, because they were of such ancient and clumsy design, kept to one side to throw away as soon as he could find better.

Then in the midst of the ruined and smoking lair his men tied their booty into bundles, some large and some small, and Wang the Tiger counted over the guns they had found and these he gave to the more trustworthy men to guard. At last he turned to the woman who was tied. She had come to herself and she lay on the ground, her eyes open. When Wang the Tiger looked at her she stared back at him angrily and he said to her harshly,

"Who are you and where is your home that I may send you there?"

But she would not answer him one word. She spat at him for answer and her face was like an angry cat's. This enraged Wang the Tiger greatly, so he called out to two of his men,

"Put a pole through her bonds and carry her to the magistrate's court and throw her into the gaol there. Perhaps she will tell then who she is!"

The men obeyed him and they thrust the pole ruthlessly through the ropes and carried the ends of the poles on their shoulders, and she swung there.

As for Wang the Tiger, when all was ready, the sun was clear of the mountain tops and he walked ahead of his men down the pass. From the lair a feeble cloud of smoke still rose, but Wang the Tiger did not turn to look at it once.

Thus they marched along the road through the country to the city once more. Many a man passing this strange throng looked cornerwise out of his eyes, and especially at the woman trussed to the pole, her head hanging down and her fox-like face pale as ashes. Every man wondered, but not one dared to ask of what had happened, lest he be drawn into some desperate brawl or other, and they were afraid and each went about his business and kept his eyes down after he had glanced a time or two. It was full day and the sun was streaming over the fields when at last Wang the Tiger and his men reached the city gates.

But when he was in the darkness of the passage through the city wall his harelipped trusty man came and led him aside behind a tree that stood there by the gate, and he whispered to Wang the Tiger, hissing with the earnestness of what he had to say,

"I have this to say that I must say, my captain. It is better not to have anything to do with this woman. She has a fox's face and fox eyes and women like this are only half human and the other half fox, and they have a very magic wickedness. Let me put my knife in her deeply and so end her!"

Now Wang the Tiger had very often heard the tales of things that women who are half fox will do, but he was so bold and fearless in himself that he laughed loudly now and he said,

"I am afraid of no man and no spirit and this is only a woman!" And he brushed the man away and went to the head of his throng again.

But the harelipped trusty man followed behind him muttering, and he muttered,

"But this is a woman and more evil than a man, and she is a fox and more evil than a woman."

XIV

WHEN Wang the Tiger came into the same courts where the night before he had done such a deed, and his men followed after him with haphazard steps because they were so weary, they found those courts cleaned and all as they had been before. All the dead had been taken away and the blood wiped and washed away with water. Every guard and servant stood in his place, and they were frightened and careful when Wang the Tiger came through the gates, and he came as arrogant as a king and everyone hastened to make obeisance before him.

But he held himself straight and haughty and he strode through the courts and the halls, pride magnificent upon his dark face. Well he knew he held this whole region now in the hollow of his hand. He turned to a guard who stood there and he shouted,

"Take this trussed woman and put her somewhere in the court gaol! Guard her and see that she is fed and not treated ill, for she is my prisoner and when I wish I will decide what her punishment is to be."

He stood and watched then while the men carried her away on the pole. She was exhausted and her face was as white as tallow. Even her lips that had been so red were white now, too, and her eyes were as black as inkstone in her paleness and she gasped for her every breath. But she still could turn those great fierce black eyes to Wang the Tiger and when she saw him watch her she twisted her face in a grimace against him, but her mouth was dry. And Wang the Tiger was astounded, for he had never seen such a woman as this, and he puzzled what he would ever do with her, for she never could be let go free so full of hatred as this, and so strong in her revengefulness.

But he put the matter from him for this while and he went in before the old magistrate. Now the old magistrate had been waiting since before dawn, and he sat there in his full robes and he had ordered foods prepared of the finest kind. When he saw Wang the Tiger come in he was all of a twitter and in great confusion, because though he was grateful for what Wang the Tiger had done, yet he knew such a man would not serve another for nothing, and he dreaded to hear what reward Wang the Tiger would ask, lest it be so great that he was more burdened than he had been by the Leopard.

So he waited in dreadful uncertainty, and when it was announced to him that Wang the Tiger was come and when he saw Wang the Tiger come in with the great measured strides such as a hero uses, the old magistrate was so confused with his fears that he did not know what to do with his hands and feet and without his knowing it they trembled and moved as though they had a life of their own apart from him. But he invited Wang the Tiger to be seated, and Wang the Tiger made the proper courteous replies, and when the rites of courtesy were over and Wang the Tiger had bowed and bowed but not too deeply, either, and the old magistrate had ordered tea and wines and meats to be brought, they sat down at last and they made a little idle talk.

But the moment came when the thing that had been done could not be avoided longer, and looking east and west and gazing every which way except at Wang the Tiger, the old magistrate opened his mouth to speak. Nor did Wang the Tiger help him, for the power was now his, and he knew very well the condition in the old magistrate's heart and he did no more than fix his steadfast eyes on the nervous old man, because he knew he frightened him thus, and the knowledge gave pleasure to Wang the Tiger because of the malice in him. At last the old magistrate began in his

194

hurried feeble old voice, very soft and whispering and low,

"Be sure I never can forget what you did last night and I can never thank you enough that I am rid of the pest under which I have suffered all these years and my old age can be peaceful now. And what shall I say to you who have delivered me, and how shall I reward you, who are more to me than a son? And how reward your noble men? Ask what you will, even to my very seat, and it is yours."

And he waited trembling and biting his forefinger. Wang the Tiger sat calm and waiting until the old magistrate was done and then he replied decently,

"I do not ask anything at all. From my youth I have been against all wicked and evil men, and what I did I did to rid the people from a pest."

Then he sat silent and waited again, and now it was the magistrate's turn and he said,

"You have the heart of a hero and I did not dream there were such as you in these days. But still I cannot close my eyes in peace even when I am dead if I do not give you thanks in some certain way, and so speak and say what will please you best."

Thus they talked back and forth and with each speech spoken in turn and very properly and courteously they came nearer to the point at last, and then Wang the Tiger made it known in winding words that he was minded to open the ranks of his men to all of the Leopard's old followers who wished to change their banner. At this the old magistrate was filled with fright and he grasped the sides of his carved chair and he rose to his feet and said,

"But are you minded to be a robber chief in his place then?"

And to himself he said that if this were so then was he undone indeed, for this strange tall black-browed fellow, who had come to him from nowhere, was fiercer to see than even the Leopard had been and he was more clever. At least the Leopard had been known to all, and it was known how much he would demand; and thinking thus the old magistrate began to groan aloud a little without knowing that he did. But Wang the Tiger spoke out straightly and he said,

"You need not fear. I have no mind to be a robber. My father was an honorable man who owned land and I have my own inheritance from him. I am not poor so that I need to rob for anything. Moreover, my two older brothers are rich and proper men. If I carve out my future way to greatness it will be by my own skill at war and by no such low trickery as robbers use. No, this is my reward and all I ask of you. Let me stay here with my men in your courts and appoint me as your own chief general in your army you have here. I and my men will come as part of your retinue, and I will protect you from robbers and I will protect your people, also. You can feed us and give us certain revenues that are our due, and you can give me the shelter of the name of the state."

Now the old magistrate listened to this in bewilderment and he said feebly,

"But what shall I do with the general I have already? I shall be torn between you, for he will not go down lightly from his post."

To this Wang the Tiger made brave answer,

"Let us fight it out as honorable men do, and if he wins, I will go away and let him have my men and my guns. If I win, he is to go away and leave me his."

Then the magistrate, groaning and sighing, for he was a scholar and a follower of sages, and he loved peace, sent out and called for his general to come in. And after a while the man came, a little pompous round-bellied man who wore war garments of a foreign sort, and he grew a little sparse beard and he brushed his scanty eyebrows up and did his little best to look fierce and brave. He dragged a long sword at his heels as he came in and he came stamping his feet down hard at each step. When he bowed, he bowed from his waist and he tried to be very ferocious.

Then halting and sweating, the old magistrate somehow made known to him what the matter was and Wang the Tiger sat there coldly and he looked away and seemed to think of other things. At last the old magistrate was silent and he hung his head and he wished himself dead and he thought to himself that he would soon be dead between these two, for he had always thought his own general fierce enough since the man had a hot swift little temper of his own, but Wang the Tiger was far swifter and deeper in his anger, as any man could see who looked at that face of his.

Now the little pot-bellied general was angry enough at what he heard and he laid his little fat hand on his sword and made as though he would dart at Wang the Tiger. But Wang the Tiger saw the movement almost before it was made, although at the time he had been staring seemingly into the peony terrace in the court, and he drew his wide lips back from his white teeth and pulled down his heavy black brows and folded his arms across his breast and he stared so heavily at the little general and with such a dire look, that the little man faltered and thought better of what he did and swallowed his anger as best he could. And indeed he was not a fool. He saw his day was over, for he did not dare to measure himself against Wang the Tiger. He said at last to the old magistrate,

"I have thought for a long time that I ought to return to my old father, for I am his only son and he grows very old. But I have never been free to go because my duties here at your honored court have been so arduous and continuous.

Besides this filial duty that is mine there is the illness in my belly, which seizes me every now and again. You know of this illness, my lord, and how because of it I have not been able to go as I have so longed to do against those robbers and all these years I have chafed at my inability which Heaven itself put upon me. So now I gladly retire to my old village home to do what I should for my old father and to nurse also my increasing illness."

This he said and he bowed very stiffly and the old magistrate rose and bowed also and he murmured,

"Be sure you shall be well rewarded for all your faithful years."

And the magistrate looked after the little general regretfully as he withdrew and he sighed and he thought to himself that after all he had been a very easy man of war and if he had not put down the robbers still he was not hard to have in the courts except when his little tempers flew up over some small question of meat and drink and these were easily settled. And then the old magistrate stole a look at Wang the Tiger and he was very ill at ease because Wang the Tiger looked young and harsh and very fierce and ill-tempered. But he only said in his peaceable way,

"Now you have the reward you wish. You may have the courts the old general had as soon as he is gone, and you may take the soldiers. But there is one thing more. What shall I say to those above me when it is known I have changed my general, and what even if the old general goes to complain of me?"

But Wang the Tiger was clever and he answered at once, "It will all bring glory to you. Tell them you hired a brave and he put down the robbers and you have retained the brave as a private guard. Then do you force the general—and I will put my force behind yours—to write and ask that he be allowed to retire and he must name me in his place, and so shall the glory be yours, that you hired me and through me you routed the robbers."

Then, although unwillingly, the old magistrate saw this was no mean plan and he began to be somewhat cheered except that he was still afraid of Wang the Tiger and he feared his ruthlessness lest it ever be turned against himself. But Wang the Tiger let him be afraid, for this suited him, and he smiled his cold smile.

Now did Wang the Tiger settle himself into those courts, for the winter was come down out of the north. He was well pleased with all he had done, for his men were fed and clothed and his revenues began to come in and he could buy them winter garments and they were all warm and fed.

When he had arranged everything for them and the deep of the winter drew on and the days passed each other in regular procession, Wang the Tiger bethought himself suddenly one idle day of the woman he had still in the gaol. He smiled to himself harshly when he thought of her and he shouted to the guard at his door,

"Go and fetch that woman out of the gaol I sent there some sixty days or so ago! I had forgot that I have not fixed her punishment and she tried to kill me." Then he laughed silently and said again, "She is tamed by now, I dare swear!"

So he waited in some pleasure and interest to see how tamed she would be. He sat alone in a hall of his own and beside him was a large iron brazier of coals. Outside the snow of deep winter fell heavily and the court was filled with the snow and it hung thickly on every branch and tree, for there was no wind on that day, only a very bitter, silent cold, frozen with the dampness of the falling snow. But Wang the Tiger waited idle and warm beside the brazier of coals, and he was wrapped well in a sheepskin robe, and a tigerskin was thrown across the back of his chair to keep the chill away.

It was nearly an hour before he heard a commotion in the silent court and he looked toward the door. The guard was coming with his prisoner, but he had two other guards to help him. Even so she twisted this way and that and she strained against the ropes that bound her. But the guards forced her into the door and in the struggling the snow swept in with them. When they had her fast at last and standing before Wang the Tiger, the guard said in apology,

"General, forgive me because so long a time has passed before I could obey your command. But we have had to force this young hag every step. She lay naked in her bed in the gaol and we could not go in for decency's sake, for we are respectable men with wives of our own, and so the other women in the gaol had to force her clothes upon her. She bit and scratched and fought against them but at last they had enough on her so that we could go in and tie her and drag her out. She is mad—it must be she is mad. We have never seen a woman like this. There are those in the gaol who say even that she is not a woman but a fox changed into a woman for some evil purpose of the devils."

But the young woman shook back her streaming hair when she heard this. Her hair had been cut short once, but now it was grown nearly to her shoulders. She screamed forth,

"I am not mad unless it be with hate against *him!*" and she cursed and she thrust her chin out at Wang the Tiger and she spat at him and would have spat on him except that he drew back hastily and the guards seeing her purpose jerked her back so that her spittle fell hissing upon the hot coals of the brazier. At this the guard stared and he said again with conviction,

"You see she is mad, my general!"

But Wang the Tiger said nothing. He only fastened his eyes on this strange wild creature, and he listened to her speech, for even when she cursed it was not the speech of a common or ignorant woman. He looked at her closely and he saw that although she was slender and now gaunt to thinness, she was still handsome and haughty, and she did not look like a thick country wench. Yet her feet were big and they looked as though they had never been bound, and this was not as it should in those parts for a woman who came from a good family. He could make nothing of her, therefore, with all these contradictions, and he only stared on at her and he watched her fine black brows twisting above her angry eyes and her thin pouting lips drawn back from her smooth white teeth, and as he watched it came to him that she was the most beautiful woman he had ever seen. Yes, even with her face pale and pinched and angry she was beautiful. So at last he said slowly,

"I have never known you at all. Why should you hate me?"

And the woman answered passionately, and she had a clear, piercing voice, "You killed my lord and I will not rest until I have revenged him. Though you kill me I will hold my dead eyes open until I am revenged for him!"

At this the guard was horrified and he lifted his sword and he cried, outraged, "To whom do you speak, vixen?" And he would have smote her across the mouth with the flat of his sword except that Wang the Tiger made a sign that she was not to be touched. Then Wang the Tiger said in his still way,

"Was the Leopard your master?"

And she cried in the same piercing, passionate voice, "Yes!"

Then Wang the Tiger leaned forward indolently and he said quietly and very scornfully,

"I have killed him. Now you have a new master, and it is I."

At this the young woman lunged forward as if she would have fallen upon him and killed him if she could and the two guards struggled with her, and Wang the Tiger watched them. When they had her fast again so she could not move, the sweat poured down her temples and she was gasping and half weeping, but she stood and fixed her furious eyes on Wang the Tiger's face. Then he met her eyes and stared at her and she stared back at him in defiance, and as though she did not fear him and would not look away and as if she had determined to down his look before she lowered her own bold eyes. But Wang the Tiger only stared on indomitably and without any anger visible, and with a mighty and calm patience and for all his depth of anger he had a power of such strong patience if he were not angry.

As for the woman, she stared on for a long time. But at last, although he still stared unmoved, her eyelids fluttered and she gave a cry and turned and she said to the guards,

"Oh, take me away to the gaol again!" And she would not look at him any more.

Then Wang the Tiger, smiling in the mirthless way he had, said to her,

"You see, I said you have a new master."

But she would not answer him anything. She stood suddenly drooping and she parted her lips and panted a little, and at last he told the guards to take her away again and this time she went without any struggle, glad to go away from him.

Then Wang the Tiger was all the more curious to know who she was and he was very curious to know how she came to be in the robbers' lair and he had it in his mind to know her story. So when the guard came back shaking his head and saying, "I have had wild ones in my hand in my day, but not like this tigress," Wang the Tiger said to him,

"Tell the chief of the gaol that I must know who she is and why she was in the lair."

"She will not answer any question," said the guard. "No, she says nothing. The only change in her was that at first she would not eat but now she eats ravenously, yet not as though she were hungry but as though she ate to be strong for a purpose. But she will not tell anyone who she is. The women are curious and they have tried every cunning way to question her but she will not tell. Torture may force it from her, but even then I do not know, for she is so fierce and bitter a thing. Do you order torture, my general?"

Wang the Tiger thought for a while, then and at last he set his teeth together and he said, "If there is no other way, let it be by torture. She is to obey me. But it is not to be torture to her death." And after a while he said again, "And break none of her bones and do not mar her skin."

At the end of the day the guard came to him once more to make report and he said in consternation, "My general, high above me, it is not possible to make that woman say anything so long as we must torture her so gently as to break no bones and not mar her skin. She laughs at us."

Then Wang the Tiger looked at him gloomily and he said, "Let her be for the time then. And give her meats and some wine to eat and to drink." And he put the matter into the recesses of his mind, until he could think what to do with her.

Then while he waited for a thought to come to him, Wang the Tiger sent his trusty harelipped man southward to his old home and he bade the man tell his brothers all that had befallen him and how great his success was and how he had won it and lost but a few men, and how he had entrenched himself in his region. He warned the man, however, saying,

"You are not to boast too much of what I have done, for this small place and this little county seat is but the first step up the high mountain of glory before me, and you must not let my brothers think I am as high as I plan to go, or they will come hanging on me and beg me to foist up this son of theirs or that and I want no more of their sons, no, even though I have not the son of my own I wish I had. Tell them the small measure of my success, and tell it so that they will be encouraged to give me the moneys I need still, for I have five thousand men now to feed and clothe, and they eat like wolves. But tell them I have begun and I shall go on until I have this province in my rule and after that more provinces. There is no boundary to my way."

To all this the trusty man gave his promise, and he went his way south dressed as a poor pilgrim who goes to worship at some distant temple.

As for Wang the Tiger he set himself then to the settling of his men and it was true he had every right to take pride in what he had done. He had established himself honorably and not as a common robber chief and he was established in the magistrate's court and as part of the government of that country. And everywhere by river and lake his fame went forth through that region and everywhere people spoke of the Tiger, and when he opened his lists for anyone to take service under him, as he now did, men flocked to his banners. But he chose them carefully and he rejected the old and unfit and such as looked weak or half blind or imbecile, and he paid off such of the state soldiers as did not seem able or strong, and there were many of these who had been in the army merely to have food to eat. Thus Wang the Tiger gathered to himself a mighty army of nearly eight thousand men, all young and strong and fit for war.

He took the hundred he had in the beginning, except the few who had been killed in the brawl with the robbers or who had been burned in the lair, and these he raised into captains and sergeants over the new men. But when all this was done, Wang the Tiger did not, as many men in his place would have done, sit in idleness and ease to eat and drink. No, he made himself rise early, even in the winter, and he taught and trained his men and he forced them to learn every skill of war and battle that he knew himself, and how to feint and to attack and to ambush, and how to retreat without loss. Everything he could he made up his mind he would teach them, for he had no purpose to stay forever in this small court of a county magistrate. No, his dreams were swelling in him, and he let them grow as great as they would.

XV

Now the two elder brothers of Wang the Tiger had been waiting with hearty impatience to hear how he did with his venture, but each brother showed it in his own way. Wang the Eldest, since his son had hanged himself, pretended to have no more interest in his brother, and he mourned his son whenever he thought of him. His lady did, also, but her mourning found comfort in complaining against her husband and she said, often,

"I said from the first he ought not to go. I said from the first that it was an ill thing for a family like ours to send so good a son for a soldier. It is a low common life, and I said so."

At first Wang the Eldest had been foolish enough to make answer to her and to say,

"Now, lady, I did not know you were unwilling, and it seemed to me you were ready enough, the more because he was to be no common soldier but my brother would raise him as he raised himself."

But this lady had made up her mind as to what she had said, and she cried out vehemently,

"You never do know what I say because your mind is always on something else—some woman or other, I suppose! I said plainly and often that he ought not to go—and what is your brother but a common soldier? If you had listened to me, our son would have been living and well today and he was our best son and framed to be a scholar. But I am never listened to in my own house!"

She sighed and made a piteous face and Wang the Eldest looked east and west and he was very uneasy to have called this storm on himself and he did not answer a word, hoping that the force of her anger would spend itself more quickly thus. The truth was that now her son was dead the lady continually moaned that he had been her best son after all, although when he lived she scolded him too, and found fault with him, and thought her eldest son the best by much. But now the eldest was not good enough for her in anything and so the dead son seemed better. There was that third and hunchbacked one, but she never asked for him after she heard he liked to live with Pear Blossom, as he now did wholly, and she said if anyone spoke of him,

"He is not strong and the country air is good for him."

She sent a little present to Pear Blossom sometimes in lieu of thanks, some small, useless thing or other, a little bowl of flowered pottery or a bit of cheap cloth only partly silk but brave in show or color, such as Pear Blossom never wore. But Pear Blossom always thanked her prettily, whatever the gift, and sent back fresh eggs or some produce of the land, careful always to return something and so owe nothing. Then she took the cloth and gave it to the fool, or she made a gay coat or shoes to please the poor thing, and she gave the pottery bowl to the hunchback if he liked it, or to the farmer's wife who lived there in the earthen house, if she fancied the flowery town stuff more than her own blue and white ware.

As for Wang the Second he waited in his own way to hear what his younger brother did, and he listened secretly here and there and he heard rumors that the robber chief to the north of them had been killed by a new young brave, but he did not know if it were true or not or if the brave were his brother or not. So he waited and saved his money until the trusty man came, and he sold Wang the Tiger's lands when he could do it prudently, and he put the money out at very high interest, and if he turned the money over a time or two more than he told anyone, this he considered his just wage for all the trouble he had for his brother, and he did no injury to his brother thus, for no one else would have done as well as he did for Wang the Tiger.

But on the day when the harelipped trusty man stood upon the threshold, Wang the Second could scarcely wait to hear his tale, and with an unused eagerness upon his face he drew the trusty man into his own room and poured tea out for him, and then the trusty man told what he had to say, and Wang the Second heard it through to the end without a word.

When it was finished, and the trusty man told it exactly and well and he ended as Wang the Tiger had told him to end, saying,

"Your brother and my general says we are not to be hasty and say he has climbed his mountain because this is but his first step and he holds but a small county seat and he dreams of provinces."

Then Wang the Second drew his breath in a little and he asked,

207

"But do you think he is sure enough so that I can safely risk my own silver on him?"

Then the trusty man answered, "Your brother is a very clever man and many a man would have been content to settle into the robbers' lair and maraud the region and so rise somewhat high. But your brother is too wise for that, knowing that a robber must turn respectable before he can be a king, and so he has the power of state behind him. Yes, although it is only a small magistrate's seat, still it is the state and he is a state's general, and when he goes out to fight with other lords of war and when he finds a cause of quarrel with someone as he will when the spring comes, then he can go out as one with authority and not as rebel."

Such caution as this pleased Wang the Second very much, and so he said with more than usual heartiness, the hour being near to noon,

"Come out and eat and drink with us, if you will bear our common meal," and he took the man with him and set him at their family table.

Then when Wang the Second's wife saw the trusty man she cried a greeting to him in her hearty way and she said,

"What news of my little pocked son?"

The trusty man rose to his feet then and answered that her son was very well and he did well and the general was minded to raise him up, doubtless, for he kept him always about his person. But before he could say a word, the woman shouted that he was to sit and not stand in courtesy. So when he had sat down again he thought to tell them about how the lad had gone to the robbers' lair and how tricky he was and how neatly he had done what he had to do. But he stopped himself, because he knew that women are so strange and their tempers are uncertain, and mothers are the strangest of all, for they see fears and harms about their children where there are no such things. He contented himself with silence, therefore, when he had said enough to please her.

In a few minutes she had forgotten all she asked, for she was busy about many things, and she bustled here and there fetching bowls and setting them out on the table, and she held a babe at her breast as she worked. The child suckled tranquilly, while with her free arm she was zealous in dipping out food to the guest and to her husband and to the clamoring, hungry children who did not eat at the table, but stood at the door or on the street with their bowls and chopsticks, and when their bowls were empty they came running in for fresh rice and vegetables and meats.

When the meal was over and they had finished their tea after they ate, Wang the Second took the trusty man to his elder brother's gate, and there he bade the man wait until he could call his brother out and then they would go to a tea house to talk. But he told the man not to show himself lest the lady see him and they would need to go and hear her talk for a time. And so saying Wang the Second went inside and through a court or two to his elder brother's own rooms, and there he found him lying fast asleep on a couch beside a brazier of red coals, snoring after his noon meal.

But when Wang the Eldest felt his brother's light touch on his arm he started out of his sleep with a snort, and after being dazed for a while he understood what was wanted and he struggled up and drew on the fur robes he had laid aside, and he followed his brother softly so that he would not be heard. No one saw them go out except his pretty concubine who thrust her head out of a door to see who passed, and Wang the Eldest held up his hand as a sign of silence, and she let him go, for if she were timid and fearful of the lady, she was a kind, mild creature, too, and she could lie kindly and she would say she had not seen him, if she were asked.

They went together to the tea house and there the trusty man told his story over again, and Wang the Eldest groaned in his heart that he had not a son to give his younger brother, and he was jealous that his second brother's son did so well. But he kept it to himself for once, and he only spoke well to the man and he agreed to all his brother said in the matter of moneys to be sent back, and he waited until he reached his home again.

Then suddenly it seemed as though his heart overflowed with jealousy and he went and sought out his eldest son. The young man lay in the curtained bed in his own room, and he lay there idle and flushed and reading a loose lascivious tale called *The Three Fair Women,* and he started when he saw his father come in and he hid the book under his robe. But his father did not even see it he was so full of what he had come to say and began in haste,

"Son, do you still wish to go to be with your uncle and rise with him to a high place?"

But the young man had outgrown that moment in his life and now he yawned delicately, and his mouth was as pretty and pink as a girl's when he opened it thus and he looked at his father and smiled idly and he said,

"Was I ever so foolish as to want to go for a soldier?"

"But you will not be a soldier," urged his father anxiously. "You will be from the first much higher than soldier, and next your uncle." Then he lowered his voice, coaxing his son, "Your uncle is a general already and he has established himself by the wisest guile I ever heard of, and the worst is over."

But the young man shook his head wilfully, and Wang the Eldest, half angered and half helpless, looked at his son lying there on his bed. Some truthful sight came to this man at this instant, and he saw his son for what he was, a young man dainty and fastidious and idle, without any single ambition for anything except his pleasure, and his only fear that he was not better dressed and less in fashion than other young men whom he knew. Yes, Wang the Eldest saw his son lying on the silken quilts of his bed, and the young man wore silk to his very skin, and he had satin shoes on his feet and his skin was like a beauty's skin, oiled and perfumed, and his hair was perfumed and smoothed with some foreign oil also. For the young man studied to make his body beautiful in every way, and well nigh he worshipped it for its softness and beauty, and his reward was that there were many who praised him for it among those whom he played with at night in gaming houses and playhouses. Yes, he was a young lord in a rich man's house, as anyone could see, and none would have dreamed that his grandfather was one Wang Lung, a farmer, and a man of the earth. For this one instant did Wang the Eldest see his eldest son, although he was a man muddled and confused with many small things, and he was frightened for his son and he cried out in a high voice very different from his usual rolling tones,

"I am afraid for you, my son! I am afraid you will come to no good end!" Then he cried out more sharply than he ever had to this son of his, "I say you shall go and hew out some sort of a way of life and not grow old here in idle slothful pleasure!" And he wished in a sort of fright, which he did not understand in himself, that they had seized on the moment of the lad's ambition. But it was too late; the moment was gone.

When the young man heard the unwonted sound of his father's voice he cried out half afraid, half petulant, sitting up suddenly in his bed,

"Where is my mother? I will go and ask my mother if she will have me go or not, and I will see if she is so anxious to be rid of me!"

But Wang the Eldest, hearing this, fell back into himself again, and he said hastily and peaceably,

"We-well—let be—you shall do as you please since you are my eldest!"

And the cloud descended upon him again and the moment of clarity was gone. He sighed and thought to himself that it was true that young lords could not be as other common youths were, and he said to himself that it was true his brother's wife was a very common woman, and doubtless his pocked son was little better than a servant to his uncle. So Wang the Eldest consoled himself vaguely and he shuffled as he went out from his son's room. As for the young man, he lay back on his silk-covered pillow again, and he clasped his hands under his head and smiled his indolent smile, and after a while he felt for the book he had hidden and took it out and began to read it ardently once more, for it was a naughty, zestful book that a friend of his had commended to him.

But Wang the Eldest could not forget his vague despondency and it hung on him still so that for the first time his life did not seem so good to him as he thought it was. It was a very sore thing to him that when he had seen the trusty man gone again, his pilgrim's wallet filled with silver and his belt stiff with silver about his waist, and his bundle filled with it so that he could hardly heave the thing to his back, that he could not think of anything Wang the Tiger could do for him yet, and it seemed a sore thing to him and his life very weary because he had no son to whom he could look for glory and he had nothing but this land that he hated and yet did not dare to part with altogether. His lady even saw his despondency and in his extremity he told her some of his trouble, and she had taught him so well that in his secret heart he did believe her wiser than himself, although he would have denied it stoutly if anyone had asked him if he did. But this time she gave him no help, for when he tried to tell her how great his younger brother had become she laughed shrilly and with scorn and she said,

"A general at a small county seat is no great lord of war, my poor old man, and you are silly to be so envious of him! When he is lord of war in the province it will be time enough to tell off our younger son to him, and more likely it will be your smallest son who is only a suckling now at the other's breast!"

So Wang the Eldest sat silent then and for a time he did not go out as zestfully as he had to his pleasure places, and not even talk with his many friends seemed the worth it had before. No, he sat alone and he was not one to sit thus either, for he was a man who liked to be where there were people running to and fro in a commotion of some sort or other, even though it were but household bustle and servants bickering with a vendor and children crying and quarreling and the usual uproar of daily living. He liked even this better than to sit alone.

But now he sat alone because he was wretched and he did not know why he was except that for the first time it came to him that he was not so young as he was once and his age was creeping on him unawares, and it seemed to him he had not found the good in life he might have found and he was not so great as he should have been. Chiefest of all his vague miseries was one not vague, and it was the land he had from his father. It was a curse to him for it was his only livelihood and he must give it some oversight or he would have nothing to eat, he and his children and his wives and servants, and it seemed to him as though there were some vile magic in that land, and it was always seed time and he must go out to it or time to fertilize and he must see to it or it was harvest and

213

he must stand in the hot sun and measure out grain or it was time to collect his rents; and there was all the hateful round of the land, forcing him to labor when he was by nature a man of leisure and a lord. Yes, even though he had an agent, there was some shrewdness in this man, even against his will, that made his gorge rise to think the agent grew rich at his expense, so that although he hated it he dragged himself each season to the place where he could oversee what was done.

He sat now in his own room and now under a tree in the court outside it if the winter sun were warm enough and he groaned to think how he must go out year after year or the robbers who rented his land from him would give him nothing. Yes, they were forever howling, "Ah, we have had floods this year," and "Ah, we have such a drought as never was," or else it was, "This is the year for locusts," and they and his agent had a hundred tricks against him who was their landlord, and for the weariness of his strife with them he blamed and he loathed the land. He longed for the day when Wang the Tiger would be great enough so that his elder brother need no longer go out in heat and cold; he longed for the day when he could say, "I am brother to Wang the Tiger," and it would suffice. Once it had seemed much that men had come to call him Wang the Landlord, for this was his name now, and it had seemed an honorable good name until this moment.

The truth was this that Wang the Landlord found it very hard because all his life so long as his father Wang Lung had lived he had received money freely from him enough to pay for all he needed, and he never labored over its coming. But after the inheritance was divided he labored more than he ever had and yet with all this labor to which he was unaccus-

214

tomed he had not all the silver he needed, and his sons and wives never seemed to care how he labored.

No, his sons would wear the very best and they must have this fur in the winter and that dainty light fur to line their robes in the spring and autumn and all kinds of silks each in its season, and it was a hardship fit to break their hearts if they must wear a coat a little too long or a little wider in the cut than was this year's fashion, for they feared more than anything the laughter of the young town dandies who were their companions. So with the eldest son, and now the fourth son was learning this also. Although he was but thirteen years old, he must have his little robes cut thus and so and a ring on his finger and his hair scented and oiled too, and a maid to serve him only and a man to take him out; and because he was his mother's darling and she feared for him at the hands of evil spirits, he wore a gold ring in one ear, too, to deceive the gods and make them think him a girl and worthless.

As for his lady, Wang the Landlord could never persuade her that there was less silver in the house than there had once been and if he said when she wanted a sum of him, "But I have not so much to give you and I can only give you fifty pieces now," she would cry out, "I have promised it to the temple for a new roof over a certain god, and if I do not give it I shall lose my dignity. Indeed you have it, for I know you spend money like water on wining and gaming and on all those low women I know you have and I am the only one in this whole house who looks to the things of the soul and to gods. Some day I may have to pray your soul out of hell, and you will be sorry I had not the silver then!"

So Wang the Landlord had somehow to find the silver, although he hated it very much to see his good money going into the hands of the smooth and secret priests whom he hated and did not trust, and of whom he heard certain very evil things. Yet he could never be sure, either, that they had not some knowledge of magic and he could never be sure, although he pretended disbelief in gods as things fit only for women, that there was not some power in them too, and this was another confusion in him.

The truth was that this lady of his was so deep now in her intimacy with gods and temples and all such things that she grew very holy and she spent many hours in going to this god and that, and it gave her the greatest pleasure to pass into a temple gate leaning as a great lady does upon her maids, and as she came in to see the priests of the temple and even the abbot come to her obsequious and bowing and full of flattery and full of talk that she was a favorite of the gods and a lay nun, and very near the Way.

When they talked thus she simpered and smiled and cast her eyes down and deprecated, but before she well knew what she did oftentimes she had promised them this and that and a sum of money more than she really wished to give. But the priests took care to give her full praise and they put her name up in many places as an example to all devout persons, and one temple even presented her with a wooden ensign painted vermilion red and there were gilt letters on it signifying how this lady was so devout and good a follower of the gods. This ensign was hung in a lesser hall of the temple, but where many might see it. After this she was the more proud and holy and devout in her looks, and she studied to sit calmly always and to fold her hands and often she went holding her rosary and muttering the syllables of her prayer while others gossiped or talked idly. Therefore being so holy she was very hard with her husband and she would have what silver she needed to keep up the name she had.

When Wang the Landlord's younger wife saw what the

lady had she wanted her little share, too, not for the gods, although the girl learned to prate of them to please the lady, but still she wanted her silver. And Wang the Landlord could not think what she did with it, because she did not dress herself in fine flowered silks or buy jewels and gold things for her dress and hair. Yet the money went from her quickly, too, and Wang the Landlord did not complain lest the girl go and weep before the lady, and the lady reproach him that since he had taken such an one he ought to pay her something. For these two women liked each other in some strange cool way, and they stood together against their husband if they wanted something for themselves.

One day Wang the Landlord did find out the truth, however, for he saw his younger wife slip out to a side gate and take something from her bosom and give it to one who stood there, and Wang the Landlord peered and he saw the man was her old father. Then was Wang the Landlord very bitter and he thought to himself,

"So I am feeding that old rascal and his family, too!"

And he went into his own room and sat and sighed and was very bitter for a while and he groaned to himself. But it was no use, and he could do nothing for if she chose to give what she had from her husband to her father and not to spend it on sweetmeats and clothing and such things as most women love, she had this right, except that a woman ought to cleave first to the house of her husband. But Wang the Landlord did not feel he could contend with her and he let it pass.

And Wang the Landlord was the more torn in himself, for he could not control his own desires, even though he did now honestly try for the first time in his life when he was nearly fifty years old, to spend less for his love of women. But he had his weakness with him yet, and he could not bear to be thought a niggard among them when his fancy fixed itself.

Besides these two women in his house, he had the singing girl established as a transient wife by common agreement in another part of the city. But she was a pretty leech, and although he had finished with her soon, she held him by her threats of killing herself and of loving him above all the world, and she cried on his bosom and fixed her little sharp fingers into the deep flesh on his neck and she hung to him so that he did not know what to do with her.

With her she had her old mother also, a vile hag, and she in her turn screeched out,

"How can you cast off my daughter who has given you all? How would she live now, seeing that she has not been in a playhouse all these years you have had her and her voice is gone and others have taken her place? No, I will defend her and I will take her case to the magistrate if you cast her off!"

This frightened Wang the Landlord very much, for he feared the laughter of the town against him if they heard all this old woman's ribald talk that she would vent against him in court if she could, so that he fumbled hastily for what silver he had. When the two women saw he was afraid, they plotted and made every opportunity they could for storm and weeping, knowing that when they did, he would pay them in haste. And the strangest thing of all was that with so many troubles, this great fat weak man still could not keep himself free, but must still be overcome with his desires at a feast somewhere and pay a new little singing girl he saw, even though when he came home and was himself on the next day, he groaned at his own folly and cursed his own fulsom heart.

But now, pondering all this during these weeks of his despondency he grew frightened at his own zestlessness, and he did not even care to eat so much as he had, and when he found his appetite for food waning he was frightened lest he die too soon, and he said to himself that he must rid himself of some of his troubles. And he determined that he would sell a good large share of his land and live on the silver, and he thought to himself secretly that he would spend what was his and his sons must care for themselves if there was not enough left for their lifetime. And it seemed to him suddenly that it was a vain thing for a man to stint himself for those who live on after him. He rose wilfully then and he went to his second brother and he said,

"I am not fitted for the cares of a landlord's life, for I am a city man, a man of leisure. No, I cannot with my increasing weight and years go out at seed time and harvest, and if I do one day I shall drop dead with the heat or the cold. I have not lived with common people, either, and they cheat me before I know it and out of all my land and my labor. Now this I ask of you. Act as my agent and sell a good half of my lands for me now and let me have the money as I need it, and what I do not need put out at interest for me, and let me be free of this accursed land. The other half I will keep to leave to my sons. But there is not one of them who will help me with it now, and when I say to my eldest son that he is to go for me sometimes to the land he is always pressed with a meeting with some friend or he has a headache and we shall starve if we continue as we are now. Only the tenants grow rich from the land."

Then Wang the Second looked at this brother of his, and he despised him in his heart, but he said smoothly,

"I am your brother, and I will not take any commission at all for selling it and I will sell it for you to anyone who bids highest for it. But you must say what your lowest price is for each lot."

But Wang the Landlord was very eager to be finished with his land and he said quickly,

"You are my brother and sell it for what you think fair. Shall I not trust my own brother?"

He went away then in high good humor because he was rid of half of his burden and he could go his way for a time and wait for silver to come into his hands as he longed to do again. But he did not tell his lady what he had done, because she might cry out against him that he had given them over into the other's hand, and she would say that if he wished to sell, he ought to sell it himself to some among the many rich men with whom he feasted and with whom he seemed in such deep friendship, and Wang the Landlord did not wish to do this, for in his heart, for all his bluster, he trusted his brother's wit more than he did his own. And now having done this, his heart rose again and he could eat once more, and once more his life seemed good enough to him and he thought to himself there were others more troubled than he, and he was ardent again.

Now Wang the Second grew more content than ever for he had all in his own hands. He planned that he would buy the best of his brother's lands for himself. It was true that he paid a fair price for them, for he was not a dishonest man as men are reckoned, and indeed he told his elder brother that he bought a little of the best land to keep it in the family. But how much of the land he bought Wang the Landlord did not know, for Wang the Second had him sign the deeds when he was somewhat drunken and he did not look to see what name was on it, but being full of the good humor of drunkenness his brother seemed excellent to him and wholly to be trusted. He would not have been willing had he known to see so much of his land pass into Wang the Second's keeping, perhaps, and so Wang the Second made much of the poorer pieces he sold to tenants or to whom it was who wished to buy. And it was true that Wang the Second did sell much land thus. But

Wang Lung had been very wise in his day and he bought far more good land than any other kind, and so when all the business was over Wang the Second had in his own personal possession and for his sons the best and the choicest of all his father's land, for he had so bought the best of his younger brother's inheritance also. And with all this land he planned he would supply much of the grain to his own markets and increase his stores of silver and gold, and he grew powerful in the town and in that region, and men called him Wang the Merchant.

But unless he knew it no one would have dreamed this small meager man was so rich, for Wang the Merchant still ate the plain spare bit of food he always did and he took no new wife into his house as most men will when they are rich, for show if for nothing else, and he wore the same sort of small patterned silk gown of a dark slate grey that he had always worn. In his house they added no new furniture, and in his courts there was no flower nor any waste thing, and what had been there before now was dead, for his wife was thrifty and raised flocks of fowls and these ran in and out of the rooms to pick up bits of food the children dropped, and they ran about the courts and plucked every grass blade and green leaf, so that the courts were bare except for a few old pines, and the earth grew hard and packed.

Nor would Wang the Merchant let his sons be spendthrift nor idle. No, he planned for each one, and each had a few years of schooling to learn to read and write and to count skilfully upon the abacus. But he would not let them stay long enough to be held scholars in any wise, for scholars will not labor at anything, and he planned apprenticeships for them and they were to come into his business. The pocked one he considered his younger brother's, and the next one he planned to make his steward on the land, but the others he apprenticed when their time came and when each was twelve years old.

In the earthen house Pear Blossom lived on with the two children and every day of her life was like the one before it, and she asked no more than that it should be so always. She grieved no more for the land, for if she did not see the elder she saw the younger son of her dead lord come out before harvest time to estimate the growth of grain and to see the seed weighed off and all such things. Yes, and she heard, too, how Wang the Merchant, for all he was a townsman, was sharper as landlord than his brother even, for he knew to a ten catty weight what a field still standing in green grain would give, and his narrow little eyes were always sharp to see if a tenant pressed his foot secretly against the side of a load to weigh it down or if he poured water into the rice or the wheat to make it swell. His years in the grain market had taught him everything that country people do to cheat the merchant and the townsman, for they are enemies by nature. But if Pear Blossom asked whether any ever saw him angry when he found out a trick, the answer always came with unwilling admiration that he was never angry. No, he was only implacable and calm and more clever than any of them, and the nickname he had in that whole countryside was this, "He Who Wins in Every Bargain."

It was a scornful name and full of hatred, and all the country people hated Wang the Merchant very heartily. But he did not care and he was even pleased to know what they called him, and he knew because an angry farm wife shouted it at him once with curses when he saw her sink a great round stone into the heart of a basket of grain about to be weighed, and she had done it when she thought his back was turned.

More than a time or two did a farm woman curse him, for

a bitter-tongued woman is bolder than any man, and if a man were discovered in a trick he looked sullen or sheepish as his nature was, but a woman would curse and she would cry out after him,

"How is it that in one generation you forget how your father and your mother toiled on the land even as we do and they starved too, as we must, when you grind our blood and bones as you do now?"

Wang the Landlord had grown afraid sometimes when the people grew bitter, for he knew the rich may well fear the poor, who seem so patient and humble and who can be so bold and ruthless when they turn to rend whom they hate. But Wang the Merchant feared nothing, and it was nothing to him even when one day Pear Blossom saw him pass and she called to him and came out and said,

"If so be, sir, my lord's son, that you can be a little less exact with the people, I should be glad. They labor very hard and they are poor and like children in ignorance, oftentimes. It goes against my heart to hear the cruel things they say, sometimes, about my lord's sons."

But Wang the Merchant only smiled and went his way. It was nothing to him what any said or did, so long as he had his full profits. His was the power and he feared nothing, for he felt himself secure in his riches.

XVI

Now the winter wore on very long and cold in those parts and in the time of bitter winds and in the fury of wind-driven snows Wang the Tiger could but stay on in the magistrate's courts in the place that was now his and wait for the spring to come. He entrenched himself in his place and he steadily demanded from the magistrate this tax and that for his eight thousand soldiers. Yes, there was even a tax put on all land for his benefit and it was called the tax for the protection of the people by the state soldiery, but this soldiery was really Wang the Tiger's own private army, and he taught them and trained them and made them ready to enlarge his power for him when he saw the moment was come. Every farmer in that whole region paid something on every field he had and he paid it out for Wang the Tiger; and because the robbers were gone and the lair burned and they need not fear the Leopard any more, the common folk were full of praise for Wang the Tiger and they were ready to pay him well, but still they did not know how well this was.

There were other taxes also that Wang the Tiger had the magistrate lay for him, some on shops and markets, and every traveller who came through that town, which was a pass between north and south, paid a tax and every merchant paid a tax on the goods he took back and forth for sale and barter, and so the money poured steadily and secretly into Wang the Tiger's stores. He was sharp enough, too, to see that it did not touch too many hands in passing, knowing that no hand in this world will readily release as much silver as it grasps. He appointed his own trusty men to see to the collecting of it and although these spoke smoothly to all and he commanded them so to speak, yet he gave them the power over anyone they found taking more than his share, and he told each trusty man that he would punish them himself if they failed him. He was safer than most from treachery for everyone feared him for a ruthless man. Yet they knew him to be just, too, and they knew he did not kill any man carelessly or for mere pleasure.

But as Wang the Tiger waited for the winter to be gone

he chafed very much in spite of his success, for this life in the magistrate's courtyards did not suit him. No, and there were none who could be his friends, for he would not bring himself to intimacy with any, knowing that as long as people feared him he could hold his place the more easily among them; besides, he was one who did not by nature love to take part in feasting and friendship, and he lived alone except for his pocked nephew whom he kept near him always lest he need something, and his trusty harelipped man who was his chief guard.

The truth was that now the magistrate was so old and given to his opium pipe, everything ran slackly about him and his courts were filled with cliques and jealousies and crowded with underlings and underlings' relatives who sought an easy way to live. This man turned against that, and there were deep angers and revenges and quarrels continually. But if these were brought to the old magistrate's ears he turned himself to his opium or he thought of something else, for well he knew he could not settle everything, and he lived alone with his old wife in an inner court and he only came out when he must. But he tried to do his state duty still, and every audience day at dawn he rose and put on his official robes and he went into his audience hall and ascended the dais there and sat down in the chair from whence he heard his cases.

He did his poor best, too, for he was a good and kind man at heart, and he supposed he meted out justice to such as came before him there. But he did not know that every suppliant who came before him had paid his way through from the very gateman at the gates, so that any man who had not silver enough for high and low could not hope even to reach that audience hall, and the very councillors who stood in the presence of the magistrate had each received his share. Nor did the old magistrate know he leaned so heavily on these councillors of his. No, for he was old and easily confused and often he did not catch the point of a case and he was ashamed to say he did not, or he dozed somewhat toward the end of the hour, and did not hear what was said, and he was afraid to ask again, lest men think him not able. So he turned naturally to his councillors who never failed to flatter him and when they said, "Ah, this man is evil and that man has the right of it," the old magistrate would agree hastily and say—"It is what I thought—it is what I thought," and when they cried out, "Such an one ought to be well beaten because he is so lawless," the old magistrate would quaver forth, "Yes—yes, let him be beaten!"

Now in these idle days Wang the Tiger often went to the audience hall to see and to hear and to pass the time away, and when he went he sat to one side and his trusty men and his pocked nephew stood about him as a guard. Thus he heard and saw all this injustice. At first he said to himself that he would pay no heed to any of these things, for he was a lord of war and these civil affairs were no business of his, and he would spend his care on his soldiers, seeing that they did not share in the loose, idle life of the courts, and many a time when he saw that which made him angry in the audience hall he went out and was furious with his soldiers and forced them to marches and to practices of war, whatever the winds were that day, and so he relieved his heart of the pressure of its anger.

But he was a man just at heart and when he saw the injustice go on time after time he could not bear it at last, and he grew surcharged with anger against some of the councillors who had the ear of the magistrate, and especially against the chief councillor. Yet he knew it was no use to say anything to the weak old man. But still, when he had sat sometimes and listened to cases and when he had seen injustice done a hundred times, he grew so pent in himself that he would rise and stride away and he muttered to himself many times,

"If spring does not come quickly I shall kill someone against my will!"

As for the councillors, they did not love him, either, because he secured so much revenue and they mocked him for a coarsely bred fellow and one beneath them in polish and learning.

Now Wang the Tiger's anger burst forth one day in a sudden way that he himself had not expected, and it began with a small matter enough, even as a mighty storm will begin sometimes with only a little wind and a handful of ragged cloud.

It happened on a certain day before the new year, when men are out everywhere to collect debts and those who owe hide as best they may so that they cannot be found until the first day of the new year when debts cannot be collected from anyone, that the old magistrate had his last audience day of the old year and he sat upon his dais. On that day Wang the Tiger had been very restless because he was so idle. He would not game because he did not want his soldiers to see him at it and feel the more free themselves to do it, and he could not read overmuch because novels and tales weaken a man, they are so full of dreams and the stuffs of love, and he was not scholar enough for the old philosophies. Therefore being sleepless also, he rose and went with his guard and sat awhile in the audience room to see who would come that day. But in his heart he was pent and impatient for the spring, and especially because the last ten days had been so cold and so filled with a downpour of constant rain that his men cried out against being taken out of their quarters.

There he sat, and it seemed to him that his was the dreariest life, and there was not one soul to care if he lived or died, and so he sat, listless and glowering in his usual place. Presently he saw a certain rich man come in whom he knew, having seen him here before. This man was a usurer of the town, a smooth-faced, fat man, with very small, smooth, yellow hands that he flourished with a sort of evil grace as he spoke, and he continually pushed back his long silken sleeves from his hands before he waved them. Many times Wang the Tiger had watched his hands and seen how small they were and how soft and full and how pointed the finger tips were with their long nails, and he had watched the man's hands when he did not hear what he said, even.

But today the usurer came in with a poor farmer and the farmer was very frightened and ill at ease, and he threw himself before the magistrate with his face to the ground, and remained there speechless, begging for mercy. Then the usurer told his case and it was that he had loaned a sum of money to this farmer, and had accepted his land as security. This was two years ago, and now the money with its interest had mounted above the worth of the land.

"Yet in spite of this," the usurer cried, and he pushed back his silken sleeves and moved his smooth hands and made his voice rich and reproachful, and he was very unctuous, "in spite of this, O honored magistrate, he will not move from his land!" And the man rolled his little eyes around in indignation at this wicked farmer.

But the farmer said nothing at all. He continued to kneel there with his face bent and leaning upon his two hands forked together. At last the old magistrate asked him,

"Why did you borrow and why do you not pay?"

Then the farmer looked up a little and he fixed his eyes on the magistrate's footstool, and he continued to kneel, and he said anxiously,

"Sir, I am a very common man and poor, and I do not know how to speak to such as you, honored Sir. I am very common and I have never spoken to one higher than the head in our village, and I do not know how to speak here, and yet I have no one to speak for me, seeing that I am so poor."

Then the old magistrate said kindly enough,

"You need not fear—only speak on."

Then the farmer after opening his lips a time or two soundlessly began to speak, but still he did not lift his eyes at all, and it could be seen that his spare body was shivering in his patched and ragged clothes from which the old wadding stuck forth out of the holes like old sheep's wool. His feet were bare and thrust only into shoes woven out of reeds and these had now fallen from his feet, so that his hard and horny toes rested stiffly upon the damp stone floor. But he did not seem to feel this, and he began in a weak voice and he said,

"Sir, I had a little land from my fathers. It is very poor land and it has never fed us full. But my parents died early and there were only I and my wife, and if we starved we did it and that was all. But she bore a child, a son, and then after years another, a girl. When they were little it was still not so hard. But they grew and we had to wed the son and his wife had a child. Sir, think of it, the land was not enough for my wife and me and now we have these. The girl was long too young to be wed and I had her to feed somehow. Two years ago I had a chance to betroth her to an old man in a village near us, for his wife was dead and he needed one to mend his household. But I had to give her a wedding garment. Sir, I had nothing so I borrowed a little money—only ten pieces of silver, to most men nothing, but to me very much and more than I had. I borrowed it from this usurer.

In less than a year the ten pieces had grown into twenty of its own accord, for I had no more than the ten to spend. Now in two years it is forty. Sir, how can dead silver grow like that? There is only my land. He says go, but where shall I go? Let him come and drive me off, I say. There is nothing else than this."

When the man had finished saying this he remained perfectly silent. Wang the Tiger stared at him and it was the strangest thing that he could not keep his eyes from the man's feet. The farmer's face was drawn and sallow and told of his life and of his never being full fed since he was born. But his feet told the whole tale. There was something eloquent in this man's two bare feet, knotted and gnarled in the toes, and the soles like the dried hide of a water buffalo. Yes, looking at the man's feet Wang the Tiger felt something welling up in him. Nevertheless, he waited to see what the old magistrate would say.

Now this usurer was a man of the town and well known and he had feasted with the magistrate many times and he kept the good will of the court with him because he paid silver to high and low in every case he had and he had many. The magistrate hesitated, therefore, although it could be seen he was somewhat moved, too. At last he turned to his chief councillor, a man near his own age but strong and straight for his years, and his face was smooth and handsome still, although his scanty whiskers that grew in three parts from his cheeks and chin were white. The magistrate asked this man,

"What do you say, my brother?"

This man smoothed his few white whiskers then and he said slowly as though he pondered justice, but the memory of silver was warm on his palm,

"It cannot be gainsaid that this farmer did borrow money

and he has not returned it, and money borrowed must run into interest and this is according to the law. The usurer lives by his loaned moneys as a farmer does by his land. If the farmer rented his land out and received no rent he would complain and his complaint would be just. Yet this is only what the usurer has done. It is just, therefore, that he be paid his due."

The old magistrate listened to this carefully, nodding his head from time to time, and it could be seen he was moved by it, too. But now suddenly the farmer lifted his eyes and for the first time he looked in a kind of daze from one face to the other. Yet Wang the Tiger did not see his face or how his eyes looked. He only saw the man's two old bare feet curl upon each other in an agony, and suddenly he could not bear it. His immense anger rushed forth and he stood up. He clapped his hands together hard and he roared in a great voice,

"I say the poor man shall have his land!"

When all the people gathered in the court heard this roar come out of Wang the Tiger every head turned toward him, and the trusty men Wang the Tiger had, leaped to him and stood with their guns pointed fiercely and seeing them everyone shrank back and kept silent. But Wang the Tiger felt his anger released now and he could not stay it if he would and he pointed his finger at the usurer and stabbed it through the air again and again as he spoke and he shouted in a great voice, his black brows darting now up, now down above his eyes,

"Again and again have I seen this fat, biting insect here with some tale like this and he has greased his way in with silver to high and low! I am weary of him! Away with him!" And he turned to his guard and shouted, "After him with your guns!"

Now when the people heard this they thought Wang the Tiger had gone suddenly mad and everyone turned and ran for his life. Yes, and swiftest of all to run was the fat usurer and he reached the gate ahead of them all and he went through it with a squeak like a rat that barely escapes. He was so swift and he knew so well the winding alleys that although the trusty men pursued him he was gone and they could not find him, and when they had run so far they could only draw themselves up and look at each other with blank faces and pant awhile. And after they had looked a little more they went back through the hubbub that had risen now in the streets.

When they reached the court again there was an uproar indeed, for Wang the Tiger seeing what he had begun, grew reckless and he called his soldiers and cried out,

"Clear me these courts of everyone—all these cursed sucking worms and all their dirty women and children!"

And his soldiers fell with zest to doing what he said and the people ran out of the courts like rats from a burning house. Yes, in less than an hour there was not a soul there except Wang the Tiger and his own men, and in the magistrate's own courts the old magistrate and his lady and their few personal servants. These Wang the Tiger had commanded were not to be touched.

When Wang the Tiger had done all this, and it had been done in such a burst of rage as he had seldom had in his life before, although he was given to such angers, too, he went into his own room and he sat down by the table and leaned on it and breathed heavily for a while. And he poured himself out some tea and drank it slowly. After a time he saw that he had set a pattern for himself this day that he must follow out somehow. But the more he thought the more he did not regret it, for now he felt free in his heart of all his despondency and gloom, and he felt light and brave and free and when his harelipped man stole in to see what he needed and his pocked lad brought in a jug of wine for him, he cried out to them, laughing his silent laugh as he did,

"Well, at least I have cleared out a serpent's nest this day!"

When the people of that town heard of the rebellion in the court there were many who were pleased for they had known what corruption was there, and while some were afraid and waited to see what Wang the Tiger would do next, there were many who came clamoring about the court gates and they cried out that there should be a time of feasting set and that the prisoners ought to be freed out of the gaol so that everyone could rejoice together.

But the one who had benefited most by the uproar, and it was the poor farmer, was not among that crowd. No, although he had been delivered this once he could not believe that any good fortune could be in store for him, and when he heard the usurer had escaped, he groaned and fled back to his land, and he went to his house and crept into his bed and if anyone came to ask his wife or children where he was they said he had gone away somewhere and they did not know where he was.

When Wang the Tiger heard what the people demanded he remembered that there were in the gaol some dozen or so of men whom he had seen thrown in for one unjust cause or another and they were hopeless of coming out, for most of them were poor and had not money enough to secure their freedom. And so he was willing and he told his trusty men to free the people in the gaol, and he called out to his men that they were to have three days of feasting, and he sent for the cooks of the magistrate's court and he had them come into his presence and he said to them loudly,

233

"Prepare the best dishes of your native parts, the hot peppery dishes and the fish dishes to go with wine, and everything with which we can make merry."

He ordered good wines, too, and strings of firecrackers and rockets and all such things as please the people. And everyone was glad.

But just before the trusty men went to fulfil his command concerning those in the gaol Wang the Tiger suddenly thought of something, and it was that woman who was in the gaol, too. He had wanted her out a score of times during this winter, but each time he had not known what to do with her either, so he had contented himself with commanding that she be well fed and not chained as some were. Now when he thought of the prisoners free, he thought of her and he thought to himself,

"But how can I free her?"

And he wanted her free and yet he wanted her not so free that she could go away, and he was astonished at himself when he found he cared whether she came or went. He was astonished at his own heart, and being bewildered, he called his harelipped trusty man secretly into the room where he slept and he said,

"But what of that woman we had from the lair?"

Then the trusty man answered gravely, "Yes, there is she, and I wish you would let me tell the Pig Butcher to put a knife to her throat in a way he has so that little blood flows."

But Wang the Tiger looked away and he said, slowly,

"She is only a woman." And he waited awhile and said, "At least I will see her again, and then I can know what I ought to do."

The trusty man looked very downcast at this, but he said nothing and went away, and as he went Wang the Tiger called after him that the woman was to be brought at once

234

to him in the hall of justice where he would go to wait for her.

He went into the hall of justice then and stepped up on the dais into the old magistrate's seat out of some strange impulse of vanity he had, and he thought he would like to have the woman see him there in the great carven seat raised as it was above the other seats, and there was no one to say him nay, for the magistrate did not come out of his own rooms yet, having sent word he was ill of a flux. There Wang the Tiger sat very stiff and haughty and he kept his face smooth and proud as a hero's ought to be.

At last she came in between two guards, and she wore a plain cotton coat and trousers of some dull blue common stuff. But this common garb was not what had changed her. She had eaten well, and the gauntness of her body was changed to a fulness that was still slender. Pretty she could never be because her face was too marked for prettiness, but she was very bold and beautiful. She came in steadily and freely and she stood before Wang the Tiger, quiet and waiting.

He looked at her in greatest astonishment, for he had not dreamed of a change like this, and he said to the guards,

"Why is she so still now, seeing how mad she was before?"

And they shook their heads and moved their shoulders and said, "We do not know, except that when she went out from our captain last time she went broken and weak as though some evil spirit had passed from her, and she has been like this ever since."

"Why did you not tell me?" said Wang the Tiger in a low voice. "I would have had her freed."

The guards were astonished at this and they said to excuse themselves,

"Sir, how could we know that our general cared what came to her? We waited for your commands."

Then words flew of their own accord to the tip of Wang the Tiger's tongue and he all but cried them out, "But I do care!" He did but barely stop them for how could he say such a thing out before all these guards and before this woman?

"Loose her from those bonds!" he shouted suddenly.

Without a word they loosed her and she stood free and they all waited to see what she would do, and Wang the Tiger waited also. She stood there as though she were still bound and she did not move. Then Wang the Tiger called out to her sharply,

"You are free—you may go where you will!"

But she answered, "Where shall I go, seeing I have no home anywhere?"

And saying this, she lifted up her head and looked at Wang the Tiger with a sudden seeming simplicity.

At that look the sealed fountain in Wang the Tiger was unstopped and such a passion rushed out into his blood that he began to tremble within his soldier's clothes. Now it was his eyes that dropped before hers. Now she was stronger than he. The room was filled with the air of this passion that had been stopped so long and men stirred uneasily and stared at each other. Suddenly Wang the Tiger remembered they were there and he roared at them,

"Get you gone, every one of you, and stand outside the door!"

They went away then, crestfallen, for they saw well enough what had befallen their general, even that which may befall any man, high or low. They went out then, and waited upon the threshold.

When there were none but these two left in the hall, Wang the Tiger leaned forward out of his carven seat and he said in a hard, hoarse voice,

"Woman, you are free. Choose where you will go and I will send one to take you there."

And she answered simply, with all the boldness gone out of her, except that she could look at him in the eyes while she said it,

"I have chosen already. I am your bondswoman."

XVII

IF Wang the Tiger had been a coarse and common man and without feeling for what was lawful and decent he might have taken this woman, since she had no father or brother or any man to stand for her, and he might have done as he liked with her. But that hour in his youth which had been like a blow upon his heart made him fastidious still and it made his pleasure more keen to think he could wait, with all his passion, until he could have her as a wife. Moreover, he wanted her as wife, for mingled with all his personal passion for her, which fell more deeply on him hour by hour, was the craving also to have a son by her, his son, his first-born son, and only a true wife can bear a man his true son. Yes, half of the exultation of his secret longing for her was this, to think what a son they would form between them, he with his power and great tall body and all he had to bestow, and she with her fox-like beauty and her spirit of fearlessness. To Wang the Tiger when he dreamed of it, it seemed his son lived already.

In great haste, then, he called his harelipped trusty man and he bade him thus,

"Go to my brothers and tell them I want my share of the silver that was left to me when I should want to wed. I need it now for my marriage, for I have set my will upon this woman. Tell them to give me a thousand pieces of silver, for I have presents to give her and my men must have a very great feast on such a day and I must buy myself a new robe fit for the day. But if he gives you eight hundred, come back with it, and do not delay for the rest. And bid my brothers come and see the marriage, too, they and all they care to bring with them."

The trusty man listened to this in greatest consternation, and his lower jaw hung hideously and he stammered forth in an agony,

"Oh, my general—oh, my captain—to that fox! But take her for a day—a time—not wed—"

"Be silent, fool!" Wang the Tiger roared at him then, starting up from his seat at the man. "Did I ask your counsel? I will order you beaten like a common criminal!"

The man hung his head then silent, but tears rose into his eyes and he went on his errand very heavily, for he felt the woman would bring his master nothing but evil and he muttered many times as he went along the road,

"Yes, and I have seen these fox women! Yes, and my general will never believe any evil I tell him! These fox women do always fasten themselves on the best men—it is always so!"

Thus he went along the road, his feet stirring the dust that lay thick through the dry winter days, and men passing him stared at him curious because of his muttering and because of his tears that rolled down his cheeks sometimes without his knowing it, and when they saw he paid no heed to anything except what was in his own heart, they set him down as mad, and gave him the wider half of the road.

But when this trusty man came with his message to Wang the Merchant, that one was for once startled out of his secret calm and he looked up from his table where he sat casting up accounts, for the trusty man, finding him not at his house, had come straight to his grain shop, and there he was at his desk in a corner behind the counters. He looked up and said in agitation, his pen arrested in his hand,

"But how can I suddenly withdraw so much money from the places where I have it loaned out? My brother ought to tell me when he is betrothed and so give me warning of a year or two. Such haste is scarcely decent in a wedding!"

Now Wang the Tiger knew his brother and how loath he was to part with money and so he had also told his trusty man before he went,

"If my brother delays you are to press him to the point and tell him plainly I will have the money if I have to come and fetch it myself. I will carry this thing through in three days after you return, and you are not to be away more than five. There is need for haste, for I do not know how long it will be before I have an army march down on me from above, for I cannot hope to remain unnoticed when the provincial ruler hears what I did in these courts. He will send men against me, even, and there can be no feasting and wedding on a battlefield."

Now it was true enough that what Wang the Tiger had done by violence he must expect to be heard in the courts above him and it was true that he might be punished. But there was a deeper truth than this, and it was that Wang the Tiger was so hungry for this woman he could not wait for her longer than he must, and he knew he was useless as a warrior until he could have her safely for himself, and so set his mind free for something else. Therefore he had urged his trusty man and he grew fierce in his urging and he added,

"Well I know that merchant brother of mine will howl that he has his money where he cannot get it. You are not to heed him. Tell him I have my sword still, and the very swift and fine sword that I took from the Leopard when I killed him!"

But the trusty man kept this threat as a last resort and he did not use it up at the first, and not until Wang the Merchant seemed about to delay on another score, and it was that it was a shame to the family to wed into it a woman who had no family and no home, and had been a trollop, perhaps, as such women are. But the trusty man did not tell him it was a woman out of a robbers' lair. No, although he was sorely tempted to tell it and tempted to hold back the woman by any means, yet he knew Wang the Tiger well enough to know he would have what he set himself to have, and so he used his threat.

Then Wang the Merchant had to scour about and get what silver he could, and he was in great distress of mind that he was compelled to call in money suddenly like this and lose its interest, and he went very gloomily to his elder brother and said,

"The sum of money due our younger brother for his marriage he calls for now, and he is going to wed some trollop or other whom we have never heard of! He is more like you than me, after all."

Wang the Landlord scratched his head at this and cast about for an answer, and then decided on peace, and he said,

"It is a strange thing, for I thought he would call upon us when he felt the need and when he was established, and ask us to betroth him properly, since our father is dead who should have done it for him. Yes, I had a maid or two in mind even." And in his heart he thought that surely he would have chosen a maid better than anyone else, seeing he knew women so well, and all the best maids, at least by hearsay, who were in the town.

But Wang the Merchant had been driven very irritable with the exigency and he sneered and said,

"Be sure you have a maid or two in mind! But that is nothing to me. The thing is what can you give of this thousand he wants, for I have no such great amount of cash to take out of my girdle suddenly like this!"

Wang the Elder stared heavily at his brother, then, and he sat staring with his hands on his fat knees, and he said huskily,

"You know all I have. I never have any ready silver. Sell a piece of my land again."

Then Wang the Merchant groaned a little, for it was not a good time to sell before the New Year, and he had counted on the harvests of wheat to which the land was all planted. But after he had gone back to his shop and had fingered his abacus awhile and cast up his loss and profit, he found it would pay him to sell more land rather than to draw his money out of the places of high interest where he had it, and so he sold a fair field, and when he let it be known, many came to buy of him. He sold the land for a thousand pieces and a little odd sum over, but he gave the trusty man only nine hundred pieces, and held back the rest, lest Wang the Tiger demand more.

But the trusty man was a simple fellow, and he remembered that his master told him he was not to delay for a hundred pieces or so, and he went away with what he had. And Wang the Merchant hastened to put out at interest what had not been asked for, and he was a little comforted that he had saved this much, at any rate.

There was but one untoward thing in this transaction he made, and it was that when he sold the land he sold a piece or two not far from the earthen house, and Pear Blossom happened to be out on the threshing floor in front of the house.

When she saw the knot of men gathered about the field, she shaded her eyes with her hand and looked through the sunshine and she knew what was being done. She hastened then to Wang the Merchant's side and motioned him back a little from the others, and she opened her eyes with reproach and said to him,

"Again do you sell the land?"

But Wang the Merchant would not be troubled with her when he had so much else to trouble him, and he said bluntly,

"My younger brother is to be wed, and there is no other provision for the sum that is rightfully his for such a purpose except to sell a piece."

Then Pear Blossom shrank back in the strangest way and she said no more. No, she went slowly back to the house, and from that day on her life narrowed itself yet more, and what time she did not spend in caring for the two children, as she called them always, she spent assiduously in listening to the nuns who came to visit her, and she besought them now to come every day. Yes, even in the morning, when it is ill luck to see a nun, and many will spit upon a nun if she cross their path before noon, because it is so ill an omen, Pear Blossom welcomed them always.

Eagerly she foreswore eating any more meat her life long, and it was not hard for her, either, because she had always shrunk so from taking any life at all. Yes, she was such an one that even on a hot summer's night she would close the lattices so that the moths would not fly in and burn themselves in the candle flames, and this she counted as the saving of life. Her greatest prayer was that the fool might die before her so that she need never use the packet of white poison that Wang Lung had left to her to use if she must.

She learned of these nuns and far into the night she told off her prayers and she had always wrapped about her wrist the little rosary of beads of fragrant wood. This was all her life.

Now after the trusty man had gone, Wang the Merchant and Wang the Landlord consulted together as to whether they ought or not to go to their brother's wedding. They each longed to share such success as he had had, but the trusty man had made much of the need for haste lest a battle be made by those above, and so the brothers were afraid, also, because they did not know how strong Wang the Tiger was and whether, if he lost, he would be heavily punished and they perhaps entangled in the punishment because they were his brothers. Wang the Landlord longed especially to go and see what sort of a woman his younger brother had, for the trusty man told enough to whet his interest. But when his lady heard of the affair she said gravely,

"It is a very strange and unusual thing to have such a brawl as we have heard. No, if he is punished by those above him in the state, then we may be all punished, for I have often heard it told that if a man commits a crime of rebellion against the state, his family may be killed even to the very ninth-removed cousin."

It was true that in the past such punishments were made, when kings and emperors strove to sweep the country clean of crimes, and Wang the Landlord had seen such things told in plays and he had heard of them in story tellers' booths, where he loved to pass time away, so that now, although he was too high for such low pastimes and dared not join a common crowd in such a place, he still listened eagerly if a passing story teller came into the tea house to tell his tale. Now, remembering, he turned yellow with fright and he went to Wang the Merchant and said,

"We had better have some sort of a signed paper saying

243

our brother was an unfilial son so that we have cast him out of our house, so that if he fails in a battle or is punished we will not be entangled with him, we and our sons." And he thought to himself at that moment that he was glad his son had not wanted to go, after all, and he took pleasure in pitying his brother and saying, "I do feel for you with your own son in such a danger!"

Now although Wang the Merchant merely smiled, yet when he had thought awhile it seemed to him a good, cautious thing to do. So he wrote a paper saying how and in what ways Wang the Third, nicknamed the Tiger, had been unfilial and no longer belonged to the house, and he had his elder brother sign it first and then he signed it and he took it to the magistrate's court and paid a sum of money to have it secretly stamped. Then he took the deed and put it safely away where none might find it unless he needed it.

Thus the two brothers felt safe, and they looked at each other when they met in the tea house one morning, and Wang the Landlord said,

"Why should we not go and feast merrily now, seeing we are safe?"

But before they could consider it, for they were not men who at their age could take a journey easily, there came a rumor over that whole region, told from mouth to mouth, and it was that the ruler of the province had heard with great wrath that some small country upstart, half robber, half runaway soldier from an old southern general, had seized the seat of government in one of the counties, and an army was to be sent against him to capture him. This ruler was responsible to those yet higher than he, and if he did not manage this affair he would be blamed.

When this rumor came filtering through from wayside inn and tea house, and be sure there were those who ran with

pleasure to tell it to the two brothers, then Wang the Landlord and Wang the Merchant gave up their plan speedily,
and each stayed close in his house for a time, and each was
glad he had not boasted too soon that he had a brother in a
high place, and it was a comfort to them to think of the
paper, signed and stamped at court. If anyone spoke of their
third brother before them Wang the Landlord said loudly,

"He has been wild and runaway all his days!"

And Wang the Merchant drew his meager lips together
and said,

"Let him do what he likes, for it does not concern us and
he is scarcely our brother."

Wang the Tiger was in the midst of his wedding feast
when this rumor reached him also, and in the midst of three
days of mighty feasting throughout the courts. He had ordered
the killing of cows and pigs and fowls, and he ordered everything to be paid for as it was taken to be killed. Although
he was so strong in this region now that he could have taken
what he liked without price and none would have dared to
withstand him, yet because he was a just man he paid for
all.

This justice moved the common people toward him very
much so that they praised him to each other and man said
to man,

"There could be far worse than this lord of war who rules
over us. He is strong enough to keep robbers away and he
does not rob us himself, beyond the taxes, and I do not see
that we could ask for more than this under heaven."

But still at this time they did not come out too openly for
him yet, because they had heard the rumor also, and they
waited to see if he could be victorious or not, for if he lost
they would be blamed if they had showed loyalty to him.

But if he gained then they could take courage to come out for him.

Still they had let Wang the Tiger take what he needed for the feast, although it taxed the people much to feed so many at a time, and he would have the best for once, and he had better than the best even for himself and his bride and his trusty men and the women who cared for the bride. These women were some half score of those about the courts, the wife of the gaoler and of such harmless persons who do not care who is over them and they came creeping back to their places the next day after the overthrow, ready to swear loyalty to anyone who fed them. And Wang the Tiger would have these women properly about his bride, for he was very careful toward her and did not go near her for the days before he married her; no, although he could not sleep at times in the night for thinking of her and wondering who she was and burning for her. But stronger than this was the feeling he had for her to make her the mother of his son, and it seemed to him it was his duty to his son to be careful in all he did.

Different indeed was she from Pear Blossom, and because of that early image of a woman set into his memory he had always thought, if he thought, that he would like mild, pale women best. But now he did not care, and he said to himself wildly that he did not care who she was nor what, so that he had her and had her sealed to him forever through their son.

During those days no one came near him for anything, for his trusty men saw that he was wholly given over to his desire. But they consulted together secretly, for they had heard the rumor and they put their strength to hastening the wedding, so that it could be over and their leader slaked and ready to be himself and lead them on when the need came.

More quickly, then, than Wang the Tiger even could hope,

the feasts were prepared and the wife of the gaol keeper stood for the woman and the courts were thrown open to all such as cared to come and see and feast. But few men of the city came and fewer women, because they were afraid. Only the homeless ones and such as live nowhere and have nothing to lose came in as any may come in to a marriage and ate heartily and stared their fill at the strange bride. But when they went in to fetch the old magistrate and bring him to a seat of honor on such a day, as Wang the Tiger had commanded should be done, he sent out word that he grieved he could not come for he had a flux and could not rise from his bed.

As for Wang the Tiger, throughout that day of his wedding he moved in a dream and he scarcely knew what he did except that the hours of the day moved so slowly that he did not know what to do with himself. It seemed to him that every breath he drew lasted an hour and that the sun would never crawl up the sky to noon, and when it had, that it would stay forever. He could not be merry as men are at their weddings, for he had never been merry, and now he sat as silent as ever, and there was not one to joke at his expense. He thirsted exceedingly all that day, and he drank much wine, but he could eat nothing, for he was as full as though he had eaten a mighty meal.

But into the courts of feasting men and women and the crowds of poor and ragged and the dogs from the streets came in by scores to feast and to eat and to pick the bones that were left, and in his own room Wang the Tiger sat silent and half smiling as in a dream and so the day wore on at last to night.

Then when the women had prepared the bride for the bed he went into her room and she was there. It was the first woman he had ever known. Yes, this was a curious, unheard-

247

of thing, that a man could come to be more than thirty years old and be a soldier and a runaway from his father's house since he was eighteen, and never had he gone near a woman, so sealed his heart had been.

But that fountain was flowing free, now, and naught could ever seal it again, and seeing this woman sitting there on the bed, he drew his breath in sharply, and she hearing it, lifted her eyes and looked at him fully.

So he went to her and he found her silent but passionate and frank upon her marriage bed, and he loved her mightily from that hour, and since he had known no other, she seemed to him faultless.

Once in the middle of the night he turned to her and he said in a husky whisper,

"I do not even know who you are."

And she answered calmly, "What does it matter except that I am here? But some time I will tell you."

And he let it pass, content for the time, for they were neither of them usual folk, and both their lives were not such as are commonly lived.

But the trusty men did not let Wang the Tiger have more than the night, and the next morning at dawn they waited for him, and they saw him come out of his door, calm and refreshed from his marriage chamber. Then the harelipped man said, bowing,

"Sir, and honored, we did not tell you yesterday since it was a day of joy, but we have heard rumors from the north and the provincial ruler has heard that you have seized the government and comes down against you."

And the Hawk said in his turn, "I heard it from a beggar who came from that way and he said he passed ten thousand men upon the way marching down upon us."

And the Pig Butcher added his tale, stammering through his thick lips in his haste to speak as he had been told,

"I—I also heard it—when I went out to the market to see how they stick their pigs in this city and a butcher told me."

But Wang the Tiger was all softened and at ease and for the first time he could not bring himself to think of war and he smiled in his slight way and said,

"I can trust my men, and let them come." And he sat down to drink a little tea before he ate and he sat at a table beside a window and it was broad day and a thought came to him suddenly, and it was this, that there is a night at the end of every day, and he seemed to know it for the first time, now, so meaningless had all other nights of his life been except this one night.

But there was one who heard what his trusty men said, and she stood by the curtain and looked through a crack of it, and she saw they were dismayed to see their leader sunk in some pleasing thought of his own. When Wang the Tiger rose and went out of the room to go to the one where food was eaten, she called clearly to the harelipped man and she said,

"Tell me all you have heard."

He was very loath to talk to a woman of what was none of her affair, and he muttered and made as if he had nothing to tell until she said imperiously,

"Do not play the fool with me, who have seen blood and fighting and battle and retreat these five years since I was grown! Tell me!"

Then wondering and abashed before her bold eyes fixed on his and not dropped as the eyes of women usually are, especially when they are newly wed and should be full of shame, he told her as though she had been a man what they all feared and how they were in danger because more men

249

marched against them than they had, and many of their men were untried in their loyalty if a battle came. She sent him away quickly then saying he must beg Wang the Tiger to come to her.

He came as he had never come to any summons, smiling more softly than anyone had ever seen him smile. She sat down upon the bed and he sat down beside her and took up the end of her sleeve and fingered it and he was more abashed in her presence than she was in his and he kept his eyes down, smiling.

But she began to speak swiftly in her clear, somewhat piercing voice,

"I am not a woman such as will stand in your way if there is a battle to be fought and they tell me an army marches against you."

"Who told you?" he answered. "I will not trouble myself for three days. I have given myself three days."

"But if they come nearer in three days?"

"An army cannot come two hundred miles in three days."

"How can you know what day they started?"

"The tale could not have reached the provincial seat in so short a time."

"It could have!" she said swiftly.

Now here was a strange thing. These two, a man and a woman, could sit and talk of something far from love and yet Wang the Tiger was as knit to her as he had been in the night. He was amazed that a woman could talk like this for he had never talked with one before and he had always thought them pretty children in tall bodies, and one reason why he feared them was because he did not know what they knew nor what to say to them. He was so made that even with a woman paid for he could not rush to her as a common soldier does, and half his diffidence with women was because

250

he feared the speech he must make with them. But here he sat and talked with this woman as easily as though she were a man and he listened to her when she said on,

"You have fewer men than the provincial army has, and when a warrior finds his army smaller than his enemy's then he must use guile."

At this he made his silent laugh and said in his gruff way, "Well I know that, or I would not have had you for mine now."

She dropped her eyes quickly at this as though to veil something that might show itself in them and she bit the edge of her lower lip and she answered,

"The simplest guile is to kill a man, but one must catch him first. The same simple guile will not do now."

Then Wang the Tiger answered with pride, "I will pit my men against thrice their number of state soldiers. I have trained them and taught them this whole winter and hardened them with boxing and running and fencing and with all feints of war and none of them is afraid to die. Moreover, it is known what state soldiers are, and they will always turn to the strongest side, and doubtless the soldiers of this province are not better paid than any others like them."

Then she said with some impatience, and she drew her sleeve out of his fingers as she spoke,

"Still you have no plan! Hear me—I have a plan made while we talked. There is the old magistrate you have guarded in his court. Use him as a hostage of a kind."

Now she spoke so earnestly and soberly that Wang the Tiger listened to her, yet was amazed that he did, for he was not a man who often took counsel with others, thinking himself sufficient for anything. But he listened and she said,

"Take your soldiers out and take him also and force him and tell him what he is to say, that he shall say what you command. Let him go out to meet the provincial general with a trusty man on either side of him who will hear what he says, and if he does not say what you have told him, let them have their swords ready and plunge them into his bowels, and that shall be a sign for battle. But he has a gall no larger than a hen's. He will say what he is told, and let him say that nothing has been done without his consent, that the rumor of a rebellion is only because his own old general rebelled and if it had not been for you who delivered him the seals of state would have been stolen and his own life gone."

Now this seemed excellent good guile to Wang the Tiger, and he listened with his eyes fastened on her face as she spoke. He saw the whole plan there before him and he rose and laughed noiselessly to think what she was and he went out to do what she had said, and she came close behind him. He commanded a trusty man to go and fetch the old magistrate out and bring him to the hall of audience. Then the woman had a fancy and it was that they would go and sit in the audience room, he and she together, and let the old magistrate come before them, and Wang the Tiger was willing because they must frighten the old man thoroughly. So they sat themselves down on the dais, Wang the Tiger in a carven chair, and the woman beside him in another chair.

Soon the old magistrate came tottering in between two soldiers, and he came out trembling and his robe thrown about him anyhow. He looked half dazed about the hall, and he saw not one face he knew. No, even those servants of his who had returned looked away when he came in and found this excuse and that to go away on some other business. There were only the faces of soldiers about the walls of the hall, and every man had his gun and every man was loyal to Wang the Tiger. Then he looked up, his old lips trembling and blue, his mouth open, and he peered up and there sat

Wang the Tiger with his two brows drawn down, fierce and murderous to see, and beside him a strange woman whom the old magistrate had never seen or heard of and he could not think where such an one as she had come from. He stood trembling and timid and ready to die because such an end to his life had come to him as this, who was a man of peace and had been a Confucian scholar in his day.

Then Wang the Tiger shouted in his rough and bitter way, with little courtesy,

"You are in my hand now and you must follow my commands if you would live on here! We march against the army of the province tomorrow, and you are to go with us, and when we meet the army you are to go first with my two trusty men and meet the general who comes against me. Tell him that you have chosen me your lord of war and that I saved you from a rebellion in your own courts and I stay here by your choice. My two trusty men will be there to hear all you say; if one word goes wrong it is your end and your last word. But if you speak well and as I tell you, you may return here and you may take your old place again upon this dais, and I will save your face for you and it need not be known whose is the power here in these courts, for I have no mind to be a petty magistrate, nor will I have another here in your place, so long as you do what I command."

What then could the weak old man do but give his promise and he said, groaning,

"I am caught on the end of your spear. Let it be as you say. I am an old man and I have no son, and what does my life matter to me?"

And he turned and went away shuffling and groaning as he went to his court where his old wife was, who never came out at all. It was true he had no sons, for the two children she had given him died before they could speak.

Now whether the thing could have been done as Wang the Tiger planned or not none knows, but again his destiny helped him. It was now full spring and over the land the willows budded again and the peach trees burst into swift bloom, and while farmers stripped off their winter coats and worked bare backed in the fields again, rejoicing in the mild winds and the warm gentle sun upon their clogged flesh, the lords of war awoke also, and the restlessness of spring filled the countryside. And the lords of war awoke quarrelsome and full of lust of war against each other and old troubles were burnished and made new and old differences sharpened, and every man grew ambitious to achieve some new place for himself while the fresh spring lasted.

Now the chief seat of government of the nation at this time was in the hands of a weak, unready man, and there were many lords of war who cast longing eyes at that seat and thought how easy it would be to seize it. Many counted over such as stood in the way and some banded together and consulted as to how they could take the power of the nation and unseat this unstable and ignorant man whom others had put there, and how they could place their own choice there to serve their own purpose.

Among these lords of war Wang the Tiger was still one of the very least and he was scarcely known among the great ones except as when men of battle gossip among themselves at some meeting or feast, and one might say,

"Did you hear of the captain who split himself off from his old general and has set himself up in such and such a province? He is a good brave, it is said, and he is called the Tiger because of his angers and fierceness and his two black brows."

Thus the chief lord of war in the province where Wang the Tiger now was had heard of him and he had heard how

254

Wang the Tiger had routed the Leopard and had approved the deed. Now this chief lord was one of the great lords of war of the nation and he was one of those who had it in his mind to unseat the weak ruler if he could, and if he could not put himself on the seat at least to put his man there, so that the revenues of the nation would come to his own hands.

During this spring, therefore, when restlessness rose everywhere, strange flowers of ambitions blossomed. There were proclamations pasted on city gates and on walls and all such places where people pass, and these proclamations were sent out by the lord of war of that province. He said that since the ruler was so evil and the people greatly oppressed, he could not endure such crimes as these before heaven. Although he was weak and witless, yet must he come forth to save the people. Having so written, he prepared for war.

As for the people, since few of them could either read or write, they did not know this their savior, but they groaned aloud because fresh taxes were put upon their lands and upon their harvests and upon their carts and in the towns upon shops and goods. If they groaned aloud or complained, there were those minions of the lord of war who heard them and cried out,

"How ungrateful a people are you, who will not pay even for your own salvation! And who else should pay for the soldiers who are to fight for you and make you safe?"

So the people paid what they must, however unwillingly, fearing if they did not either the wrath of the lord they had or of a new lord who might come in and conquer them and devour them afresh, being rapacious with his victory.

Having determined on this war, therefore, the lord of the province was eager to marshal to him every small captain and general, so when he heard of the rebellion Wang the Tiger had made, he said to the civil ruler of the province,

255

"Do not bear too heavily down upon that little new general whose name is Wang the Tiger, because I hear he is a good angry fierce fellow and I want such as he is under my ensign. This whole nation will divide itself, perhaps this spring, and if not this year then next or next, and the lords of the north will declare against the lords of the south. Let this man be treated gently then."

Now although it is said that lords of war should be subservient in a nation to the civil governors of the people, it is a thing known and proved that the power goes always to the armed man and the man with weapons, and how can a weaponless man, even though he has the right, oppose a man of war in the same region with him, who has soldiers to his command?

Thus it was that destiny helped Wang the Tiger in that spring. For when the armies of state came marching against him, Wang the Tiger led his men out and he sent the old magistrate ahead in his sedan and he ambushed many good strong men near in case of treachery. When they came to a meeting place the old magistrate came out of his sedan and stumbling through the dust of the country road, he went, dressed in his magistrate's robes, and leaning upon the two trusty men. The general who had been sent from the state came to meet him, and after the rites of courtesy had been observed, the old man said in his faltering way,

"You have it wrongly, my lord. This Wang the Tiger is no robber but my own captain and my new young general who protects my court and he saved me from a rebellion in my own retinue."

Now although the general did not believe this, having heard the truth from his spies, and although no one believed it, still he had his orders that Wang the Tiger was not to be offended and that he was not to lose a man in a brawl so little as this when every gun was needed for the greater war. When he heard what the old magistrate said, therefore, he only rebuked him slightly saying,

"You should have sent word of this before because we have been at an expense to bring men to punish what I thought was a rebel. There shall be a fine imposed on you to pay for the expense of an idle errand and it is ten thousand pieces of silver."

When Wang the Tiger heard that this was all he exulted very much and he led his men back in triumph again. And he imposed in his turn a tax beyond what was usual upon all the salt in that place and in less than twice thirty days he had the ten thousand pieces and some over, for that place had much salt and it was even sent out to other places and some said to other countries, too.

When this was over Wang the Tiger was more strong than ever in his power and he had not lost a man, either. It seemed to him that for this honor was due to his woman and he honored her for her wisdom.

Yet he still did not know who or what she was. Passion was still his chief pastime with her, but he wondered sometimes what her story was. Yet if he asked her she always put him off, saying,

"It is a long tale, and I will tell you some day in a winter when there can be no war. But now it is spring and time for battle and for enlarging yourself, and not for idle talk."

And she put him off restlessly, her eyes bright and hard.

Then Wang the Tiger knew the woman was right, for over all the country the news came winged that there was to be such a war that spring among the lords of war as had not been in ten years of wars, and the people were dismayed, not knowing from what point the war would strike them, hearing of it coming here or coming there. Yet there was the

257

land to till and they tilled it, and in the cities the merchants had their shops and men must live and children be fed. So the people went on about their lives, and if they groaned at a coming terror, they did their work while they waited to see what would happen to them.

In his region all the eyes of the people were turned to Wang the Tiger, for his rule over them was now open and established and they knew the taxes went through his hands. Although the old magistrate was still there for a show of state, he was an old image and everything was decided by Wang the Tiger. Yes, Wang the Tiger even sat at the magistrate's right hand in the audience hall, and the old magistrate looked to him when the judgment moment came, and the money that used to be paid to the councillors now went into Wang the Tiger's hand and to his trusty men. But Wang the Tiger was still himself, for if he took from the rich, if a poor man came and he knew it, he would let him speak for himself freely. There were many poor who praised him. But all the people turned to Wang the Tiger in this spring to see what he would do, for they knew if he joined in the great war they must pay the soldiers he would need and buy his guns.

As for Wang the Tiger, he had considered the matter well, alone and with his woman and also with his trusty men, but he was still puzzled as to what was best for him. The lord of war of the province had sent out commands to every little separate general and captain and small lord of war and said,

"Follow under my ensign with your men, for now is the hour when we can all rise up a step or two in the tide of war."

But Wang the Tiger did not know whether to come at his call or not, because he could not see which side would win. If he cast in his name with the losing side he would set himself back and perhaps ruin himself, seeing he was so newly risen up. So he took thought for himself and he thought and he sent out his spies to see and to hear and to find out what was the stronger and the winning side, and he said while they were out he would delay and declare himself for no one, and he would wait until the war was fought nearly to an end and the victory plain and then he would make haste to declare himself, and so on the last swelling wave he might ride with others to its crest, and not lose a man or gun, either. He sent out his spies, then, and waited.

In the night he talked about it with his woman, for their love and his ambition were linked in the strangest way, and when he had slaked his thirst and lay at his ease he talked with her as he had never done to anyone in his life. He poured out to her every plan he had and he ended every dream with this saying,

"Thus will I do, and when you give me a son, he will be the meaning for it all."

But she never answered this hope of his and when he pressed on it, she grew restless and spoke of some everyday thing and again and again she said,

"Have you your plans ready and made for the last battle?" and she said often, "Guile is the best warfare, and the best battle is the one at the end when victory is sure and swift."

And Wang the Tiger never noticed any coldness in her at all, he was so hot himself.

All through that spring he waited therefore, although waiting chafed him in usual times, and he could never have borne it now if he had not had this woman new to him and there at his hand. Summer came on and the wheat was cut and all through the valleys the sound of the flails beat all day into the still, hot sunshine. In the fields where the wheat had stood the sorghum cane grew tall and rank and put forth its tassels and while Wang the Tiger waited, wars sprang up

259

everywhere, and this general and that in the south banded together for the moment like generals of the north, and still Wang the Tiger waited. And he hoped greatly that the generals of the south would not win, for it went against some gorge in him to link himself ever again with those little dark and stunted men. It went against him so much that he brooded sometimes, and said to himself sullenly that if the south won he would go and hide in his mountains for a while and wait for a new turn of war.

But he did not wait in complete idleness. He trained his men with fresh zeal and he enlarged his army once more, and enrolled in it many good young fellows who came to him and over the new ones he set the old and other soldiers, and his army swelled to ten thousand men, and to pay for this he added somewhat to his taxes on wine and on salt and on travelling merchants.

His only trouble at this time was that he had not enough guns, and he saw he must do one of two things; either he must get guns by guile, or he must conquer some little near captain and take his guns and ammunition. Now this was because guns were very hard to find, being foreign things and brought in from foreign parts, and Wang the Tiger had not thought of this when he had chosen his region an inland region, and he had no coastal port he controlled, and other ports were guarded so that he could not hope to smuggle guns through them. Moreover, he knew no foreign tongue, nor had he any near him who did, and so he had no way yet to deal with the foreign merchants, and so it seemed to him that after all he must have a little battle somewhere, for many of his men were without guns.

One night he told this to his woman, and she took a sudden interest and put her mind to it, for often she could be listless and paid no heed to him at all. Now when she put her mind to it she said very soon,

"But I thought you said you had a brother who is a merchant!"

"I do have such a one," said Wang the Tiger, wondering, "but he is a grain merchant and not a merchant for guns."

"Yes, but you see nothing!" she cried at him, in the impatient, high way she had. "If he is a merchant and deals with sea coasts, he can buy guns and smuggle them in his goods somehow. I do not know how, but there must be a way."

Now Wang the Tiger thought this over awhile and again it seemed to him this was the cleverest woman, and he made a plan on what she had said. The next day he called his pocked nephew to him, grown tall in this past year, and he kept the youth by him continually for small special things he needed to have done, and he said,

"Go to your father and pretend you are home for a visit and nothing more but when you are alone with him tell him I need three thousand guns and I am hampered sorely because I have not them. Men grow everywhere, but not guns for them, and they are useless to me without each man his gun. Tell him he is a merchant and one who deals with the sea coast and he can think of a way for me. I send you, because the thing must be kept secret, and you are my own blood."

The youth was glad enough to go, and he promised secrecy eagerly, and he was proud with his mission. And again Wang the Tiger waited, but he still received men under his ensign, only he chose his men carefully and tested each as to whether or not he feared to die.

XVIII

THE lad went winding his way homeward, then, over the countryside. He had taken off his soldier's garb and had put on the clothing of a farmer's son and with these coarse blue garments and his face brown and pocked he looked nothing but a country lad, and fit grandson for Wang Lung. He rode upon his old white ass, with a ragged coat folded under him for a saddle, and he kicked the ass under the belly with his bare feet to hasten it sometimes. No one who saw him riding thus and often half asleep under the hot sun of summer would have dreamed that he carried a message that was to bring three thousand guns into that peaceful country. But when he did not sleep he sang his song of soldiers and war, for he loved to sing, and when he did this a farmer would look up at him uneasily from his work in the fields and stare after the youth, and once a farmer shouted after him,

"A curse on you to be singing a soldier's ditty—do you want to bring the black crows around us again?"

But the youth was gay and careless and he spat here and there in the dust of the road to show how careless he was, and to show he would go on singing if he wished to sing. The truth was he did not know any other songs than these, having been so long among reckless and fighting men, and it cannot be expected that soldiers will sing the same songs that farmers sing in their quiet fields.

On the third day at noon he came to his home and as he slid off his ass at the place where the side street parted from the main street, there was his eldest cousin lounging along and he stared and stopped in a yawn he was making and said, in greeting,

"Well, and are you a general yet?"

Then the pocked lad called back quickly and wittily,

"No, but I have taken at least the first degree!"

This he said to mock his cousin a little because everyone knew how Wang the Landlord and his lady had always talked a great deal of how they would make a scholar of this son and how next season he was to go up for examination at such and such a seat of learning and so become a great man. But the season went and the year passed into another, and he never went. Now the pocked youth knew this cousin of his was on his way not to any school but to some tea house, being just up, doubtless, from his bed, and languid after the night he had had somewhere. But the son of Wang the Landlord was dainty and scornful and he surveyed his cousin and said,

"At least being a first degree general has not put a silk coat on your back!"

And he walked on without waiting to hear any answer, swaying himself as he walked so that his own silk robes, the color of the green of a willow tree newly leaved, swayed also with his lordly steps. But the pocked youth grinned and stuck his tongue out toward his cousin's back, and went to his own door.

When he stepped into the court of his own home all was as it ever was. It was time for the noon meal, and the door was open into the house and he saw his father sitting down alone to the table to eat and the children ran anywhere and ate as they always did, and his mother stood at the door with her bowl to her lips and her chopsticks pushing the food into her mouth and as she chewed she chattered to a neighbor woman, who had come in to borrow something, about a salt fish that a cat had stolen the night before, although it was hung high on a beam, too. When she saw the son she shouted at him,

"Well, you are back in time to eat, and you could not have struck it better!" and she went on with her chatter.

The youth grinned at her but he said nothing except to call her name out, and he went inside and his father nodded to him, a little surprised, and the son called his name dutifully and then went and found himself a bowl and a pair of chopsticks and filled his bowl from the food on the table and then went to one side and sat down edgewise on his seat as sons should do if they sit in the presence of those above them.

When they had eaten, the father poured a little tea into his rice bowl, but sparingly, for he was sparing in all he did, and he drank it down in small, meager sips, and then he said to his son,

"Do you bring any word?"

And the son said, "Yes, I do, but I cannot tell you here." This he said because his brothers and sisters crowded around him and stared at him silently, since he was strange to them, and they listened eagerly for any word he might say.

By now the mother was back also to fill her bowl again, for she was a very hearty one to eat and ate a long time after her husband was finished and gone, and she stared too at her son and said,

"You have grown a good ten inches, I swear! And why have you a ragged coat like that on? Does your uncle give you no better? What do they feed you to make you grow like that—good meat and wine, I swear!"

And the lad grinned again and said, "I have good clothes but I did not wear them this time, and we eat meat every day."

At this Wang the Merchant was aghast and he cried with unwonted interest,

"What—does my brother give his soldiers meat every day?"

The lad hastened to say, "No, but now only because he

prepares them for a war and he wants them fierce and full of blood. But I have meat because I do not live with the common soldiers and I may eat what my uncle and his woman leave in their bowls—I and the trusty men."

At this his mother said avidly, "Tell me about that woman of his! It was a strange thing he did not ask us to the wedding."

"He did," said Wang the Merchant hastily, seeing no end to this talk if it began. "Yes, he did ask us, but I said we would not go. It would have cost a pile of silver and you would have wanted new clothes and this and that for a show if you had gone."

To this the woman said with much spirit and in a loud voice,

"Well, and you old miser, I never go anywhere and—"

But Wang the Merchant cleared his throat and said to his son,

"Come with me for there is no peace here," and he rose and brushed his children aside, but not ungently, and he went out and his son followed him.

Wang the Merchant walked ahead of his son down the street to a small tea house where he did not often go, and he chose a table in a quiet corner. But the house was almost empty, for it was an hour when there were not many guests, for farmers had sold their loads and gone home, and city guests had not come in for the afternoon's talk. There in peace then did Wang the Merchant's son tell him his mission.

Wang the Merchant listened very closely to it all and he said not a word until his son had said his say, and when it was over he did not let his face change. No, where Wang the Landlord would have been astonished and rolled his eyes and sworn it was a thing impossible to do, Wang the Merchant had by now grown so secretly rich that nothing was

265

impossible to him and if he ever hesitated, it was to see if the thing would benefit him or not when done. He had his money in all sorts of places and men borrowed of him for everything they could. He had even his money in Buddhist temples, loaned to priests on security of temple lands, for in these days the people were not devout as they had been, and only women and usually old women, too, were the ones to heed the gods, and many temples grew poor and left off their flourishing estate. And Wang the Merchant had his money in ships upon the rivers and upon the seas, and he had money in a railway, and he had a very good sum in a brothel in the city, although he was never a guest at his own brothel, and his elder brother never dreamed that when he went to play at that great new house opened but a year or so ago, that it was his own brother's house. But it was a business that brought good return, and Wang the Merchant reckoned on the common nature of men.

Thus his money flowed out in a hundred secret channels, and if he had recalled it suddenly, thousands would have suffered. Yet he ate no more than he ever did and no better, and he did not game as any man will who has more than he can eat and wear, nor did he let his sons wear silk coats, and seeing him and how he lived, none would have dreamed how rich he was. Therefore he could think of three thousand foreign guns and not be astounded as Wang the Landlord would have been. Yes, looking at those two brothers, if one had met them together in the street, one would have said that Wang the Landlord was the very rich one, for he spent his money so easily and he was so monstrous fat and rolling in his silk and satin robes and his furs and his sons all silk clad too, except the little hunchback who lived with Pear Blossom and grew to quiet manhood there beside her, forgotten day after day.

266

So Wang the Merchant pondered for a time in silence, and he said at last,

"Did my brother say what security I am to have for so much money as this to buy these guns? I ought to have good security, seeing that it is against the law to buy them."

And the youth said, "He said, 'Tell my brother he must take all the land I have left for security if he cannot trust my word until I can collect revenue to pay for them. I have my hand over all revenues in this region, but I cannot give out a vast sum at once and not make my men suffer.'"

"I do not want more land," said Wang the Merchant, reflecting, "and this has been a hard year here, near to famine, and land is cheap. All he has left will not be enough. His wedding fee ate deep into the lands."

Then the youth said earnestly, and his little bright black eyes shone in his face he was so earnest,

"Father, it is true my uncle is a very great man. You should see how everyone fears him! But he is a good man too, for he does not kill only to kill. Even the ruler of the province fears him. He is not afraid of anything—no, who but he would have dared to marry a woman whom everybody calls a fox! And if you give him these guns it will mean more power to him than ever."

Now the words of his own son cannot move a father too much, but still there was some truth in this and the thing that decided Wang the Merchant was that it would pay him well to have a brother who was a powerful lord of war. Yes, if the time of a great war came on such as was rumored in these years and if the war moved here—and who can tell how a war will move?—his great possessions might be seized and despoiled, if not by enemy soldiers, then perhaps by the lawless poor. For Wang the Merchant now had his wealth no more in lands, and the lands he had were as nothing be-

267

side his houses and shops and money-lending business, and such wealth may be taken away so quickly in a time when men are free to despoil, that in a few days a rich man may be made poor if he has no secret power from somewhere to help him and protect him, in a sudden need such as may come at any time.

So he thought to himself that these guns might be a protection for him, too, one day, and he thought a while longer of how he could purchase them and how smuggle them in. This he could do, for he now owned two small ships of his own to carry rice to an outer country near by. It was against the law to send rice out in this way, and he had to do it secretly, but he made a great profit on it and it paid him to give bribes, for the rulers were lax, and if they were paid, they overlooked his two little ships which he kept small on purpose, and vented their anger and zeal for law upon foreign ships or again upon some others that did not bring them any good.

And Wang the Merchant thought of his two ships coming back empty sometimes from that other country or else only half loaded with cotton stuffs and foreign knick-knacks, and he thought he could manage easily enough to smuggle foreign guns among those wares, and if he were caught he would put money out here and there and he would give his two captains something to close their mouths and make silence worth while for all. Yes, he could do this. Then he said to his son, looking about first to see that none was near, no guest or officious servant, and he spoke through his teeth without moving his lips and very softly,

"I can get the guns to the coast and even to a certain point where the railway runs nearest my brother, but how can I get them to him over a day and more of dry land and no way of travel except by foot or beast's back?"

Now Wang the Tiger had not said anything of this to the youth, so he could only scratch his head foolishly and stare at his father and he said,

"I must go back and ask him that."

And Wang the Merchant said, "Tell him I will manage to put the guns into goods of another sort and marked with other names and put them at a point, and then he must get them somehow from there."

So with this the lad went back to his uncle, and he went the very next day. But that night he slept in his own home and his mother cooked him a dish he loved of little steamed loaves of bread with garlic and pork inside, a very dainty dish. He ate himself full of these and what were left he thrust into his bosom to eat on the way. Then seated upon his ass he wound his way back again to Wang the Tiger.

XIX

THERE happened during the next month a thing such as Wang the Tiger in his arrogance would not have believed true if he had been told. The fever of war spread over that whole region when it was known that great lords above waged a war and split the country into two parts. In that fever little war-like spirits arose everywhere, and men who were idle and without work or those who would not work and lovers of any adventure and sons who did not love their parents and gamesters who lost in their gambling and every little discontented man seized on this time to come out and make a showing of some sort.

In this very region where Wang the Tiger now ruled in the name of the old magistrate, these rebellious men joined themselves into bands and they gave themselves the name of

The Yellow Turbans, because they wore strips of yellow about their heads, and they began to prey upon the country. At first they did it in small timid ways, exacting from some farmer food as they passed or they went into a village inn and ate and went on without paying or only partly paying for their meal, showing such fierce looks and raising their voices so high and quarrelsome that the innkeeper was afraid to make an ado and so swallowed his loss as best he could.

But these Yellow Turbans grew bolder as their numbers swelled, and they began to long for guns, for their only guns were the few that runaway soldiers among them had. They grew more bold, therefore, in their marauding among the common people, although they still did not come near any large towns or cities, but kept themselves to small villages and hamlets. At last some of the more courageous among the farmers came to Wang the Tiger and told him and they made report of how the marauders grew bold because they were unchecked and they would come in the night to rob and if they did not find all they liked they would kill a household of farming folk and think nothing of the deed. But Wang the Tiger did not know whether to believe the tale or not, for when he sent spies out to ask other farmers, there were weak ones who were afraid to tell and they denied the whole matter, and so Wang the Tiger for a time did nothing, thinking lightly of it when his whole mind was set on the right moment to declare himself in the great war.

But the time of the great heat of summer came on and many armies marched through to the south and there were some of these soldiers who were lured away to the robber band and the robbers grew greatly in numbers and daring. At this season of the year also the sorghum cane grew very high in those parts and it made a very perfect hiding place for robbers and they grew so bold and it came to such a pass that people did not dare to travel off the highway except in a large number together.

Now whether Wang the Tiger would have believed how bad it was or not cannot be said, for he was somewhat at the mercy of his men and he must believe what his spies and his own trusty men thought and they overpraised him and made him think none would dare to stand before him. But one day there came in from the country to the west two brothers, two farmers, and they carried a hempen bag with them. They would not open this bag for anyone to see, and they said steadfastly to all questions asked them,

"This bag is for the general."

And supposing they brought a gift to Wang the Tiger, the guards let them through the gates and they went to the hall of audience and there Wang the Tiger sat, for it was the hour when he often did so. When the two brothers came before him they made their obeisances, and then without a further word they opened the hempen bag and took from it two pairs of hands, one the hands of a very old woman, worn and hard with work and the dark skin cracked and dry, and the other the hands of an old man calloused in the palms with the holding of the handle of a plow. These hands the two brothers held up by the stumps where the blood now was black and dried. Then the elder of the brothers, a very earnest, angry man of middle age, his face square and honest, said,

"These are the hands of our old parents and they lie dead! Two days ago the robbers marauded in our hamlet and when my old father cried out that he had nothing they cut off his two hands, and when my old mother bravely cursed them they cut off hers also. We two brothers were in the fields but our wives escaped and came screaming to us and we ran back with our forks. But the robbers were gone, for there had been no great band of them, only eight or ten, and our parents were old. Yet not one in the village dared to lift his hand to help them lest they suffer at some later time. Sir, we let you have the revenues and we pay you a heavy tax over and above what we must pay the state, and we pay on land and on salt and on all we buy and sell and we do it to be protected from robbers. What will you do?"

And they held up the worn, stiff old hands of their parents.

Now Wang the Tiger did not, as many a man in his place would have done, grow angry at such bold speech. No, he was astounded at the tale, and he grew angry, not because the farmers had dared to tell him, but that such a thing could be in his regions. He shouted out for his captains and they came in, one by one as they were found here and there, until there were some fifty of them in the hall.

Then Wang the Tiger himself picked up the dead hands from where they lay helplessly upon the tiled floor and he showed them to all and he said,

"These are the hands of good farming folk who were marauded and robbed in the daytime when their sons worked in the fields! Who goes first against these marauders?"

The captains stared and the sight roused them and they were roused to think that robbers dared to rob in lands belonging to them and they muttered together and said here and there,

"Shall we let this go on in a land where we have the first right?"—"Shall these accursed thieves grow great in our own lands?" and they cried out, "Let us go against them!"

Wang the Tiger turned then to the two brothers and he said, "Return to your homes in peace and confidence. Tomorrow these will go out and I shall not rest until I find out who the head of these robbers is and deal with him as I dealt with the Leopard!"

Then the younger brother spoke, and he said, "Most Gracious, we think there is no head yet and they wander in little bands separate from one another except as their name links them, and they look for one strong man to hold them together."

"If this is so," said Wang the Tiger, "it will be the easier to scatter them."

"But not to stamp them out," said the older brother bluntly.

Then the two farmer brothers waited on there as though they had more to say and did not know how to say it, and at last after being impatient for a while in himself because they did not go, Wang the Tiger perceived they mistrusted him and he grew somewhat angry and said,

"Do you doubt that I am strong enough who killed the Leopard, a mighty robber in his day and he lived on you more than twenty years?"

The two brothers looked at each other and the elder one swallowed his spittle and said slowly,

"Most Gracious, it is not that. But we have something to say to you in private."

Wang the Tiger turned to the captains who still stood about and he shouted to them to be gone and prepare their men. When they were all gone except the one or two whom Wang the Tiger always kept about him, the elder brother fell on his face and he knocked his head three times upon the tiles and he said,

"Do not, Most Gracious, be very angry. We are poor men and when we ask a favor we can but ask it and we have no money to pay bribes to insure it."

And Wang the Tiger said in surprise, "What is it? I do not ask for bribes if you ask a thing I can do."

The man answered humbly, "When we came here today our village brothers tried to hold us back because they said if we brought the soldiers it would be worse than the robbers for they demand so much and we are poor men who must work if we eat. The robbers come and go, but the soldiers live on in our houses and look at our maids and eat what we keep for the winter and we dare not oppose them because they have weapons. Most Gracious, if your soldiers are to come like this, then keep them, and we will suffer what we must."

Now Wang the Tiger was a good man and he was furious when he heard this and he rose and shouted for his captains to come again, and when they came back in twos and threes he roared at them and made his face very black and he drew his brows down at them and he said,

"This region I rule over is small enough so that the men can go out and be back the third day and so they shall do! Every man of mine shall be away no more than three days and if any quarters himself upon the people I will have him killed! If they overcome the robbers and rout them I will reward them with silver and food and wine but I am no robber chief and I have no robber band!" And he glared at the captains in so fierce a way that they promised him hastily.

Thus Wang the Tiger did, and he sent the brothers away with his promise and they took the hands of their parents and put them reverently into the hempen bag again, so that the old pair might be buried whole and with all their parts, and they returned to their village full of the praises of Wang the Tiger.

But when Wang the Tiger had sent the brothers away and took time to think what he had promised, he was in some dismay to find where his kind heart had carried him, and he sat in his own room very sober, for he had no mind to lose his good men and his guns in a brawl with robbers. He knew, too, that there must be some in his army such as are in every

274

army, who are idle and looking for a better place, and these might even be enticed away to the robbers and take their guns with them. So he sat there brooding and thinking he had been too hasty and too moved by the token the brothers brought.

And as he sat there, a messenger came with a letter and it was from his brother, Wang the Merchant. Wang the Tiger tore the end and took the letter out and read it and there in devious, winding words, his brother told him that the guns were come and would be left at a certain place on a certain day, and they were hidden in bags of grain brought for making flour in the great northern mills.

Now Wang the Tiger was in as great a puzzle as he ever had been for he had to fetch the guns somehow and yet his men were scattering over the countryside against robbers. He sat awhile and cursed the day to himself, and as he sat the woman he loved came in. She was unusually gentle and languid as she walked, for it was the middle day of the great heat of summer, and she wore only a white silk coat and trousers, and she had unbuttoned the collar of her coat at the throat, so that her neck showed out, very soft and full and paler than her face.

Now Wang the Tiger for all his cursing and trouble saw her and he was caught and held at the sight of her pretty throat and he held his trouble back for an instant and he longed to lay his fingers there upon her pale neck, and he waited until she came near. She did come near and leaned upon the table and she said to him, looking at the letter he still held,

"Is there anything wrong with you that you look so black and angry?" Then she waited and laughed a little, a small high laugh, and she said, "I hope it is not I, for I would be afraid you might kill me with such black looks as you have now!"

Wang the Tiger held the letter out to her saying nothing, but his eyes fixed upon her bare throat and upon the smoothness of the turn it made into her bosom. He had come to such a pass with this woman that even in this short time he told her everything. She took the letter and read it, and he could take thought to be proud that she could read and he deemed her beautiful beyond anything as she bent over the letter, her thin, sharply marked lips moving a little as she read. Her hair was smooth now and oiled and knotted at her neck into a little net of black silk thread, and in her ears were hung gold rings.

She read the letter and then put it into its envelope again, and laid it on the edge of the table, and Wang the Tiger watched her quick light hands, thin and quick, as she did this, and then he said,

"I do not know how to get those bags of grain. I must get them by some guile or force."

"That is not hard," said the woman smoothly. "Guile and force are easy. I have a plan already in my head, made as I read the letter. You need only to send a band of your men as though they were robbers, the robbers that men tell of now-a-days, and let them seem to rob the grain for themselves, and who will know you have anything to do with it?"

Now Wang the Tiger laughed his noiseless laugh when she said this because it seemed to him so wise a plan and he drew her to him, for he was alone in the room and the guards went outside the door whenever she came, and he satisfied himself with his hard hands on her soft flesh, and he said,

"There has never been a woman so wise as you! When I killed the Leopard that day how I blessed myself in that deed!"

And after he had satisfied himself he went out and called for the Hawk and he said,

"The guns we need are at a place about thirty miles from here, where the two railroads cross, and they are in bags of grain as though to be transshipped there to the northern mills. But take five hundred men and arm yourselves and dress yourselves like some breed of robbers and go there and seize those bags and seem to carry them away to a lair. But have carts and asses ready at a near place and bring the bags here, grain and all."

Now the Hawk was a clever man and he trusted to his wits and to guile, whereas the Pig Butcher trusted to his two great fists that were as large as earthen bowls, and a wily deed like this pleased him, and so he bowed. Then Wang the Tiger said further,

"When all the guns are here, be sure I shall reward you and every soldier shall have a reward measured to what he has done."

Then when this was done Wang the Tiger went back into his room. The woman was gone, but he sat back in his arm-chair of carved wood, which had a woven reed seat for cool-ness, and he unfastened his girdle and his coat at the throat, for the day grew to a monstrous heat, and he sat and rested himself and thought of her throat and the turn it made into her bosom and he marvelled that flesh could be so soft as hers, and how skin could be so smooth.

Not once did he note that the letter his brother had written was gone, for the woman had taken it and thrust it deep into the bosom of her robe, where not even his hands had reached it.

Now when the Hawk had been gone for a half a day Wang the Tiger walked alone in the cool of the night before he went in to sleep, and he walked in the court near a side gate that was open to the street, a small street where few people passed, and those only by day. And as he walked he heard a cricket cheep. At first he paid no heed to it, because he had so much to dream of. But the cricket cheeped on, and at last he heard it and it came to him that this was not the time of the year for a cricket and so out of idle curiosity he looked to see where it was hid. It came from the gate and as he looked out into the gathering dusk he saw someone crouched and shapeless by the gate. He put his hand to his sword and stepped forward and there in the gathering dusk he saw his nephew's pocked face turned palely toward him and the lad whispered breathlessly,

"No sound, my uncle! Do not tell your lady I am here. But come into the street when you can and I will wait for you at the first forks. I have something to tell you and it must not wait."

The youth was off like a shadow then, but Wang the Tiger would not wait, since he was alone, and he went after the shadow, and came first to the spot. Then he saw his nephew come sliding along in the darkness of the walls, and he said in great astonishment,

"What ails you that you come creeping along like a beaten dog?"

And the youth whispered, "Hush—I have been sent to a place far from here—if your lady saw me here and she is such a clever one I do not know who she has watching me—she said she would kill me if I told, and it is not the first time she has threatened me!"

When Wang the Tiger heard this he was too astonished to speak. He lifted the lad half off his feet and dragged him into the darkness of an alley and he commanded him to speak. Then the lad put his mouth to Wang the Tiger's ear and he said,

"Your woman sent me with this letter to someone, but I do not know to whom, for I have not torn it open. She asked me if I could read and I said no, how could I, being country bred, and she gave me this letter, then, and told me to give it to a certain man who would meet me at the tea house in the north suburb tonight and she gave me a piece of silver for it."

He thrust his hand into his bosom and brought out a letter and Wang the Tiger seized it without a word. Without a word he strode through the alley to a small street where an old man opened a little solitary shop to sell hot water, and there, by the flickering light of the small bean oil lamp that was hung upon a nail on the wall, Wang the Tiger tore open the letter and read it. And as he read he saw plainly there was a plot. She—his woman—had told someone of his guns! Yes, he could see she had met someone and told him, and here in the letter she laid a last command. She wrote,

"When you have the guns and are gathered, I will come."

Now when Wang the Tiger read this it was as though the earth he stood upon whirled out from under his feet, and as though the heavens came down to crush him. He had loved this woman so heartily and so well that he never dreamed she could betray him. He had forgot every warning his trusty harelipped man gave him, and he never saw the man's down-cast looks these days, and he loved the woman to such a point that he longed exceedingly for but one more thing, and it was that she would give him a son. Yes, he asked her again and again and with what ardor, every time, whether she had conceived or not. He had so loved her he did not dream she could withstand him in her heart. At this very hour he had been waiting, even, to go to his love; waiting for the night.

Now he saw she had never loved him. She could plot like this at the very hour when he waited for the turn of war and

279

his own great step forward. She could plot like this and lie all night in his bed and pretend sorrow when he asked concerning his son. He was suddenly so angry he could not draw his breath. That old black anger of his rose in him blacker than he had ever known it to come. His heart beat and roared in his ears, his eyes blurred, and his brows knitted themselves until they pained him.

His nephew had followed him and stood in the shadow by the door. But Wang the Tiger flung him aside, without a word, and never seeing that in the strength of his anger he threw the lad down cruelly upon the sharp stones of the road.

He strode back to his courts on the wings of his anger and as he went he took his sword out of its sheath, the Leopard's fine steel sword, and he wiped it upon his thigh as he walked.

He went straight into the room where the woman lay in her bed, and she had not drawn the curtain because of the heat. There she lay, and the full moon of that night had risen over the wall of the court and its light fell upon her as she lay upon the bed. She lay naked for coolness and her hands were flung out and one lay curling and half open upon the edge of the bed.

But Wang the Tiger did not wait. Although he saw how fair she was and fair as an image of alabaster in the moonlight, and underneath his rage he knew there was a pain in him worse than death, he did not stay. For the moment he remembered wilfully how she had tricked him and how she would have betrayed him, and in this strength he lifted up his sword and he drove it down smoothly and cleanly into her throat, upturned as her head hung over her pillow. He twisted it sharply once, and then he brought it out and wiped it on the silken coverlid.

There came a single sound from her lips but the blood choked it so he did not know what she said and she did not move except that the instant his sword was in her throat, her arms and legs flew up and her eyes burst open. Then she died.

But Wang the Tiger would not stop to think what he had done. No, he strode out into the court and he shouted, and his men came running, and he threw his commands at them harsh and sure in his anger. He had to go now without a moment's delay to the succor of the Hawk and see if he could not reach the guns before the robbers did. All his men left he took with him except two hundred whom he left under the captaincy of his harelipped man and he led the others out himself.

As he passed through the gate he saw the old man who watched there come out of his bed yawning and dazed at all the sudden commotion and Wang the Tiger shouted at him as he rode by on his horse,

"There is something in my room where I sleep! Go and carry it out and fling it into a canal or some pond! See to it before I return!"

And Wang the Tiger rode on very high and proud and nursing his anger. But inside his breast it was as though his heart dripped blood secretly into his vitals and however he brooded and blew upon the flame of his anger, his heart dripped steadily and secretly within. And he groaned restlessly of a sudden, although none heard it in the dull thudding of horses' feet upon the dusty road. Neither did Wang the Tiger himself know that he groaned over and over again.

All over that countryside did Wang the Tiger roam with his men that night and the next day, seeking the Hawk, and the sun beat down upon them for the day came windless. But Wang the Tiger would not let his men rest because he had that within himself which could not rest and toward the evening upon the highway that ran north and south he met the

Hawk at the head of his band of walking soldiers. At first Wang the Tiger could not be sure if these were his own men for the Hawk had done what he had been told to do, and he had told his men to wear their ragged inner garments and tie a towel about their heads and Wang the Tiger had need to wait until they came near to see who they were.

But at last Wang the Tiger saw these were indeed his own men. He dismounted then from his red horse and sat down under a date tree that was there beside the road, for he was exceedingly spent from within, and he waited for the Hawk to come near. The more he waited the more afraid he grew that his anger might die down, and he forced himself to remember, with a furious pain, how he had been deceived. But the secret of his pain and anger was that although the woman was dead, yet he still loved her; although he was glad he had killed her, yet he longed for her with passion.

This angry pain made him very surly and when the Hawk was come Wang the Tiger growled at him, scarcely lifting his eyes, and his eyes nearly hidden under his brows,

"Well, I will swear you have not the guns!"

But the Hawk had a voluble good tongue of his own in that peaked face of his and he had a very ready and proud temper and this temper made him brave and he answered with heat, and without any courteous words,

"How did I know the robbers would have been told of the guns? They had been told by some spy or other and they went before us. How can I help it if they were told before you told me?" And as he spoke he threw his gun upon the ground and folded his arms on his bosom and he stared mutinously at his general, to show he would not be put down.

Then Wang the Tiger, seeing justice still, rose wearily from the grass where he sat and he stood under the date tree and leaned against its rough trunk, and he unbuckled his belt and drew it more tightly about him before he spoke. But at last he said wearily and with a great bitterness,

"I suppose all my good guns are gone, then. I shall have to fight the robbers for them. Well, if we must fight we will!" He shook himself impatiently and spat and roused himself and went on with more vigor, "Let us go and find them and press hard on them, and if half of you lie dead after the fray, why, then you are dead and I cannot help it! My guns I must have and if a gun costs me ten men or so, why, I will find ten men more for every gun and the gun is worth it!"

Then he mounted his horse again and held the beast hard when it danced to and fro with impatience that it was taken from the succulent grass that was there, and the Hawk stood there moodily watching and at last he said,

"I know well enough where the robbers are. They are gathering together in the old lair and I can swear they have the guns with them. Who their leader is I do not know, but they have been busy for a few days now, and have given the countryside peace while they gathered together, as though they were ready to choose a leader."

Now Wang the Tiger knew well who their leader was to have been but he said no more except to give his men orders to march against that lair and he said,

"We will go there and you are to fire at them. When the firing is over, I will parley and every man who brings a gun may join my ranks. For every gun you see and pick up and bring to me you shall have a piece of silver." And so saying, he mounted his horse once more.

Once more Wang the Tiger rode over the winding valley paths and over the low foothills until he came to the double-crested mountain, and his men came raggedly behind him. The farming folk looked up from their fields and wondered and the soldiers shouted,

"We go against the robbers!"

To this sometimes farmers made answer back heartily, "A good deed!" But more there were who said nothing and they looked sourly at the soldiers as they tramped into their fields of grain and cabbages and melons, because they did not believe that any good could come of soldiers, they were so weary of them.

Once more did Wang the Tiger ascend the foothills and at the base of the double-crested mountain where the pass wound up between cliffs, he dismounted and led his horse and so did all his men who rode. But he paid no heed to them. He walked along as though he were alone, his body bent to the mountain, and he thought of the woman and how strangely he had come to love her and he loved her still so that he was weeping in himself and he could scarcely see the mosses of the steps. But he would not repent that he had killed her. No, in spite of his love he understood in some dim part of him that such a woman who could deceive him so perfectly as she had when she accepted with smile and with frankness his passion, such a woman could only be true if she were dead, and he muttered to himself,

"She was a fox, after all."

So he led his men steadfastly up that mountain and when he was near to the head of the pass he sent the Hawk and fifty men ahead to see what was in the lair, and he waited in the shade of a cluster of pine trees, for the sun beat down exceedingly hot. In less than an hour the Hawk came back and he said he had circled about the place and he gave report: "They are all unready for they are building up the lair again."

"Did you see anyone above another?" said Wang the Tiger.

"No, I did not," answered the Hawk. "I crept so close I could even hear what they said. They are very ignorant and unlearned in robbery for the pass is not guarded, and there

284

they are quarreling among themselves for the houses least ruined."

This was good news, and Wang the Tiger shouted to his men and at their head he ran swiftly up the pass and as he ran he gave great shouts and he commanded his men to rush into the lair and kill at least a robber apiece, and then stop so that he could parley.

So they did, and Wang the Tiger stood to one side and his men rushed in and shot off a round and everywhere the robbers dropped dead and writhing and crying bitterness as they died or lay dying. It was true they were all unprepared and thinking only of their houses and of how they would establish themselves, and there must have been three or five thousand of them gathered in that lair, like ants in a mound, all piling earthen walls and carrying timbers and straw for roofs and planning for future greatness. When they were surprised like this every man dropped what he did and ran hither and thither and Wang the Tiger saw there was not one to tell them what to do and that they had no certain leader. For the first time some slight weak ray of solace came into Wang the Tiger's heart, for well he knew who would have marshalled them, and it came to him that sooner or later he would have had to fight against the woman he loved and better to kill her as he did.

When he thought of this his old belief in his destiny rose in him once more and he shouted to his men in his lordly way and commanded them to stand and he cried out to the robbers who were not shot,

"I am Wang the Tiger who rules this region, and I will not brook robbers! I am not afraid to kill and not afraid to die. I will kill every one of you if you think to join others against me! Yet I am a merciful man too, and I will make a way out for those of you who are honorable men. I return to my encampment now in the county seat. Within the next three days I will accept into my ranks any man of you who comes with a gun, and if he brings two guns he shall have a free gift of silver for the extra gun he has."

When he had shouted this out, Wang the Tiger called to his men sharply and they all went clattering down the pass again. Only he made certain of this, that some of his men went down backward and that they kept their guns upon the pass, lest there come a shot or two from some bolder robber. But the truth was those robbers were very ignorant men. They had fallen in with the plot of the woman who had been the Leopard's, and they went eagerly to fetch the guns, yet few of them knew how to hold a gun, and those few only runaway soldiers, and they did not dare to fire upon Wang the Tiger lest it be nothing but twisting a tiger's whiskers and he come rushing back upon them, and destroy them all.

There was complete silence in that mountain and not a sound came from the lair, and as Wang the Tiger went on his way there was only the slight rise and fall of the winds in the pines and a bird calling in a tree. And he led his men down the pass. Back through the fields he led them and as he went the soldiers said everywhere in exultation to the farming folk,

"Three days and the robbers will be gone, we swear!"

Some of the folk were glad and thankful, but most of them were guarded in their looks and words and waited to see what Wang the Tiger would want of them, for they had never heard of a lord of war who did anything for a countryside without asking much in return for all he did.

Then Wang the Tiger went back to his own courts and he gave his soldiers each a fee of silver coins and he ordered wine of a good enough quality to be given to every man, enough to comfort him but not to make him drunken. And he had a few kinds of special meats for them. Then he waited for the three days to pass.

One by one or in pairs or in fives and eights and tens the robbers began to come straggling into that city from everywhere, bringing guns with them. Seldom did any man bring two guns, for if he had laid his hand on more than one gun he brought with him a younger friend or a brother or some other one, for truly many of these men were in need and without food enough to eat and they were glad to seek sure service under a leader somewhere.

Wang the Tiger commanded that every sound man not too old he received into his army, and from such as he did not want he took the guns and paid them something. But to such men as he received he gave food and good clothing.

When the three days were over he allowed three more days of mercy and after these three more, and men came in day after day until the courts and the soldiers' camps were bursting and Wang the Tiger was forced to quarter his men into the houses of that town. Sometimes a man who was the father of a family would come to complain that his house was crowded and his family squeezed into a room or two. But if he came and Wang the Tiger saw he was young or that he was bumptious in his complaining, then Wang the Tiger threatened him and said,

"Can you help it? Bear it then! Or would you rather have robbers in the region to despoil you?"

But if the one who complained were an old man or if he came courteously and spoke gently, then Wang the Tiger was courteous, too, and he gave him some silver or a gift of some sort, and said courteously,

"It is only for a short time, for I shall march to the war soon. I shall not rest content always with so small a county seat for my capital."

And he said everywhere to all, and he said with some savage bitterness because he had no woman of his own any more and it galled him in some secret unknown way to think of any man with any woman,

"If any soldier of mine looks on a woman forbidden, tell me, and he is dead!" And he quartered the new soldiers in the houses nearest him, and he threatened them heartily if they did so much as look at a good woman.

To every soldier also Wang the Tiger paid what he promised him. Yes, although he was now hard pressed for silver, since nearly four thousand new men had joined him from the robbers and he had only two thousand and odd out of the three thousand guns he had his brother buy for him, yet he paid every man and kept them all content. But he knew he could not always do this unless he could think of some new tax, for he was now drawing upon his own secret stores, and this was a dangerous thing for a lord of war to do, lest if he be suddenly put down, and must retreat somewhere for a time, he has nothing then to feed to his men. And Wang the Tiger set himself to think of some new tax.

Now the spies that Wang the Tiger had sent out began to gather in again at this time, for the summer was coming to an end, and they all brought the same news, and it was that the southern generals were repulsed once more and again the north was victorious. This Wang the Tiger believed the more readily because during the last few weeks he had not been hard pressed as he had been before by the provincial general to send his forces out to battle for him.

So Wang the Tiger made haste, then, and he sent his nephew and his trusty harelipped man and they took his letter to the capital of the province and he wrote a courteous letter regretting he had been so long putting down the robbers in that land, but now he was ready to join his forces to the north against the south, and he sent gifts.

But his destiny helped him very cleverly again, for on that very day when the pair reached the capital with this letter, truce was sworn and the rebels went south to recover themselves, and the northern armies were given their days of looting for booty as a reward of their victory. So when the general of that province received Wang the Tiger's allegiance he sent back a courteous acceptance, but he said that this war was over and the autumn come. Yet doubtless there would be other wars and spring would come again, and Wang the Tiger was to hold himself ready for such a time.

This was the answer the pair took back to Wang the Tiger and he received it and was well content, for his name he knew would be among those of the victorious generals, and he had not lost a man and not a gun, and he had his great army whole.

XX

THEN the golden winds of autumn blew clear out of the west and over the land once more, and the farmers reaped their harvests and the full moon swung once more to its height and the people rejoiced in the coming of the mid-autumn festival and they made ready to give thanks to the gods for these goods, that there had been no great famine and only a crop or two scarce, that the robbers had been put down once again, and that wars had not come near their region.

And Wang the Tiger took account of himself where he was and how much he had achieved and he found he was better this year than last. Yes, he now had twenty thousand soldiers under him quartered in the town and in its suburbs and he had altogether nearly twelve thousand guns. Moreover, he was now known and reckoned among the lords of war, for the weak and unready ruler whom the war had left still sitting in his place had sent out a proclamation of gratitude to all those generals who had helped him to remain when the generals of the south had tried to end his government, and Wang the Tiger's name was among the others to whom he gave thanks and titles. It is true that the title given to Wang the Tiger was not high and it sounded longer and better than it was, but still it was a title, and for this honor he had not entered a battle or lost a gun.

There remained to him this one great difficulty and it was that at the time for the feast, when it is a time of reckoning for all who lend or borrow, Wang the Merchant sent word that he must receive the money for the guns, for others pressed him for payment. Then Wang the Tiger grew quarrelsome and he parleyed with his brother and sent a man to say that this time he would not pay for the whole of the guns he had lost and he said to his brother through this messenger,

"You should have warned your agents not to turn the guns to the first who came for them."

To this Wang the Merchant answered with reason,

"But how did I know that the ones who brought my own letter for proof and used your name for a sign were not your men?"

This Wang the Tiger could not answer, but he had the power of his armies to use for an argument and so he said back again in great anger,

"I will pay half the loss and no more and if you do not agree to this I will pay nothing, and I do not need to do in these days what I do not wish to do."

Then Wang the Merchant, being a man prudent and full of philosophy if he could not mend a thing, agreed to it and

290

he bore his half well enough because he could raise the certain rentals he had and he put the interest up somewhat in a place or two where he knew he could not be refused and so he did not hurt himself.

But Wang the Tiger at first scarcely knew how to get the sum that he must pay, because he needed so much for his vast army that although a stream of silver ran into his hands every month and even every day yet it all ran out again, too. He called his trusty men into his own room and said to them in private,

"Is there any revenue we could have which we do not have now?"

And his trusty men scratched their heads to warm up their brains and they looked at each other and here and there and they could not think of anything. The harelipped man said,

"If we make the revenues too heavy on foods and goods the people must have every day they may turn against us."

This Wang the Tiger knew was true, for so the common people have done always if they are too pressed and must turn or else starve, and although Wang the Tiger was by now very well entrenched in that region, still he was not great enough to be wholly careless of the people. So he must think of something new and at last he thought of a chief industry in that town and of a tax he could put upon it, and it was the tax of a copper coin or two on every wine jar made in that region.

Now the wine jars of that region were famous, and they were made of a very fine pottery clay and glazed blue and when the wine was poured into them a seal of the same clay was put over the mouth and stamped with a sign, and that sign was known everywhere for a sign of good wine in a good jar. When Wang the Tiger thought of this he slapped his thigh and shouted out,

"The pottery makers grow richer every year, and why should we not make them share a tax with the others?"

All the trusty men agreed to it as a very good thought, and so Wang the Tiger laid the tax that very day. He laid it courteously and he sent word for the heads of the business and told them he protected them for he protected the sorghum lands where the cane grew for their wine, and if he did not there would be no wine for their jars, and he said he needed money to protect the lands, and his soldiers must be fed and armed and paid. But behind all this courtesy were the glittering weapons of his thousands and although the pottery makers met together secretly and grew very angry and talked of a hundred ways and of rebelling and of many things, they knew in the end they could not refuse for Wang the Tiger could do what he liked and there were many worse than he, and this they knew.

They were willing, then, since they must be, and Wang the Tiger sent his trusty men to estimate what the output of the jars was and every month there was a good full sum of silver given to Wang the Tiger, and in three months or so he paid Wang the Merchant. Then, since the pottery makers were used by this time to the tax, Wang the Tiger let it come on into his hands and he did not say the need for it was not so sharp as it had been. Indeed he did need all he could secure, for he had a long road yet before the end of his ambition was come, and he was restless with his ambition and he busied himself in many things.

Then when he took thought and saw that he could not take much more from the people of his lands and keep them content, he cried to himself that he was too great for so small a place and in the next spring time he must enlarge himself far beyond the confines he now had, for this region was so small that if a great famine came, such as might come any year under the cruelty of heaven, he would be undone. He had been protected thus far by his good destiny, for there had been no vast famine yet since he came to this place, and only small ones in this place and that.

Then the winter drew on when there can be no war and Wang the Tiger entrenched himself warmly. He saw to it that so long as the rain and the winds did not beat too bitterly nor the snow fall too deeply, his men went out every day for training and exercise. He himself trained the best and cleverest, and these taught the others. Especially did Wang the Tiger take stock of his guns. Every month he had them counted before his eyes and tallied with his account, both in number and kind, of what he had, and he continually told his men that if there was at any time a gun not there by its tally, he would shoot a man or two or three to keep the proportion what it was. Not one dared to disobey him. More than ever they feared him, for they all knew by now that he had killed even the woman he loved. He could be so angry even as that, and they all dreaded his anger, and leaped if he so much as twisted his black brows together.

Then winter came down out of the bitter north and the dark days came when Wang the Tiger could not go out nor force his men out and he faced at last what he knew was waiting for him and that against which he had been so busy. He was idle and he was alone.

Now did he wish he were like other men who turn eagerly to gambling or to the drinking of wine or to feasting or to the seeking out of some woman to divert them from any trouble they may have. But Wang the Tiger was not so. He had eaten plain food and liked it better than a feast, and the thought of any woman sickened him. Once and twice he tried to game, but he had not the temper for it. He was not quick at dice or at seizing a chance and when he lost he grew angry and felt for his sword and those who gamed with him were alarmed when they saw his brows begin to twist and his mouth grow more surly than it was and when they saw his big hand fly to his hilt, and they made haste to let him win every time. But this wearied Wang the Tiger, too, and he cried out,

"It is a fool's game, as I ever said it was!" and he flung himself away furious because he was not diverted nor eased at all.

Worse than the day was the night that must come and he hated it more than the day, for he slept alone and he must sleep alone. Now this loneliness by day and by night was not a good thing for such a man as Wang the Tiger for he had a heavy bitter heart that did not see mirth as some do, who have even more to bear than he, and the lonely sleep was not good either, for he had a strong and craving body. Still there was not a soul whom he could take for friend.

It was true that the old magistrate lived still in a side court with his old wife who was now dying of a consumption, and he was in his way a good and learned old man. But he was so unused to men like Wang the Tiger and so frightened that he could only fork his two old hands together and make haste to say whenever Wang the Tiger spoke to him,

"Yes, Honored—yes, General!"

And Wang the Tiger was wearied of this after a while and scowled at the old scholar so fearsomely that he turned the color of clay and he scuttled out of the rooms as soon as he dared, his faded robes dragging on his thin old body.

Yet Wang the Tiger held back his impatience, too, for he was a just man and he knew the old magistrate did the best he could and often he sent him away quickly before his impatience grew too high lest he might grow angry and do damage to the old man and his hand fly out before he meant it to do so.

There were his trusty men also, three good and true warriors, and the Hawk was indeed a very good warrior and better than a thousand common soldiers in his cleverness of guile. Still he was but an ignorant man and he could only talk of the ways there are to hold a weapon and the ways there are of sparring with fists and of kicking with the right foot and the left in a circle before the enemy can recover himself, and such ways and feints of battle, and when he had told these over and over and told how he had done this and done so in some fight or other he had had somewhere, he had told all he knew and Wang the Tiger wearied of him even while he valued him.

There was that Pig Butcher and he was very able with his great, nimble fists and his thick body that he could throw against a gate and crush it in, yet he was but heavy, stammering company on a winter's night. And there was the trusty harelipped man, the truest best soul although no great warrior, either, and best when sent on some message, and his hissing and spitting when he talked could be no pleasure. Nor would Wang the Tiger stoop to talk with his nephew who was a generation beneath him, nor would he descend to feasting and carousing with his own soldiers, for he knew that if a leader does this and if he lets himself be common and play among his own men and lets them see him weak and drunken, on the day of battle they will not reverence him or hear his command, and indeed Wang the Tiger took great care never to appear before his own men unless he wore his full accoutrements of war and unless he had his sharp sword he had used in such a way that now he loved and hated it too. Yet it was so keen a blade that he could never find its mate in the world, and he used to take it out and look at it and muse sometimes when he was alone and think how if he brought it down upon a cloud even it would cut it in two. Her throat had been as soft as that and so the blade had done that night.

But even if Wang the Tiger had had friends in the day there must come the night at the end of every day and he must be alone then perforce and he lay upon his bed alone, and the nights in winter are very long and black.

Through such long black nights must Wang the Tiger lie alone and sometimes he lit a taper candle and read his old books he had loved as a lad and which had first turned his mind to soldiering, the stories of the three kingdoms and of the robbers that bordered a great lake, and he read many doughty tales like these. But he could not read forever. The candle burned down to the end of its reed wick, and he grew cold and he must lie alone at last in the black and bitter night.

Then, although every night he put off this hour, yet the hour came when he remembered the woman he loved and he mourned for her. But he did not in all his mourning wish her living again, for he knew and he steadfastly told himself that she could never have been one whom he could have trusted and the sweetness of his love had been that he had opened his whole heart to her. No, dead he could trust her, but if she had been alive and he had prevented and pardoned her, still he would have been afraid of her always. The fear would have divided him, so that only half his heart would have gone on in his cause and he would never have risen to be great.

So he told himself in the night. Yet he pondered painfully on this, that the Leopard, who had been but an ignorant fellow, risen but a little above his robber band, could have so won the love of the woman, who was no common woman, that even though he were dead, yet did she cleave to him and even against her living love she clave to the dead man still.

For Wang the Tiger could not believe she had never loved him. No, he remembered over and over with hunger when he thought of it how frank she had been and passionate upon this very bed where he now lay. He would not believe that such passion had sprung up where no love was. And he grew wretched and weak and felt that somehow he must be a lesser man, for all his pride and place, than the Leopard he had killed, because his living hold upon the woman had been less than the memory of the dead man in her. He could not understand all this, but only he felt it must be so.

And feeling himself less of a man than he thought, his life stretched ahead of him long and meaningless and he doubted himself that he could ever be great and if he did then for what use, seeing he had no son for whom to achieve greatness, and it would all die with him and what he had go to others. He did not love his brothers or his brothers' sons enough to struggle in war and guile for them. And he groaned to himself in the dark and silent room and he groaned out,

"When I killed her I killed two, and the other was the son I might have had!"

Then he remembered again and he always saw her now as she looked when she lay dead, her strong fair throat pierced and the bright blood gushing out. When he saw her thus again and again, he could not bear it, and suddenly he could not lie any longer on this bed, no, although it had been washed and painted freshly and the blood stains were gone and the pillow was new, and although no one had ever mentioned to him what had happened there nor had he ever known where they took her body. He rose from the bed and he wrapped his quilts about him and sat miserable and shivering upon a chair, until the feeble dawn came and showed pale and chill through his lattices.

So the winter nights wore on the same, night after night,

and at last Wang the Tiger cried out to himself that this could not be, for these sad and lonely nights were making him less than a man and they were sucking the ambition out of him. He grew afraid for himself because nothing seemed good to him any more and he was impatient with all who came near, and most of all did he grow impatient with his nephew and he said bitterly,

"This is the best I have, this grinning pocked ape, son of a tradesman—this is nearest I have to my own son!"

At last when it seemed he must go mad a turn came in his own spirit and it came to him one night that the woman even though dead was ruining him as surely as she would have done if she had been alive and gone the way she planned. And suddenly he hardened himself and it seemed he spoke to her own ghost to defy her and he said in his own heart,

"Cannot any woman have sons, and do I not desire a son more than any mere woman? I will have a son. I will take a woman or two or three until I have a son. I have been a fool that I do always cling so to one woman—first to a woman I never even knew beyond a few scattered words such as a man may speak to a slave in his father's house and I went sore for that woman nearly ten years, and then there was the one I had to kill. Shall I never be rid of her too and shall I go sore for her another ten years and be too old to beget a son then? No, I shall be as other men are and I will see if I cannot make myself free as other men do and take a woman and leave her again when I please."

On that very day he called his trusty harelipped man to him and he called him into his own private room and he said,

"I have need of a woman, any woman of a decent kind, and go and tell my brothers that my wife is dead and tell them to find me something since I am busy with the wars that must come in the spring time and I do not care to deviate my thoughts from the wars."

The harelipped man went gladly on this errand then, for he had seen with jealous eyes at least a little of what his general suffered and had guessed the cause, and he thought this good cure.

As for Wang the Tiger, he could but wait to see what time would bring and what his two brothers would do for him, and while he waited he forced himself to plan his wars and to think how he would enlarge himself. And he schemed how to weary himself into sleep at night.

XXI

By winding ways, lest men mark his harelip and wonder at his frequent coming, the trusty man came to the town and thence to the great house where the Brothers Wang lived. He asked and found that Wang the Merchant was at this hour, which was nearly noon, in his counting house, and there the trusty man went at once to give his message. Wang the Merchant sat in his own part of the counting house, a small dark room which gave off the main market, and he was fingering an abacus and reckoning certain profits he had made on a ship's load of wheat. He looked up and listened to the trusty man's tale, and when he had heard he said, astounded, his little eyes staring, and his meager mouth pursed,

"Now I can get even silver more easily for him than I can get a woman. How should I know where to turn for a woman? It is an ill thing he has lost the one he had."

The trusty man, sitting cornerwise upon a lowly seat to show he felt his place, answered humbly saying,

"All I ask, my master's brother, is that you find a sort of woman who will not trouble our general and make him love her. He has a strange deep heart and he so fixes himself on one thing that it is a madness with him. So he loved this woman who died and he has not forgotten her yet, no, although months have passed he does not forget her and such constancy in a man is not good for his health."

"How did she die?" asked Wang the Merchant curiously.

But the trusty man was very faithful and discreet and he stopped himself as he was about to answer, because he bethought himself that when men are outside the ranks of soldiers and not acquainted with war-like things, they grow squeamish and they cannot bear killing and dying as soldiers must, whose trade it is to kill and be killed if they cannot save themselves by guile. So he said simply,

"She died of a sudden flow of blood," and Wang the Merchant let it be at that.

Then he sent the trusty man away, first bidding a clerk to take him to some small inn and feed him with rice and pork, and after they were gone Wang the Merchant sat and mused and he thought to himself,

"Well, and here is a time when that older brother of mine will know more than I, for if he knows anything at all it is women, and what woman do I know except the one I have?"

Then Wang the Merchant rose to go out and find his brother, Wang the Landlord, and he took from a nail in the wall his grey silk robe that he wore when he went out but took off in his counting house to spare it wear, and he went to his brother's house and he asked the gateman to know if his master were at home that day. The gateman would have led him in, but Wang the Merchant would wait, and the gateman went in and asked a slave and the slave replied that he was at a certain gaming house. When Wang the Merchant heard this he went to that piece, choosing his way as delicately as a cat over the cobbled street, because it had snowed in the night and the day was so cold that even yet the snow lay there, and there was only a little path in the middle made by vendors and those who must go out for a living or as his brother did, for pleasure.

He came to the gaming house and he asked a clerk and heard that his brother was within at a certain door, and Wang the Merchant went to it and opened it and found Wang the Landlord there gaming with certain of his friends in a small room made hot with a brazier of coals.

When Wang the Landlord saw his brother's head come in at the door he was secretly glad to be disturbed and called away, for he was not over-skilled at gaming, since he had learned the thing late in life. Wang Lung, his father, would not have let a son of his gamble in city gaming houses if he had known it. But Wang the Landlord's son was quick and able enough because he had gamed all his life long, and even the second son had been able to gain a little pile of silver at any game he had a share in.

So when Wang the Landlord saw his brother's head come in at the partly opened door he rose readily and said in haste to his friends,

"I must stop, for my brother needs me for something," and he took up his fur coat he had laid aside in the heat of the room and went out to where Wang the Merchant waited. But he did not say he was glad he had come, because he was too proud to tell that he lost at gaming, since a clever man should win. He only said,

"Have you something to say to me?"

Wang the Merchant answered in his scanty way, "Let us go where we can talk, if there is such a place in this house."

Then Wang the Landlord led the way to a place where

there were tables for tea drinking, and they chose a lonely table set a little apart from the others, and there the two brothers seated themselves, and Wang the Merchant waited while Wang the Landlord ordered tea and then wine and then bethinking himself of the hour, he ordered some meats and dishes of food. At last the serving man was gone, and Wang the Merchant began forthright,

"That younger brother of ours wants a wife, for his woman is dead and he has sent to us this time. I thought here is a thing you can manage better than I."

This Wang the Merchant said drawing down his lips in a secret smile. But Wang the Landlord did not see it. He laughed out loud and his fat cheeks shook and he said,

"Well, and if I know anything at all it is such things, and you are right but it would not do to say it before my lady, though!"

And he laughed and looked sidewise out of his eyes as men will when they talk of these matters. But Wang the Merchant would not joke with him and he waited. Wang the Landlord sobered himself then and he said, further,

"But this comes at a very good time, for I have been looking over the maids of this town for my son, and I know all the likely maids. I have a plan now to betroth the eldest one of my sons to a maid nineteen years of age, a daughter of the younger brother of the magistrate—a very good, honorable maid, and my son's mother has seen some of the samples of her embroidery and handiwork. She is not pretty but very honorable. The only trouble is my son has some silly thought of choosing a wife for himself—he has heard of such new ways in the south.

"But I tell him it is not known here to do such things, and besides he can choose others he likes. As for that poor hunch-

302

back, his mother wants a priest in the family, and it seems a pity to waste a good straight son in such a way—"

But Wang the Merchant was not interested in all these doings of his brother's family, for it is known as a matter of course that every son must be wed sooner or later and his own sons also, but he did not waste his time on such things, deeming them women's duty, and he had put it all into his wife's hands, saying only that such maids as came into his house must be virtuous and stout and hard working. So he broke in now with impatience,

"But are any of the maids you saw fit for our brother, and are their fathers willing to have them go into a house to wife one already wed as he has been?"

But Wang the Landlord would not hasten himself over such a dainty job as this and he let his memory linger upon the maids, this one and that, and on all he knew from what he had heard of them and he said,

"There is a very good maid, not too young, whose father is a scholar and he has made her into something of a scholar, too, he having no son and needing to teach someone what he knew. She is what they call now-a-days a new woman, such as have learning and do not bind their feet, and because she is strange in this way, her marriage has been delayed, because men have not dared to take a woman like this for their sons, lest a trouble come out of it. But I hear there are many like her in the south, and it is only because this is a small old city, doubtless, that men here do not know what to make of her. She goes on the street even and I have seen her once and she went very decorously and did not stare about her, either. With all her learning she is not so hideous as might be feared, and if she is not very young yet she cannot be more than twenty-five or six. Do you think my brother would fancy such a one who is not like a usual woman?"

To this Wang the Merchant answered with reserve, "But do you think she will make a good housewife and be useful to him? He reads and writes himself as well as many a man does, and if he did not he could hire it done for him by some scholar. I do not see that he needs all this learning in a wife."

Then Wang the Landlord, who had been dipping food into his bowl busily, the serving man having come to and fro many times with dishes, paused and held his porcelain spoon in mid-air full of a soup and he cried,

"He can hire a servant too, I swear, or a jade, and it is not all in what a woman can do that makes her a good wife. The chief thing is whether or not she fits a man's fancy or not, especially if he is one like my brother who will not seek out other women. Sometimes I think it would be a pleasant thing to tickle a man if his wife could sit and read poetry to him or some tale of love as he lies on his bed to sleep."

But this was distasteful to Wang the Merchant and he picked delicately at a dish of pigeons stewed with chestnuts and thrust his chopsticks carefully between the bones to find the bit he relished and he said,

"I would rather fit my fancy to a woman careful in the house and who had children and who could save money."

Then Wang the Landlord grew suddenly angry in the wilful way he had even since his childhood and his great full face turned a dark red and Wang the Merchant saw they would never agree on this, and it was not a thing to waste his day upon, for women are but women, whoever they may be otherwise, and one will serve the final purpose of a man as well as another, so he said quickly,

"Ah, well, and that brother of ours is not poor, and let us choose two wives for him then. Do you choose the one you think best, and we will wed him to her first, and then awhile later send him the one I choose, and if he likes one better than the other let him, but two are not many for such a man as he in his position."

Thus they compromised, and Wang the Landlord was pleased that the one he chose was to be the wife, although when he thought, it seemed no more than his due, for no man could lie with two wives on his wedding night, and, after all, he was the eldest son in this family and the head. So they agreed and then parted and Wang the Landlord went bustling to do his part and Wang the Merchant went back to his house to find his wife and talk with her.

When he reached his home she was at the gate standing in the snowy street, her hands wrapped in her apron to warm them, but ever and again she brought them out to probe the crops of fowls that a vendor had there to sell. The snow had made such fowls cheaper than usual since they could not find their own food and she wished to add a hen or two to her stock and as Wang the Merchant came near she did not look up but continued to peer at the fowls. But Wang the Merchant said to her as he passed, to go into the house,

"Have done, woman, come here."

Then she made haste and chose two hens and after quarreling over their weight upon the scales to which the vendor hung them by their legs tied together, they agreed upon the price and she came into the house and thrust the hens under a chair and then sat down cornerwise on it to hear what her husband had to say to her and he said in his dry, scanty way,

"That younger brother of mine wants a wife, for his has died suddenly. I know nothing of women, but you have had your eyes hanging out these two years looking for wives for our sons. Is there one we could send there?"

His wife answered readily, for she delighted in all such things as birth and death and marriage and her constant talk was of these,

"There is a very good maid who lived next door to me in my own village, and she is so good I have often wished that she were young enough for our eldest. She is the pleasantest-tempered maid, and very saving, and she has no fault at all except that her teeth grew black even when she was a child from some worm that ate them away, it is said, and now they drop out sometimes. But she is ashamed of this and keeps her lips drawn down to hide them, so they are not easily seen, and because of this she talks very little and very low. Her father is not poor either, and he owns land, and he will be glad to have her wed so well, I know, seeing that she is already a little beyond the age."

Then Wang the Merchant said dryly, "If she cannot talk much that will be worth something. See to it, and after the wedding we will send her." And he told his wife that two women were to be chosen, and she said loudly,

"Well, I feel sorry for him if he has to have one of your brother's choosing for what does he know except lewd women, and I vow if his lady has anything to do with it she will choose a nunnish creature, for I hear now she is so daft over priests and nuns she would have the whole house praying and mumming. It is well enough, I say, to go to the temple once in a way if there is someone sick of a fever or if a woman is childless or something, but I daresay the gods are like all of us, and we do not love best the people who are for ever troubling us and calling at us for this and that!"

And she spat on the floor and rubbed the place with her foot, and forgetting the hens under her chair, she thrust her feet back and struck them and they set up a mighty squawking, so that Wang the Merchant rose and called out impatiently,

"I never saw such a house! Must we have hens everywhere?"

And when she reached under hastily to drag the fowls out

306

and explain how the price for them was less than usual now, he broke in to what she began to say and said,

"Let be—let be—I must go back to my markets. Attend to the thing and this day two months or so we will call her. Only keep all the costs well in mind for the law does not require that we pay over again for my brother's wedding."

Thus the thing was done and the two maids were betrothed and the deeds drawn up and Wang the Merchant entered the costs carefully into his counting books, and that day month was the day set for the wedding.

Now the day was near the end of the old year, and Wang the Tiger when he had been told of it, made ready to go to his brothers' house to wed once more. He had no heart to do the thing and yet he had determined he would and so he gave over any thought or wavering and he made ready his three trusty men he appointed to watch in his stead, and he left his nephew to be messenger if any trouble should rise while he was gone.

When he had done this he made a feint of asking permission of the old magistrate to leave for five days and six days for the journey to come and to go, and the old magistrate made haste to give his permission. And Wang the Tiger took precaution to tell the old magistrate that he left his army and his trusty men, lest there be some vague hope of rising against him somehow. Then clothing himself in his next best garments and taking his best with him in a roll upon his saddle, Wang the Tiger went south to his home, taking with him a small guard of fifty armed men, for he was a man of such courage that he did not, as many lords of war do, surround himself with hundreds of inner and outer guards.

Through the wintry country Wang the Tiger rode, stopping at village inns by night, and riding on again over the frozen earthen roads. There was no sign yet of spring, and the land lay grey and harsh, and the houses made of the grey clay and thatched with the grey straw, seemed but part of the land. Even the people, bitten with the winds and dust of the northern winter were grey of the same hue, and Wang the Tiger felt no joy rise in his heart these three days, as he rode toward his father's home.

When he was come he went to his elder brother's house, since there he was to be wed, and when he had given them brief greeting he said abruptly that before he wed he would do his duty and go to do reverence at his father's grave. And this they all approved, and especially Wang the Landlord's lady, for it was a decent, proper thing to do, seeing that Wang the Tiger had been so long away, and he had not shared in the regular times that the family paid such respect to their dead.

But Wang the Tiger, although he knew his duty and when he could he did it, now performed it partly because he was restless and dreary in himself, and he did not know why he was either. But he could not bear to sit in his brother's house idle, and he could not bear his brother's unctuous pleasure at the coming wedding, and he was oppressed in himself and he must needs think of some excuse to be out and away from them all, because this house did not seem his home.

He sent a soldier then to buy the paper money and the incense and all such things as are useful to the dead and with these he went out of the city with the men at his horse's heels, their guns on their shoulders. He took a little faint comfort to see how people stared at him on the street and although he held his face stiff and stared ahead seeming to see and to hear nothing, still he heard his soldiers shout out roughly,

"Way for the general, way for our lord!" And as he saw the common people shrink back against the walls and into the gateways he was a little comforted because he was so great to them, and he held himself erect in his state and pomp.

Thus he came to the graves under the date tree which by now had grown knotted and gnarled, although when Wang Lung had first chosen that place to lay his dead, it was a smooth young tree. Now other date trees had sprung from it, and Wang the Tiger, having dismounted while he was yet a long way off to show his respect, came slowly to these trees and one of the soldiers stood and held the red horse, and Wang the Tiger walked slowly and stately in his reverence until he came to the grave of his father. There he made obeisance three times, and the soldiers who carried the money and the incense came forward and arranged it, the most at Wang Lung's grave and the next at the grave of Wang Lung's father and the next at the grave of Wang Lung's brother, and the least at O-lan's grave, whom Wang the Tiger could remember but dimly as his mother.

Then Wang the Tiger went forward again in his slow and stately way and he lit the incense and the paper and he knelt and knocked his head the number of times he should before every grave and when this was finished he stood motionless and meditated, while the fire burned and the silver and the gold paper turned to ash and the incense smouldered sharp and fragrant upon the wintry air of that day. There was no sunshine and no wind, a grey chill day such as may bring snow, and the warm slight smoke of the incense curled clearly in the chill air. The soldiers waited in completest silence while their general communed as long as he wished with his father and at last Wang the Tiger turned away and walked to his horse and mounted it and went back along the path he had come.

But while he meditated he had not thought at all of his father Wang Lung. He thought of himself and of how when

309

he lay dead there would not be one to come and do him reverence as son to father, and when he thought of this it seemed well to him that he was to be wed and he bore a little better the dreariness he had in his soul for the hope of a son.

Now the path on which Wang the Tiger rode skirted the threshold of the earthen house and passed by the edge of the threshing floor that was its door yard, and the noise of the soldiers roused the hunchback youth who lived there with Pear Blossom and he came hobbling out as quickly as he could and stood staring. He did not know Wang the Tiger at all, or even that this was his uncle, and so he only stood there by the path and stared. For all he was now nearly sixteen years old and soon to be a man, he stood scarcely taller than a child of six or seven, and his back rose curved like a hood behind his head and Wang the Tiger was astonished at the sight of him and he asked, drawing his horse back,

"Who are you who live here in my earthen house?"

Then the lad knew him, for he had heard he had an uncle who was a general and he often dreamed of him and wondered what he was like, and now he cried out, yearningly,

"Are you my uncle?"

Then Wang the Tiger remembered, and he said slowly, still staring down at the lad's upturned face,

"Yes, I have heard somewhere that my brother had a brat like you. Strange, for we are all so straight and strong and so was my father, too, the straightest, strongest old man, even in his age."

Then the lad answered simply, as though it were a thing to which he were long used, and he stared avidly at the soldiers as he said it, and at the high red horse,

"But I was dropped." Then he stretched out his hand toward Wang the Tiger's gun and he peered up out of his strange aged face and his little, sad sunken eyes, and he said eagerly,

"I have never held one of those foreign guns in my hand and I would like to hold it for a moment's time."

When he stretched up his hand thus, a little dried, wrinkled hand like an old man's, out of a sudden pity for this poor warped lad Wang the Tiger handed him down his own gun to feel and to look at. And as he waited for the lad to have his fill of it, one came to the door. It was Pear Blossom. Wang the Tiger knew her instantly, for she had not changed much except to grow thinner even than she had been, and her face, always pale and egg-shaped, was now covered with fine thread-like wrinkles drawn lightly into the pale skin. But her hair was as smooth and black as ever. Then Wang the Tiger bowed very stiffly and deeply but without descending from his horse, and Pear Blossom gave a little bow and would have turned quickly away except that Wang the Tiger called out,

"Is the fool still living and well?"

And Pear Blossom answered in her soft small voice, "She is well."

And Wang the Tiger asked again,

"Do you have your full due every month?"

And she answered again in the same voice, "I thank you, I have all my due," and she held her head down as she spoke and looked at the beaten ground of the threshing floor and this time when she had answered him she went swiftly away and he was left staring at the empty doorway.

Then he said suddenly to the lad,

"Why does she wear a robe that is like a nun's?" for he had seen without knowing he did that Pear Blossom's grey robes were crossed at her throat as a nun's are.

The lad answered, scarcely thinking of what he said, so longing and fixed was his heart upon the gun as he fingered it and smoothed its wood,

"When the fool is dead she will go into the nunnery near

311

here and be a nun. She eats no meat at all now and she knows many prayers by heart and she is a lay nun already. But she will not leave the world and cut off her hair until the fool dies, because my grandfather left her the fool."

Wang the Tiger heard this and he was silent a moment in some vague pain and at last he said pityingly to the lad,

"What will you do then, you poor hunched ape?"

And the lad made answer, "When she goes into the nunnery I am to be a priest in the temple because I am so young I must live for a long time and she cannot wait for me to die, too. But if I am a priest I can be fed and if I am ill and I am often ill with this thing I carry on me, then she can come and tend me, since we are kin." This the boy said carelessly. Then his voice changed and grew half sobbing with some passion, and he looked up at Wang the Tiger and cried out, "Yes, I am to be a priest—but, oh, I wish that I were straight and then I would be a soldier—if you would have me, Uncle!"

There was such fire in his sunken dark eyes that Wang the Tiger was moved by it, and he answered sorrowfully, for he was a merciful man at heart,

"I would have you gladly, you poor thing, but shaped as you are, what can you be now but a priest!"

And the lad hung his head out of its strange socket and he said in a small, low voice,

"I know it."

Without another word he handed the gun back to Wang the Tiger and he turned and limped away across the threshing floor. And Wang the Tiger went on his way to his marriage.

This was a strange marriage to Wang the Tiger. He was in no burning haste this time, and day and night were alike to him. He went through it all silently and decorously as he did everything he had to do unless a rage came over him.

312

But now love and rage seemed forever equally far from his dead heart, and the red-robed figure of the bride was like some dim, distant figure with which he had nothing at all to do. So also the guests, and so the figures of his brothers and their wives and children, and the monstrous fat figure of Lotus, leaning on Cuckoo. Yet he looked at her once, too, for she panted as she breathed she was so heavy with her flesh and Wang the Tiger could hear this thick gusty breathing as he stood to bow to his elder brothers and to those who sponsored the woman and to the guests and to all those to whom he must bow in ceremony.

But when the wedding feast was brought he scarcely tasted this dish or that, and when Wang the Landlord began his jokes, since there should be merriment even at a man's second wedding, and when a guest took up the laughter, it died away into feebleness and silence before Wang the Tiger's grave face. He said nothing at all at his own wedding feast except that when the wine was brought he took up the bowl quickly as though he were thirsty. But when he had tasted it he set the bowl down again and he said harshly,

"If I had known the wine would be no better than this I would have brought a jar of the wine of my own region."

After the days of wedding were over, he mounted his red horse and went away and he did not cast one look behind at the bride and her serving maid who came behind him in a mule cart, with the curtains drawn. No, he rode on as seeming solitary as he had been when he came, his soldiers at his heels, and the cart lumbering behind them. Thus Wang the Tiger brought his bride to his own regions, and in a month or two and a little more the second woman came under her father's care, and her he received also, since one or two were the same to him.

Then the New Year drew on and its festivals and these

313

passed, and it was the time when spring first begins to stir in the earth, although no sign of it could yet be seen in any leaf upon a tree. Yet there were signs, too, for the snow, if it came on a chill grey day, did not lie but melted in the sudden heat of a warm wind that blew fitfully out of the south, and the wheat plants in the fields, while they did not yet grow, took on a fresher green, and everywhere farmers stirred themselves out of their winter idleness and looked to their hoes and their rakes and fed their oxen a little better to prepare them for labor. By the roadsides the weeds began to send up shoots and children roamed everywhere with their knives and pointed bits of wood and tin if they had not knives, to dig the fresh green stuff for food.

So also did the lords of war bestir themselves in their winter quarters and soldiers stretched their full-fed bodies and wearied of their gaming and brawling and idling about towns where they were entrenched and they stirred themselves to wonder what their fortunes could be in the new wars of the spring, and every soldier dreamed a little and hoped that one above him might be killed and give him place.

So also did Wang the Tiger dream of what he would do. Yes, he had a scheme, and it was a good one, and now he could put himself to it for it seemed to him that his gnawing, nagging love was dead. Or, if not dead, then buried some- where, and whenever he was troubled by its memory he went deliberately to one of those two wives of his, and if his flesh lagged, he drank wine deeply to rouse it.

And being a very just man, he showed no favor to one wife above the other, although they were very different, too, the one learned and neat and pleasing in a plain and quiet way, and the other somewhat uncouth, but still a woman of virtue and of good heart. Her greatest fault was her black- ened teeth, and that she had a very foul breath if one came

314

near her. But even so Wang the Tiger was fortunate in that they did not quarrel, these two women. Yet doubtless his justice helped this, for he was scrupulous and he went to them each in turn, and the truth was they were the same to him and alike nothing.

But he need no longer lie alone unless he wished. Still, he never grew familiar with either woman, and he always went in to them haughtily and for a set purpose and he made no speech with them and there was no frankness as there had been between him and the one dead and he never gave himself freely.

Sometimes he pondered on this difference that a man may feel toward women, and when he did he told himself bitterly that the one dead had never been truly frank with him, no, not even when she seemed as free as a harlot, for all the time she hugged her design against him in her heart. When he thought of this Wang the Tiger sealed his heart again and calmed his flesh with his two wives. And he had this for a hope and for a fresh light to his ambition, and it was that from one of the twain surely he might have his son at last. In this hope Wang the Tiger encouraged his dreams of glory once more and he swore that in this very year in this very spring he would go forth to a great war somewhere and win for himself power and wide territories, and he saw the victory already his own.

XXII

THEN as spring blossomed and the white cherry trees and the pale pink peach blooms lay like light clouds over the green land, Wang the Tiger took counsel with his trusty men as to war and they waited for two things. The first was to see how the war would renew itself between the lords of north and south, for the truce they had made the year before was very slight and tenuous and it was but a truce of the winter when it is not convenient to do battle in wind and snow and mud. Aside from this, the lords of north and south so differed in their nature, the one being large in body and slow and fierce, and the other little tricky men, good in guile and ambush, that with such difference in temper and even in blood and language, it was not easy for them to agree upon long truce. The other thing for which Wang the Tiger waited and his trusty men with him was for the return of the many spies he sent out early in the year. And while they waited Wang the Tiger took counsel with his trusty men as to what territory they might attach to what they had and so enlarge the region.

Now they took counsel together in the great room which Wang the Tiger used for his own and there they sat, each according to his rank, and the Hawk said,

"North we cannot go, for we are in allegiance with the north."

And the Pig Butcher said loudly, for it was his way to speak whatever the Hawk said, like a rude echo, for he did not like to be thought less wise than the Hawk, and yet he himself could not think easily of a new thing to say,

"Yes, but even so, it is a very poor and meager land there, and the pigs are so accursed and so thin they are no use butchering. I have seen those pigs and I swear their backs are sharp as curved scythes, and a sow's pigs can be counted before ever she gives them birth. It is not a country anyone wants to wage a war to gain."

But Wang the Tiger said slowly,

"Yet south we cannot go, for if we do we will strike my own and my father's folk, and a man cannot tax his own people freely and with an easy mind."

Now the harelipped man spoke little and never until the others had their say out, and now he said in his turn,

"There is a region where my native land once was, but it is nothing to me now, and it is to the southeast of this, between here and the sea, a very rich country, and one end of it lies against the sea. There is a whole county spread out edgewise along a river there that flows to the sea, too, and it is a good country, full of fields and it has a low ridge of hills, and the river is full of fish. The county seat is the only large town, but there are many villages and market towns and the people are thrifty and do well."

Wang the Tiger heard this and he said,

"Yes, but such a good place is not likely to be without its lord of war. Who is it?"

Then the trusty man named the name of one who had once been a robber chief and the very year before this one had thrown in his lot with the south. When he heard this name, Wang the Tiger decided swiftly that he would go against this robber chief, and he remembered to this day how he hated the men of the south and how tasteless their soft rice and peppered meats had been and there was nothing for a man to set his good teeth down upon to chew it, and he remembered the hateful years of his youth and he cried out,

"The very place and the very man, for it will enlarge me and it will count in the general wars, as well!"

As swiftly as this was the thing decided and Wang the Tiger shouted to a serving man to bring wine and they all drank and Wang the Tiger gave his commands that the soldiers were to be prepared for movement and they were to march to the new lands as soon as the first spies returned to tell of what the great war was to be this year. Then the trusty men rose to take their leave and to fulfill these commands, but the Hawk lingered after the others went away, and he leaned and whispered into Wang the Tiger's ear, and his voice was hoarse and his breath hot upon Wang the Tiger's cheek, and he said,

"We must let the soldiers have the usual days of looting after the battle, for they mutter among themselves and they complain that you hold them in so tight and they do not have the privileges under your banner that other lords of war give. They will not fight if they cannot loot."

Then Wang the Tiger gnawed the stiff black hair he had let grow these days about his lips and he said very unwillingly, for he knew the Hawk was right,

"Well, then, tell them they are to have the three days when the victory is ours, but no more."

The Hawk went away well pleased, but Wang the Tiger sat sullen for a while, for the truth was he hated this looting of the people, and yet what else could he do, seeing that soldiers will not risk their lives to fight without this reward? So, although he agreed to it, he was ill at ease for a time, for he could not but see in his mind the picture of the suffering of those people, and he cursed himself for a man too soft for the trade he had chosen. And he forced himself to be hard and he told himself that after all it must be the rich who lose most, since the poor have nothing of worth to anyone, and the rich can bear it. But he was ashamed he was so weak and not for anything would he have had a man of his know he shrank from seeing pain, lest he be despised.

Then the spies returned, one after the other, and each in his turn reported to their general, and they said that although no war as yet was broken forth, yet the lords of north and of south were buying weapons from outer countries and war must come, for everywhere armies were being enlarged and strengthened. Now when Wang the Tiger heard this he decided that he would begin without delay upon his own private war, and on that very day he commanded his men to assemble themselves upon a field outside the city gates, for there was so vast a number they could not gather together inside, and he rode there upon his high red horse with his bodyguard behind him, and to his right his pocked nephew sat, no longer upon an ass, but now upon a good horse, for Wang the Tiger had given him a position there. And Wang the Tiger held himself erect and exceedingly proud, and his men all stared at him in silence, for indeed he was such a warrior as is not often seen in the world for great good looks and heavy fierce brows and on his lips the hair he had let newly grow made him look older than his forty years. Thus before them he sat motionless and he let them stare at him awhile, and suddenly he lifted his voice out in a shout and he called to all his men,

"Soldiers and heroes! Tomorrow six days and we will march to the southeast and we will take that region. It is a rich and fertile land bordering upon a river and the sea, and what I gain there I will share with you. You are to divide under my two trusty men, and the Hawk will lead from the east and the Pig Butcher from the west. I myself with my picked five thousand men will wait to the north and when you have attacked from two sides and hold the city fast, which is the center to the region, I will rush in and close and crush the last resistance. There is a lord of war there, but he is only a robber, and well you have shown me how you can deal with robbers, my good fellows!"

Then he added, but very unwillingly although he had hardened himself for it, "If you are victorious you are to have freedom in that city for three days. But on the dawn of the fourth day your freedom ends. He who does not answer the call of the bugles I shall cause to be blown for a sign to you, him will I kill. I am not afraid to die and not afraid to kill. These are my commands. You have them!"

Then the men shouted out and they stirred restlessly and as soon as Wang the Tiger had gone away they grew very eager and greedy and anxious to be off and every man looked to his weapons and cleaned and sharpened all and he counted the bullets he had. At that time many a man bartered with others for bullets, and those who were weak in their desire for wine or for a turn at a wench paid over their bullets as far as they dared for that for which they yearned.

On the dawn of the sixth day Wang the Tiger led his mighty army out of the city. Yet great as it was he left a small half behind, and he went to the old magistrate who now lay on his bed and never rose from it he grew so weak, and Wang the Tiger told the old man that he left the army to protect him and his court. The magistrate thanked him in his feeble courteous way, but well he knew the army was left a guard upon him still. And the harelipped man was its head, and it was a hard place, for the soldiers were discontented to be left behind, and Wang the Tiger was compelled to promise them a dole of extra silver if they did well and guarded faithfully and he promised them that the next war would be theirs. So they were content a little, or at least less discontent.

Then at the head of his army Wang the Tiger went out, and he caused it to be told among the city people that he went to wage war again for them against an encroaching enemy from the south, and the people were afraid and eager to please him, and the guild of merchants there gave him a sum for a gift, and many from the city followed the army as they left the city that day and they stayed to see Wang the Tiger's ensign set up and the sacrifice made to it of a killed pig and incense so that good fortune might attend the war.

When this was over Wang the Tiger went on in good

earnest and he had not only his men and their weapons to wage the war, but he had brought a goodly sum of silver, too, for he was too clever a general to plunge at once into battle, and he would parley and wait and see how silver could be used, and at least if silver was useless at first in the end it might serve something and buy over some important man to open the gates of the city to them.

It was now the middle of spring and the wheat was two feet high or so over miles of that countryside and ready to head, and Wang the Tiger cast his eyes far and wide over that green land as he rode. He had a pride in its beauty and fruitfulness for it was his own to rule and he loved it as a king may love his realm. Yet he was wise and with all his eye for its beauty he could keep his wits sharp for some new place to fix a tax to maintain this vast army he now had and for his private store he must increase, also.

Thus he passed out of his own region, and when he had come far enough south so that he came to groves of pomegranate trees and saw them putting out from their gnarled grey branches the tiny flame-colored new leaves that come late and after all other trees are leaved, he knew he was in the new lands. He looked everywhere then to see what these were, and everywhere he saw fruitful, nurtured fields, and well fed beasts and fat children and he rejoiced at it all. But as he passed with his men the folk upon the lands looked up at them and scowled to see them and women who had been the moment before talking and laughing in their gossip together grew silent and pale and stared and many a mother put her hand over her child's eyes. And if the soldiers burst into some song of war as they did often when they marched, then men in the fields cursed aloud to hear the quiet air broken like this. The very dogs rushed furiously out of the villages to nip the strangers, but when they saw so vast a horde they were

321

dismayed and shrank away with their tails curled under their bellies. Every now and again an ox broke loose from where it was tied and fled as fast as it could because of the noise of so many men passing, and sometimes if it were yoked it ran plow and all and the farmer plowman after it. Then the soldiers guffawed loudly, but Wang the Tiger if he saw it stopped courteously until the man had his beast in hand again.

In the towns and hamlets also the people were silent and stricken when the soldiers came pushing through the gates clamoring and laughing and hungry for tea and wine and bread and meat, and shop keepers scowled over their counters because they feared their wares gone and they not paid for them, so that some drew the wooden doors over their open shops as though the night were come. But Wang the Tiger had early given command that nothing should be seized without payment and he had given his men money for such things as they needed to eat and to drink. Yet well he knew that the best general cannot control so many thousands of lawless men, and although he had told his captains he would hold them responsible, yet he knew no small amount of evil must surely be done, and he could only shout, "If I hear of it I will kill you!" and he trusted that the men would subdue themselves somewhat, and he did not try to hear everything.

But Wang the Tiger planned this way to control his men to some degree. When they came to a town he made them stay in a suburb and he went with only a few hundred first and he sought the richest merchant in that place. When he had found him he commanded him to gather together the other merchants and he waited in the richest merchant's shop. When they were all there before him very fearful and courteous, then Wang the Tiger was courteous, too, and he said,

"Do not fear that I shall be extortionate and take more than I ought. It is true I have many thousands of men in the suburb, but give me only a fair amount for my expense on this march and I will lead my men on and we will not stay here but the night."

Then the merchants, all pale and fearful, would put forward the spokesman they had chosen and he would stammer forth a sum, but Wang the Tiger knew well it was the lowest they could name, and he would smile coolly but he drew down his brows while he smiled, and he said,

"I see the fine shops you have, the oil shops and the grain markets and the silks and the cloths and I see your people how well they are fed and clothed and how good your streets are. Do you cry your town so small and poor as this? You shame yourselves by such a sum!"

Thus courteously he would force their sum upward, and he never threatened them coarsely as some lords of war do and cry out that he would set his soldiers free in the town if he did not get so much and so much. No, Wang the Tiger used only fair means, for he always said that these men must live too and they ought not to be asked for more than in reason they ought to be able to give. And the end of it and the fruit of his courtesy was that he had that for which he asked and the merchants were glad to be rid of him so easily and rid of his horde.

Thus Wang the Tiger marched his men to the southeast where the sea was and each time he stopped in a town he had a sum of money the merchants gave him and at dawn he went on and the people were glad. But in poor hamlets or small villages Wang the Tiger did not ask for anything unless it were a little food, and the least he could take.

Seven days and seven nights did Wang the Tiger thus lead his men and at the end of those days he was even somewhat enriched by the sums of money he had had, and his men were all in great high heart and well fed and very hopeful.

At the end of the seven days he was within less than a day's journey of the city he planned to take as the heart to this whole region and he rode to a low hill from where he could see it. There that city lay like a treasure encircled by its wall, and set into the rolling green fields, and Wang the Tiger's heart leaped to see it so beautiful and under so fair a sky. There the river ran also, as he had heard it did, and the south gate of the city touched the river, so the city seemed like a jewel hung upon a silver chain. In greatest haste then did Wang the Tiger send his messengers to that city guarded with a thousand men, and he declared to the lord of war who held that city that he who was Wang the Tiger had come down out of the north and he came to save the people from a robber and if the robber would not withdraw peacefully and for a sum to be named then must Wang the Tiger march against the city with his tens of thousands upon thousands of brave armed men.

Now the lord of war in that place was a very doughty old robber and he was so black and hideous a man that the people had nicknamed him after the fearful black god who stands in the entrance halls of temples to be guardian there, so the lord of war was called Liu the Gate God. When he heard the boldness of this message that Wang the Tiger had sent he fell into a mighty rage and he bellowed with his wrath awhile before he could give an answer, and when he could, he answered thus:

"Go back and tell your master that he may fight if he wishes. Who fears him? I have never heard of this little dog who calls himself Wang the Tiger!"

The messengers returned then and repeated this faithfully to Wang the Tiger and he was mightily angry in his turn and he was secretly hurt that the lord of war said he had never heard the name of Wang the Tiger, and he wondered

324

within himself if he were less than he thought. But outwardly he ground his teeth together in his black beard and he called to his men and they marched against the city that very day and encamped themselves all about it. But the gates were locked against them so that they could not go in, and Wang the Tiger bade his men quarter themselves until dawn, and he had a row of tents put up around the city moat so that his men could watch to see what the enemy did and bring him the news.

Now at dawn Wang the Tiger rose very early and he roused his guard and all his men were called by the blowing of bugles and drums and when they were assembled Wang the Tiger gave his commands that they were to be ready for battle when he called, even though it might be that they waited for a month or two. Then with his guard he went to a hill that was to the east of the city and there was an old pagoda there and he climbed up into it and his men he left below to guard him and to terrify the few old priests that were in a temple there, and he saw that while the city was not large, perhaps with not more than fifty thousand souls or so, still the houses were well built and the roofs were of a dark tile and piled upon each other like scales upon a fish's back. He went down then and back to his men and he led them across the moat, but as he did so, a shower of shots dropped from the high city wall, and Wang the Tiger withdrew again in haste.

Wang the Tiger could do no more then but wait, and he took counsel with his captains and these counselled a siege, for a siege is surer than a battle, since people must eat. This seemed a good thing to Wang the Tiger also, because his men must of a certainty be killed if he attacked the city now, and the gates were so strong, and the great beams so joined together with plates of iron, that Wang the Tiger did not know how to prevail against them. Moreover, if they guarded the locked gates so that no food could go in day after day, after a month or two the enemy must be weakened and submit, whereas if they fought now the enemy would be strong and well fed, and it could not be said certainly where the victory would turn. Thus Wang the Tiger reasoned and it seemed to him the better thing to wait until he could do battle and be sure of victory.

Therefore he ordered his soldiers to guard that whole city wall, but to stand back from it far enough so that shots could not reach them but would fall harmlessly into the moat. The soldiers did so encircle the walls and no one could come out or go in, and the soldiers fed on the produce of the land about there and they ate the fowls and the vegetables and the fruits and the grains that the farmers had, and since they paid something for all they took, the farmers did not join against them, and Wang the Tiger's army fared very well. The summer came on in its season and the land was good and the season was prosperous, for it was in these parts a year neither dry nor wet, although it was rumored that toward the west no rains had fallen behind the mountains and there would be famine in that place. When Wang the Tiger heard this, he said to himself that again his good destiny was over him that there was plenty here for him.

Thus a month passed and more and Wang the Tiger waited day after day in his tent and no one came out of that locked city. And he waited twenty more days and he grew very impatient and so did his men also, but the foe was doughty still, and if they went across the moat shots still popped out from the city wall. Wang the Tiger wondered very much and he said in his anger,

"What can they have left to eat that anyone has yet the strength to hold his weapon?"

And the Hawk, who stood by, spat in admiration of so good and brave an enemy and wiping his mouth on his hand he said,

"They must by now have eaten the dogs and the cats and the beasts of every kind and even the rats to be caught in their houses."

Thus the days passed and there came no sign out of the besieged city until the end of the second month of summer. Then as Wang the Tiger went out one morning as he did every day to see if there were any smallest change, he saw a white flag waved above the north gate where he was encamped. And in great haste and excitement he bade a man of his raise a white flag, too, and he exulted for he thought the end was come.

Then the north gate opened a little, and only wide enough to let one man through and it was shut and they could hear the scraping of the iron bars. And Wang the Tiger watched breathless on the other side of the moat where his camp was, and he saw a young man walking slowly toward him, carrying a white flag upon a bamboo pole. Then Wang the Tiger called to his men to stand in line, and he took his place just behind and they waited for the man, and he came near and he called out when he could be heard,

"I come to talk of peace and we will pay you a sum and all we have if you will go away in peace."

Then Wang the Tiger laughed his noiseless laugh and he said, sneering,

"Do you think I have come so far for money alone? I can get money in my own regions. No! Your lord of war must surrender to me for I need this city and this region and it shall be part of my own."

Then the young man leaned upon his pole and he looked

at Wang the Tiger with a look of death and he entreated, saying,

"Have mercy and take your men away!" And he fell on his face before Wang the Tiger.

But Wang the Tiger felt his anger begin to creep up in him as he always did when he was opposed and he was roused and he shouted,

"I will never go away until the land is mine!"

Then the young man rose and he threw back his head proudly and he said,

"Then stay, and spend your life here, for we can bear it!" and without another word he turned back toward the gate.

Then Wang the Tiger felt his old black anger come up in him and he said to himself that he was amazed that an importunate enemy should send so discourteous a messenger, who had not even performed any rites of courtesy, and to himself he thought that this was the most impudent young man he had ever seen, and the more he thought the more angry he grew and suddenly and before he knew it clearly himself he was furious and he called to a soldier,

"Lift me your gun and shoot that fellow!"

The soldier obeyed instantly and he shot very well for the young man fell face down upon a narrow bridge that crossed the moat and his flag fell into the water and the pole floated idly upon the surface of the moat and the whiteness of the flag was sullied with the muddy stream. Then Wang the Tiger commanded his men to run forward and fetch the young man, and they did, running swiftly lest a shot come down from the wall, but not one did come, and Wang the Tiger marvelled a little and wondered what this might mean. But he wondered still more when the young man lay before him dead and fast turning the hue of death, for this young man was not starving at all. No, when Wang the Tiger

328

ordered his clothes to be stripped from him so that he might see his flesh, there the young man lay, not fat but still filled out well so that it could be seen he had been fed with something.

Then was Wang the Tiger somewhat dashed at the sight and he was discouraged for the moment and he cried,

"If this fellow is as fat as he is, what have they to eat that they can last so well against me?" And he cursed and said, "Well, and I can spend my life at this as well as they can!"

Because he was so angry from this day he commanded his soldiers to make themselves easy and to take their comfort, and thereafter when he saw them taking food or goods from the people in the suburbs about that city or from farming folk here and there, he did not stop them as he once would have, and when a farmer came to complain or any came to swear against a soldier that he had come into a private house and done what he should not, Wang the Tiger said sullenly,

"You are an accursed lot, you people, and I believe you are sending food secretly into this city or else how can they be so long fed?"

But the farmers swore they were not and many times one would say piteously,

"What do we care what lord is over us, and do you think we love this old robber who has kept us half starved with his taxes? Sir, if you will only treat us with mercy and keep your men back fom evil, we will even be glad to have you in his place."

But Wang the Tiger grew surly as the summer wore on, and he cursed the heat and the myriads of flies that breeded upon the piles of filth the many soldiers must make, and the mosquitoes that came out of the stagnant moat, and he thought with impatience of the city where his own courts were and where his two wives waited for him, and all his anger made

329

him not so kind as he had been and his men grew very lawless and he let them be so.

There came one night in the time of the great heat, a very hot bright moonlight night and Wang the Tiger walked outside his tent for coolness, for he could not sleep. He walked alone except for his bodyguard who strolled yawning and half asleep behind him as he walked to and fro. And Wang stared as he ever did at the walls of the city and they stood high and black in the moonlight and it seemed unconquerable to him. And as he stared he grew very angry again, and indeed his anger was never cooled in these days, and he swore to himself very bitterly that he would make every man and woman and even the children in the city suffer for all the discomfort of this war he was waging. At that moment he saw a moving spot upon the blackness of the wall, a spot more black and moving downward. He stared and stood still. At first he could not believe he saw it but the longer he stood and stared the more he could see that there was something small and dark moving like a crab among the vines and the dry small trees that clung to that old wall. At last he saw that it was a man. Yes, the man reached the bottom and he dropped and came out into the moonlight and Wang the Tiger saw that he waved a white cloth.

Then Wang the Tiger commanded that one go to meet him bearing a white flag also, and he commanded that the man be brought to him and he stood and waited there and he strained his sight to see what this man was. When the man was come he threw himself at Wang the Tiger's feet and beat his head on the ground to beg for mercy. But Wang the Tiger shouted,

"Stand him on his feet and let me see him!"

Two soldiers came forward then and lifted the man and Wang the Tiger stared and as he stared he grew so angry that he felt a thickness in his throat, for this man was not yet starved. No, gaunt he was and very thin and black, but he was not starved and Wang the Tiger bellowed,

"Are you come to surrender the city?"

And the man said, "No, the chief will not surrender yet for he still has food, and we who are about him have some food given us every day. The people starve, it is true, but we can let them, and we are able to hold out yet awhile and we hope for help from the south for we have let a man over the wall secretly to go for it."

At this Wang the Tiger felt very insecure and he said doubtfully, holding back his anger as best he could,

"Why have you come if not to surrender?"

And the man said sullenly, "I do come only for my own sake. The general under whom I serve has used me very ill. Yes, he is only a coarse and hateful creature, wild and un-tutored, and I am a man of gentle blood. My father was even a scholar and I am used to courtesy. He has put me to great shame before my own soldiers. Now a man may forgive much, but he can never forgive being put to shame and it is insult not only to me but to my ancestors for whom I stand in these times, and his ancestors were, if he knows them at all, such as would be held serfs by mine."

"But how could he put you to such shame as this?" asked Wang the Tiger, and he was secretly much astonished at this turn.

And the man answered with a sullen passion, "He belittled me for the way I held my gun and this is my greatest skill and I can fell what I aim for without a miss."

Then a light began to come over Wang the Tiger, for well he knew that laughter and belittling can breed the bitterest hatred in a man's heart even against a friend, and a man will do anything for revenge if shame is put on him, especially

331

if he be a high proud fellow such as this man was in his looks. And Wang the Tiger said plainly,

"Tell me what your price is."

Then the man looked about him and here were the soldiers of Wang the Tiger's bodyguard, listening and their mouths ajar, and he bent and whispered,

"Let me go into your tent with you where I can speak out."

Then Wang the Tiger turned and strode into his tent and he commanded the man to be brought there and he left no more soldiers with him than five or six or so to guard against possible treachery from this man. But there was no treachery in this one, only revenge, and so Wang the Tiger found, for the man said,

"I am so filled with hatred and rage that I am willing to climb back over the wall and open the gate to you and I ask only one thing, that you will take me under your own banners and the few men who follow me whom I do not hate, and protect us, lest if the robber is not killed, I shall be sought for and killed, for he is a bitter enemy."

But Wang the Tiger would not have such generous help free and unrewarded with no more than this, and so he said, looking hard at the man as he stood before him between the two soldiers who held him,

"You are a very proper man not to bear insult and no good fellow will. I am glad to have so good and brave a man with me. Go back, then, and tell your fellows and all the soldiers that I will take them under my own banners, all who surrender themselves and their guns, and not one of them shall be killed. As for you, you shall be a captain in my army, and I will give you two hundred pieces of silver and five pieces to every man with his gun that you bring also."

Then the man's twisted face lightened and he cried warmly,

"You are such a general as I have been searching for all my life long, and I will surely open the gate to you at the moment when the sun is at its zenith on this very day now dawning!"

With this the man turned abruptly and went back and Wang the Tiger rose and went out of his tent and watched the man as he climbed nimbly and skilfully over the wall, catching hold of the roots and the gnarled trees as a monkey might, and so he climbed and disappeared over the wall.

By now the sun rose like a copper rim over the edge of the fields and Wang the Tiger commanded his men to be roused but quietly and without any noise lest some enemy see a commotion and suspect a new plan. But many of the men knew already that one had come out of the city and they had risen in the night and made ready without lighting a single torch. And indeed the light of the moon had been so bright that it was like a pale sun and the men could see such things even as how their triggers were set and where a string should pass through the eyelet of a shoe. By full sunrise every man was in his place and Wang the Tiger gave orders that to each meat should be given to eat and a full deep drink of wine to make his heart warm and brave, and thus fed and comforted the soldiers waited for the drum to beat that would send them forward.

Then as the sun rose high and full and beat down with a breathless heat upon the plain where the city lay, Wang the Tiger shouted from where he stood and his men gathered as they had been told to do in six long lines and when they heard their general shout every man shouted also, and the noise ran like an echo among them. And as they shouted every man lifted his weapon in his hands, each man a gun and a knife, and they all ran forward. Some crossed the moat by the bridge, but many ran across the shallow moat and clambered dripping up the further bank and they pressed against the city wall and clustered about the north gate. But the captains would not let Wang the Tiger stand too near the front, for they did not know at this last moment whether the man would be true or not or whether there would be treachery. Yet Wang the Tiger trusted the man because he knew that revenge is the surest sort of hatred.

Thus they waited, and not a sound came out of that city, and there was no sound of guns upon the city wall. Then as the sun swung upwards into its place in the zenith, Wang the Tiger stood stiff and watching, and he saw that great iron gate swing a little and one stooped and peered and there was a little crack of light along its top. He shouted once, and they rushed forward and Wang the Tiger with them and they pressed against the gate and burst it wide and they poured into the streets of that city like water freed from a dam, and the siege was ended.

Then Wang the Tiger did not stand a moment, but he commanded to be led instantly to the palace where the robber chief lived, and he shouted and roared at his men that they were not free yet and not until he had found the old chief. Then swiftly because of the haste of their greed his men hurried him to that palace, asking as they went and laying ruthless hold on any terrified man they saw. But when Wang the Tiger entered the courts of that palace with a great flourish of drums and bugles it was empty, for the robber chief had fled. How he had known of the betrayal could not be said, but as Wang the Tiger's men had poured into the north gate the old robber and his loyal followers escaped out of the south gate and were fleeing across the countryside. Wang the Tiger hearing this from soldiers who had not gone with him rushed upon the south wall of the city and looked out and far in the distance he could see but a flying cloud of dust. He was in two minds for a while whether or

334

not to pursue it, but it came to him that he had what he wanted and it was the city and the key to this region, and what did a robber and his few men mean?

So he went down then and back into the deserted palace, and there the many soldiers of the enemy who were left came to do obeisance and to beg his protection. He was pleased to see their number, for they came to him as he sat in the chief hall, and they came in tens and in twenties, the thinnest, most haggard men he had ever seen except in famine years. But they had their weapons and when they knelt before him and held out their hands to show their submission, Wang the Tiger accepted them and ordered that every man be fed as much as he was able to eat and that he be given five pieces of silver. But when the man who had betrayed the robber chief came in at the head of his company Wang the Tiger gave him the two hundred pieces of silver he had promised him and he gave it with his own hands and he commanded that captain's garb be brought and given to the man, too. Thus did Wang the Tiger remember what the man had done for him, and he rewarded him and took him into his own ranks.

When this was all finished then Wang the Tiger knew that the time had come when he must redeem his promise to his men, for he had held them as long as he could and they would not be longer held. And Wang the Tiger gave the command for their freedom, wishing he need not while he did. It was a strange thing that now that he had what he wanted his anger against the people was gone, and he shrank from making them suffer. Yet he must keep his word, too, to his men, and when he had given them their freedom for three days he shut himself into the palace and closed the gates and he was alone except for his bodyguard. Yet even these hundred men or so were very restless and demanded their turn, and at last Wang the Tiger had to tell them off and call others back in their place, and when these others came in with their eyes all red and lustful and their faces dark and flushed so that they could not subdue their wild looks, Wang the Tiger turned his eyes away and he would not think of what was going on in that city. When his nephew, whom he kept always by him, grew curious to go out and see what was to be seen, Wang the Tiger burst out on him, glad of one on whom he could with reason fix his anger, and he roared, "Shall my own blood go ravening out like these coarse and common men?"

And he would not let the young man move out of his sight, and kept him busy about his person fetching this or that to eat or to drink or some change he must have in his garments, and when weak cries came through even into the fast closed courts, Wang the Tiger was more imperious and more angry than ever with his nephew, so that the youth was kept all in a sweat with his uncle's temper, and he did not dare to answer him a word.

The truth was that Wang the Tiger could not be cruel unless he was angry, and indeed this was a weakness in a lord of war that he could only kill in anger, whose means to glory is death, and he knew it was his weakness that he could not kill coldly or carelessly or for a cause. And he thought it weakness that he could not keep his anger against the people and he told himself he ought still to hate them because they had been so dull and stubborn and had not thought of a way to open the gates to him. Yet when his soldiers came sheepishly to ask for their food, he cried at them in a confusion of fury and pain,

"What, must I feed you even when you loot?"

To this they made answer, "There is not a handful of grain in this whole city and we cannot eat gold and silver and silks.

336

These we find but no food, for the farmers are still afraid to come in with their produce."

And Wang the Tiger suffered and was sullen because he saw that what they said was true and he could not but order them fed, although when he did, he shouted in his surliest tones. But once he heard a hearty rude fellow cry coarsely,

"Yes, and the wenches are all so thin they are like plucked fowls and there is no pleasure in them at all!"

Then suddenly Wang the Tiger could not bear his life and he went away into a room by himself and he sat and groaned for a while before he could harden himself again. But he did harden himself once more. He thought of the fair lands and he thought how he had enlarged his power and how he had in this war more than doubled the country over which he ruled, and he told himself that it was his trade and his means of greatness and last and best he thought of the two women he had and how from one of them surely his son would be born, and he cried to his own heart,

"Cannot I for that one bear that others should somewhat suffer for three little days?"

Thus he hardened himself for the three days and he held himself to his promised word.

But on the dawn of the fourth day he rose up early from his restless bed and he ordered signals given and horns blown everywhere and it was a sign to all his soldiers that their looting was over and they must come back to his commands. And because he rose up that morning more than usually fierce and black in his looks and his black brows darted up and down over his eyes, none dared to disobey him.

No, none except one. As Wang the Tiger strode out of the gate that had been fast locked these three days he heard a feeble crying in an alley near by, and being made oversensitive to these cries now, he turned his long steps there to see

337

what it was. In that alley he saw a soldier of his on his way back to the ranks, but he had seen an old woman pass and on her finger was a thin, gold ring, a poor, small, worthless thing, too, for the old woman was only some working wife, and she could not have any great good thing. But the soldier had been overcome with a sudden desire for the last bit of gold and he wrenched at the old woman's hand and she cried out at him, wailing,

"It has been on my finger nigh upon thirty years and how can I loose it now?"

And the soldier was in such haste, for the bugle was blowing, that there before his own eyes Wang the Tiger saw the man whip out his knife and cut off the old woman's finger clean, and her poor scanty blood had still strength enough to spurt out in a feeble stream. Then Wang the Tiger gave a great roaring curse, for the soldier had not seen him he was in such haste, and Wang the Tiger sprang at the soldier and he drew out his keen blade as he sprang and drove it straight through the man's body. Yes, although it was his own man Wang the Tiger did it, because his anger came up in him so to see this wretched, starved creature dealt with as she had been before his very eyes. The soldier fell without a sigh and his own blood gushed out in a hearty, red stream. As for the old woman she was terrified at such fierceness, even if it was to succor her, and she wrapped her smarting stump in her old apron and ran and hid herself somewhere and Wang the Tiger did not see her again.

He wiped his sword on the soldier's coat, then, and he turned away lest he repent what he had done, and it was useless to repent, since the man was dead. He stayed only to command one of his guards to take the dead man's gun.

Then Wang the Tiger went through that city and he was astonished beyond any measure to see the few wretched people

there were and how they came crawling out into their doorways and sat listless on the benches upon their thresholds, too
weak to lift their heads even to look at Wang the Tiger as he
came striding along in the bright sunshine of autumn, and
his guards glittering and clattering behind him. No, they sat
there as though they were dead, so dull and still they were,
and some strange shame and astonishment was in Wang the
Tiger's heart so that he did not stay to talk with any man.
He held his head very high and he pretended he did not see
the people and only the shops. There were many goods in
these shops such as he had not seen before, since this city was
on the river to the south, and the river ran to the sea, and such
goods could be brought in. Yes, Wang the Tiger saw many
curious foreign things he had not seen before, but they were
carelessly placed now and covered with dust as though no one
had come to buy for a long time.

But two things he did not see in this city. He saw no food
anywhere for sale, and the market place was empty and silent
and there were no vendors or hucksters in the streets such as
make busy any town and city, and he saw no little children.
At first he did not notice how quiet the streets were and then
he noticed and wondered for the reason of the quietness and
then it came to him that he missed the noisy voices and
laughter of the children with which every house is filled in
usual times, and he missed their darting and running upon
the streets. And suddenly he could not bear to look at the
thin dark dull faces of the men and women who were left.
He had done no more than any lord of war may do, and it
could not be counted to him for a crime, since there was no
other way in which he could rise.

But Wang the Tiger was truly too merciful a man for his
trade and he turned and went back to his courts because he
could not bear to see this city now his, and he was cast down

339

and ill humored and he swore at his soldiers and he roared at them to be out of his way, for he could not endure at all the sound of their loud, satisfied laughter and the sight of their satiate glittering eyes, and he looked with rage upon the gold rings they had on their fingers and the foreign watches they had hung on them and many such things they had taken. Yes, he even saw gold rings on the fingers of his two trusty men, upon the Hawk's hard hand a ring of gold, and a jade ring upon the thumb of the Pig Butcher, that was so large and coarse a thumb the ring stuck half way upon the joint and would go no further. But still he wore it so. Seeing all this Wang the Tiger felt very far and separate from all these men and muttered to himself that they were low and beast-like fellows and he was lonely to the depths of his being and he went and sat alone in his room in mighty ill humor and bellowed for the smallest cause if anyone came near him.

But when he had sat thus a day or two and his soldiers, seeing how angry he was, were frightened and calmed themselves somewhat, Wang the Tiger hardened himself once more and he told himself that such were the ways of war and he had chosen this way of life and heaven had destined him as he was, and he must finish what he had begun. So he rose and washed himself, for he had sat these three days unwashed and unshaven, he was so angry, and he clothed himself freshly, and he sent a messenger to the magistrate of the city that he must come and submit himself. Then Wang the Tiger went into the guest hall of this palace and sat down there and waited for the man to come.

In an hour or two the magistrate came with what haste he could muster and he came in leaning on two men, a very ghastly, pale figure of a man he looked. But he bowed to Wang the Tiger and waited and Wang the Tiger saw this man was well born and a scholar by his gentle looks. He rose therefore and bowed in return and he motioned that the magistrate was to be seated. Then Wang the Tiger was seated too and he could but sit and stare at this other, for the magistrate's face and his hands were the strangest and most dreadful color, and it was the hue of a liver that has been dried for a day or two, and he was so thin one would have said his skin was glued to his bones.

Then Wang the Tiger cried out suddenly in the midst of his wonderment, "What—did you starve too?"

And the man answered simply, "Yes, since my people did also, and it is not the first time."

"But the man they sent out to make truce the first time was fed well enough," said Wang the Tiger.

"Yes, but they fed him specially from the first," answered the magistrate, "so that if you would not make truce you would see they had stores left to eat and could hold out longer."

Then Wang the Tiger could not but approve such good guile as this and he cried out in wonder and admiration of it, and he said,

"But the captain who came out was well fed, too!"

The magistrate answered simply, "They fed the soldiers best and to the last the best they could. But the people starved and many hundreds of them are dead. All the weak and the very old and the young are dead."

And Wang the Tiger heaved a sigh and said, "It is true I saw no babes anywhere." And he stared awhile at the magistrate and then he forced himself to say what he must and he said, "Submit yourself to me now, for I have won the right to take that other lord of war's place over you and over this whole region over which he ruled. I am the ruler now and I add this to my dominion I have already to the north. The revenues shall come into my hand now, and I will demand of

341

you a certain sum fixed and beyond that a proportion of revenues every month."

This Wang the Tiger said with some few courteous words afterwards, for he was not devoid of such courtesy. The magistrate answered in his weak and hollow voice, moving his dry lips over teeth that seemed too large and white for his drawn mouth,

"We are in your power. Only give us a month or two to recover ourselves." Then he waited awhile and he said again with great bitterness, "What is it to us who rules over us if we can only have peace and if we can only pursue our business and have a livelihood and nurture our children? I swear I and my people are willing to pay you in all reason if you will only be strong enough to keep off other lords of war and let us live secure in our generation."

This was all Wang the Tiger cared to know, and now his merciful heart smote him to hear the man's feeble, breathy voice and he cried out to his soldiers,

"Bring in food and wine and feed him and the men with him!" And when he had seen this done, he called his trusty men to him and he commanded again, "Go out now into the countryside and take soldiers and compel the farmers to come in with their grains and their produce so that the people may buy and eat and recover themselves again after this very bitter war."

So did Wang the Tiger show his justice to all the people and the magistrate thanked him, and he was moved with his gratitude. Then Wang the Tiger saw how courteous and gently born and reared this magistrate was for even half starved as he was and his eyes glittered at the food that was set on a table before him, he restrained himself and he dallied and delayed, his trembling hands clasped tightly together, until all the polite and courteous things were said that should be said from guest to host and until Wang the Tiger could seat himself in the host's place. Then the poor man fell upon the food, and still he tried to hold himself back and in very pity Wang the Tiger at last made excuse that he had some affair to which he must go. He went away then and let the man eat alone, for his underlings ate separately, and afterwards Wang the Tiger heard his men say in wonder that the dishes and bowls needed no washing so clean the starving men had licked them.

Then Wang the Tiger took the sweetest pleasure in seeing the markets of that city fill again and in seeing the food begin to lie in vendors' baskets along the sides of the streets and on the counters, and he thought he could see day by day that men and women grew fatter and the dark livid hue left their faces and they won back their clear and golden color of health. All through the winter Wang the Tiger lived in that city, arranging for his revenues and shaping affairs anew, and he rejoiced when children began to be born and women suckled babes again, and the sight stirred some deep in his own heart that he did not understand, except that a longing fell on him to return to his own courts and for the first time he wondered concerning his own two women. And he planned to return to his own house at the end of that year.

Now when Wang the Tiger had finished his siege of the city the spies whom he kept out in other parts had come to him and told him that there was a great war waging between north and south and again they came and said the north had won that war once more. Then Wang the Tiger made haste and he sent a band of men bearing gifts of silver and of silks and he wrote a letter to the general of the province. This letter Wang the Tiger wrote himself, for he was a little vain of his learning, since few lords of war are learned, and he set on it his own great red seal that he had now he was grown great.

In the letter he told how he had fought against a southern general and had defeated him and had taken this region that ran by this river for the north.

Then the general sent back a very good answer, full of praise for Wang the Tiger's success, and he gave him a very fine new title, and all he asked was that a certain sum be sent him every year for the provincial army. Then Wang the Tiger, since he knew he was not strong enough yet to refuse, promised the sum, and thus he established himself in the state.

As the end of the year drew near and Wang the Tiger took stock of his position, he found he had more than doubled his territories, and except for the mountainous parts which were bare, the lands were good and fertile producing both wheat and rice in measure, and besides this, salt and oils of peanuts and sesame and beans. Now, moreover, he had his own way to the sea and he could bring in much he needed and he could be free of Wang the Merchant his brother, when he wanted guns.

For Wang the Tiger longed very much to have great foreign guns, and the longing came to him especially because among the things the old robber chief had left were two very strange, huge guns such as Wang the Tiger had never seen before. They were of a very good iron without bubbles or holes of any sort in it, and so smooth that some clever ironsmith must have shaped them. These guns were heavy, too, so heavy that more than twenty men must put forth their utmost strength to lift them up at all.

And Wang the Tiger was very curious about these guns and he longed to see how to fire them, but no one knew how to do it, nor could they find any bullets for them. But at last two round iron balls were found hid in an old storehouse, and it came to Wang the Tiger that these were for the great guns, and he was in great delight and he had one of the guns taken

344

out into an open spot in front of an old temple which had a waste place behind it. At first no one would come forward to try the gun, but Wang the Tiger offered a very good reward of silver, and at last the captain who had betrayed the city came forward, wanting the reward and hoping to gain favor, and he had seen the guns fired once, and he set all in readiness and very cleverly he fastened a torch on to the end of a long pole and set fire to the gun from a distance. When they saw the smoke begin they all ran a long way off and waited, and the gun blew off its great charge and the earth shook and the very heavens roared and smoke and fire streamed out, so that even Wang the Tiger was staggered and his heart stopped for an instant's fear. But when it was over they all looked and there the old temple lay in a heap of dusty ruins. Then Wang the Tiger laughed his noiseless laugh, and he was struck with delight at so good a toy as this and so fine a weapon of war, and he cried out,

"If I had had a gun like this there would have been no siege for I would have blown the city gates in!" And he thought a moment and he asked the captain, "But why did not your old chief turn them upon us?"

To this the captain said, "We did not think of it. These two guns he captured from another lord of war with whom I was once also, and they were brought here but never fired, and we did not know these balls were here and we did not think of these guns as weapons at all, so long they have stood here in the entrance court."

But Wang the Tiger treasured these great guns very much and he planned he would buy more balls for them and he had them brought and set where he could often see them.

When he had taken stock of all he had done, Wang the Tiger was well pleased with himself and he prepared to return to his home. He left a good large army in that city led by his own old men, and the newest men and the new captain he took back with him. After some pondering, he left in highest command in this city two whom he could trust. He left the Hawk and he left his nephew, who was grown now into a goodly young man, not tall but broad and strong and not ill to look at except for his pocked face which would be marred like that even when he lay dead of old age. It seemed to Wang the Tiger a good pair to leave, for the young man was too young to take command alone, and the Hawk could not be wholly trusted. So Wang the Tiger set them together and he told the young man secretly,

"If you believe he thinks of any treachery, send a messenger to me on wings by night and by day."

The youth promised, his eyes merry with his joy to be lifted up so high and left alone, and Wang the Tiger could go and be at ease, for a man can trust those of his own blood. Then having done all well and made all secure, Wang the Tiger returned victorious to his own home.

As for the people of that city they set themselves steadfastly again to build up once more what had been destroyed. Once more they filled their shops and set to work their looms to make silk and cotton cloths, and they bought and sold and they never talked except of such renewal, for what was passed, had passed, and Heaven lays its destiny upon all.

XXIII

WANG THE TIGER made haste on his homeward journey, although he said it was to see if his army were peaceful as he had left it. And he truly thought this was the chief reason, for he did not understand himself that he made haste for a deeper cause than this and it was to see if he had any son born to him or not. He had been away from his house close upon ten months out of a year, and although he had twice received letters from his learned wife in that time they were such very proper letters and full of such respect, that the sheet was full of these words, and little else said except that all was well enough.

But the moment he stepped into his own courts triumphantly, he saw at a glance that Heaven was over him still and his good destiny still held, for there in the sunny court, where the south sun shone warm and there was no wind, sat his two wives, and each held a babe, and each babe was dressed in scarlet from head to foot, and upon their doddering little heads were crownless scarlet caps. The unlearned wife had sewed a row of small gold Buddhas upon her child's cap, but the learned wife, because she was so learned, did not believe in these tokens of good fortune, and she had embroidered flowers upon her child's cap. Except for this, there seemed no difference in the pair of children, and Wang the Tiger blinked at them amazed, for he had not thought of two. He stammered out,

"What—what—"

Then the learned wife rose, for she was quick and graceful in speech and she spoke prettily always, very smoothly and throwing in a learned phrase or a line from some old poem or classic, and she made a show of her shining white teeth as she spoke, and she said, smiling,

"These are the babes we have borne for you while you were away, and they are strong and sound from head to foot," and she held up her own for Wang the Tiger to see.

But the other wife would not have it held back that she had borne a son, for the learned wife's was a daughter, and she rose too and made haste to say, although she spoke seldom

347

because of her blackened teeth and the gaps where she had none, and now she held her lips close and she said,

"Mine is the son, my lord, and the other is a girl."

But Wang the Tiger said nothing at all. Indeed he could not speak for he had not known all it would be to have something of his own making belong to him like this. He stood and stared for a while speechless at these two minute creatures who seemed not to see him at all. No, they looked placidly at him as though he had always been there like a tree or a bit of the wall. They winked and blinked at the sunlight and the boy sneezed overloudly for his size so that Wang the Tiger was yet more astonished at such a gust coming out of so small a fragment. But the girl child only opened her mouth as a kitten does, and yawned very widely, and her father stared at her while she did. He had never held a child in his arms, and he did not touch these two. Nor did he know what to say to these two women at such a time, seeing that his speech had always been of warlike things. He could only smile somewhat fixedly, therefore, even while the men who were with him exclaimed in joy and admiration at the son their general had, and when he heard these exclamations he muttered out of his deep pleasure,

"Well, and I suppose women will breed!" and he went hastily into his apartments, being too full of joy for his own comfort.

There he washed and ate and he changed his stiff garments of war for a silk robe of a deep dark blue, and when it was all finished it was evening. Then he sat down by the brazier of coals, for the night came on quiet and chill with frost and there Wang the Tiger sat alone and reflected on all that had come about.

It seemed to him that destiny favored him at every point, and so favored there was nothing to which he could now attain. Now that he had a son his ambition took on meaning and what he did, he did for a purpose. As he thought his heart swelled in him, and he forgot every sorrow and loneliness he ever had, and he shouted suddenly into the stillness of the room,

"I will make a true warrior out of that son of mine!" and he rose and slapped his hand against his thigh in his pleasure.

He strode about the room then for a while, smiling without knowing he did, and he thought what a comfortable thing it was to have a son of his own, and he thought how now he need depend no more on his brothers' sons, for there was his own son to continue his life after him and to increase his domains of war. Then another thought came to him and it was that he also had a daughter. He spent a little time then wondering what he would do with her, and he stood by the latticed window and fingered the hairs of his beard, and thought of his daughter with reticence because she was a girl and at last he said to himself in some doubt,

"I suppose I can wed her to some good warrior when the time comes, and it is all that I can do for her."

From this day on Wang the Tiger saw a new purpose in those two women of his, for from them he saw springing yet more sons, true and loyal sons who would never betray him as might another who had not his own blood in him. No longer did he use those two women to free his own heart and flesh. His heart was freed at the first sight of his son, and of his flesh he hoped for his sons, trusty soldiers to stand beside him and support him when he grew old and weak. So he went regularly to his two wives, and not more to one than the other, for all their secret gentle striving for his favor, and he was very well content with them each in her own way, for he sought from them equally but the one thing, and he did not hope for more from the one than from the other. It trou-

349

bled him no more that he did not love a woman, now that he had his son.

Thus the winter passed in content. The New Year festival came and passed also, and Wang the Tiger made more merriment than usual because the year had been so good, and he rewarded all his men with wine and meats and with a bounty of silver. To each man he gave also such small things as they craved, tobacco, a towel, a pair of socks, and other small things. To his wives also he made a bounty and at the festival the whole house was very merry. There was but one untoward thing and it came after the feast day, so that no joy was curtailed. This was that the old magistrate died one night in his sleep. Whether he took too much opium, being heavy with his sleep, or whether the bitter cold overcame him in his drugged heaviness, could not be known. But the matter was reported to Wang the Tiger and he ordered a good coffin and all to be done for the gentle old man, and the very next day after it was all finished and the coffin ready to be sent to his old home, for the magistrate had not been native to the province, one came again to tell that his old wife had taken what was left of her husband's opium and so followed him of her own will. Nor could any grieve, for she was old and sickly and she never came out of her own courts, and Wang the Tiger had never seen her in his life. He ordered another coffin, therefore, and when all was ready he sent them with three serving men to be taken to their own city in the next province. Then Wang the Tiger sent report in proper form to those above who should know of it, and he sent his trusty harelipped man with the letter and with him some soldiers, and Wang the Tiger said secretly to the trusty man,

"There are things not to be said except by mouth to ear, and so I have not written this. But if the chance comes to you let it be known that I must have a say in who shall be the civil magistrate here."

The trusty man nodded his head at this and Wang the Tiger was content. In such confused times as these he did not fear the hasty coming of any governor, and he could rule very well himself. So he forgot the matter and he took for his own wives the innermost rooms where the old magistrate had lived and soon he had forgot that any had ever lived here except himself and his own.

The year drew on then to spring again, and Wang the Tiger made up his mind, since he had been so fortunate this year in everything and he had good reports from his new lands and the silver flowed in regularly from all his many revenues so that his soldiers were paid and content and loud in his praise, that he would return for the spring festival to his father's house and pass the feast day with his brothers. It was a fitting thing for a great house to do, the more especially as it is a season when the sons should repair their father's grave. Wang the Tiger, moreover, had a little reckoning yet to do with his second brother, and he was ready now to be free of such borrowing, and he wished to be free. Therefore Wang the Tiger sent some soldiers to tell his elder brothers, with all decent courtesies, that he and his wives and his children and their servants would come by the feast day. To this the two brothers, Wang the Landlord and Wang the Merchant, returned very courteous words of welcome.

When all was ready, then, Wang the Tiger mounted his high red horse and at the head of his guard rode forth. But this time they must needs ride slowly for there were the mule carts where the two women rode and other mule carts for the maid servants. And Wang the Tiger did ride slowly and he was proud to do it for such a cause. Riding thus at the head of his cavalcade, his women and his children, he took his place

351

in the generations. Never did his lands look so fair to him nor so prosperous as they did in this time of bursting spring, of budding willow and unfolding peach blossoms. And seeing the faint tinge of green and peach in every valley and upon every hillside, and seeing the deep brown of moist earth turned to the spring sunshine, he remembered suddenly his father and how every spring he loved to pluck a sprig of willow and a sprig of blooming peach and carry them in his hand or put them above the door of the earthen house, and thinking of his father and of his own son, Wang the Tiger felt his place in the long line of life, and he was never any more separate as he had once been, nor alone. For the first time he forgave his father wholly for certain deep angers he had against him as a youth. Nor did he know he forgave. He only knew that some bitterness left in him since his angry boyhood slipped out of him and was blown away as though on a healthy wind, and he was peaceful with himself, at last.

So Wang the Tiger came to his father's house and he came in triumph and not so much as youngest son and youngest brother, but as a man in his own right by what he had achieved and by the son he had begotten. And they all felt his achievement, and his brothers met him and welcomed him very nearly as though he were a guest, and his brothers' wives contended with each other as to who should be most voluble and ready in her welcome.

The truth of it was that the lady of Wang the Landlord and the wife of Wang the Merchant had struggled with each other as to who should house Wang the Tiger and his family. The lady took it as a matter of course and her right that they should come to her lord's house, for now as Wang the Tiger's fame began to be known she felt it would be an honorable thing to have him as guest and she said,

"It will be fitting, for we chose his wife for him, a very

learned and pleasant lady, and she can scarcely be at home with your brother's wife, who is so ignorant. Let her keep the lesser wife if she wishes, but we must have our brother and his lady here. He may be moved by one of our sons or he may be able to do us some great good. At the very least he will not be subject to her hints and desires!"

But the wife of Wang the Merchant said to him importunately and often, and she would not give up her wish at all,

"How can our brother's woman know how to feed such a number, and she only used to feeding nuns and priests with their poor vegetable stuffs?"

There came to be such anger that these two women quarreled face to face over the matter, and, seeing the coming and the going and hearing the loud talk that grew more loud as the festival day drew near, and seeing that nothing could be decided and that each wife for pride's sake would not give up a smallest point, the two husbands met together in their old trysting place in the tea house, for they were united as they never could have been otherwise by the enmity of their two wives. There they consulted together and Wang the Merchant, who had made his plan, said to his brother,

"Let it be as you say, but what do you think if we put our brother and his retinue into that court our father left empty? True, it belongs to his wife Lotus, but she is so very old now and uses it not at all since she has given up gaming, and if we put them there we can divide the expense between us, and this we can use as a reason to our two ladies and so have peace again."

Now once Wang the Landlord would have wished to use some way he had thought of alone, but as he grew older and so monstrous in his girth he grew exceedingly slothful and he was drowsy much of the day, and he would do anything to avoid trouble. This plan then seemed very good to him, and he wanted to have his powerful younger brother's favor, but still he did not care so much if his second brother did not have more than he. In his growing indolence he had passed the time when he loved guests as he once did, and he was glad not to have those in his house now to whom he must be courteous in season and out of season and so weary himself. He agreed willingly, therefore, and each man went home to his wife and told her the plan. It was a very good compromise for all, for none lost her way altogether, and each determined secretly to seem to be the one responsible for their comfort, and yet each was pleased that the vast cost of wines and feasts and bounty for serving men and women would be halved, and to all of them this was a sound reason enough.

Then those old courts where Wang Lung had lived in the years of his later middle life were swept and garnished and made clean. It was true that Lotus never went into them, and the serving maids sat in them sometimes but that was all. Lotus was grown very huge and old now, and Cuckoo was her only companion except her slaves, for as she grew old Lotus's eyes were filmed and she could not even see at last to cast dice in gaming or to see what the numbers were in any of the games of chance she loved. One by one the old crones who had used to come to her died, or were bedridden, and only Lotus lived on, alone with those who served her.

Her slaves she used very bitterly, and as her eyes failed her tongue grew cruelly sharp, so that the brothers had to pay maid servants very high wages or they could not bear her tongue. As for the slaves who were bought and could not leave if they liked, two of them killed themselves, one of them swallowing her poor glass earrings and the other hanging herself on a beam in one of the kitchens where she

354

worked, rather than endure longer Lotus's cruelties. For Lotus would not only wield her tongue coarsely, shrieking out such words as maids cannot bear to hear, but she would nip them cruelly. Her fat old fingers, that were so useless in the strange beauty they still kept and they were smooth and beautiful when all other beauty had faded from her, those old fingers could nip and pinch a young girl's arm until the blood came purple under the skin, and sometimes when this did not satisfy her, Lotus would take the coals out of her pipe and press them into tender young flesh. There was not one whom she did not treat thus if she could except Cuckoo, and she feared Cuckoo, and leaned upon her for everything.

For Cuckoo was what she ever was. In her age, and she was very old now also, she seemed to grow more thin and dry and withered and yet she had a strength in her old frame that was almost what it had been in youth. Her eyes were sharp and her tongue harsh and her face, although wrinkled all over, was still red. She was greedy, too, as ever she had been, and if she guarded her mistress against the thievery of other serving women, she herself thieved most hardily from Lotus. Now that Lotus's eyes were filmed, Cuckoo took what she liked from Lotus and she swelled her own private store, and Lotus, being so old, forgot what jewels she had and what fur garments and what garments of satin and silk, and so she did not know what Cuckoo took. If by chance she remembered and cried out for something of a sudden, Cuckoo diverted her if she could, and if Lotus was perverse and would not forget, Cuckoo went and fetched the thing from her own boxes and gave it to Lotus. But when, after fingering it a time or two Lotus forgot again, Cuckoo took it and kept it once more.

Nor did a slave or serving woman dare complain, for

Cuckoo was the real mistress there, and even the brothers deferred to her, for they knew they could find no one to take her place and they dared not anger her. When therefore Cuckoo said Lotus had given her this or that, the maids were silent, for they knew well that if they complained, Cuckoo was so bitter and evil she could have put poison into a bowl of food and thought nothing of it, and sometimes she would boast of all the skill she had in poisoning to keep them afraid. As for Lotus, she leaned on Cuckoo for everything, as she grew blind, and now because of the mighty weight of her flesh she walked no more except from her bed to the great chair of carved black wood where she sat a little while after noon and then back to her bed again. Even so she must be supported by four slaves and more, for those pretty little feet of hers which had once been Wang Lung's pride and pleasure were nothing but stumps beneath the great and monstrous body which in other days had been slender as a bamboo and passionately beloved by Wang Lung.

When one day Lotus heard the commotion in the courts next hers and when she asked and heard that Wang the Tiger was coming with his women and children to pass the feast day and worship at his father's grave with his brothers, she grew petulant and she said,

"I cannot have brats here! I have always hated brats!"

This was true for she was a childless woman and had always some strange hatred against little children, and especially when she passed her time of such fruitage. Then Wang the Landlord who had come in with his brother, soothed her and he said,

"No, no, we will open the other gate so that he need not come near you at all."

Then Lotus cried again in her old, querulous way,

"I forget what son he was of that old man of mine! Was

he the one who used to stare at that pale slave I once had and he ran away when that silly old man of mine took her for himself?"

Then both brothers looked at each other aghast and they were astonished at this tale and had never heard it, and Wang the Merchant said hastily, for Lotus was now very free and obscene in her old age and talked of her early life so that neither brother allowed his children to come near her for she did not know decency from indecency and all her old life would come bubbling to the surface of her lips sometimes, and he said,

"We know nothing of this. Our brother is now a famous lord of war and he will ill brook such talk as this against his honor."

But Lotus when she heard this laughed and she spat upon the tile floor and she cried out,

"Oh, and you men are so full of your honor but we women know what poor stuff your honor is made of!" And she listened for Cuckoo to laugh also, and she cried out, "Eh, Cuckoo?" and Cuckoo, who was never far away, gave her thin shrill cackle of laughter, for she was pleased to see these two middle-aged men, each grave and important in his own way, put to such confusion. As for the two brothers, they hurried away to direct the serving men in all that must be done.

When all was ready Wang the Tiger came with his house, and he took up his abode in these days in the court where his father had lived. It was empty for him, now, and swept at last of every presence except his own and his son's and he could forget that anyone had ever lived there except himself and his son.

Then the festival came to this whole house, the festival of spring, and everyone laid aside his private grudge for the once; even the wives of the two elder brothers, when they came together in the family, were formal and courteous with each other. Everything was done in its proper order and in the way it should be done, and there were certain duties at this time which the sons of Wang Lung had toward their father.

It happened that two days before the festival day was Wang Lung's birthday. Wherever he was, on this day he was ninety years old, and since his sons were together they determined to perform their whole filial duty and Wang the Tiger was very ready because since he had his own son his anger against his father had gone of its own accord and he was left ready and eager to take his place in the line of father and son and father and son.

On this birthday of Wang Lung's, therefore, his sons invited many guests and a great feast was prepared, such a feast as they would have made if their father had been with them, and there was rejoicing and congratulation and there was every dish such as is proper at a birthday feast. And they had Wang Lung's tablet there and made obeisance to it and they did him honor on his birthday.

On the same day Wang the Landlord hired priests and he spared no money and each son gave his share, and the priests chanted all their chants for Wang Lung's spirit to give it rest and joy in the happy courts where it now was, and they decked the hall with their sacred emblems and signs, and for half a day the courts were filled with the rise and the fall of their chanting voices and the dull thick sound of the wooden sticks upon their drums of wood.

All this did Wang Lung's sons do in his memory. Beyond this they and their wives and their sons went out to the place where the graves of their fathers were, and Wang Lung's sons saw to it that every grave was made straight and smooth and heaped high with fresh earth. Each grave was shaped to a point and upon the point a clod of earth was put, and white paper cut cunningly into long strips was fastened beneath the clod and streamed in the sweet spring wind of that day. And Wang Lung's sons bowed to the earth before his grave and they set incense to burn, and they brought their sons to bow, and proudest of them all was Wang the Tiger, for he took his own fair son and he bowed the child's little head, too, and he was knit to his fathers and to his brothers through this child, his son.

And as they went home again they saw that over the whole countryside, wherever there were fathers' graves and grandfathers' graves, there were sons who did what they had done for Wang Lung this day, for it was a day of remembrance. Then Wang the Landlord was more moved than he usually was, and he said,

"Let us do this more regularly than we have in past years, for we have but ten more years and our father will be a hundred years old, and then he will have been born again into another body in this world, and we cannot feast his birthday, for it will be a new birth and he will be unknown to us."

And Wang the Tiger, grave in his fatherhood, said, "Yes, we ought so to do for him as we hope our sons will do for us when we are where he is now."

And they went homewards in silence and gravity, each feeling his kinship to the others more than was wont with any of them.

After these duties were over, they all set themselves to the merriment of the festival, and when the day of the festival came to evening the air was unexpectedly warm and sweet and a little slender perfect moon hung in the sky, clear and pale as amber. On this night they all gathered in the court where

359

Lotus lived, for she had that day turned plaintive all of a sudden and she said,

"I am a lonely old woman and they never come near me nor hold me as one of this house at all!"

And she moaned and wept tears out of her blind old eyes so that Cuckoo went and told the brothers, and they yielded to her because this day their hearts were unexpectedly tender toward their father and what had been his. Instead, therefore, of feasting in the courts of Wang the Landlord, where his lady would have had the family gather, they went to the court where Lotus lived. It was a large and beautiful court, too, with pomegranate trees brought from the south in one corner, and in the center was a small octagonal pool where the new little moon shone reflected. There they all ate cakes and drank wine, and the children rejoiced in the moon's light and they ran everywhere hiding in and out of the shadows and running out again to seize a cake or sup a little wine. They all ate their fill of the steamed delicacies and cakes suitable to this festival, some stuffed with pork chopped fine, and some with brown sugar and very dainty. There was so much that even the slaves ate freely and the servants filched and ate behind doors or when they went on a pretense to fetch more wine. Nor was it missed what they took, or if the mistresses' sharp eyes noted it, at least for once nothing was said, so that no reproof might mar the night.

And as they ate and drank, Wang the Landlord's eldest son, who was a very pretty musician, played upon a flute, and his next brother, a lad with nimble, delicate fingers, played upon a harp whose strings he struck lightly with two slender bamboo sticks, and they played ancient songs to the spring, and sang a plaint or two of some dead maiden's to the moon. When they played so well together, their mother

360

was very proud, and she commended them often and cried loudly as soon as one song was finished,

"Play something else, my sons, for it is pretty to play like this under the new moon!" And she was proud of their slender, lovely looks.

But the wife of Wang the Merchant, whose sons were plainly taught and who knew no toying with music, yawned and talked aloud to this one and to that one, but most of all to the wife she had chosen for Wang the Tiger. She made very much of this one and she was pointed in her ignoring of the learned wife; she scarcely glanced at Wang the Tiger's daughter, but she could never be done with smelling and nuzzling the boy child, and one might have thought it all due to her that the child was a boy.

But still there was nothing open said, although the lady darted looks of displeasure at her sister-in-law and that one caught them all and took delight in pretending she did not. But no one else seemed to see, and Wang the Landlord roused himself and he ordered the servants to bring the tables for the night's feast into the courts, and they did. Then everyone set himself to the real food, and the serving men brought in one dainty dish after another, for Wang the Landlord gave this feast to them, and he had outdone himself in ordering it. There were many dishes that Wang the Merchant and Wang the Tiger had never even heard of, such as ducks' tongues stewed with spices and ducks' feet with the dainty black skin peeled from them, and there were many such fine dishes that tickled the tongue very well.

Of all those who ate and drank heartily that night none ate and drank more heartily than Lotus, and the more she ate the more she was moved with merriment. She sat in her great carved chair and there was a slave beside her to put some of every dish into her bowl, but sometimes she would dip for herself, and a slave guided her hand then and she dipped her porcelain spoon into the dish and put it eagerly to her trembling old mouth and supped it loudly. Meats and all she ate, for she had her teeth all strong and sound still.

Then as she grew more merry she paused sometimes in her eating to tell a lewd coarse tale or two that made the young men laugh as much as they dared but they dared not laugh too much before their elders. But she listened for their choking and bursting laughter, and was encouraged to other tales. Wang the Landlord himself could scarcely keep his face decent except that his lady sat there stiff and silent and he could look at her and be grave. But the ruddy wife of Wang the Merchant guffawed loudly and the more loudly when she saw that her sister-in-law would not laugh at all. Even Wang the Landlord's second wife bit her lips, and while she would not laugh because her lady did not, still she was fain to hold her sleeve across her face and smile behind it.

But Lotus grew so free at last when she listened and heard men laugh that for shame's sake she must be silenced, and so the two older brothers plied her with wines to make her drowsy and the more since they feared she would say some very lewd thing about Wang the Tiger and anger him, and they feared his anger. Because of this tongue of Lotus's they had not urged Pear Blossom to come to the family feast, and when she answered the messenger they sent that she could ill leave her charges, they let her be, deeming it were best to rouse no memories in Lotus.

Thus the night passed happily and midnight came and the moon swung high, and soft clouds came up and seemed to swing the moon here and there. The babes were asleep in their mothers' bosoms, for the youngest in every family sought long ago his mother's breasts, except the youngest of

Wang the Landlord's lady, who was by now a proud and slender girl of thirteen, grave because she was betrothed not long ago. But Wang the Landlord's second wife was a warm mother, and she had two in her arms, one a child of a year and more, and the other newly born but a little over a month, for Wang the Landlord still liked her. As for Wang the Tiger's wives, each held her own, and his little son slept with his head thrown back over his mother's arm and the moonlight fell full on his face, and Wang the Tiger looked often at that small sleeping face.

But after midnight the merriment waned, and the sons of Wang the Landlord slipped away one by one, for they had other pleasures waiting, and it wearied them to sit long with elderly folk. They went easily and carelessly, and the second son of Wang the Merchant looked longingly after them, but he dared not go because he feared his father. The servants also grew weary and longed for their rest, and they withdrew and leaned in this doorway and that, yawning mightily, and muttering to each other,

"Their children waked at dawn and we had to tend them and now the old ones feast to midnight and we must tend them still! Will they never let us sleep?"

But at last they did separate, but not before Wang the Landlord was drunken, and his lady called for his serving men to come and let him lean upon them and so go to his bed. Even Wang the Tiger was nearer drunken than he had ever been, but he could walk into his own court. Only Wang the Merchant was as smooth and neat as ever, and his wrinkled yellow face was scarcely changed at all, and not red even, for he was one of those who grow more pale and quiet as he drinks more deeply.

But of them all not one had eaten and drunk as Lotus had, and indeed, old as she was now and nearly seventy-eight years old, she had eaten and drunk too well. In the middle hours between midnight and dawn she moaned and was very restless, for the wine she had drunk seemed to come up in her and heat her to a mighty fever and all the meats and oily dishes she had eaten lay heavy in her as stone. She turned her head this way and that upon her pillow and was ill at ease and called out for one thing and another, but nothing eased her. Then suddenly she gave a strange hoarse scream and Cuckoo ran to her, and when she heard Cuckoo call out, Lotus muttered something and stared out of her filmed eyes and tossed her arms and legs and was suddenly still. Then her fat old face grew dark and purple and her body rigid and stiff, and she began to draw her breath in quick, stammering gusts, loud enough to be heard in the next court. Wang the Tiger would have heard her if he had not been somewhat drunken and so sleeping more heavily than his wont.

But his learned wife slept lightly always and she heard the cry and rose and came in. She had some slight knowledge of old medicines from her father, who was a physician, and now she drew aside the curtain and the light of earliest dawn fell upon Lotus's frightful face. Then the learned woman cried out, aghast,

"It is the old lady's end come on her if we cannot purge her of her wines and meats!"

She called for hot water and for ginger and for all the medicines she knew and she tried them all. But it was no use, for Lotus was deaf to all calls and entreaties now, and her teeth were so locked that even when they forced her blackened lips apart, her teeth were locked inside. It was the strangest thing that in an old body like this her teeth should still be sound and white and good, and they lost her her life now, for if there had been a hole somewhere or a gap

364

where a tooth was gone, they would have poured the medicine in somehow, and Cuckoo could even have taken a mouthful and spurted it in with her own lips. But the sound whole teeth were fast and locked.

So Lotus lay breathing and snorting through half the next day, and suddenly, without ever knowing this was her end, she died. The purple of her face faded away and she turned as pale and as yellow as old wax. Thus did the feasting time end in this death.

Then the two elder brothers saw to the making of her coffin, but they had to let her lie a day or so, for the coffin had to be built twice as big as common, and there was none to be found made ready that was broad enough.

And while they waited Cuckoo truly mourned this creature she had tended all these years. Yes, she truly mourned her, even though she went about and collected all she could of the things that were Lotus's still, opening this box and that and taking all of any value, and she sent her stores out secretly through a hidden back gate, so that at last when Lotus was put into her coffin those who served her marvelled that she had scarcely a coat fit to be buried in and they wondered what she had done with the good sum of silver she had as Wang Lung's widow, seeing she had not gamed it away of late years. Yet for all her thieving Cuckoo mourned for Lotus, and she wiped a few scanty tears away, which if they were few were the only tears she had ever shed for anyone, and when the coffin was filled with lime, for Lotus had begun to stink very soon, and when the lid was sealed down and it was carried out the gate to the temple where it was to lie until a day of burial was chosen, Cuckoo walked after the coffin and hurried her old feet to keep in sight of it until it was put into the empty room of the temple among many other coffins already there. Then she turned away and went to some place of her own she had somewhere, and came no more to the house of Wang, and she mourned Lotus truly and as truly as she was able.

Before the ten allotted days were past Wang the Tiger was weary of his brothers and their sons and the hour of close kinship they had felt in the festival was gone. But he sat the days out and he watched the coming and going of his brothers' sons as he went to this house and to that sometimes and it seemed to him that these sons were but poor weak fellows and promised no great good. The two younger sons of Wang the Merchant looked no higher than to be clerks and they had no ambition except to idle over a counter and laugh and gossip with the other clerks if their father was not by to see them at it, and even the younger one who was but twelve years old was apprenticed in a shop and spent his every moment that he dared in tossing pennies with the urchins on the street who gathered at the shop door to wait for him, and because he was the master's son none dared to say anything against him nor to refuse him a handful of pennies if he clamored for them out of the shop's till, although they all kept a sharp eye out to see if the lad's father came so that he might run back to his place while Wang the Merchant passed. And Wang the Tiger saw that this brother of his was so engrossed in his money making that he never saw his sons at all, nor thought of how they would one day spend as eagerly what he so eagerly gathered together, nor that they only endured their clerking until he died and left them free so that they need not work.

And Wang the Tiger saw the sons of his elder brother, how finicking and dandyish they were, and how they must have everything that touched them soft and fine, cool silk in summer, and warm soft furs in winter. Nor would they eat well and robustly as young men ought to do, but they dallied with their food and complained of this because it was too sweet and of that because it was too sour and salt, and they pushed one bowl after another away from them, and the slaves were kept hurrying hither and thither for them.

All this Wang the Tiger saw with anger that it was so. One night he walked alone in the court that had been his father's and he heard the sound of a woman's giggling laugh. Suddenly a little girl, who was child of some servant or other, ran past the round gate of his court, and she was frightened and breathless and when she saw Wang the Tiger there she stooped to scuttle past him. But he laid hold of her little arm suddenly and shouted at her,

"What woman laughed?"

The child shrank away terrified at his glittering eyes, but he had fast hold of her and she could not twist herself free, and she cast down her eyes and stammered,

"The young lord took my sister aside."

Then Wang the Tiger asked sternly,

"Where?"

The child pointed to the back of the next court to an empty room that Lotus had used as a granary, but now it was empty and locked loosely with a great hasp. Then Wang the Tiger dropped the child's arm and she ran like a rabbit, but he strode to that place where she pointed and he saw the hasp was wide enough so that the doors stood apart from each other nearly a foot, and a slender young body could easily pass through. He stood there in the night and listened, and he heard a woman's laughter, tittering and giggling, and he heard some voice whisper words he could not catch but he heard them come hot and breathless from the man's throat. Then his old sickness against passion rose in him and he was about to beat upon that door except that he stayed himself in the act and he thought with scorn,

"What business is it of mine that there is still such a thing in this same house?"

And he went back weary and sickened to his court. But some strange power even in his disgust made him restless and he walked about the court and while he waited the moon rose late. Soon out of that inner empty room he saw a young slave slip between the hasped doors and she smoothed her hair and he saw her smiling there in the light of the moon and she glanced about her swiftly and went swiftly and soundlessly in her cloth shoes across the tiled empty court which had been Lotus's. Only once she stopped under the pomegranate tree and it was to fasten her loosened girdle.

And after a time, and all this time Wang the Tiger had stood motionless, his heart throbbing with some sort of disgust that was half sick and half sweet, he saw a young man come sauntering by and he sauntered as though he were out to see the night and nothing more. Then Wang the Tiger shouted suddenly,

"Who is it?"

There answered a very pleasant voice, idle and light,

"It is I, Uncle!"

Wang the Tiger saw it was indeed his elder brother's eldest son, and some gorge rose in Wang the Tiger's heart and he could have sprung upon the young man because he told himself he hated lewdness so bitterly, and most of all he hated it in his own blood and he could not bear it. But he held his hands hard to his sides, for well he knew one cannot kill a brother's son and well he knew his own temper that if he let it come up he could not stop it where he would. So he only gave a great snort and he turned blindly away into his room and he grunted to himself,

"I must get me out of these courts where one of my brothers is a miser and the other a rake! I cannot breathe this air, for I am a man of freedom and of battle and I cannot keep my angers bottled in me as men must who live like this with women in courts!" And he wished suddenly with some strange desire that there was a need for him to kill someone and shed blood in a cause so that he could free his heart of a charge it had which he could not understand.

Then to calm himself he forced his thoughts to his little son and he crept into the room where the child slept in his mother's bed, and he looked down upon the child. The woman slept heavily as country women will and her mouth was open and her breath came out very foul so that even as he bent over his little son Wang the Tiger was fain to cover his nostrils under his hand. But the child slept serene and still, and looking at his quiet face grave in sleep, Wang the Tiger swore that his son should not be like any of these. No, this boy should be hardened from his youth up and reared to be a great soldier and he should be taught every sort of skill and he should be made into a man.

On the very next day, therefore, Wang the Tiger took his two wives and his children and all those who had come with him and they made their farewells, after they had feasted together with their kinsmen. But in spite of the farewell feasting it seemed to Wang the Tiger that he was the less near to his two brothers, after all, for this visit, and when he saw his elder brother, sleepy and peaceful and sunken in his flesh, and how his heavy eyes never lightened except at some lewdness, and when he saw his second brother, and how his face grew more narrow and his eyes more secret as his age came, it seemed to him they were like men who were blind and deaf and dumb because they did not see what they were or what they had made their sons.

369

But he said nothing. He sat glowering and silent and he dwelt with a mighty pride upon the thought of his own son, and the man into which he would shape him.

So they parted, and on the surface all was smooth and courteous and they bowed deeply to each other and the elder brothers and their ladies and serving men and maids came out to the street and they called a hundred good wishes. But Wang the Tiger said to himself that he would not soon come back to his father's house.

With the greatest content, therefore, did Wang the Tiger return to his own lands and the lands seemed the best he had ever seen and the people the sturdiest and best and his house was home, and all his men welcomed him and they fired firecrackers at his coming and there were smiles of welcome everywhere when he swung himself down from his red horse and a score of soldiers idling about the courts leaped forward to catch the bridle as he tossed it aside, and it pleased Wang the Tiger to see them do it.

He set himself therefore as the spring widened, and everywhere spread into early summer, to round his men afresh and train them again day after day. He sent out his spies again and he sent out men to see how his newly taken lands were, and he sent his trusty man everywhere to bring him revenues and he sent guards fully armed to bring the treasure to him safely, for in these days it was far more than one man could carry in a sack upon his shoulders as once he had.

But in the evenings when the day was over and he sat in his court alone in the warm spring night, at such times when there are many men whose hearts grow wayward and yearn for some love or other beside what they have tried, Wang the Tiger yearned after his son. Then he had the child brought to him continually, although he did not know how to play with any child, not even his son. He commanded the nurse to seat herself where he could see the child, and he sat and stared at every movement the boy made and at every transient look that flickered across his face. When the boy learned to walk Wang the Tiger could scarcely contain himself for pleasure and when he was alone at night and no one to see him in the courts he took the girdle that the nurse passed around the child's waist and he held it and walked round and round while the boy staggered and panted in the loop of the girdle.

If any had asked Wang the Tiger what he thought while he stared at his son, he would have been in the greatest confusion, for he did not know himself. Only he felt swelling up in him great dreams of power and glory and sometimes out of his fullness he pondered on how in these times a man could rise to any power and place if he had might enough and could make men afraid of him, for there was no emperor and no dynasty in these times, and anyone might struggle and shape events if he would. And feeling this in himself Wang the Tiger would mutter into his beard,

"And such a man am I!"

Now there came a strange thing out of this love Wang the Tiger had for his son and it was that when Wang the Tiger's learned wife heard how he had his son brought to him every day, she dressed her daughter in bright new garments one day and she brought her in all fresh and pink and she had put little silver bracelets upon the child's wrists and tied her black hair with pink bits of yarn, and she forced the child upon her father's attention thus. When Wang the Tiger was embarrassed and turned his eyes aside not knowing what he ought to say, the mother said in her pleasant voice,

"This little daughter of ours craves your notice, too, and she is no whit less strong and fair than your son."

Wang the Tiger was somewhat taken aback with this

371

woman's courage for he did not know her at all, except in the darkness of the nights in her turn, and so he could mutter out of courtesy,

"She is fair enough for a girl."

But the child's mother was not satisfied with this, for he scarcely looked at her daughter, and she pressed on and said,

"No, my husband, at least look at her, for she is no usual child. She walked three months before the boy did and talks now as though she were four instead of two and under. I have come to ask for a favor to me that you will give her learning also and share your goods with her as you do with your son."

To this Wang the Tiger said in astonishment,

"How can I make a soldier out of a girl?"

Then in her steadfast, pleasant way the mother said,

"If not a soldier, then some skill in a school, for there are many such in these times, my husband."

Suddenly Wang the Tiger heard that she called him by that name that no woman ever had, and she did not call him "my lord" as other women would, and he was embarrassed and out of his confusion he looked at the child because he could think of nothing to say. Then he saw that truly this girl was a very enticing little one, very round and fat and she had a tiny red mouth that she moved in smiles, and her eyes were large and black and her hands were fat and the nails very perfect and complete. He saw them because her mother had stained the nails red as women will do sometimes for children very loved. The child's feet were cased in little pink silk shoes and the mother held them both in her one hand while the other she passed about the child's middle as she leaped up and down upon her mother's hand. When the mother saw him looking at the girl babe she said gently,

"I shall not bind her feet, and let us send her to a school

and make such a woman out of her as there are here and there in these days."

"But who will wed such a maid?" cried Wang the Tiger astonished.

To this the mother replied tranquilly, "Such a maid can wed whom she likes, I believe."

Wang the Tiger took some thought at this and he looked at the woman. He had never looked at her before, deeming it enough if she served his purpose, and now as he looked he saw for the first time that she had a wise good face and a manner which made her seem composed and able to do what she liked, and when he looked at her she did not fear him and she looked back at him without giggling or drawing her mouth down as the other wife might have done. And he thought to himself in some wonder,

"This woman is more clever than I thought and I have not seen her very well before," and aloud he said courteously and he rose as he spoke, "When the time comes I will not say nay to you if it seems a wise thing."

Now it was a curious thing that she who had been so composed always and had lived content so far as Wang the Tiger knew or cared, now when she saw this new courtesy in the man seemed moved in some strange way. The color came dull and red into her cheeks and she looked at him earnestly and in silence and with yearning creeping into her eyes. But Wang the Tiger, seeing her change thus, felt the old repulsion against women well into his heart and his tongue was locked and he turned away and muttered that he had forgot something he had to do that hour, and he went away quickly, shaken in himself, and he did not like her when she looked at him in such a way.

But the fruit of the hour was that sometimes if the mother sent a slave with the girl at the time when he called for his

373

son to be brought so that the two came together, Wang the Tiger did not send the girl away. At first he feared the mother might return and make a custom of talking with him, but when he saw she did not, he let the girl be there for a while and he stared at her, for her sex made him shy of her even though she was but a child staggering hither and thither. Still she was a winning thing and he watched her often and laughed silently at her tempers and her broken words. His son was large and grave and not given to laughter, but this girl was small and quick and full of merriment and her eyes were forever seeking her father's, and if she were not watched she abused her brother and snatched what he had away from him, being so quick. Without knowing it Wang the Tiger came to notice her in a certain fashion, and he knew her for his child among others if he saw a slave holding her at the gate in a crowd to see what went by upon the street, and sometimes he even stopped to touch her hand and see her flash her eyes at him to smile.

Then going into his house when she had thus smiled, he was content and at last he felt no more alone but a man among his own, both women and children.

XXIV

Now Wang the Tiger had it always in his mind that he must enlarge his place and his position for his son's sake, and so he told himself often and he planned how he would do it, where he would creep in and make the victory at the end of some common war, how he would push southward of his river and seize the next county or two in a famine year when the people were pressed by drought or flood. But it happened that for a few years there was no great common war, and one weak and unready man after another came and went upon the central seat of government and if there was no sure peace still there was no great outburst of war, either, nor such a time as a lord of war could take to come out too boldly.

For a second thing, it seemed to Wang the Tiger that he could not as he once had done put his whole heart into his ambitions for enlarging himself, for there was this son of his to plan for and to tend, and after that were all his soldiers and the matters of the domain, for none had ever come to take the old magistrate's place. Once or twice a name had been sent to Wang the Tiger but he had always rejected it quickly because it suited him better to be alone, and now as his son grew out of babyhood into his childhood Wang the Tiger thought sometimes that if he could put the state off for a few more years it would be a very good thing for himself to be the magistrate there when he was too old to be a warrior and when his son could take his place at the head of the army. But he kept this plan secret in himself for it was too soon yet to tell it forth. And indeed, the boy was now only six years old. But Wang the Tiger was in such haste for him to grow into a man that while sometimes the years went fast, yet at other times he thought they would never pass at all, and looking at his son he did not see him for the little lad he was, but for the young man, the young warrior, he would have him be, and without knowing it he forced the child in many ways.

When his son was but six years old Wang the Tiger took him away from his mother and out of the courts of the women, and brought him into his own courts to live with him. This he did so that the boy would not be made soft by women's caresses and women's talk and ways, but partly he did it because he was in such haste for the boy's constant companionship. At first the boy was shy and lost with his father and he wandered about with a look of fright in his eyes and when Wang the Tiger made a mighty effort and put out his hand to draw the child near the boy stood stiff and withdrawn and barely suffered his father, and Wang the Tiger felt the child's fear and he yearned over the child, but he was speechless because he did not know what to say, and he could only let the lad go again. At first it had been Wang the Tiger's purpose to cut the child's life off clean from the mother and from the life of any woman, for he had only soldiers to serve him, but soon it could be seen that so clean a cut was beyond the endurance of so small and childish a heart. The boy did not complain at all. He was a grave and silent lad, patient to endure what he must, but he was never joyful. He sat by his father when his father called to him so to do, and he was dutiful to stand at once when his father came into the room where he was, and he read his books with his old tutor who came every day to teach him, but he never spoke more than he must.

One night Wang the Tiger watched him thus at his night meal, and the lad felt his father watching him and he bent his head over his bowl very low and made as though he ate, but he could not swallow. Then Wang the Tiger grew angry for indeed he had done everything he could think of for this child of his and that very day he had taken the lad with him to review his armies, and he set the lad across his saddle in front of him as he rode, and his heart swelled as the men cried out to the little general, as they called him. The lad had smiled faintly, and had turned his head away until Wang the Tiger forced him saying,

"Hold your head high—they are your men—your soldiers, my son! You shall lead them out one day to war!"

Thus forced the boy held up his head somewhat, but his

376

cheeks were a burning dark red, and when Wang the Tiger leaned over he saw the boy did not look at the men at all, but looked far off into the fields beyond the grounds where the armies marched and when Wang the Tiger asked him what he saw he lifted his finger and pointed at a little sunburned naked lad in the next field who lay across a water buffalo's back, staring at the brave show of soldiers, and the boy said,

"I would like to be that boy and lie on the buffalo's back."

Wang the Tiger was not pleased at such a common, low wish as this and he said sternly,

"Well, and I think my son might wish higher than to be a cowherd!"

And he bade the boy harshly that he was to look at the army and see how they marched and wheeled and how they held their guns aloft to charge, and the boy obediently did what his father said, and did not again look at the little herd.

But Wang the Tiger had been troubled the whole day for what his son had wished and now he looked at the child and he saw him bend his head lower and lower and he saw the boy could not swallow because he was weeping. Then Wang the Tiger was stricken with fear that his son was in some pain, and he rose and went to the child and took his hand and he cried out,

"Are you in a fever or something?"

But the small hand was cool and moist and the boy shook his head, and he would answer nothing for a long time even though Wang the Tiger forced him and he called for his harelipped trusty man at last to help him with his son. When the man was come Wang the Tiger was so torn with his anxiety and his fear and some anger, too, because the child was so stubborn, that he shouted to the man,

"Take this young fool out and see what you can find wrong with him!"

By now the boy sobbed desperately and he had put his head down on his arms to sob and hide his face, and Wang the Tiger sat there angry and near to weeping himself and his face worked and he pulled at his beard. Then the trusty man lifted the child in his arms and took him away somewhere and Wang the Tiger waited in agony for a while, staring at the boy's untasted bowl. When the man came back again but without the child, Wang the Tiger roared at him,

"Speak out and tell me all!"

Then half hesitating the man answered,

"There is no illness in him at all, and he only cannot eat because he is so lonely. He has never lived alone before and without a child and he longs for his mother and for his sisters."

"But at his age he cannot play and idle his time away and with women," said Wang the Tiger, half beside himself, and he tore at his beard and twisted himself in his seat.

"No," said the man calmly, for he knew his master's temper and did not fear him, "but he might return sometimes to see his mother, or his sister might come a few times to play, since they are both but children still, and by such means the parting might be eased for the lad, else he will be ill."

Then Wang the Tiger sat silent awhile and he sat and suffered such mortal jealousy as he had never suffered before since that woman whom he had killed came back to torture him because she had loved the dead robber better than him. But now it was jealousy because his son did not love him wholly and longed for others than his father, and Wang the Tiger suffered because while he found his joy and pride in his son, his son was not content with even so great a love, nor did he value it, and for all he was surrounded with his father's love, he yearned for a woman. And Wang the Tiger

378

said to himself violently that he hated all women and he rose out of his seat passionately and he shouted at the trusty man saying,

"Let him go then, if he is such a weakling! What do I care what he does if he is to be a son, after all, such as my brothers have?"

But the trusty man answered gently,

"My general, you forget he is only a little child."

And Wang the Tiger sat down again and groaned awhile and said, "Well, did I not tell you let him go?"

Thereafter once in five days or so the boy went into his mother's court, and every time he went Wang the Tiger sat and gnawed his beard until the boy came back and then he questioned him this way and that as to what he had seen and heard, and he said,

"What were they doing there?"

And the boy made answer always, half startled by the passion in his father's eyes, "Nothing, my father."

But Wang the Tiger would persist and he cried, "Were they gaming or sewing or what? Women do not sit at nothing unless they gossip, and that is something, too!"

Then the boy put his mind to it and he knit his brows and made painstaking, slow answer,

"My mother cut out a little coat for my youngest sister out of some red flowered cloth, and my eldest sister, whose mother is not mine, sat and read a book to show how well she could do it. I like her better than my other sisters, because she understands when I speak to her and does not laugh at nothing as they do. She has very big eyes and her hair comes below her waist when it is braided now. But she never reads very long. She is restless and she likes to talk."

This pleased Wang the Tiger and he said with pleasure,

"So all women are and they are given to talking about nothing!"

It was the strangest jealousy in Wang the Tiger's heart, for it drew him still further away from those others of his own household and he went more and more seldom to either of his wives. And indeed it looked as time went on as if this lad was to be his only son, for Wang the Tiger's learned wife had never any more children than the one daughter, and the ignorant wife had two daughters, some years apart, and it came to be, that whether Wang the Tiger was not hot in his blood and had no great taste for women, or whether the love of his son made him content, he went at last no more to the courts of his wives. Partly it was some strange shame in him that after his son came to sleep in his room with him he was ashamed for the lad's sake to rise and go out at night to a woman. No, as time went on Wang the Tiger did not, as many lords of war do when they grow rich and strong, fill their courts with feasting and with women. His treasure he poured into guns and more guns and soldiers, except the certain sum he laid by and increased steadily against the time when some disaster might befall him, and he lived sternly and simply and alone except for his son.

Sometimes, and it was the only woman who ever came into their courts, Wang the Tiger let his eldest daughter come in to play with his son, her brother. The first time or two her mother brought her there and she sat for a moment or so. But Wang the Tiger was very ill at ease to have her there, the more because he felt this woman reproached him for something or even that she yearned for something from him, and suffered under some loss he did not understand, and so he rose and went away with a few courteous words to explain his going. At last it seemed she ceased to expect anything from him and he saw her no more, and a slave brought the girl in to play at the rare times when she came.

But in a year or two even the girl came no more, and the mother sent word that she took her daughter to some school for learning, and Wang the Tiger was glad, because the girl came into the austere courts where he lived and she disturbed him because she wore so bright a coat and because she thrust a red pomegranate flower into her hair or a white jasmine that was very fragrant and she loved best of all to put a spray of cassia flowers into her braid, and Wang the Tiger could not bear cassia flowers, because the scent was so sweet and hot and he hated such scent. She was too merry, too, and wilful and domineering and all the things he hated in a woman, and he hated most of all the light and laughter in his son's eyes and the smiles upon his lips when his sister came. She alone could stir him into gayety and to running and play about the court.

Then Wang the Tiger felt his heart close in possession about his son and his heart closed against his daughter, and the faint impulse he had felt toward her when she had been a babe was gone now that she grew into a slender girl, and into the promise of a woman, and he was glad when her mother prepared to send her away and he gave silver freely and readily and he did not begrudge it at all, for now he had his son to himself.

He made haste before his son could be lonely again to fill his life full with many things and he said to his son,

"Son, we are men, you and I, and now cease to go into your mother's courts except at those times when it is fitting to pay respect to her, for it is a very subtle easy way to waste a life with women, even with mother or sister, for they are still but women and still ignorant and foolish. I would have you learn every sort of soldier's skill, now, both old and new. My trusty

381

men can teach you all you need to know of old, the Pig Butcher how to use fist and foot, and the harelipped one how to wield sword and staff. And for the new ways I have heard of and never seen, I have sent to the coast and hired a new tutor for you, who learned his ways of war in foreign countries, and he knows every sort of foreign weapon and way of war. He is to teach you first and what time besides he has left he is to teach our army."

The boy answered nothing but he stood as his wont was when his father spoke to him and he received his father's words in perfect silence. And Wang the Tiger looking at the boy's face tenderly saw no sign of anything he felt there, and he waited awhile and when the lad did not speak but only to say,

"May I leave the room if it is your will?" Wang the Tiger nodded his head and sighed without knowing why he did, or even that he sighed.

Thus Wang the Tiger taught and admonished his son and he saw to it that every hour of the boy's life, beyond eating and sleeping, was filled with some learning or other. He made the boy rise early and practice his feints of war with the trusty men and when he had finished and had eaten his early meal he spent the morning with his books and when he had eaten again the new young tutor took him for the afternoon and taught him every kind of thing.

Now this new tutor was a young man such as Wang the Tiger had never seen before. He wore western clothes of war and spectacles upon his nose, and he had a very straight, swift body. He could run and leap and fence, and he knew how to set fire to all kinds of foreign weapons of war. Some he held in his hand and threw and they burst into flames, and some he fired like a gun with hand on a trigger, and there were many other kinds. And Wang the Tiger sat by as his son learned all these ways of war, and although the Tiger would not have said it, he learned of many things he himself had never even seen or heard of, and it came to him that it was a small thing to have been so proud of those two old foreign guns, and the only great guns he had. Yes, he saw he knew very little even of war, since there was more to know than he had dreamed, and now he would often sit far into the night talking to his son's new tutor, and he learned of all sorts of clever ways of killing, the death from the air that drops down upon men, and the death that is in the bowels of the sea and comes up to kill, and the death that can fly more miles than men can see and drop and burst upon an enemy. Wang the Tiger listened to this in greatest wonder and he said,

"I see the people of the outer countries are very clever at killing and I did not know it."

Then he began to ponder it all and one day he said to the tutor,

"I have a good rich territory in my hand and we do not have a complete famine more than once in ten or fifteen years, and I have a little silver put together. Now I see I have been too satisfied with my men, and I see that if my son is to learn all these new ways of war he must have an army skilled in such things, too. I will buy some of these machines that are used for war now-a-days in outer countries, and you shall teach my men and shape an army fit for my son when he comes to it."

The young man smiled his quick and flashing smile and he was very willing and he said,

"I have tried to teach your men, but the discourteous truth is that they are a very ragged straggling lot and too content to eat and drink. If you will buy some new machines and if you will set hours of the day when they shall march and learn, I will see if they are to be shaped."

Now Wang the Tiger was displeased secretly at such discourteous truth, for he had put many days of his life into teaching his men, and he said stiffly,

"You must teach my son first."

"I will teach him until he is fifteen," said the young tutor, "and then if you will permit me to advise one so high as you, I will say he should be sent to a school of war in the south."

"What, can men learn war in a school?" said Wang the Tiger wondering.

"There is such a school," replied the young tutor, "and such as come out of it are captains at once in the state's army."

But Wang the Tiger grew haughty at this and he said, "My son has no need to go and search for some little captain's place in the state army as though he had not an army of his own," and after a while Wang the Tiger said again, "Besides, I doubt if any good thing can come out of the south. I served under a southern general in my youth and he was an idle, lustful creature, and his soldiers little monkeys of men."

The tutor, seeing Wang the Tiger was displeased, smiled and took his departure and Wang the Tiger sat on and he thought of his son and it seemed to him that surely he had done everything for his son that could be done. And he searched his heart painfully to remember his youth and he remembered that he had longed once for a horse of his own. The very next day therefore he bought a little black horse for his son, a strong good beast from the plains of Mongolia, and he bought it from a horse dealer whom he knew.

But when he gave it to the boy, and he called him out to see what he had for him, and there the little black horse stood in the court, a red saddle of new leather upon his back, and a red bridle studded with brass, and the groom who held the horse and whose sole duty was to tend it from this day on had in his hand a new whip of red braided leather. Wang the Tiger thought to himself proudly that it was such a horse as he himself might have dreamed of as a lad and thought too good to be alive, and he looked eagerly at his son to catch the pleasure that must break into his eyes and smile.

But the boy did not come out of his gravity at all. He looked at the horse and said, composed as he always was,

"My thanks, my father."

And Wang the Tiger waited, but no light came into the boy's eyes, and he did not leap forward to seize the bridle nor to try the saddle, and he seemed waiting to be allowed to go away.

Then Wang the Tiger turned away in furious disappointment and he went into his room and shut the door and he sat down and held his head in his hands and yearned over his son with anger and with bitterness of unrewarded love. But when he had grieved awhile he hardened himself again in his old way and he said stubbornly,

"Yet what more can he want? He has all I dreamed of when I was his age and more than I dreamed. Yes, what would I not have given for a teacher so skilled as he has, and for a fine foreign gun such as he has, and now a little shining black horse and the saddle and bridle red, and a red whip set into a silver handle!"

Thus he comforted himself, and he commanded the lad's tutor to spare no teaching of this son of his, and not to heed the languors that the boy might have, for these are common to all lads who grow, and they cannot be heeded.

But at night when Wang the Tiger woke up and was restless he heard his son's quiet breathing in the room and a suffering tenderness filled his breast and he thought to himself over and over,

"I must do more for him—I must think of something more I can do for him!"

Thus did Wang the Tiger spend his years upon his son and he might have slipped all unknowing into age, so engrossed was he, had not a certain thing come about that shook him out of his too great fondness and stirred him up to war again, and to his destiny.

It was on a day in spring when his son was nearly ten years old, for so did Wang the Tiger measure the years now by his son, and he sat under a budding pomegranate tree with the boy. The lad had been rapt before the little flame-like new leaves of the tree and he had cried out suddenly,

"I do swear that to me these little fiery leaves are more beautiful than the whole flower, even!"

Wang the Tiger was looking at them, painstaking in his attention to see what his son saw if he could, when there came a great commotion at the gates and one came running to Wang the Tiger to announce someone coming. But before the serving man could get the words from his mouth Wang the Tiger saw his pocked nephew come staggering in, lame from his swift riding, and he was haggard and weary with his riding by night and day, and the dust had settled into his deep pocks so that he was very curious to see. Words came slowly to Wang the Tiger so long as he was not angry and he could but stare at the young man and the young man gasped forth,

"I came on a winged horse by day and by night to tell you that the Hawk is plotting to divide himself from you and he has set up your army for his own and he has taken for his base the very city you besieged, and he is in some league with the old robber chief who has been itching these years for his revenge. I have known he held back revenue these last

386

months and I feared some such outcome, but I have waited to make sure lest raising a false alarm the Hawk be offended and kill me secretly somehow!"

All this tumbled out of the young man's mouth and Wang the Tiger stared out of his deep eyes and his eyes seemed to recede beneath his forehead as his black brows drew down more heavily and he felt his good hot rage come up to help him and he roared out,

"That accursed dog and thief—and I raised him up from a common soldier! Everything he owes to me, and he turns on me like the wild cur he is!"

And feeling his good, war-like anger rise higher and higher in him Wang the Tiger forgot his son and he strode to the outer courts where his captains lived and his trusty men and some of his soldiers, and he roared that five thousand men were to prepare to follow him within the forenoon and he shouted for his horse and for his keen and narrow sword. Everywhere those courts, which had lain quiet and at peace with the spring, became now like a turmoiled pool, and out of the women's courts the children and the slaves peeped with frightened faces dismayed at so much shouting of weapons and war, and the very horses were excited and their hoofs clattered and pranced upon the tiles of the courts.

Then Wang the Tiger, when he saw all was astir as he had commanded, turned to the weary messenger and he said,

"Go and eat and drink and rest yourself. You have done very well and for this I shall raise you up. Well I know that many a youth would have joined the rebels, for it is always in the hearts of young men to rebel, but you have remembered our bond of blood to stay by me. Be sure I shall raise you up!"

Then the young man looked east and west and he whispered,

"Yes, but, my uncle, will you kill the Hawk? He will sus-

387

pect when he sees you come for I told him I was ill and must go back to my mother for a while."

Then Wang the Tiger promised in a great, furious voice, and he cried,

"You need not beg me, for I will burnish my sword upon his flesh!"

And the young man went away very content.

Then by forced marching Wang the Tiger led his men out the three days to the new territory and he led out his old and trusted men, and he kept at home those who had joined his ranks from the besieged city and the captain who had betrayed the robber chief lest they betray him also in his turn. He promised his good men that they should have their turn now to loot the city if they were brave for him, and he would give them besides a month's extra wage in silver, so they marched with good hearts and ready feet.

They did so well that before the Hawk had any idea of such a mishap he heard that Wang the Tiger was upon him. The truth was that the Hawk had no knowledge of how wily and full of clever guile was the young man who was Wang the Tiger's nephew, for the youth was so merry and his tongue so smooth and his pocked face so full of seeming ignorance except of a jest or of some bit of horseplay among the soldiers, that the Hawk thought all he did unseen. He was very glad when the youth said he was ill of some pain in his liver and that he must go home to his mother, and he planned that now he would put out his proclamations of rebellion and he would discover which men were loyal to him and the others he would put to death. To the men who would rebel with him he promised the freedom of the city for booty.

In these days, therefore, the Hawk fortified himself and he commanded food to be brought into the city, for well enough he knew Wang the Tiger's temper that he would not be still and let things be, and in great terror the helpless people prepared themselves again for a siege. Even on that very day when Wang the Tiger came into the city gate he saw farmers coming by the score with their loads of fuel upon their poles across their shoulders, and donkeys and mules came with bags of grain crossed upon their backs, and men carrying baskets of squawking fowls or driving herds of cattle and carrying pigs trussed upon poles and squealing furiously as they felt themselves borne along, their heads hanging and feet up. And Wang the Tiger gnashed his teeth to see it all, for he knew that if he had not been told in time of the plot, he would have had a very difficult siege with all this food in the city, and the Hawk was a far greater foe than the witless old robber chief had been, for he was a clever man and very fierce and he had besides the two foreign weapons of war and he could set them on the city wall and turn them upon the besiegers. When Wang the Tiger thought of all he had missed so narrowly, his anger rose until his eyes were red and he gnawed and chewed at his beard. He let his anger rise then as deep and high as it would and he forced his horse on and shouted to his men that they were to go straight to the courts where the Hawk was encamped.

Now there were already those who had run to tell the Hawk that he was undone, for Wang the Tiger was already upon him, and the Hawk felt despair drop on him out of the skies. He hesitated but a moment to think whether or no he might brazen the hour out by guile, or whether he might rather escape by a secret way, and he had no hope at all that his men would dare to stand by him now, since Wang the Tiger brought so vast an army in. He knew he stood alone. But in that moment's hesitation he was lost, for Wang the Tiger came galloping through the gates crying that the Hawk was to be caught at any cost and held for him to kill, and he turned himself off his saddle as he shouted and his men swarmed through the courts.

Then the Hawk, seeing his end was on him, ran and hid himself. Although he was a brave man, he ran and hid himself in the pile of grass in one of the kitchens. But what hope had he against the hordes that poured to find him who were fierce with their hopes of promised reward? Nor did the Hawk have any hope from his followers beyond that if one saw where he was hid, he would not tell it. He waited there in the grass, and if he hid, still did not tremble, for he was a brave man.

But he must be found, for they ran searching everywhere for him eager to find him and claim reward, and the gates front and back were guarded and the small gate of escape, and the walls to the courts were very high. So the Hawk was found by a handful of soldiers, and they saw an end of his blue coat in the grass and they ran out and clapped the door to, and yelled for others to come, and when some fifty men or so came running they went in cautiously, for they did not know what weapons the Hawk might have, although he was weaponless, except for a small, short dagger, useless against so many, for he had run out in distraction as he sat eating his morning meal. They fell upon him in a heap, then, and pinioned him and led him to their general, and the Hawk went sullenly, his eyes wild and the straw sticking in his hair and his clothes. Thus they led him to where Wang the Tiger sat in the great hall waiting, his sword drawn and shining like a narrow silver serpent stretched across his knees. He glowered at the Hawk from under his dark brows and he said harshly, "So you have turned traitor against me, who raised you up from a common soldier and made you all you are!"

The Hawk answered sullenly and without raising his eyes from the shining thing on Wang the Tiger's knees,

"You taught me how to rebel against a general, and what were you but a runaway son, and who raised you if not the old general?"

Now when Wang the Tiger heard so rude an answer he could not bear it, and he shouted to the crowded soldiers who stood to see all they could,

"I thought I would drive my sword through him, but it is too clean a death for him! Take him and slice his flesh into strips as they do to criminals and those too wicked to live, to unfilial sons and traitors to the state!"

But the Hawk, seeing his end was come, and before any could stop him, pulled his small short dagger out of his bosom, and he plunged it into his own belly and gave it a great twist and left it sticking there out of his belly, and he stood staggering a moment, and he looked at Wang the Tiger as he died, and he said in his hard and reckless way,

"I do not fear to die! Another twenty years and I shall be born again in some other body—again a hero!" And he fell with his dagger still twisted in his entrails.

And Wang the Tiger, staring at what had come about almost before he could draw a breath, felt his anger ebbing out of him as he stared. He had been cheated of his revenge and yet for all his anger he was remorseful, too, that he had lost so brave a man as this rebel. He was silent for a while and at last he said in a low voice,

"You to the right and left of me, take his dead body away and bury it somewhere, for he was a lone man. I do not know whether he had father or son or any home." And after a while he said again, "I knew he was brave but I did not know him so brave as this. Put him into a good coffin."

And Wang the Tiger sat on awhile and sorrowed, and the sorrow made his heart soft so that he held his men back for a time from the looting he had promised. While he sorrowed, the merchants of that city came and craved an audience of him, and when he let them in to see what they desired of him, they came and with courtesy and much silver they besought him not to allow his men to be free in the city, saying that the people were in great terror. And being soft for the time, Wang the Tiger took the silver and promised to give it to his men in lieu of booty, and the merchants were grateful and went away praising so merciful a lord of war as this.

But Wang the Tiger had an ado to comfort his soldiers, and he had to pay them each one a good sum and he ordered feasts and wines for them before they would leave off their sullen looks and Wang the Tiger had to call upon their loyalty to him and promise them some further chance some other time of war before they settled to themselves again, and ceased their curses of disappointment. And indeed Wang the Tiger had to send twice to the merchants for other sums of silver before the thing was settled and the men satisfied.

Then Wang the Tiger prepared to return to his home once more, for he longed exceedingly to see his son, for he had left in such haste he had scarcely thought to plan for him these days he was away. This time Wang the Tiger left his trusty harelipped man to hold the city with the soldiers until his nephew could return and the Hawk's men he led back with himself, leaving in their place certain tried and old men he had brought out when he came. And as precaution Wang the Tiger took the two great foreign guns with him, for he found the Hawk had had an ironsmith of the city make round balls for them and he had gunpowder to fire the guns, and Wang the Tiger took them so that he need never again fear them turned upon himself.

Now as Wang the Tiger marched back again through the streets of the city, the people looked as he passed and cast eyes of hatred upon him, for a tax had been levied upon every house to make up the vast sum that Wang the Tiger had needed to reward his soldiers and to pay his own cost of the expedition. But Wang the Tiger would not notice these looks, and he hardened himself and he reasoned in his own mind that these people ought to be willing to pay for peace, for if he had not come and delivered them they would have suffered greatly at the hands of the Hawk and of his men. For the Hawk was very cruel and men and women were nothing at all to him, and he had been used to wars from his childhood. The truth was Wang the Tiger felt that these people were very unjust to him, who had these days of hard marching, and they did not perceive they had been saved from anything and he thought to himself sullenly,

"They have no gratitude for anything, and I am too soft of heart."

He hardened his heart with such thoughts, therefore, and he was never quite so kind again to common people as he once had been. He narrowed his heart still more, and he took no trusty man in the Hawk's place for he said to himself drearily that not one could be trusted who was not of his blood, and in this narrowness he leaned yet more upon his beloved son and he comforted himself saying,

"There is my son, and he alone will never fail me."

He hastened his horse then, and hurried his march, yearning for the sight of his son.

As for the nephew of Wang the Tiger, he waited until he had heard the Hawk was killed and the news made him very blithe and merry and he went to his home for a few days and there he told everyone how brave and wily he had been, and how he had been too clever for the Hawk, although the Hawk was so clever and wise a warrior, and old enough to be another generation. So he boasted everywhere, and his brothers and sisters stood about him in greatest delight to hear him, and his mother cried out,

"Even when this son suckled I knew he was no common child, for he did pull so hard and lustily at my breast!"

But Wang the Merchant sat and listened with his meager smile fastened upon his face, and if he was proud of his son he would not praise him and he said,

"It is a good thing to remember, nevertheless, that of the thirty-six ways out of difficulty the best way of all is to run away." And he said, "Good guile is better than good weapon."

And it was his son's guile that pleased him most of all.

But when the pocked youth went to his uncle's court to pay respect to Wang the Landlord and his lady, and he told his doughty tale there, Wang the Landlord was strangely jealous. He was jealous for his dead son, and he was jealous for these other two sons of his whom he admired for their lordly looks and ways and yet for whom he had vague fears, too, that there was something wrong in them. So although he seemed courteous when his brother's pocked son told his tale, yet he lent but one ear, and while the young man talked in his eager way, the old man kept calling out for tea and for his pipe, and that he was chill now that the sun was down and he would have his light spring fur robe. As for the lady, she inclined her head to her nephew the very least she could in decency of mannerliness, and she took up a bit of embroidery and feigned to be very busy with it, matching this silk to that in the pattern, and she yawned loudly and often, and asked her lord this and that of some matter in the house or about the tenants on the land they still had left. At last the young man saw she was weary of him and he stopped his tale and went away, somewhat dashed. And before he had gone far he heard the lady raise her voice and say,

"I am glad no son of ours is a soldier! It is such a low life and it makes a young man very coarse and common."

And Wang the Landlord answered listlessly, "Aye—I think I will go to the tea house for a while."

Now the young man could not know that these twain thought of their dead young son, and he felt his heart sore in him until he came to the gate. But there stood Wang the Landlord's second wife, her last babe in her arms. She had sat listening to the young man's tale, and had slipped out ahead of him and she said to him wistfully,

"But to me it was a very good, brave tale."

And the young man went back to his mother comforted.

Three times ten days did this pocked nephew of Wang the Tiger stay in his home, for his mother took this chance to wed him to his betrothed, the maid whom she had chosen for him a few years before. Now this maid was the daughter of a neighbor, who was a silk weaver, but not a poor and common weaver who hires himself to others. No, the maid's father had his own looms and he had twenty apprentices and made bolts of many-colored satin and flowered silks, and there were not many of his trade in the city, so that he did well at it. The maid, too, was clever at it, and she could, if the spring lingered on too chill, nurse the silkworm eggs against her own warm flesh until they hatched into worms, and she could feed the worms, as they should be fed to grow, upon the mulberry leaves the apprentices gathered, and she knew how to wind the silk from the cocoons. All such skill she had, a rare skill in that town, for the family had come the generation before from other parts. It was true that the young man she was to wed had no such use for her skill; still, Wang the Merchant's wife felt it was something for a maid to have such knowledge and it made her thrifty and busy.

As for the young man, it was little to him what the maid

395

could do, but he was glad to be wed, for he was now nearly twenty-four and troubled often with his desires, and he was pleased that the maid was neat and middling pretty and she seemed not to have any great temper of her own, and it was enough for him that she was so.

When the wedding was over, therefore, and it was good enough but without great display, he returned to the city to which Wang the Tiger had appointed him, taking his wife with him.

XXV

EACH spring that drew itself out of the long winter, Wang the Tiger felt in him the stirring of his ambition to greater wars and each spring he thought to look about him and see what he could do to enlarge himself. He sent out his spies to hear what the general wars of the year were likely to be and how he could fit some private war to the greater one, and he waited, he told himself, until the spies returned and until the year was warm enough and until the hour came when he could feel his destiny call him. But the truth was that Wang the Tiger was over his youth and now that he had his son he was held and content, and he had not that old restlessness in him to be out and at war. Each spring he told himself he must for his son's very sake go forth and achieve what he had set out to do in his lifetime and each spring there seemed to be some immediate good reason why he must put off his campaigns until another year. Nor were there any great and single wars in those years of his son's youth. There were but many small lords of war over that whole country, each holding his own small domain, and not any great man came out to be above them all. For this reason, also, Wang the Tiger felt it safe to wait another year and when the year came past its spring, yet another year, and he felt sure that some time or other when his destiny struck, he would still go forth to whatever victory he would choose.

There came on a certain spring, when his son was close upon thirteen years of age, a messenger from Wang the Tiger's two brothers, and he came upon a mission very grave, and it was no less than that Wang the Landlord's eldest son lay languishing in the city gaol of his town. The two brothers sent the messenger to beseech the aid at the provincial court of their brother, Wang the Tiger, so that the young man might be released. Wang the Tiger heard the tale, and it seemed to him a very good chance to test out his power at the provincial seat and his influence with the general of that province. He put off his war he had thought of, therefore, for yet another year, and he undertook to do what his brothers asked of him, and not without some pride, that they the elders had come to beg of him, the younger, and not without some scorn that a son of theirs could be cast into gaol, such a thing as never could befall his own good son.

Now the matter was thus and this was how Wang the Landlord's eldest son came to be put into a gaol.

This son of Wang the Landlord's was now in the twenty-and-eighth year of his age and he was not wed nor even betrothed. The reason for this very strange thing was that he had gone in his youth for a year or two to a new sort of a school in the town, and there he had learned many things, and one of the things he learned was that it was a vile slavery to an old custom for a young man to be wed by his parents to a maid they chose for him, and that all young men ought to choose their own maids to wife, maids whom they had seen and had talked with and could love. When, therefore, Wang the Landlord made a survey of all the marriageable maids to fix upon one for his eldest son, this son was very rebellious in the matter and he flung himself about and pouted and said he would choose his own wife.

At first Wang the Landlord and his lady were outraged at this notion, and for once they were agreed upon a thing, and the lady cried out to her son with heat,

"And how can you see a decent maid so close as to talk with her and know if you like her or not? And who so able to choose as your parents who formed you and who know your every turn of mind and nature?"

But the young man was full of argument and temper and he pushed his long silken sleeves back from his white smooth hands, and he tossed the black hair back from his pale forehead and he cried out in his turn,

"Neither you nor my father know anything except old dead customs, and you do not know that in the south all the sons of wealthy and learned people let their sons choose for themselves!" And when he saw his father and mother look at each other, and when he saw his father wipe his brow with his sleeve and his mother purse up her lips, he cried again, "Well, and betroth me, then, and I will leave my home and never see you more!"

This frightened the parents beyond measure and Wang the Landlord said in haste,

"But tell us what maid it is you love and we will see if it can be arranged."

Now the truth was that the young man had seen no such maid as he could love for wife, for the women he had known were such as could be easily bought, but he would not tell that he had seen no maid he loved, and he only pouted out his red lips and stared sullenly down at his pretty finger nails. But he looked so violent and so wilful that this time and every time his parents spoke of the matter they pacified him in the end again and again by saying, "Well, well, let it be for now!" Twice, indeed, had Wang the Landlord need to cry off the bargain with some maid he had begun to negotiate for, because when the young man heard of this he swore he would hang himself on a beam as his brother had done, and this terrified his mother and father so that they gave in to him every time.

Yet as time went on both Wang the Landlord and his lady grew the more eager to see their son wed, for he was their eldest son and chief heir and his sons must be the chief among their grandsons. Well, too, did Wang the Landlord know that the young man went to this tea house and to that and spent his youth here and there, and while he knew that all young men are so who have no need to labor for what they eat and wear, still as Wang the Landlord passed out of his own lustiness into a quieter age, he grew very uneasy at this son of his and both Wang the Landlord and his lady feared that if their son did not wed soon he would come some day with an idle maid out of a tea house for wife, such an one as it is well enough to take for a concubine but is a shame for a wife. But the youth, if they spoke their fears to him, talked ruthlessly of how in these new days young men and women were freed from their parents' rule, and how men and women were free and equal, and he said many such foolish things, so that these two parents could do nothing but hold their peace, for the young man's tongue was so glib and swift there was no answering him and they early learned to be silent while he poured out his fiery discontents and flashed his eyes from one to the other of the old pair, and every second flung back his long cut hair and smoothed it back with his soft white hand. But after such speeches when he was gone again, for he was very restless and never there for long, the lady looked at her husband with reproach and she said,

"You have taught him these things with your own lewd

ways and he learned from his own father to satisfy himself with these flower girls instead of with an honest woman."

She drew her sleeve across her eyes as she spoke and wiped one eye and the other, and she felt herself very ill used. As for Wang the Landlord he was in great alarm for he knew that this mild beginning could lead up to a great storm, for the older the lady grew the more righteous and ill-tempered she grew also, and he rose hastily to go away and he said very meekly,

"You know that now as I pass into my age I do not go as once I did, and I try to hear your counsel, and if you have a way out of this turmoil, I promise I will follow what you say."

Now the truth was that this lady could not herself think of any way to manage this turbulent son, and she must ease herself somehow and Wang the Landlord saw that her temper was rising in her, so he made all haste to go away out of his house. And as he passed through his court he saw that other wife of his there in the sunshine nursing a child, and he said to her hastily,

"Go in and fetch something for your mistress, because she is waxing angry. Take her tea or one of her prayer books or something, and praise her and say some priest or other said this or that about her or some such thing!"

The woman rose obediently, holding her child in her arm as she went, and as he went out into the street and thought where he might turn, Wang the Landlord blessed the hour he saw this second woman of his, for if he had been alone with his lady it would have been ill for him. But this second woman grew with the years even milder and more placid than she had been, and in this Wang the Landlord was very fortunate, since two women with a common lord will often-times quarrel and lead a noisy life, especially if one of them or both of them love their lord.

But this second woman comforted Wang the Landlord in many small ways and she did things that the servants would not. For the servants knew who had the authority in this house of Wang the Landlord's, and when he roared for some servant, man or maid, the servant called out, "Oh, aye, aye!" but he lagged or did not come, and if Wang the Landlord grew peevish, the servant made excuse, "The mistress commanded me thus and thus," and so silenced his master.

But this second wife served him secretly, and she it was who comforted him. When he came back from his few lands out of humor and weary, she saw to it that he had hot tea in his pot or if it were summer that there was a melon cool in the well, and she sat by and fanned him while he ate, and she fetched water to bathe his feet and brought fresh hose and shoes. To her also he poured out all his grievances and his hatreds, and chief of these was the grievance he had against his tenants and he told her all his bitter tales and he would say,

"Yes, and today that old snag-toothed woman who is mother to the tenant on the west land poured water into the basket of grain the steward weighed—he is such a fool, or else knave, and they pay him not to see—but I saw how the scale leaped!"

To such she made answer, soothing him, "I do not believe they cheat you much, you are so clever and the cleverest wisest man I ever knew."

His bitterness against his rebellious son he poured out to her, too, and she soothed him there also, and now as he went along the street he planned how he would tell her his lady blamed him cruelly and he dwelled upon the sweetness of her answer, how she would say as she had many times,

"To me you are the best man, and I ask no better, and I swear my lady does not know what men all are and how you

401

are better than them all!" Yes, out of the weariness of his son and his lady and all his troubles with the little land he had and dared not sell altogether, Wang the Landlord clung to this second woman of his and he thought in his heart, that of all the women he had followed only this one was comfortable to him and he said to himself, for reason, "She is the only one out of all I feed who knows me for what I am!"

And his heart swelled with especial bitterness against his son this day, because he had put fresh trouble upon his father.

Now as Wang the Landlord on this day walked along the streets so pondering, his son was on his own way to the house of a friend and it came about that in the strangest way he met the maid who could please him. This friend whom the young man sought was son of the chief of police of that town, and Wang the Landlord's son gamed with him continually in preference to all others, for since such gaming was against a new law that had been made, if there was trouble the son of the chief of police could escape and his friends could escape, since his father was so weighty a man in the town. On this day Wang the Landlord's son thought to game awhile and take the anger out of his heart and divert himself from the trouble his parents were to him, and therefore he went to his friend's house.

When the door was opened to him he gave his name to the serving man, and he sat and waited in the guest hall, brooding and impatient with all his troubles. Suddenly an inner door opened and a very pretty and young lady came in alone. Now if she had been a usual maid and had seen a young man sitting there alone, she must have covered her face with her sleeve and turned back with all speed. But she did not. She looked very calmly at Wang the Landlord's son, and she looked at him fully and slowly, but without coquetry, and she was not shy at all, and meeting this full calm look it was the young man's eyes which first fell. He saw, as anyone could see, that she was a proper maid enough for all her boldness, and she was such an one as belonged to the new times. Her black hair was cut short about her head and her feet were not bound, and she wore the long straight robe that new maidens wear, and since it was now late spring, the robe was made of a soft silk the color of a gosling's down.

Now for all his lordly talk, the truth was that this son of Wang the Landlord's had very little chance to meet with such maidens as he desired to wed. He spent his days when he was not gaming or feasting and playing somewhere in reading tales of love. Nor did he like the old tales, but he read most ardently the newly written tales of love that is free between man and maid, and he dreamed of well-born maidens who were not courtesans and yet were not shy and timid before men, but like men are with men except they be maids still, and such an one he sought. Yet he knew not one, for as yet such freedom was more in books than in truth. But now it seemed to him that here was truly the one he sought and his ready heart flamed to her cool, bold look, for that heart of his was like a fire laid and waiting for the torch to set it rushing into conflagration.

In that one moment he loved this maid so mightily that he was struck dazed, and although he said not one word and she passed on her way, he sat still dazed, and when his friend came in he gasped, his mouth dry, and his heart beating fit to burst against his breastbone,

"Who is the lady who passed?"

His friend said carelessly, "It is my sister who is in a foreign school in a coastal town, and she is home for the spring holiday."

Then Wang the Landlord's son could not but ask on, faltering,

"Is she not wed, then?"

The brother laughed and said, "No, she is the wilfullest maid, and she is forever quarreling with my parents on this, for she will not have any man they choose for her!"

Wang the Landlord's son heard this and it was like a cup of wine held to thirsty lips, he said no more and went on to his game. But as he played, he was distraught, for he felt the flames licking up about his heart and the fire burned in him. He excused himself soon and hastened to his home and to his own room and he shut the door and there alone he felt himself knit to this maid by every tie. And he murmured to himself that it was a shame she must suffer from her parents too, as he did, and he told himself he would not come to her except by such free means as men and women use in these free times. No, he would have no go-between, not parent nor even his friend her brother. Then in fever and haste he took out the books he had read and studied them to see what sort of a letter such heroes wrote to their free loves, and then he wrote her such a letter, too.

Yes, he wrote to that maid, and he put his name to what he wrote, and he began the letter with all the courteous proper words. But he said also that he was a free spirit and so he saw her, also, and she was therefore to him the very light of the sun, the very hue of a peony flower, the very music of the flute, and in an instant's time she had plucked his heart out of his bosom. Then when he had written this, he sent it by his own private servant, and having sent it he waited at home in such a fever that his parents did not know what was wrong with him. When the servant came back to say the answer would come later, the young man could but wait on, and yet he loathed his waiting and he hated all in the house and he slapped his younger brothers and sisters without mercy if they came near him and complained against the servants, and

404

even the good-natured concubine his father had, cried out, "You behave as a dog that will go mad!" And she drew her own children out of his reach.

But after three days a messenger brought an answer, and the young man, who spent his days hanging about the gate, seized it and made off to his room and tore the letter in his haste to open it. He pieced the two torn parts together and made it out. She wielded her brush very boldly and prettily and when she had written words of courtesy and words to justify her boldness, she said, "I also am a free spirit, and I will not be forced by my parents in anything."

Thus delicately did she put her preference for him, and the young man was beside himself with pleasure.

In such a way, then, had the matter begun, and the two could not be content even with many letters, but they must meet somehow, and so they did meet a time or two at the side gate to the maid's house. They were both afraid, although they neither wished to show it, and in such hasty meetings and in many letters written back and forth and much bribing of servants and disguising of their names in their letters, this love burned hotter and hotter, and since neither man nor maid had ever done without anything they dearly wanted, so they could not now. At their third meeting the young man said very ardently,

"I cannot wait and I must wed you and so I will tell my father."

To this the maid answered very wilfully, "And I will tell my father I will poison myself if I am not to have you, too."

So they did tell their fathers, and while Wang the Landlord was glad enough to have his son's fancy fix itself on a maid of such a good house and set himself at once to arrange the match, the maid's father turned stubborn and he would not have the young man for his daughter. No, since he was chief of police it was his business to have his spies everywhere, and he knew things that others did not about this young man and he cried out at his daughter,

"What, that do-nothing of a dandy who spends his time in every idle house of pleasure?"

And he commanded his servants that his daughter was to be locked into her own courts until she went back to her school, and when she came flying in furiously to talk with him and implore him he would not pay any heed to her. No, he was a very calm man and while she argued he hummed a tune and read a book, and when she grew too angry and said things a maid should not, he turned on her and said,

"I always knew I should have held you in this house and not sent you to a school. It is this schooling that spoils maids now-a-days, and if I had it to do again, I would have kept you decent and ignorant as your mother is and so wed you early to a good man. Yes, and I will do it yet!" and he roared at her so suddenly that she faltered and was afraid.

Then these two young things wrote very pretty despairing letters to each other and the servants grew rich on bribes, and ran back and forth. But the young man pined in his home and did not go out to game or play, and his parents saw him pine and they did not know what to do. Wang the Landlord sent a secret bribe by devious ways to the chief of police, and though he was a man ready for a bribe, yet this time he was not ready, and so they all despaired. As for the young man, he would not eat and he talked of hanging himself and Wang the Landlord was distracted altogether.

Now one evening as the young man walked near the back of the house where his love lived, he saw the small gate of escape open, and the maid servant who carried her letters, squeezed through, and she beckoned to him to come. He came faltering and fearful, yet driven by his own heart, and when he was come, there inside the little court by the gate, stood his love, and she was very determined and wilful and full of plans. Yet now that they were face to face their words did not come easily either, and not nearly so easily as words upon paper, and the truth was the young man was much afraid lest he be discovered there where he ought not by any means to be. But the maid was wilful, and being learned, she would have her desire and she said,

"I will not heed these old ones. Let us flee together somewhere and when they see us gone, for very shame they will let us wed. I know my father loves me, for I am his only daughter and my mother dead, and you are your father's oldest son."

But before the young man could match his ardor to hers, the chief of police stood suddenly there at the door of the house that gave upon the court, for some servant that bore ill will to the young girl's maid had told for revenge, and the chief of police shouted to his attendants,

"Bind him and put him in gaol, for he has taken away my daughter's honor!"

Now it was a very unlucky thing for Wang the Landlord's eldest son that his love's father was chief of police and could throw whom he liked into gaol, for another man would not have had such power and must have paid money to have him imprisoned. But with the word the attendants haled the young man away, and the maid shrieked and hung herself upon the young man's arm, and cried she would not marry any other and that she would swallow her rings.

But that calm old man, her father, turned to the serving maids and said,

"See to her, and if she is left alone and by any chance does what she says, I will hold you for her death."

And he went away as though he did not hear her moans

and cries, and the serving maids did not dare to leave her, being afraid for themselves, and so the young girl had no choice but to live on.

As for the chief of police, he sent word to Wang the Landlord that his son was in the gaol because he had attempted the honor of his own daughter, and having sent this message he sat in his hall and waited. Then was the household of Wang the Landlord in the greatest confusion and Wang the Landlord was completely distracted and did not know what to do. He sent a good bribe immediately of all the silver he had about him, and he struggled into his finest robes and went to the chief of the police himself to apologize. But that man was in no mood to have the thing so easily settled, and he sent word out to the gate that he was ill from so much worry and could see no one, and when the bribe was brought in he sent it back again saying that Wang the Landlord had mistaken his character and he was not such an one as to be tempted thus.

Then Wang the Landlord went groaning back to his house, and he knew the bribe was too small, and since it was just before wheat harvest he was very short of silver, and he knew he must ask his brother's help. There was his son in gaol, too, and he suffered for that, and he must send food and bedding lest he suffer there. When this was done and Wang the Merchant called, Wang the Landlord sat in his own room and waited, and his lady forgot all usage and in her distress she came in where he sat leaning his head on his hands, and she called on this god and that to witness to all she had to bear in this house.

But for once Wang the Landlord sat not moved more than he was, for all her cries and reproaches, for he was frightened to his heart's bottom to have his son like this in the power of the chief of police. But Wang the Merchant came in very

408

collected and he made his face smooth as though he did not know what was wrong, although the tale was flying everywhere, and being so good and nasty a tale, every servant knew it already and his wife knew it and had told him all and more than all, and she had said with greatest relish, over and over,

"Well I knew no good would come out of that woman's sons and their father so lustful as he is, too."

But now Wang the Merchant sat and listened to the tale as it came from the young man's father and mother, and they made his crime very light, and Wang the Merchant looked judicial and as though he took for granted the young man's innocence and thought only of some wily way to free him. Well he knew his elder brother wanted to borrow a vast sum, and he planned deeply as to how this could be avoided. When the tale was told and the lady was weeping freely at the end, he said,

"It is true that silver is very useful when dealing with officials anywhere, but there is one thing better still and it is power of arms. Before we spend all we have, let us beseech our brother, who is now a very high general, that he exert himself and use his influence in the provincial court and have a mandate sent down from above to our magistrate here who will command the chief of police to release your son. Then a little silver may be used here and there to help the cause."

Now this seemed a wonderful and good plan to them all and Wang the Landlord marvelled that it had not come to him, and on that very day and in that very hour he sent a messenger to Wang the Tiger and thus it was that Wang the Tiger heard of it.

Now Wang the Tiger besides the duty he had to help his brothers, saw it was a very good chance to test his power and influence. So he wrote a proper, humble letter to the general of the province and he prepared gifts and he sent all by his trusty man and a guard to keep the gifts safe from robbers. Now that general when he received the gifts and read the letter, pondered awhile, and it seemed to him that here was a useful way to bind Wang the Tiger to him in case of a war and if he did this favor, Wang the Tiger would feel an obligation and it seemed a cheap way to secure this favor by letting a young man out of gaol and he cared nothing at all for so small a fellow as the chief of police in a single town. So he sent the word that Wang the Tiger asked, and then he told the ruler of that province, and the ruler sent a mandate down to the magistrate of the county, who sent his mandate down to the magistrate of the town where the House of Wang lived.

Now Wang the Merchant was more tricky than ever, and he was more clever, and he followed each step with enough silver so that every man who touched the affair felt himself rewarded but still not so much that a greedy spirit might be roused to look twice at the source of so much money. In his turn, the chief of police received the command also and Wang the Landlord and Wang the Second watched very carefully for this moment when it came, for they knew a man will not suffer being put to public shame, and so when they knew he had received the command, they went to him with goodly bribes and with many apologies and they begged the chief of police as though for their own sakes, feigning that they knew nothing of all that had passed from above. No, they made obeisances and they besought him as a man of mercy, and at last he accepted the money carelessly and largely as a man will who confers a favor. Then he ordered the young man released and he reproved him and sent him home.

As for the two brothers, they gave a mighty feast to the

chief of police and so the matter was ended, for the young man was free again, and his love somewhat the cooler for the gaol.

But that maid was more wilful than ever and she clamored anew to her father. This time he was somewhat more willing, now that he understood how powerful this family of Wang was, and how strong a lord of war one of the three brothers was, and how much money Wang the Merchant had, and he sent a go-between to Wang the Landlord and he said,

"Let us wed these two and seal our new friendship."

So the matter was carried through and the betrothal was made and the wedding on the first lucky day to be found thereafter and Wang the Landlord and his lady were filled with relief and happiness. As for the bridegroom, although he was somewhat dazed at this sudden turn, yet he felt some of his old ardor return and he was very well content and the maid was full of triumph.

But to Wang the Tiger the whole affair was of no great moment except for this; he knew himself now for a man of power in that province and he knew that the general held him to be one whose favor he wished to hold to himself, and his heart swelled with pride. When this whole matter was finished, the spring had turned well into summer and Wang the Tiger said to himself that since he had been so busy and the year was now so late, he would put off his planned war until yet another year. He did this the more easily, because he was now sure of his position, and yet more easily, because in the beginning of that summer his spies began to return to him and they said that some sort of war was rumored well to the south, but they did not yet know what war it was, nor who its head. When Wang the Tiger heard this he understood fully the value of his army to the provincial general and why he sought to hold his favor. And he waited then for another spring, to see what it would bring forth.

And as always he did, Wang the Tiger spent his life with his son. The lad came and went gravely about his duties and it was Wang the Tiger's pleasure to watch the lad in his silent way. Often he gazed at his son, and he loved to dwell upon his serious face, half child, half youth. Many a time when he thus studied his son's face as it bent over some book or task, Wang the Tiger was caught by a strange familiar look in the boy's high square cheek, or in the firmness of his mouth. It was not a beautiful mouth, but very firm and fixed for so young a lad.

And it came to Wang the Tiger one night that his son had his look from his grandmother, Wang the Tiger's own mother. Yes, Wang the Tiger knew it was his mother's look, although he could only remember her clearly when she lay dying, and the boy's ruddy face was very different, too, from her pale, dying face. But deeper in Wang the Tiger than any clear memory was some feeling that told him his son moved in his mother's slow and silent way, and that her gravity was upon his son's lips and in his eyes. And when Wang the Tiger felt this vague familiar thing in his son, it seemed to warm his heart the more, and he loved his son more deeply yet and for some reason he did not understand he was knit to him yet more closely.

XXVI

Now the son of Wang the Tiger was such a sort of lad as this; he was faithful in every duty and he did all that he was told to do. He studied to perform the feints of war and the postures that his teachers set before him, and he rode his horse well enough, if not easily as Wang the Tiger did. But the lad did all as though he had no pleasure in any of it and as though he forced himself to everything as a task. When Wang the Tiger asked the tutor how his son did, the tutor answered hesitating,

"I cannot say he does not do well, for he does all well to a point, and he does very exactly what he is told, but beyond that he never goes. It is as though he kept his heart back."

This answer troubled Wang the Tiger very much for it had seemed to him before this that his son had no good hearty anger in him, and he was never angry and he had neither hatred nor desire in him for anything, but only he went gravely and with patience to all he had to do. Now Wang the Tiger knew that a warrior cannot be so; no, a warrior must have spirit and anger and wilfulness in him and a ready passion and he grieved and wondered how to change his son in this.

One day he sat by and watched the lad in the court as he fired at a target under his tutor's direction, and although the lad stood quietly and lifted his arm quickly and did not hesitate to pull firmly upon the trigger when the call came, yet it seemed to Wang the Tiger that he saw his son brace himself and a look come over his smooth boy's face as though he hardened himself within, so that he might do what he must, because he hated it so much. Then Wang the Tiger called to his lad and he said,

"Son, put your heart into it, if you would please me!"

The lad looked quickly at his father then, the pistol still smoking in his hand, and a strange look stole into his eyes and he opened his lips as though to speak. But there sat Wang the Tiger, and he could not look gentle if he would, those brows of his heavy and black, and his mouth sullen in his stiff black beard even when he did not mean it so, and the lad looked away again and sighed a little and he said in his patient way,

"Yes, my father."

Then Wang the Tiger looked with vague pain at his son, and for all his stiff hard looks his heart was soft, but he did not know how to speak out of his heart. And after a while he sighed and he watched in silence until the lesson was over. Then the lad looked doubtfully at his father and he said,

"May I go now, my father?"

And it came to Wang the Tiger that this lad of his went often away somewhere alone and many times he slipped away and Wang the Tiger did not know where, except that he knew the guard he had appointed to follow his son wherever he went followed him doubtless. But Wang the Tiger on this day looked at his son with a question in his mind, whether the lad went where he should not, and he saw him that he was a child no longer, and smitten with a sudden jealousy, Wang the Tiger made his voice as gentle as he could and he asked,

"But where do you go, my son?"

The boy hesitated and hung his head and at last he said half afraid,

"To no one place, my father. But I like to go outside the walls of the city and walk about the fields awhile."

Now if the boy had said he went to some bawdy place Wang the Tiger could not have been so taken aback and he said astounded,

"Now what can be there for a soldier to see?"

And the boy kept his eyes down and he fingered his little leather belt and he said in a low voice, in his usual patient way,

"Nothing—but it is quiet and pleasant to see now when the fruit trees are abloom, and I like to talk with a farmer sometimes and hear how he plants his land."

Then Wang the Tiger was completely astonished and he did not know what to do with this son of his, and he mut-

414

tered to himself, that here was a strange son for a lord of war to have, who had hated from his youth up the ways of farmers upon the land, and suddenly he shouted out more angrily than he meant to do, because he was somehow disappointed and yet he did not know why he was,

"Do what you will then, and what is it to me?" And he sat on awhile heavily, for his son had slipped, swift as a freed bird, away from his father.

Wang the Tiger sat on and he meditated painfully, and yet he did not know why his heart was so sore, either. At last he grew impatient and he hardened himself somewhat and he told himself that with such a son he ought to be content, since the lad was not profligate and he did what he was told, and so Wang the Tiger put the matter away from him once more.

Now during these several years there were rumors of some new great discontent shaping itself up into a war somewhere, and Wang the Tiger's spies brought back tales of young men and young women in the schools of the south shaping themselves in a war and they brought tales of common folk upon the land shaping themselves for war and such things had never been heard of before, because such things are the trade of lords of war and have nothing to do with common people. But when Wang the Tiger in astonishment asked why they did battle and in what cause his spies did not know, and Wang the Tiger told himself it must be some school or other where some teacher did a wrong, or if it were the common people it must be some magistrate too vile and the people could not endure him more and they rose to kill him and put an end to what they could not bear.

But at least until he could see how new war shaped and how he could fit himself to it Wang the Tiger waged no wars of his own. No, he conserved his revenues and he bought such tools of war as he wished. Nor did he need to ask his brother Wang the Merchant to help him for Wang the Tiger had now his own port at the river's mouth which he owned and he hired ships and smuggled his own weapons in from outer countries easily enough. If there were those above him who knew it they were silent for they knew he was a general on their own side and every gun he had was a gun for them in the struggle that must come one day, since peace cannot last forever anywhere.

In such ways did Wang the Tiger strengthen himself as he waited, and his son grew and came into his fourteenth year.

Now these fifteen years and more that Wang the Tiger had been a great lord of war he had been lucky in many ways and the chief way was that there had been no great whole famine in his regions. Small famines there had been in one place or another, for thus it must ever be under a cruel heaven, but there was no famine over all his regions together, so that if one part starved, he need not press hard upon it, but he could raise his taxes in some other part where the people did not starve, or at least not so bitterly. This he was pleased to do, because he was a just man and he did not willingly take from dying people the little they had as some lords of war will do. For this the people were thankful and they praised him, and many throughout his region said,

"Well, and we have seen worse lords of war than the Tiger, and since there must be such lords, it is lucky we have this one who only taxes us for his soldiers and he does not love feasting and women and the things that most such men love."

It was true that Wang the Tiger took care to be just to the common people as much as he could. To this day no new magistrate had come to take the old one's place in that court. There had been a certain one appointed, but hearing how fierce a man Wang the Tiger was he delayed his coming, saying that his father grew old and that he must wait until the old man died and was buried before he could come. So until he came Wang the Tiger very often dispensed his own justice in the court and he heard people who came before him and he defended many a poor man against a rich man or a usurer. The truth was that Wang the Tiger did not need to fear any rich man, and he would clap the rich man into gaol if he did not pay what Wang the Tiger would have of him, so that it came to be in that town that landlords and usurers and such people hated Wang the Tiger very heartily and they went to great lengths to avoid bringing a case before him. But Wang the Tiger cared nothing for their hatred, since he was powerful and did not need to be afraid. He paid his soldiers regularly and well and if he was harsh sometimes with a man who committed some liberty too great, still he paid them their monthly wage and this was more than many a lord of war did, who must depend upon a looting to keep his men about him. But Wang the Tiger was not driven to a war for the sake of his men, and he could delay if he pleased, and his position in that region among the people and among his own men was very good and secure by now.

But however well men do establish themselves, they have always a perverse heaven with which to reckon, and so also did Wang the Tiger. In the fourteenth year of his son's age, when he prepared the next year to send him to the school of war, there fell a very heavy famine upon every part of Wang the Tiger's regions, and it spread from one part to another like a dire disease.

It came about that the proper rains of spring fell in their season, but when the time came for their cessation, the skies rained on, and the rains held day after day and week after week, and even into the summer they held, so that the rising wheat mouldered in the fields and sank into the water, and all those fair fields were pools of muddied water. The small river, too, which was by nature but a placid stream, went roaring along swollen and furious, and it tore at its clay banks and overran them and rushed against inner dykes and burst them apart and then went sweeping down its course and poured all its mud into the sea, so that the clear green waters were sullied for many a mile out. As for the people, they lived in their homes at first, building up their tables and beds upon boards out of the water. But as the waters rose to the roofs of their houses and the earthen walls crumbled, they lived in boats and in tubs and they clung to such dykes and mounds as still stood above the water, or they climbed into trees and hung there. Nor did people so only, but wild beasts and the snakes of the fields also, and these snakes swarmed up the trees and hung festooned upon the branches and they lost their fear of men and came creeping and crawling to live among them, so that men did not know which was the greater terror, terror of water or terror of the crawling snakes. But as the days went on and the water did not fall, there was yet another terror and it was the terror of starvation.

Here was a very sore thing for Wang the Tiger to bear, and one that he had not known before. He was worse off than many another man, too, because where other men have but their own families to feed, here was he with a vast horde dependent on him and they all very ignorant men, ready to complain, and content only if they were well fed and well paid, and loyal only so long as they were given what they held to be their due. From one place and another in Wang the Tiger's territories the revenues ceased to come in fully and at last as the waters stayed through the summer and when autumn came and there was no harvest, then by the winter of that year there were no revenues except the one upon the opium which was smuggled into those parts, and even this was much shrunken, since people could not buy and so the smugglers took their goods to other places for the time. Even the salt revenues ceased, for the waters washed away the salt wells, and the potters made no more wine jars, since that year no new wine was brewed.

Now Wang the Tiger was in great distress and for the first time in all his years as a lord of war and ruler over territories, in the last month of that year he could not pay his men. When he saw what was come he knew he must save himself by harshness alone, nor dared he show pity lest they take it for weakness in him. He called his captains to him, therefore, and he shouted at them as though they had done some evil and as though he were angry at them,

"All these months you men of mine have been fed while others starved and you have had wage as well! Now your wage must be food only, for my silver is gone, and no revenues will come until these times are over. No, and in a month or so, I shall have no silver left even to feed you and I must borrow a vast sum from somewhere, if you are not to starve, and if I and my son are not to starve with you."

Now as he spoke thus Wang the Tiger made his face hard and he glared at his men from under his brows and he pulled at his beard angrily, but secretly he looked to see what his captains did. There were mutinous faces among them and when they had gone out in silence there were those whom he kept as spies about him always who came back to tell him,

"They say they will fight no war until their dues are given them."

When he had heard his spy whisper this Wang the Tiger sat gloomy for a while in his hall, and he thought on the hearts of men and how ungrateful they are, and he thought how he had fed his men well and as usual during all these hungry months when the people starved and died and they did not love him the better. Once or twice he had said to himself that he might even take some of that private store of silver that he kept for his own lest he be put to it hard in some retreat and vanquishment in some war, but now he swore his men might starve and he would not rob himself and his son for any of them.

Still the famine did not cease. Everywhere in that region the waters lay and men starved and since there was no dry land in which to bury them, their bodies were cast out upon the water and floated there. There were many bodies of children, because men grew desperate at the unceasing wail of hungry children who could not understand why they were not fed, and so in the darkness of night and despair some parents even laid their children into the water; some did it out of pity for their children, for it seemed a shorter, sweeter death, but some did it because of the little store of food they had left, and they would not divide it with any other, and when two were left in a family then sometimes those two schemed secretly as to which was the stronger.

By the New Year, and none remembered it was a festival, Wang the Tiger gave his men but half their usual food, and he himself ate no meat in his household, but only grain gruel and such poor stuffs. One day as he sat in his own room thinking on what a pass he had come to, and wondering that his good destiny was in such abeyance, there came a man out of his guard who stood day and night about his door, and the man said,

"There are six men to see you who come from your own army and to stand for all the others. They have something to say."

Then Wang the Tiger looked up sharply out of his gloom and he asked,

"Are they armed?"

To this the guard replied, "I do not see any arms on them, but who can know the heart of any man?"

Now Wang the Tiger's son sat in the room at a little desk of his own, and his head was bent over some book he studied diligently. Wang the Tiger looked at him, thinking to send him away. And the lad rose at that instant and made as though to go away. But when Wang the Tiger saw him so willing his heart hardened suddenly and he thought to himself that his son must learn how to deal with men who were rebellious or savage, and so he cried out,

"Stay!" And the lad sat down slowly, as though he did not know what to make of it.

But Wang the Tiger turned to the guardsman and he said,

"Call the whole guard to come in and stand about me, and let them bring their guns ready set as though to make attack, and call the six men in!"

Then Wang the Tiger sat himself in a great old armchair he had which had once been the magistrate's own chair, and there was a tiger skin thrown over the back of it for warmth. There Wang the Tiger sat, and his guards came in and stood to right and to left of him, and Wang the Tiger sat and stroked his beard.

The six men came in and they were young men, hardy and easily moved and daring as young men are. They came in courteously when they saw their general sitting there with his guards about him and the points of the guns glittering about his head, and the one who had been chosen to speak made his proper obeisance and he said,

"Most Merciful, we have been chosen by our comrades to come and ask for a little more food. Indeed, we are not fed.

421

We do not say anything of wage now, seeing the times are so hard, and we will not ask for arrears in our wage now. But we are not fed, and day by day we grow weaker, and we are soldiers and our whole trade stock is in these bodies of ours. We have but a poor loaf of bread a day. For this we come to you, to put the matter before your justice."

Now Wang the Tiger knew what ignorant men are and he knew that they must be kept frightened or they will not obey their leader. He stroked his beard furiously, therefore, and he coaxed his anger to rise in his breast. He thought of all his kindness to his men, how he had not used them hard in war and how he had gone against his will in letting them take their booty after siege, and how he had always paid them and seen them well clothed, and how he was himself a good man and not lustful and exorbitant in his desires as so many men are, and as he thought of all this he felt his good anger begin to rise in him that these men of his could not bear hardship with him when it was the will of heaven and no fault of his own, and the more he thought of this the more he fanned his anger and tried to increase it. When he felt some semblance of it rise in him he made haste to use its strength, for he knew what he must do, and he roared out,

"Do you come here to pull the tiger's whiskers? Shall I let you starve? Have I ever let you starve? I have my plans made ready and food is due at any hour from foreign lands. But no, you are rebels—you would not trust me!" And he gathered up all his anger and he gave a great shout to his guards, "Kill me these six rebels!"

Then those six young men fell on their faces to beg for their lives but Wang the Tiger did not dare to spare them. No, for the sake of his son and himself and his household and for the people of that whole countryside whom they might turn to maraud if he lost his command over his men, he dared not

422

spare them, and he would not let his mercy free now. He shouted,

"Shoot, you men, to right and left!"

Then those guards shot, and the whole great room was filled with roar and smoke, and when the smoke lifted, those six men lay dead.

And Wang the Tiger rose at once and he commanded, "Take them back now to those who sent them and tell them it is my answer!"

But before the guards could stoop to lift the bodies of the young men a strange thing happened. That son of Wang the Tiger's, he so grave a lad and seeming usually to see little of what went on around him, now he rushed forward in the wildest distraction such as his father had never seen upon him, and he bent over one of the young men and stared and he went from one to the other of the young men, touching them here and there swiftly, looking at them with great wild eyes, staring at their loose-flung limbs, and he cried out to his father, standing to face him, and not knowing what he did,

"You have killed them—they are every one dead! This one I knew—he was my friend!"

And he fixed such despairing eyes upon his father's eyes that Wang the Tiger was suddenly afraid in some strange way because of the look in his son's eyes and he looked down and he said to justify himself,

"I was compelled to it, or they might have led the others and risen against me and so killed us all."

But the boy choked and he muttered, "He did only ask for bread—" And suddenly his face broke into weeping and he rushed from that room, and his father stared after him stupefied.

As for the guards, they went to their business and when Wang the Tiger was alone again, he sent out of the room even the two men who were always with him day and night, and he sat alone and held his head in his hands for an hour or two and he sat and groaned and wished he had not had to kill the young men. When he could not bear it any longer he called out that his son was to come to him, and after a while the boy came in slowly, his face bent down and his eyes veiled from his father. Wang the Tiger called to him to come near, and when he was come he took the lad's strong slender hand and fondled it a little as he had never done before and he said in a low voice,

"I did it for you."

But the lad made no reply at all. He had hardened himself and bore his father's love silently and stiffly and Wang the Tiger sighed and let him go, for he did not know what to say to his son or how make his son understand his love. So Wang the Tiger's heart was very sore and it seemed to him that of all men he was the most alone in this whole world, and he suffered a day or two. Then he, too, hardened himself again and let this pass also, since he did not know what to do, and he planned that he would do something for his son to make him forget. Yes, he would buy him a foreign watch or a new gun or some such thing and so win the boy back to him. Thus Wang the Tiger hardened himself and thus he comforted himself, also.

Nevertheless, the coming of these six men out of the army did show Wang the Tiger in what dire straits the times had brought him, for he saw that he must find food if he was to hold his army true. He had said falsely that he had already found food for them from foreign parts, but now he knew he must go out somewhere and find such food. Then once more he thought of his brother, Wang the Merchant, and he told himself that in such an hour brothers must stand together and he would go and see how the times were in his father's house, and what help he could secure.

He sent out the word, therefore, among his men that he went to find food and silver for them and he promised them a plenty, and when they were all cheerful and expectant, and freshened somewhat in their hope and loyalty to him, he chose a good guard and put them over his house and he commanded his own guard to prepare for the journey, and on a day he had set he called for boats to be brought and with his son and his soldiers and their horses all in these boats, they prepared to ferry across the waters to those parts of the road where the dykes still held, and there they would mount their horses again and ride to the town where Wang the Tiger's brothers lived.

Upon those narrow dykes their horses took their pace slowly, for the water spread in a sea on either side, and the dykes were crowded with huddled people. And not people only, but rats and serpents and wild things struggled to share that space with the people, and these wild things forgot their fears and tried with all their feeble strength to contend for space. But the only life these people showed was in such brief angers as rose in them when the serpents and beasts grew too many and they struck at them spitefully. But sometimes for long spaces they did not even so contend and the serpents curled and crawled wherever they would, and the people sat in their stupor.

Through these Wang the Tiger marched, and he had need of his armed guard and of his guns, for these people would have fallen upon him otherwise. As it was, here and there and often a man rose, or a woman, and twined about his horse's legs in silence and despair, yet with a faint last hope. And Wang the Tiger was gentle enough in heart with them, and he drew his horse and would not trample them down. No, he waited until one of his guardsmen came and took the wretched creature away and threw him on the ground again, and Wang the Tiger passed on without looking back. Sometimes the man lay where he had been thrown, but sometimes he gave a wild howl and leaped into the water and so ended himself and his woe.

All the way the lad rode beside his father, and not one word did he say, nor did Wang the Tiger speak to him, since there was the coldness between them of the six dead men, and Wang the Tiger feared to ask his son anything. But the lad's face was bowed down except sometimes when he seemed to steal a look sidewise at the starving people, and such a look of horror came into his face that Wang the Tiger could not bear it and he said at last,

"These be but very common folk and they are used to this once in a few years or so, and there are tens of thousands of such as these and the ones that die are not missed in a handful of years. They spring up like new rice again."

Then the boy said suddenly, and his voice was changing now like a fledgling bird's, and it came out in a squeak because he was so charged with his feeling, and with his fear lest he weep before his father,

"Yet I suppose it is as hard for them to die as though they were governors and men like us." And as he spoke he tried to fix his mouth hard and firm, but indeed these were sorrowful sights and his lips quivered, do what he would.

Now Wang the Tiger would have liked to say some comforting word, but he was astonished at what his son had said, and it had not come to him that these common folk suffered as he might suffer, since men are born as they are born and one may not take the place of any other. And he did not wholly like what his son said, because it was too soft a thing for a lord of war who may not stop to put his own heart into

426

any man who happens to suffer hardship. So Wang the Tiger could not think of any comforting word, for it was true that nothing could be fed these days except the carrion crows that circled and whirled again slowly in great wheels above the waters, and he said no more than this,

"We are all alike under the cruel will of Heaven."

After this Wang the Tiger let his son be; seeing what thoughts the lad had, Wang the Tiger asked him no more of anything.

XXVII

Now Wang the Tiger wished very often upon that journey that he could have left his son behind. But the truth was he did not dare to do it, lest there be some among his men who were secretly sullen because of the six dead men. Yet almost as much as he feared death for his son he feared too to take him to his brothers' courts. He feared the softness of the young men there, and he feared the coarse love of money that tradesmen have. He commanded his son's tutor, therefore, whom he had brought also, and he commanded his trusty harelipped man, that they were not to leave their young master at all, and besides these he told off ten seasoned and old soldiers who were to stay beside his son day and night, and he told his son he must study his books as ever he did at home. But he did not dare to say to him, "My son, you are not to go where there are women," for he did not know whether or not the boy had thought of such things yet. All these years when Wang the Tiger had his son by him in his own courts, there had been no women there, neither servant nor slave nor courtesan, and the lad knew no women at all except his mother and his sisters, and of latter years Wang the Tiger had not let him go alone even on the rare visits of duty he made to his mother, but had told off a guard to go with him. In such ways had Wang the Tiger fortified his son, and he was more jealous for this son of his than other men are for the women they love.

Yet in spite of his secret fears, it was a sweet moment for Wang the Tiger when he came riding to his brother's gates with his son riding beside him. It had pleased some fancy of Wang the Tiger's to have his tailors and sewing men cut his son's garments exactly like his own, and the lad wore just such a coat of foreign cloth, and such gilt buttons and such shoulder pieces of gilt, and a cap like Wang the Tiger's with a sign upon it. Wang the Tiger had even, upon the lad's fourteenth birthday, sent a man into Mongolia and found two horses exactly alike, except one a little smaller than the other, and both of them strong and dark and reddish in color, and their eyes white and rolling, and so even their horses were alike. It was sweetest music to Wang the Tiger's ears to hear the people upon the street cry out, as they stopped to stare at the soldiers pass,

"See the old lord of war and the little lord of war, as like as the two front teeth in a man's mouth!"

So they came riding up to the gates of Wang the Landlord, and the lad swung himself down from his horse as his father did, and clapped his hand to his sword's hilt as his father did, and marched gravely beside his father, without ever knowing that he did all like his father. As for Wang the Tiger, when he had been received into his brothers' house, and when his two brothers and their sons came in to give greeting, one after the other as they heard he was come, Wang the Tiger looked about on them all, and he drank in the looks of admiration they gave to his son as a thirsty man drinks down his wine. In the days thereafter while Wang the Tiger was in that house, he watched his brothers' sons

428

eagerly and scarcely knowing he did, hungry to be sure his own son was far better, and hungry to be comforted for his only son.

And Wang the Tiger could find much wherewith to comfort himself. The eldest son of Wang the Landlord was now well wed, although he had no children yet, and he and his wife lived in the same house with Wang the Landlord and his lady. This eldest son grew already somewhat like his father, and he was already a little round in the belly and his pretty body was coating itself with a soft deep fat. But he had a weary look, too, and it was true he had something to weary him, for his wife would not live pleasantly with his mother, the lady, but she was pert in her new wisdom and she cried out to her husband when they were alone and he tried to exhort her,

"What—am I to be a servant to that old proud woman? Does she not know we young women are free now-a-days and we do not serve our mothers-in-law any more?"

Nor did this young woman fear the lady at all, and when the lady said with her old majesty, "When I was young I served my mother-in-law as it was my duty to do, and I took her tea in the morning and I bowed myself before her as I had been bred to do," the daughter-in-law shook back her short hair and tapped her pretty unbound foot upon the floor and she said very impudently,

"But we women today do not bow down before anyone!"

Because of such strife the young husband grew often weary, nor could he solace himself with his old diversions, for his young wife watched him and would know his every play place, and she was so bold she did not fear to follow him out into the street and cry out that she would go, too, and that now-a-days women did not stay locked in the house, and men and women were equal and with such talk she so diverted the people upon the streets that for very shame's sake the young husband gave up his old diversions, for he did believe her bold enough to follow him anywhere. For this young wife was so jealous that she would break off every habit and natural desire her husband had, and he could not so much as glance at a pretty slave and she would not let him go near a brothel with his friends without finding such a shrieking and weeping stirred up ready for him when he came home again, that it was an outrage in the house. Once a friend to whom he complained advised him saying,

"Threaten her with a concubine—it is very humbling for any woman!"

But when the young man tried this, his wife was not humbled at all, but she cried out and her round eyes flashed at him,

"In times like this we women will not endure such things!"

And before he knew what she did, she sprang at him with her little hands outspread and she clawed him on either cheek like a small cat, and there were four deep scratches red and bright on his two cheeks, and it was plain to anyone how he came by them, and he could not stir out for five days and more for shame. Nor dared he put her to any open shame, for her brother was his friend and her father chief of police and a man with power in the town.

Yet in the night he loved her still, for she could curl against him sweetly enough and coax him and be so seeming penitent that he loved her heartily then, and he softened to listen to her talk.

At such hours the burden of all her talk was that he must ask his father for a certain sum of money and they two would go away out of this house and go to some port city on the coast and live there in the new fashion and live among those of their kind. And she would fling out her pretty arms and

430

hold him and wheedle him, or she would grow angry and weep or she would lie in her bed and refuse to rise or to eat until he would promise, and so in a thousand ways she wearied her husband, until at last he gave his promise. But when he had promised and had gone to his father, and when Wang the Landlord heard it he looked up out of his heavy old eyes and he said,

"Where shall I find such a sum as you say? I cannot do it." And after a while when he seemed sunken in the sleepy indolence in which he passed much of his life now, he spoke again and he said, "A man must bear with women, for the best of them are full of strife and contention. Learned or unlearned, they are so, but the learned ones are the worst for they do not fear anything. Let the women rule the house, I have always said, and I will seek my peace elsewhere. So you must do, also."

But the young wife would not have it settled so easily, and she forced her husband to go again and again to his father, and for peace's sake Wang the Landlord grew weak at last and he promised he would plan some way, although well he knew the only way he had was to sell the most of what land he still owned. As for the young wife, when she had even the half promise, she prattled of her going and made her every plan and talked so constantly of what many ways there were to find pleasure in the coast city, and how fine the women dressed themselves and how she must buy a new gown and a coat of fur, and how all the clothes she had were less than rags and fit only for such a country place as this, that with all her talking she stirred her husband up to some eagerness to be gone, too, and to see all the wonders of which she spoke.

Now Wang the Landlord's younger son was a man, too, and he had followed in his brother's footsteps, and he was eager in only one thing and it was that he should be given no less in anything than his elder brother had. He had a secret and mighty admiration for his pretty sister-in-law, and in his heart he determined that when his elder brother left home, he would storm to follow after and see that city where there were many ladies pretty and new as his sister-in-law was. But he was wise enough to say nothing of his plan until his brother was gone, and he only idled about the house and the town, waiting, and despising all he had and saw, now that he knew how wonderful a place the coast city was and how filled with new things and fine new people, learned in every foreign thing. And he even looked at Wang the Tiger's son as though secretly belittling him, and Wang the Tiger caught the look and hated the young man for it.

But in the house of Wang the Merchant the young men were outwardly more humble and when they came home at night from their shops they sat edgewise on their seats and stared at this uncle and at this cousin of theirs, and Wang the Tiger took secret pleasure in the looks these young tradesmen cast at his son, and he marked how they stared at the lad and at the little gilded sword he wore that he took off sometimes and held across his knee for the younger children to look at and to touch with their fingers.

At such times Wang the Tiger rejoiced mightily in his son and he forgot the lad had been cold to him. He rejoiced to see his son rise sharply and neatly as his tutor had taught him to do and make his salute to his father or to his uncle as he came in, and then sit down again in a very mannerly way when his elders had taken their places. And Wang the Tiger smoothed his beard and loved his son exceedingly and he grew more merry than he had ever been in his life when he saw how much taller for his years his son was than these clerks his brother had for sons, and how much harder his son's flesh was and how straight and true his body and not languid and curved and pale as his cousins were.

During all these days that Wang the Tiger was in the houses of his brothers he guarded over his son carefully. When the lad sat beside him at feasts Wang the Tiger himself saw to his son's wine, and when the serving men had poured three times, he would not let them pour again for his son. And when the lads who were his cousins cried out to him to come and play here or there somewhere, Wang the Tiger sent his son's tutor and the harelipped trusty man and the ten old soldiers with him everywhere. Every night Wang the Tiger made some excuse and he would not be at rest until he had gone himself to his son's room and seen the lad in his own bed and alone except for the guard who watched at the door.

Now in this house of his father where his two brothers still lived so easily and well, it was as though no famine were in the land and as though no waters stood upon harvest fields, and as though none starved anywhere. Yet well enough did Wang the Landlord know and well enough did Wang the Merchant know what went on outside their peaceful home, and when Wang the Tiger had told them his straits and why he was come and when he ended saying, "It is to your interest to save me out of my danger, because my power keeps you safe, too," they knew very well he spoke the truth.

For there were starving people outside of this city also, and many of them hated the two brothers very bitterly. They hated Wang the Landlord because he still owned land and those who worked on it must share with him, who did not labor at all, the bitter fruit they wrung from the earth, and to them it seemed, when they had bent over their fields in cold and heat and in rain and sun, that the earth and its fruit belonged to them. It was a very sore thing that at harvest time they

433

must give a good half of it to one who had sat in a town house and waited for it, and that in famine time he must still have his share.

It was true that in these years when Wang the Eldest had been landlord and while he sold the land, too, he was still no easy landlord. No, for a man so weak and soft as he was, he could curse and quarrel, and his hatred of the land vented itself against these people who tilled it for him and he hated them not only for the land's sake, but because he was so hard pressed often for money enough for his house's needs and his own needs and he was doubly bitter because it seemed to him his tenants wilfully held back what was his due and given him from his father. It came to such a pass that when his tenants saw him coming they would turn their faces to the sky and mutter,

"It must be we will have rain since the devils are out!"

And often they reviled him and said,

"You are no good son of your father, for he was a merciful man even in his age when he was rich, and he remembered that once he had toiled as we do, and he never pressed us for our rent, nor demanded grain of us in famine years. But you have never suffered and mercy has never been born in your heart!"

Such hatred had there been, and it was manifest in this hard year because in the night when the great gates were locked there were those who came and beat upon that gate and they lay on the steps and moaned out,

"We are starving and you still have rice to eat and rice to make into wines!" And others cried out upon the streets as they passed the gates, and they cried even in daytime, "Oh, that we might kill these rich men and take what they have robbed from us!"

At first the two brothers paid no heed, but at last they had

434

hired a few soldiers of the town to stand about the gate and keep all off who had no proper business there. And indeed there were many rich men in that town and countryside who were robbed and despoiled as the year grew old, for robbers began to spring up, numerous and desperate, as they do in any evil time. Yet the two sons of Wang Lung were safe enough, because the chief of police and head of the soldiers of the town had married his daughter into that house, and because Wang the Tiger was near there and the lord of war. And so before that House of Wang the people did not as yet dare to do more than moan and curse.

Nor had they come to rob the earthen house which belonged to this family they hated. No, it stood up on its hillock out of the slowly receding waters, and Pear Blossom lived there safely enough through the bitter winter with her two. This was because Pear Blossom was well known by now for her pity, and they knew that she begged for stores out of the House of Wang and many came to her doors in their little boats and tubs and she fed them. Once Wang the Merchant had gone to her and said,

"In such dangerous times as these you must come into the town and live in the great house."

But Pear Blossom had replied in her tranquil, usual way,

"No, I cannot, and I am not afraid, and there are those who depend on me."

But as the winter grew deep and cold she did grow afraid at times because there were men made desperate by hunger and the bitter wind upon the icy waters where they lived in boats still or clung to tree tops as they could, and they were angry because Pear Blossom still fed the fool and the hunchback and they muttered before her very face, with her gifts in their hands,

435

"Shall those two still be fed, when good strong men, who have a whole child or two left, must starve?"

Indeed, such mutterings grew very loud and often, and Pear Blossom had just begun to wonder if she should not take these two into the town lest they be killed some time because of what they ate, and she too weak to defend them, when the poor fool, now more than fifty and two years of age, but still the same child she ever was, died in the sudden swift way such have of dying. One day she ate and played as ever she did with her bit of cloth, and she wandered out of the gate and into the water without knowing it was water and not dry land now where she usually sat, and Pear Blossom ran after, but the fool was already drenched and shivering with the icy water. From this she took a chill, in spite of every tenderness that Pear Blossom gave her, and in a few hours she was dead, since she died as easily as she lived without a will in anything.

Then Pear Blossom sent word into the town to Wang the Landlord for the coffin, and since Wang the Tiger was there, the three brothers came together, and Wang the Tiger brought his son, also. They stayed to see this poor thing put into her coffin, and she lay there for the first time in her life wise and grave with a dignity that death alone had given to her. And Pear Blossom truly grieving, was somewhat comforted to see how her child looked and she said in the quiet, murmuring way she had,

"Death has healed her and made her wise at last. She is like any of us now."

But the brothers had no funeral for her, seeing what she had been, and Wang the Tiger left his son in the earthen house while he went in the boat with his brothers and with Pear Blossom and the tenant's wife and a laboring man to the other high land where the graves of the family were, and there in a lowly place but still inside the earthen enclosure, they buried the fool.

When all was finished and they had returned to the earthen house and made ready to go back to the town again, Wang the Tiger looked at Pear Blossom and he spoke to her for the first time and he said in his calm, cold way,

"What will you do, now, lady?"

Then Pear Blossom lifted her face to him, brave for the first time in her life, knowing as she did that her hair was growing white, and her face no longer young and smooth, and she said,

"I have long said that when this child of mine was gone I would go into the nunnery near here, and the nuns are ready for me. I have lived close to them these many years and I have already taken many vows and the nuns know me and I shall be happiest there." Then she turned to Wang the Land-lord and said, "You and your lady have already made the plan about this son of yours, and his temple is very near to mine and I will still tend him, seeing how old I am now and old enough to be his mother, and if he is ill or fevered as he often is, I can go to him. Priests and nuns, they worship together at morning and evening, too, and I can see him twice a day, too, even if we may not speak."

Then the three brothers looked at the hunchbacked lad who hung about Pear Blossom, lost now that the fool was gone, for whom he often cared with Pear Blossom. He was a man now, and he smiled painfully under their looks. Wang the Tiger was somehow touched because his own son stood so tall and strong and astonished at all this he had not known about before, and Wang the Tiger said very kindly, when he saw the son smile on the hunchback's face,

"I wish you well, poor lad, and if you had been able, I would have taken you gladly as I took your cousin and I would have done as well for you as I have done for him. But as it is, I will add something to your fee in the temple and to yours, too, lady, for money always buys a place, and I daresay it is the same in temples as elsewhere."

But Pear Blossom replied softly and surely,

"I will take nothing for myself and need nothing, for the nuns know me and I know them, and all I have is theirs too when I go to cast my lot with them. But for the lad I will take something, for it will help him."

This she said in mild reproach to Wang the Landlord, for his sum he gave when he and the lad's mother decided upon this life for their son was too meager, but if he knew it for a reproach he gave no sign, and he only sat down to wait for his brothers, being very heavy and finding it a grievance if he must stand up. But Wang the Tiger still gazed at the hunchbacked lad and said once more to him,

"And would you still rather go to the temple than to any other place?"

Then the youth took his eyes off from his tall cousin at whom he stared very avidly, and he hung his head and looked down the short length of his crooked body and he said slowly,

"Yes, seeing I am as I must be." And he said after a moment, very heavily, "A priest's robe will hide my hump, perhaps."

He turned his eyes once more to his cousin, then suddenly it seemed he could not bear to look at him any more, and not even at his gilded sword, for he dropped his eyes and turned and limped quickly out of the room.

On that night when Wang the Tiger was returned to the house of his brothers, and when he went in to see his son in his bed, he found the lad awake and eager and he asked his father,

"My father, was that house my grandfather's house too?"

And Wang the Tiger answered in surprise, "Yes, and I lived there as a lad and until he founded this house and brought us all here."

Then the boy looked up out of his bed, and his head lay pillowed on his hands crossed under his head and he looked eagerly at his father and he said with ardor,

"I like that house. I would like to live in a house set in fields like that earthen house, and very quiet and trees there and the oxen!"

But Wang the Tiger answered with an impatience he could not understand, seeing that, after all, his son had said no great harmful thing,

"You do not know what you say! I know, for I was there as a lad, it is a very hateful ignorant life, and I longed every hour to be away from it!"

But the lad said with some strange stubbornness,

"I would like it—I know I would like it!"

These few words his son said very ardently, and so ardently that Wang the Tiger felt some strange small anger in him and he rose and went away. But his son lay and dreamed that night that the earthen house was his home and that he lived there among the fields.

As for Pear Blossom, she went to that nunnery and the son of Wang the Landlord went to his temple, and the old earthen house stood empty of the three who had lived there these many years. Of the family of Wang Lung no one lived there on his land, and there were but the old tenant and his wife, and these two lived on alone. Sometimes the old woman took a withered cabbage she had hid in the earth or a handful of meal she had saved, and she tied it up in a kerchief and went to the nunnery to give it to Pear Blossom, because in her years of service she had learned to love the gentle, silent

439

woman. Yes, even in these hard times the old woman took what little thing she had, and she would wait at the gate for Pear Blossom to come out, clothed as she was now in the grey nun's robe, and she would whisper to her,

"I have a new-laid egg from that one hen I still have and it is for you!"

Then she thrust her hand into her bosom and brought out a small egg and she covered it in her hand and she held it to Pear Blossom's hand and tried to slip it in and she coaxed her, whispering,

"Eat it, mistress! I swear there would be many nuns who would do it, for all their vows, and I have seen many priests eating meat and drinking wine. Stand here where none will see you and eat it fresh—you are so pale!"

But Pear Blossom would not. No, she had made her true vows, and she shook her shaven head in its grey cap and she pushed the old woman's hands gently away and she said,

"No, you must eat it, for you need it more than I, even if I could eat it, for I am well fed enough for my needs. But even if I were not fed, I could not eat it because I have taken my vows!"

Yet the old woman would not be satisfied and she forced it into Pear Blossom's bosom where her robes crossed at the throat, and then hastened into her tub and pushed it away from the door into the water so that Pear Blossom could not reach her, and she went away smiling and content. But Pear Blossom gave the egg away in the next half hour to a poor starving wretch who crawled out of the water at the temple gate. It was a mother, and she held a starveling to the shriveled bit of skin that had been once a full round breast, and pointing to it, she begged of Pear Blossom, who came at her feeble call,

"Look at these breasts of mine! Once they were round and

full and this child as fat as a god!" And she gazed down at the small dying creature whose lips were still pressed to the empty fountain. Then Pear Blossom took the egg out of her bosom and gave it to the woman and rejoiced she had so good a thing to give.

In such ways of peace did Pear Blossom live out her life from that time on, and Wang the Tiger never saw her more.

Now Wang the Merchant was very able to help Wang the Tiger in that year of straits if he would, for the truth was he had great stores of grain and if famine brought poverty to others to him and to others like him it brought yet greater riches. For, when he saw what the times were to be, he began to hoard vast bins of grains, and even though he sold some from time to time to the rich who were able to buy at the high prices he set upon it, yet he bought also of flour and of rice from other regions, and he sent his agents out even to the nearest foreign countries to buy such goods, and his granaries were heaped with food.

He had more silver now than ever he had, for as his grain flowed out to this rich house and to that market, the silver flowed back to him for it, and in this year Wang the Merchant was burdened with his silver and he was put to it to know what he could do with it and keep it safe. Being merchant, he wanted no more land, and yet there was no other security men could offer in such a time if they borrowed money of him except the land they had under the water. He took risks, therefore, at very high interest, and he put heavy mortgages upon the harvests of the future, and such mortgages that when the lands had drained themselves once more, it seemed that all the harvest of that whole region would pour into the granaries of Wang the Merchant. But not one knew fully how rich he was, for he kept even his own sons pressed for the silver they wanted to spend, and he made poor face before every one of his sons, and held them to their clerkships in his shops and markets, so there was not one among his sons, except his eldest whom he had given to Wang the Tiger, who did not look for the day when his father was gone and he could leave the shop or the markets and spend something for the play and the good garments which Wang the Merchant would not let them have now.

Nor were his sons the only ones who hated their servitude, for there were certain of the farmers in that countryside, and one of them that shelf-toothed man who had bought largely of Wang Lung's land when he was dead, and now that the land was most of it under water, he pinched and starved and saw his children near to starvation before he would borrow from Wang the Merchant, and he waited for his land to come up out of the water and while he waited he took his brood and went south to some southern city, choosing such a life rather than to let Wang the Merchant get a hold upon his land.

But Wang the Merchant was righteous enough in his own eyes, for he told himself and all who came to borrow of him that men must not expect to borrow money or buy grain in times of scarcity at the prices not higher than usual, else what profit can there be to a man who is a merchant? He did no more, therefore, than what was just in his own eyes.

Yet he was wise man enough, and he knew that men do not think of justice in such times and he knew he was very heartily hated, and he knew that Wang the Tiger was of some service to him even in the very fact that he was lord of war. He exerted himself, therefore, and he promised certain very large stores of grain to Wang the Tiger and he lent him a great sum at not very great interest, and not above twenty per cent or so on a silver piece. When they sealed the bargain one day in the tea house, Wang the Landlord, who sat by, sighed heavily and he said,

"My little brother, I wish I were rich as this merchant brother of ours, but the truth is I grow poorer every year. I have no good business such as he has, and nothing but a little money loaned and a little land left out of all my father's fields. It is a good thing for us all that we have one rich man among us!"

At this Wang the Merchant could not forbear a very sour smile and he said plainly, for he had no grace of tongue nor any wit at courtesy,

"If I have a little it is because I have worked and I have held my sons to the shops and they do not wear silk, and I have only one woman."

But Wang the Landlord would not have any such plain talk as this, although his temper had dwindled very much too, in these later years, for he knew his brother reproached him because he had sold off a large portion of such land as he had left so that his two sons could go out to the coast as they wished, and he sat and swelled awhile in himself and at last he said loudly, rousing himself,

"Well, and a father must feed his sons, I believe, and I hold my sons a little too precious to make them spend their good young strength at a counter somewhere. If I honor my father's grandsons, shall I let them starve? It is my duty to feed my children, I believe, but perhaps I do not know my duty when I keep my sons as a lord's sons should be kept!" He could not say more, for a hoarse, constant cough troubled him these years and it came rumbling out of his bosom now, and racked him. Being speechless awhile, he could only sit swelling and angry, and his eyes were sunken in his fat cheeks, and the red mounted slowly up his thick neck. But Wang the Merchant let a little smile creep upon his own thin and

443

withered cheeks, for he saw his brother understood himself reproved, and no more need be said.

Now when the bargain was signed and sealed, then Wang the Merchant would have it written down, and at this Wang the Tiger shouted out,

"What—are we not brothers?"

And Wang the Merchant said, as though in apology, "It is for my own memory—I have such a feeble memory now-a-days!"

But he held the brush to Wang the Tiger so that he must perforce take it and put his name down. Then Wang the Second said, still smiling,

"Is your seal about you, too?"

Then Wang the Tiger must take out the seal he carried in his girdle that had his name carven on the stone, and he must stamp that too upon the paper before Wang the Merchant would take it and fold it and thrust it carefully into his own girdle bag. And watching him, Wang the Tiger grew angry, even while he had what he wanted, and he swore to himself that he must enlarge his territories somehow and he wished he had not let these years slip by as he had so that once again he was dependent upon this brother.

But for the time Wang the Tiger's men were saved, and he called for his son to be made ready and for his guardsmen to gather themselves and they would go home. It was now well upon spring and the lands were drying rapidly and everywhere men were eager for new seed to put into their lands, and everywhere men forgot the winter and all the dead and they looked forward hopeful again to the spring.

So also did Wang the Tiger feel himself eager for new things and he told his brothers farewell. Then the two brothers gave him a feast of departure, and after the feast Wang the Tiger went into that place where the tablets of his

444

ancestors were kept, and he lit incense there. He had his son by him as he lit it, and while the dense sweet smoke curled upwards, Wang the Tiger made his obeisances to his father and to his father's fathers, and he bade his son bow also. Watching the gallant figure of his son thus bowing, Wang the Tiger felt a strong sweet pride rise in him, and it seemed to him that the spirits of those dead gathered close to see so fine a one as this descended from their line, and he felt he had done what he should in his family.

When all was finished and the incense burned to the ashes in the urn, Wang the Tiger mounted his horse, and his son mounted his own horse, and with their guardsmen, they rode back by dry land to their own regions.

XXVIII

IN the spring of the year when Wang the Tiger's son was fifteen full years of age the tutor whom Wang the Tiger had hired for his son came to him one day as he walked in his court alone, and he said,

"My general, I have taught the young general, your son, all that I can alone, and he needs to go into a school of war where he will have comrades with whom to march and to fight and to practice war."

It seemed to Wang the Tiger, although he knew this day must come, as though a dozen years had passed as the turn of a hand. He sent for his son to come to him there in the court and he felt suddenly weary and old and he sat down upon a stone seat that was under a juniper tree and waited for his son. When the lad came through the round gate between the courts, walking with his steady somewhat slow step, Wang the Tiger looked at him newly. It was true that the lad was

445

tall and nearly as high as a man, and his face had already taken on rougher curves and he kept his lips folded firmly and well together. It was a man's face rather than a child's. And as Wang the Tiger looked at this only son, he remembered with a sort of wonder that once he had been impatient for his son to be grown and a man, and once his babyhood had seemed endless. Now it seemed rather that he had leaped straight out of his babyhood into this new manhood. Then Wang the Tiger sighed and he thought to himself,

"I wish that school were not in the south. I wish he had not to go among those little southerners to learn!" And aloud he said to the tutor who stood pulling at a few short hairs he grew on his upper lip, "And you are sure he had better go to that school?"

The tutor moved his head to signify assent, and Wang the Tiger stared on at his son painfully and at last he asked the lad, "And yourself, my son, you wish to go?"

Now it was very rarely that Wang the Tiger ever asked his son what he liked, because he knew so well what he wanted for his son, but he had a small weak hope that if the boy refused to go he could use it as an excuse. But the boy looked up quickly, for he had been looking at a patch of white lilies that grew there under a juniper tree, and he said,

"If it were so that I could go to another school, I would like that very well."

But this answer did not please Wang the Tiger at all and he drew down his brows and pulled at his beard and said pettishly,

"Now what school is there to which you could go except a school of war, and what use would stuff out of books be to you, who are to be a lord of war?"

The boy answered diffidently and in a low voice, "There

446

be schools I have heard in these days where they learn how to till land and such things as have to do with the land."

But Wang the Tiger was astounded at such foolishness, and he had never heard of such a school and he roared suddenly,

"Now here is foolishness, if it be true there are such schools! Well, and so every farmer must needs learn how to plow and sow and reap these days! Well, and I remember very well my father used to say a man needed not to learn to farm, for he had but to look at what his neighbor did!" Then he said very harshly and coldly, "But what has this to do with you or me? We are lords of war, and you shall go to a school of war or to no school at all, but stay here and take my army after me."

His son sighed then and shrank away a little as ever he did when Wang the Tiger roared, and he said quietly and with some strange patience,

"I will go then to the school of war."

Yet there was something in this patience which still made Wang the Tiger angry and he stared at his son and pulled at his own whiskers and he wished his son would speak out and yet he knew he would be angry if he heard what his son had in his heart, and he shouted,

"Prepare yourself, for tomorrow you shall go!"

The lad saluted him then as he had been taught to do and turned upon his heel and went away without a word more.

But in the night when he was alone in his room Wang the Tiger fell to thinking of his son going so far from him and a sort of terror came on him for what might befall his son in those parts where men were so tricky and deceitful, and he called out to his guard that his trusty harelipped man was to come in to him. When he was come Wang the Tiger turned to look at the hideous faithful face and he said, half pleading and not as master to man,

447

"That son of mine, my only son, is to go to a school of war tomorrow and even though his tutor goes, how do I know what that one's heart is who has spent so many years in foreign parts? His eyes are hid behind his spectacles and his lips behind his hairs, and he seems strange to me when I think my son must trust wholly to him. Now you shall go with my son, for I know you, and there is no one else whom I know as I do you, who have been with me when I was poor and alone and you were then what you are now that I am rich and strong. My son is my best possession and you are to watch over him for me."

Now here was a strange thing, for when Wang the Tiger said this the harelipped man spoke up stoutly and he was so earnest his words came whistling through his teeth,

"My general, in this one thing I will not obey you, for I will stay by you. If the young general must go, I will pick fifty good true men, not young, and I will teach them their duty to him, but I will stay where you are. You do not know how you need a true man near you, for in an army so great as yours there are always discontents and festerings and this man angry and that man talking of some better general, and there are very ugly rumors now of some new strange war gathering out of the south."

To this Wang the Tiger answered stubbornly,

"You hold yourself too dear. Have I not the Pig Butcher yet?"

Then the harelipped man grew very scornful and he twisted his face frightfully in his agitation and he said,

"That—that fool! Yes, he is well enough at picking flies out of the air, and if I tell him whom to strike and when to strike he can deal a blow with his great fist, but he has not wit enough to see anything until he is told where to look!"

He would not be moved at all, and Wang the Tiger com-

448

manded him and bore with his rebelliousness as he would never have borne with such refusal in any other, and at last the harelipped man said over and over,

"Well, and I can fall on my sword, then—well, I have my sword and my throat here together."

In the end there was nothing to do but to give in to this man and when he saw Wang the Tiger would do so, he grew very cheerful although a moment before he had been doleful and talking of dying. He ran out that very night and chose his fifty men and he rounded them out of their sleep and he cursed them soundly as they stood dazed and yawning and shivering in the chill spring air in the court and he shouted at them through his split lip,

"If so much as a tooth aches in the young general's mouth it will be your fault, O you who ought to die, and your whole business is to go with him wherever he goes and stand about and guard him! At night you are to lie about his bed, and in the day you are not to trust anyone or listen to anyone, no, not even to him. If he grows wilful and says he will not have you and that you encumber him you are to answer, 'We are under the old general, your father, and he pays us and we must hear him only.' Yes, you are to guard him against his own self." And he cursed the fifty men very richly and completely to frighten them well, and make them know how grave their duty was and at last he said, "But if you do well, you shall receive a good reward, for there is no more generous heart than our old general's heart, and I will speak for you myself."

Then they roared out their promise, for they knew this trusty man was nearer to their general than any except his own son, and the truth was they were pleased enough to go to foreign parts and see what they had not seen.

Then when the morning came Wang the Tiger rose from

his sleepless bed and he let his son go and he went with him a way because he could not bear to part with him. Yet it was but a small respite and a little putting off of what must come, and when he had ridden awhile beside his son, he drew rein and said abruptly,

"Son, it has been said from ancient times that though a man go with his friend three thousand miles, yet must the parting come, and so it must be with you and me. Farewell!"

He sat very stiffly upon his horse then, and he received the obeisances of his son, and he sat and watched the lad leap into the saddle again and ride away with his fifty men and his tutor. Then Wang the Tiger turned his horse about and he rode back to his empty house, and he looked no more after his son.

Three days did Wang the Tiger allow himself to grieve, and he could not set his hand to do anything nor his heart to any planning until the last of the men he had sent out with his son as messengers came back to make report. They came back every few hours from different places upon the road and each brought his own report. One said,

"He is very well and rather more gay than his wont is. Twice he dismounted from his horse and stepped into a field where a farmer was and talked with him."

"And what could he have to say to such an one?" asked Wang the Tiger, astonished.

And the man replied, remembering faithfully, "He asked him what seed he planted and he looked to see the seed, and he looked to see how the ox was tied to the plow, and his men laughed to see him, but he did not care and stared sturdily at the ox and how it was tied."

Then Wang the Tiger was puzzled and he said, "I do not see why a lord of war should care to see how an ox is tied or what seed it is," and he waited and then said impatiently, "Have you no more to say than this?"

The man thought awhile and answered, "At night he stopped at an inn and he ate heartily of bread and meat and some soft rice and fish and he drank but one small bowl of wine. There I left him and came back to bring the news."

Then another came and another with such news of how his son did and what he ate and drank and so they reported until the day when the lad reached the place where he was to go by boat upon the river to the sea. Then Wang the Tiger could but wait for some letter to come, for further than this men could not follow.

Now whether or not Wang the Tiger could have borne his restlessness without his son he did not know, but two matters came to divert and draw his heart out of himself. The first was that spies came back with strange news out of the south and they said,

"We hear a very curious war is coming up out of the south and it is a war of some sort of overturning and revolution and not a good and usual war between lords of war."

Then Wang the Tiger answered somewhat scornfully, for he was very surly these days,

"It is not new at all. When I was young I heard of such a war of revolution and I went to fight in it, thinking I did a noble deed. Yet it was but a war after all, and while the lords of war united for a time against the dynasty, when they were successful and overthrew the throne they fell apart and for themselves again."

Nevertheless, the spies returned all with the same tale, and they said,

"Nay, it is some sort of a new war and it is called a people's war and a war for the common people."

"And how can common people have a war?" answered Wang the Tiger loudly, raising his black brows at these silly spies of his. "Have they guns and will they wage war with sticks and staves and forks and scythes?" And he glared so at his spies that they were discomfited and coughed and looked at each other, and at last one said humbly,

"But we only tell what we hear."

Then Wang the Tiger forgave them with majesty and he said,

"It is true, that is your duty, but you have heard nonsense." And he dismissed them. Nevertheless, he did not wholly forget what they said, and he told himself he must watch the war and see what it truly was.

But before he could take much thought there arose another affair in his own regions which pressed upon him and drove out any other thought.

The summer drew near, and since nothing is so changeful as the heaven above men, it was a beauteous summer, with mingled rains and sun, and the waters receded and left the earth open and fertile, and wherever men could find a little seed they had but to thrust it into this warm, panting earth, steaming under the sunshine, and life leaped up out of that earth, and the harvest promised food and plenty for all.

But while they waited for harvest there were many men still hungry and that year robbers again grew rife in Wang the Tiger's regions and worse than he had ever known them to be. Yes, even in his regions where he maintained his great army fed and paid, there were men so desperate they dared to form into robber bands and to defy him, and when he sent his soldiers after them, they were not to be found. They were like a band of ghosts, for Wang the Tiger's spies would run back and tell him,

"Yesterday the robbers were to the north and they burnt

the village of the Ch'ing family." Or they would say, "Three days ago a band of robbers fell upon merchants and killed them all and took their goods of opium and silks."

Then Wang the Tiger grew exceedingly angry to hear of such lawlessness and he was angry most of all because he was defrauded thus of his own revenues from merchants, which he needed sorely to make him free from Wang the Merchant and he grew so angry that he longed to kill someone. Then he rose up in his courts and shouted that his captains were to partition out his soldiers over that whole region and for every robber's head they brought in he would give a reward of a piece of silver.

Yet when his soldiers rushed out, enticed by the reward, to seize the robbers they found none. The truth was many of these robbers were simple farming folk, and they only came out when they were not pursued. But if they saw the soldiers after them they dug and hoed in the fields and told sorry tales to the soldiers of how they had suffered at the hands of such and such a band and they told of any band except their own, and their own they never mentioned, or if they heard another mention it, they looked vacantly about and said they had never known such a band as that nor ever heard such a name. But because of the reward Wang the Tiger had promised and because many of his men were greedy, they killed any man they could and brought his head in and said it was a robber's head, and none could say it was not, and so they received the reward. There were thus many men killed who were innocent, but no one dared to complain, for they knew that Wang the Tiger sent his men out in a good and lawful cause, and if they complained it might anger some soldier and draw attention to him who complained and put it in the soldier's mind that this one who complained had a head also.

But one day in the midsummer when the sorghum cane

453

was very high and much higher than men standing, the robbers spread everywhere like a sudden blaze of fire, and Wang the Tiger was angry to such a pitch that he rose up one day himself against the robbers, although he had not gone out thus for many a day and year. But he heard of a certain small band in a village, and his spies had watched and they had seen that by day the villagers were farmers and by night they were robbers. It seemed the lands these villagers had were very low and the village lay in a great hollow and the farmers had not been able to plant even so soon as others and so they were still not fed, such as had not starved in the winter and spring.

Now when Wang the Tiger had this certain knowledge of how evil these men were and how they went by night to other villages and robbed them of their food and killed those who resisted, his anger swelled up in him and he went himself with his men to that village and he commanded them to surround the village and leave no way open for any to escape. Then with other men he went galloping in and they seized every man, a hundred and seventy-three men in all, young and old. When they were caught and held and tied together by ropes, Wang the Tiger commanded them to be brought to a certain large threshing floor before the head villager's house and there from his horse he glowered upon these wretched men. Some of them wept and trembled, and some were the color of clay, but some stood sullen and fearless having already known despair. Only the old men were tranquil and accepted whatever must come, since now they were so old, and every one of them expected death.

But Wang the Tiger when he saw he had them all, felt his killing anger cool in him. He could not kill as lustily as once he did; no, he had been secretly weaker since he killed the six men and saw his son's look. And to hide his weakness now he drew down his brows and pursed his lips and he roared at them,

"You deserve to die, every man of you! Have you not known me these many years that I will not have robbers in my lands? Yet I am a merciful man. I will remember your old parents and your little sons, and this time I will not kill you. No, I will save death for the next time you dare to disobey me and rob again." Then he called to his own men who surrounded the villagers and he said, "Draw out your sharp girdle knives and cut off their ears only, for a warning that they may remember what I have told them this day!"

Then the soldiers of Wang the Tiger stepped forward and they whetted their knives upon the soles of their shoes and they cut off the ears of the robbers and heaped the ears upon the ground before Wang the Tiger. And Wang the Tiger looked at the robbers, every man with two streams of his blood running down his cheeks, and he said,

"Let these ears of yours be sign of remembrance!"

Then he turned his horse and galloped away. And as he went his heart misgave him that perhaps he ought to have killed the robbers and finished them clean and so cleansed his regions, for such a death would have warned others, and his heart misgave him that perhaps he grew weak and too merciful, now as he grew old. But he comforted himself by saying to himself,

"It was for my son's sake I saved those lives, and some day I will tell him how for his sake I did not kill an hundred and seventy-three men, and it will please him."

IN these ways did Wang the Tiger fill the months his son left him empty and alone in his house. When he had put down the robbers once more in his regions and when the harvests came on and helped him because the people were fed again, he took a small half of his army and in the autumn when it was neither cold with winds nor hot with sunshine, he went over all his lands once more, and he told himself he must see that all was ordered for his son when he returned. For now Wang the Tiger planned that when his son came back he would give over to him the generalship in these parts and he would give to him his vast army, keeping only a little guard for himself. He would be fifty and five years old and his son would be twenty years old, and a man. Dreaming such dreams Wang the Tiger rode over his lands and with his inward eye he saw here his son's son, and with his outward eye he marked the people and the land and what revenues there were and what promise of good harvest. Now that the famine had died away once more the lands did well, although land and people still showed the shadows of those two famine years, the land because it was not fully grown yet to crops, and the people because there were many still hollow cheeked and there were too few of old and young. But life had begun once more and it comforted Wang the Tiger to see many women great with child again and he said to himself, pondering,

"It may very well be that Heaven sent the famine to show me my destiny again, for I have rested too much in these last years and been too content with what I had. It may be the famine was sent to stir me up that I should be greater yet with such a son as I have to inherit all I do and gain."

For if Wang the Tiger was wiser than his old father had

been in his time and did not believe in a god of earth, yet he did believe in destiny and in heaven, and he would have said in all that befell him there was no chance at all, not in life nor in death, but that every life and every death was purposed and meet and came from heaven thus.

In this ninth month of the dying year he rode with his soldiers joyous behind him, and everywhere men greeted him somehow, because they knew him for a mighty man who had long ruled over them and justly, too, and they put smiles on their faces and if he stopped in a town, a feast was made for him by the elders of that town or village. Only the common farming folk were not courteous, and many a farmer when he saw the soldiers coming turned his back to the road and worked doggedly on in his field, and when they were passed he spat and spat again to free his heart of hatred. Yet if any soldier had asked him fiercely why he spat he would have covered his face with vacant innocence and answered,

"Because of so much dust that blew into my mouth from under the horses' feet that passed."

But Wang the Tiger did not need to care for any man, in town or countryside.

Now in his journeying he came to that city he had once besieged where his pocked nephew had lived these many years for him and Wang the Tiger sent messengers ahead to announce his coming, and he looked keenly to right and to left to see how this town had done under his nephew's rule.

This young man was no longer young; he was a man now, and with the silk weaver's daughter he had for wife he had begotten a son or two already, and when he heard his uncle came and was even at the city gates he was in greatest consternation. The truth was this fellow had lived many peaceful years here and he had lived very peacefully, and almost he had forgotten he was a soldier. He was always merry and easy in his ways, eager after pleasure and some new thing, and he liked his life here, for he had authority so that men were courteous to him, and he had no great work to do except to receive revenues and he grew fat. In these last years he had even taken off his soldier's garb and put on easier robes, and he looked like a prosperous merchant. Indeed, he was very good friends with merchants in the town, and when they paid their taxes into his hand for Wang the Tiger, he made his little profits too, as tradesmen do, and he used his uncle's name sometimes for a light tax on some new thing. But if the merchants knew it they did not blame him, seeing it is but what any man of them would do himself, and they liked the pocked fellow and they gave him gifts sometimes, knowing he might report what he pleased to his uncle and let evil descend upon them.

So Wang the Tiger's nephew lived this merry life, and his wife pleased him, for he was not over lusty, and not often tempted outside his own bed except on the few nights when some friend or other gave a feast more vast than usual and for a special treat had hired pretty maids for part of the night. To such feasts this man was always invited, both for his position in the town and for his own sake, because he was a witty clown and he had a tricky tongue that could make men roar with glee, especially if they were somewhat drunken.

Now when he heard his uncle came he hurried and bade his wife find his soldier's garb out of some box or other where she had thrust it, and he mustered out his soldiers who had lived too easily, too, and had been his servants more than soldiers, and as he pushed his fat legs into the garments he wondered how he ever had borne to wear such stiff hard garb. His belly had grown more full, too, than when he was a youth, and his clothing gaped there, so that he must needs tie a wide girdle about his middle to hide himself. But so garbed

458

somehow and his soldiers mustered somehow, too, they waited for Wang the Tiger to come in.

Now Wang the Tiger saw in a very few days all that had taken place and he saw the meaning of the vast feasts the merchants gave him and the magistrate also, and he saw very well that his nephew sweated in his soldier's garb, and he smiled coldly to himself one day when the winds died and the sun shone very hot and his nephew took off his coat he was so hot, and there his clothing gaped beneath his ill tied girdle. And Wang the Tiger thought to himself,

"I am glad I have a son who is a lordly man, and not like this one, my brother's son, who is but a tradesman after all!"

And he was negligent toward his nephew and did not praise him much and he said coldly,

"Your soldiers you control for me have forgot how to handle their guns. Doubtless they need a war again. Why do you not lead them out next spring and make them used to war?"

At this his nephew stammered and sweated, for the truth was that although he was no coward and he could have been a soldier if he had his life laid that way for him, he was not one to lead out men and make them fear him and he loved this life best now. When Wang the Tiger saw his uneasiness, he laughed his silent laugh and clapped his hand to his sword suddenly and he roared out,

"Well, Nephew, since you live so well and the town is so rich, doubtless we can raise our taxes! I am at mighty expense for my son in the south and I think to enlarge myself for him while he is away, and sacrifice yourself a little therefore and double my taxes for me!"

Now this nephew of his had made a secret bargain with the merchants that if his uncle sought to raise taxes he would cry poverty and hard times, and if he could persuade his uncle, he was to have a goodly sum for his reward. So he began feebly to do now but Wang the Tiger was not moved at all by any such moan and he cried at last very roughly,

"I see what has come about here, and there are more ways of working against me than the way the Hawk had, but my remedy is the same!"

Then with a very rueful face for the good silver lost him, the nephew made report to the merchants and they sent in their own plaint and said,

"Yours is not the only tax. We have the city tax and the state tax, and yours is already higher than any, and it scarcely profits us to do any business."

But Wang the Tiger saw it was time to show his sword and he said bluntly, after courteous words had been spoken, "Yes, but power is with me, and I will take what is not given when I ask for it courteously."

In such ways did Wang the Tiger chasten his nephew and set him down in his place again, and in such ways did he make secure his hold over that city and over all his regions.

When all was sure and settled he went back to his house and he waited for the winter to end, and he busied himself sending out his spies and in making his plans and he dreamed of great conquests in the spring, and he dreamed that even now in his age, perhaps he could yet seize the whole province for his son.

Yes, all through that long winter Wang the Tiger held himself to that dream. It was the loneliest winter, so lonely that now and again almost he went into his women's courts he was so beside himself. But there was nothing for him there, for his ignorant wife lived alone with her daughters and Wang the Tiger had nothing to say to them, and so he only sat heavily on and alone and scarcely felt them his. Sometimes he wondered of his learned wife, but she had not come home these many years but she lived near her daughter who was at some school. Once she sent a picture of herself and this young girl to Wang the Tiger, and Wang the Tiger had stared at it awhile. The girl was pretty. She had a small pert face and she looked boldly out of the picture, her eyes black and bold under her short hair, and he could not feel her his. Well he knew she would be one of those merry, talkative maids there were now-a-days, and he was speechless before them. Then he looked at that learned wife of his. He had never known her at all; no, not even in those days when he went to her in the night. He looked at her longer than at her daughter, and out of the picture she looked back at him and he felt again that unease he used to feel in her presence, as though she had something to say to him he would not hear, as though she made a demand on him for that he had not to give. And he muttered to himself, putting the picture out of his sight,

"A man has not time in his life for all these things—I have been very busy—I have had no time for women."

And he hardened himself a little and he thought it a virtue in him that not for many years had he gone even to his wives. He had never loved them.

But the loneliest hours were the hours when he sat alone in the night by his brazier. In the day he could busy himself somehow but here were the nights once more, and they hung on him dark and sad as once they had in the past. At such times he doubted himself and he felt himself old and he doubted whether even in the spring he could make any great new conquest. At such times he smiled painfully into the coals and gnawed his beard and he thought to himself sadly,

"It may be that no man ever does all he says he would," and after a while he thought again and said, "I suppose a man when his son is born, plans enough for three generations in his own lifetime."

461

But there was Wang the Tiger's old harelipped trusty man and he watched over his old master, and when he saw Wang the Tiger brooding over the coals in the night and without zest for his soldiers in the day so that he let them idle and do as they would, then the old trusty man came in without much speech and he brought with him a jug of hot good wine and a few salty meats to make thirst, and in many small ways he coaxed his master to ease. After a while Wang the Tiger did come out of himself and he drank a little and then more and he was cheered and could sleep. When he thus drank he thought before he slept,

"Well, and I have my son and what I cannot do in my one life, he will do."

In that winter without knowing it Wang the Tiger came to drink more wine than ever he had, and it was a great comfort to the old trusty man who loved him. If Wang the Tiger sometimes pushed the jug away the old man coaxed him earnestly,

"Drink, my general, for every man must have some little comfort when he grows old, and some little joy, and you are too hard with yourself."

To please him, then, and to show he valued him, Wang the Tiger would drink. Therefore he could sleep, even in this lonely winter, because he was eased like this, and when he had drunk he put his faith very ardently in his son and it slipped from his mind that there had been a difference between them. In these days it never came into Wang the Tiger's mind that his son's dreams might not be his own, and he lived for the spring.

But there came a night before the spring and Wang the Tiger sat in his room, warm and half sleeping, and his wine

462

cooled on a little table at his hand, and he had unfastened his sword and laid it beside the jug of wine.

Suddenly out of the deep quiet of the winter's night he heard in the court a commotion of horses and soldiers' feet rushing in and stopping there. He rose up half standing, his hands upon the arms of his chair, not knowing whose soldiers these could be, and wondering if he dreamed. But before he could move further, one ran in and cried gladly,

"The little general, your son, is here!"

Now Wang the Tiger had drunk very deeply that night because of the cold and he could hardly come all at once to himself, and he drew his hand across his mouth and muttered,

"I thought in my dreams it was some enemy!"

He struggled out of his sleep, then, and stood up, and went out to the court by the great gate. It was light with the flaring of torches held by many hands, and in the midst of this brightness he saw his son. The young man had come down from his horse and he stood there waiting, and when he saw his father he bowed, but as he bowed he threw him a strange, half hostile look. Wang the Tiger shivered in the cold and he drew his coat closer and he faltered a little and asked his son, amazed,

"Where is your tutor—why are you here, my son?"

To this the young man replied, scarcely moving his lips,

"We are estranged. I have left him."

Then Wang the Tiger came out of his daze somewhat and he saw there was some trouble here not to be told before all these common soldiers who came pressing about and who were ever ready to hear a quarrel, and he turned and called his son to follow him. Then they went into Wang the Tiger's own room and Wang the Tiger commanded everyone to go out, and he was alone with his son. But he did not sit down.

463

No, he stood, and his son stood and Wang the Tiger looked at his son from head to foot, as though he had never seen this young man, who was his son. At last he said slowly,

"What strange garb is that you wear?"

To this the son lifted his head and he answered in his quiet, dogged way,

"It is the garb of the new army of the revolution." And he passed his tongue over his lips and stood waiting before his father.

In that instant Wang the Tiger understood what his son had done and who he now was, and he understood that this was the garb of the southern army in that new war he had heard rumored, and he shouted,

"It is the army of my enemy!"

He sat down suddenly then, for his breath caught in his throat and choked him. He sat there and felt his old murderous anger rise up in him as it had not since he killed the six men. He seized his narrow, keen sword from where it lay and he shouted in his old roaring way,

"You are my enemy—I ought to kill you, my son!"

He began to pant heavily, because this time his anger was strange and it came up in him so swiftly and strangely that it made him suddenly sick, and he swallowed again and again without knowing he did.

But the young man did not shrink now as he had been used to do when he was a child. No, he stood there quiet and dogged and he lifted his two hands and opened his coat and bared his smooth breast before his father. When he spoke it was with a deep bitterness, and he said,

"I knew you would want to kill me—it is your old and only remedy." He fixed his eyes on his father's face and he said without passion, "Kill me, then." And he stood ready and he waited, his face clear and hard in the candlelight.

464

But Wang the Tiger could not kill his son. No, even though he knew it was his right, and even though he knew any man may kill a son disloyal to him, and it will be counted to him for justice, yet he could not do it. He felt his anger checked at the flood, and then it began to stream out of him. He flung his sword upon the tiled floor, and he put his hand over his mouth to hide his lips, and he muttered,

"I am too weak—I am always too weak—after all, I am too weak for a lord of war—"

Then the young man, who saw his father sitting with his mouth thus covered under his hand and the sword flung down, covered his breast, and he spoke in a quiet and reasonable way, as though he reasoned with an old man.

"Father, I think you do not understand. None of you men who are old understand. You do not see our nation whole and how weak and despised—"

But Wang the Tiger laughed. He forced that silent laugh of his out and he made it loud and he said loudly, except he did not take his hand away,

"Do you think there never was such talk before? When I was young—you young men, you think you are the only ones—"

And Wang the Tiger forced out that strange, unused laugh of his that his son had never heard aloud in all his life. It goaded him as a strange weapon might, and it woke an anger in him his father had never seen and he shouted suddenly,

"We are not the same! Do you know what we call you? You are a rebel—a robber chief! If my comrades knew you they would call you traitor—but they do not even know your name—a petty lord of war in a little county town!"

So Wang the Tiger's son spoke, who had been patient all his life. Then he looked at his father, and in that same moment he was ashamed. He fell silent and the dark red came up his neck, and he looked down and began to unbuckle his leathern belt slowly and let it fall to the ground, and its bullets clattered there. And he said no more.

But Wang the Tiger answered nothing. He sat motionless in his chair, his mouth behind his hand. These words of his son's entered his understanding and some power began to ebb out of him and forever. He heard his son's words echo in his heart. Yes, he was only a petty lord of war—yes, a little lord of war in a small county town. Then he muttered behind his hand, feebly and as though from some old habit,

"But I have never been a robber chief."

His son was truly ashamed now, and he replied quickly, "No—no—no—" and then as though to cover his shame he said, "My father, I ought to tell you, I must hide away when my army comes north to victory. My tutor trained me well these many years and he counted on me. He was my captain— he will not easily forgive me that I chose you, my father—" The young man's voice dropped, and he glanced quickly at his father, and there was a secret tenderness in his look.

But Wang the Tiger made no answer. He sat as though he had not heard. The young man went on speaking, and he glanced every now and again at his father as though beseeching him for something.

"There is that old earthen house where I might hide. I could go there. If they went to seek me and found me they might look and see in a common farmer no son of a lord of war!" The young man made a little smile at this as though he hoped to coax his father to something through the feeble jest.

But Wang the Tiger made no answer. He did not understand the meaning of his son's words when he said, "I chose you, my father." No, Wang the Tiger sat still and over him rolled the bitterness of his whole life. He came out of his dreams in that moment as a man comes suddenly out of mists in which he has walked for a long time, and he looked at his son and saw there a man he did not know. Yes, Wang the Tiger had dreamed his son and shaped him faithfully to his dream, and here the son stood and Wang the Tiger did not know him. A common farmer! Wang the Tiger looked and saw his son, and as he looked he felt an old, known helplessness come creeping over him again. It was the same sick helplessness he had been used to feel in the days of his youth when the earthen house was his gaol. Once more his father, that old man in the land, reached out and laid his earthy hand upon his son. And Wang the Tiger looked sidewise at that own son of his and he muttered behind his hand, as to himself,

"—No son of a lord of war!"

Suddenly it seemed to Wang the Tiger that even his hand could no longer stay the trembling of his lips. He must weep. And so he must have done except at that instant the door opened and his trusty old harelipped man came in, bearing a jug of wine, and the wine was freshly heated, smoking and fragrant.

This old trusty man looked at his master as ever he did when he came into his room, and now he saw that which made him run forward as fast as he was able, and he poured the hot wine into the bowl that stood empty upon the table.

Then at last Wang the Tiger took his hand away from his lips and he reached eagerly for the wine and put it to his lips and he drank deeply. It was good—hot, and very good. He held the bowl out again and whispered,

"More."

—After all, he would not weep.

THE
JOHN DAY

ARISE FOR   IT IS DAY.

COMPANY
INC.